"I'M NOT U... ...NE SO CLOSE TO ME."

Gray looked into his dark eyes and found she couldn't look away.

Durian smiled. "This is good for me. For us."

They stood there like that, separated by inches, his hand on her cheek. He took her right hand and pushed up the sleeve of her robe until her forearm was exposed.

A flicker of arousal started up in her. She considered pretending she wasn't thinking about sex, except it was already too late. Her chest felt like something inside was breaking apart...

He kept touching her and she didn't want to do anything that would make him stop.

He raised her arm between them, bringing her forearm to his mouth. Gray held her breath as he pressed his lips to her skin.

She knew what was coming, and she braced herself. His teeth scraped her skin, and then he pulled. She felt Durian's reaction as he drew her blood into his mouth.

The taste echoed in her, too, as did the roar of his magic moving through her...

PRAISE FOR
My Forbidden Desire...

"Wonderful...exhilarating...a jewel."
—*Midwest Book Review*

"Dark and sexy...a must-read for anyone who loves their romance honed to a dangerous edge. Jewel's heroes are walking towers of sin—hot enough to make you shiver, so wicked you'll be screaming for more."
—MELJEAN BROOK, author of *Demon Bound*

"Phenomenal...you simply can't put it down!"
—LoveRomancePassion.com

"A must-read...difficult to put down...captivating and intriguing...the perfect blend of dark paranormal with steamy romance...a taunting, tormenting, and sizzling tale."
—BookPleasures.com

"Great...unique...kept me captivated...Jewel's characters are dark and dangerous and I loved it. I could not put this book down, and I cannot wait for more."
—FallenAngelsReviews.com

"4 Stars! Hot, hot, hot fun...downright sizzles...a heavy dose of down 'n dirty...a lovely steamy escape from reality...Jewel creates an ultra-sexy bad boy...you will not be disappointed."
—TalesofWhimsy.com

"Brava to Jewel...[A] darkly perilous and sizzling world...[Jewel's] excellent characterization makes each of the players intriguing, which adds richness to the exciting plot."
—*RT Book Reviews*

"I was thoroughly entertained...Touching and deliciously sexy...Xia is an immensely appealing hero, dangerous yet vulnerable at the same time."
—**DearAuthor.com**

"A true perfect 10...All I can say is Wow!...Jewel's imagination has unleashed a paranormal novel with entirely fresh concepts and possibilities...The action is nonstop and the characters, as well as their internal struggles, are entirely believeable and engrossing. I didn't want the book to end...Jewel has truly penned a jewel...It has all of the features expected by true lovers of paranormal romances...I highly recommend."
—**RomRevToday.com**

"Simply delicious...powerful...beautifully presented... intense, deep drama that keeps you glued to the pages."
—**RomanceReviewsMag.com**

...AND *My Wicked Enemy*

"Exciting...[a] fine jewel of a tale...a strong support cast and a superb Northern California setting inside a strong mystical *High Noon* story line."
—*Midwest Book Review*

"Riveting...rich and complex...[a] magnificent, original story line...a gem of a book!...Heart-stopping adventure, emotionally intense and HOT sexual encounters, and this is just the beginning of the story...I was up all night because this story grabbed me, and would not let go. I do not regret my loss of sleep because I experienced an evening of reading pleasure, the likes of which *rarely* happens...Ms. Jewel has created a new world inhabited with characters that I care about, and cannot wait to read more about, like maybe, yesterday? Hurry to the nearest bookstore and purchase this book. Please plan ahead so that you can enjoy it in one sitting because it is impossible to put down. Kudos, Ms. Jewel!"

—SingleTitles.com

"4½ Stars!...I read this in a day, I couldn't put it down! The book starts out like it ends, by taking your breath away."

—LoveRomancePassion.com

"A mile-a-minute thrill from the first...entertaining and unique...action-packed and the romance is outside the ordinary; actually some of the sex scenes probably need a warning label...The writing is smooth and the plot is exciting...I found myself rapidly turning the pages to find out what happens next."

—RomRevToday.com

Also by Carolyn Jewel

My Wicked Enemy

My Forbidden Desire

MY IMMORTAL ASSASSIN

CAROLYN JEWEL

FOREVER

NEW YORK   BOSTON

Book design by Giorgetta Bell McRee

Forever
Hachette Book Group
237 Park Avenue
New York, NY 10017
Visit our website at www.HachetteBookGroup.com.

Forever is an imprint of Grand Central Publishing. The Forever name and logo is a trademark of Hachette Book Group, Inc.

Printed in the United States of America

First Printing: January 2011

10 9 8 7 6 5 4 3 2 1

Acknowledgment

Thanks must go out to my family for their support, especially to my nieces and nephew, Dylan, Lexie, and Hannah for looking so impressed when they see my books on the shelves. I love you guys! My son puts up with a lot from me. I think he does it for the chocolate and pizza, but also because he's a great kid. When I needed help with things medieval French, Eric Edelstein came through for me; thanks very much! My agent, Kristin Nelson, is amazing and wonderful and her support makes more difference than you can imagine. Thanks as well to my editor, Michele Bidelspach, for her insights and suggestions that make a better book.

Glossary

Blood-Twin: A bonded pair of fiends who share a permanent magical connection. They may be biologically related and/or same sex. Antisocial and prone to psychosis.

Copa: A plant derivative, of a yellow-ochre color when processed. Has a mild psychotropic effect on the kin who use it for relaxation. On mages, the drug increases magical abilities and is highly addictive.

Cracking (a talisman): A mage or witch may crack open a talisman in order to absorb the life force therein and magically prolong his or her life. Requires a sacrificial murder.

Demon: Any one of a number of shape-shifting magical beings whose chief characteristic is, as far as the mage-kind are concerned, the ability to possess and control a human.

Fiend: A subspecies of demon. Before relations with the magekind exploded into war, they frequently bonded with the magekind.

Kin: What fiends collectively call each other. Socially divided into various factions, constantly seeking power over other Warlord-led factions. The kin connect with other kin via psychic connections. They typically possess multiple physical forms, at least one of which is recognizably human.

Mage: A male who possesses magic. A sorcerer. See also **magekind**.

Magekind: Humans who possess magic. The magekind arose to protect vanilla humans from the depredations of demons, a very real threat.

Mageheld: A fiend or other demon who is under the complete control of one of the magekind.

Sever: The act of removing a mageheld from the control of a mage or witch.

Talisman: A usually small object into which a mage has enclosed the life force of a fiend, typically against the fiend's will. A talisman confers additional magical power to the mage who has it. Sometimes requires an additional sacrifice. See also **cracking (a talisman)**.

Vanilla: A human with no magic or, pejoratively, one of the magekind with little power.

Warlord: A fiend who leads some number of other fiends who have sworn fealty. Usually a natural leader possessing far more magic than others of the kin.

Witch: A human female who possesses magic. A sorceress. See also **magekind**.

My Immortal Assassin

PROLOGUE

Tigran lay supine on a metal table in the room, unable to move. There was almost nothing he could do but stare at walls covered with writing so old almost no one alive could read them. As one of a race of demonkind thought to be immortal, Tigran had been alive long enough to be familiar with the language. He understood all too well that the dire curses were meant to damn what he was, just as he understood the benedictions intended to protect the human mage who was preparing to kill him.

His movements were limited by the magic the mage had called down. Though his heart still beat, breathing strained the muscles of his torso. The mage lifted his hands over his head and Tigran understood the breaths left to him could be counted on two hands. When Tigran drew air into his oxygen-starved lungs, his chest rose slowly toward the instrument of his destruction. When he exhaled, the moment of his death receded.

He averted his eyes from the soot-blackened knife the mage held over his chest, but an afterimage of the blade burned in his head. Death was inevitable. Inescapable. This moment had been his fate since the day he'd been taken into slavery. He welcomed his freedom and embraced the cessation of his physical suffering.

So far, he'd pushed away the terror of being unable to move, of knowing that soon that honed and gleaming edge would slice through his chest. This life would end in a river of his crimson rage.

The human woman was here, and though he was horrified to think she would witness his death, he was glad not to be alone. Because she was here, there was a way in which he would live on. She wasn't one of his kind, but he regretted none of his decisions. He couldn't move his head to see her, but she was here, more terrified than he was. His. Strong enough to keep her wits. He'd chosen well. In his soul, in the very marrow of his being, she was his. There had been days when he imagined meeting her in a life in which he wasn't enslaved. How different things might have been. Without regret he had done the unforgivable to her. He'd destroyed her then remade her and she had survived and changed them both.

When he told her what was in his heart, when he entered her body with passion and desire that was more than what was required of him, even when he confessed his gratitude and admiration that she had lived through all that he had done to her, she hated the result at the same time that she loved him. She understood how little had been in his control, and that she was alive because of him.

He loved her with the cold ferocity of a knife blade through his heart.

Light flashed on the descending metal and arced away in a rainbow of impossible colors.

He opened his mind to hers, this human woman he had changed, so that he would die having done exactly what he had been commanded he do. She was the instrument of his revenge and his immortality. She was a lie that wasn't. A deception that had allowed him to defy the mage. And she had agreed to do this for him. For them both.

He reached out to her in the last moments of his life. For the final time, he told her that he loved her.

The knife descended.

His magic boiled up, resisted the pain until even he broke. He screamed into eternity when the mage's hand closed around his heart. Tigran triggered his magic and pushed out to her.

With his last breath he exulted.

He died knowing she had saved his life and praying he had given her the power to save herself.

CHAPTER 1

Durian kept his arms crossed over his chest while he waited for the human woman to come to. She was flat on her back right now, in a rather inelegant sprawl. She felt enough like magekind to set off warnings, but he already knew he had little to worry about on that account. Magekind, yes, and therefore she was his enemy, but she was something else, too. Something she shouldn't be; and that concerned him more than her insignificant talent as a magic-using human. Such it was. Which was almost nothing.

That, in itself, was remarkable.

If he was reading her correctly—and he knew that he was—she was also one of the kin, one of a species of demonkind better known to the magekind as a fiend. Just as he was. That ought to be near impossible. Unfortunately for her, there weren't many ways—two or three at most—for someone born human to end up with magic that could only have come from someone like him.

Her eyelids fluttered, but he knew she'd been conscious long before he saw the color of her irises. An icy blue, fittingly cold for what she was. Her eyes closed again, but her thoughts and emotions were alive in his head.

"There is no point," he said, "pretending you're not yet awake."

She moved her leg and winced. Her eyes opened all the way. She looked at him straight on with her cold blue eyes. The anima behind her gaze fascinated him. "Is he dead?"

He straightened his sleeve in order to hide his surprise at the question. "No."

"Shit." She moved her other leg.

The situation, whether she realized it or not, was about as dire as it got for someone like her. In these days of the kin enforcing the rules against harming humans, a surprising number of the magekind—demonkind's traditional enemy—were ignorant about the kin. He had to allow that she might, possibly, be one of the ignorant ones. He waited until she had more of her wits about her before speaking again.

"The only reason I didn't terminate you for what you did, human, is my curiosity about why you tried to kill Christophe dit Menart."

She pushed herself to a sitting position and looked around. She blinked a few times but didn't, as he well knew, see much of anything useful. "Where the hell are we?"

Durian didn't answer since it was abundantly clear she was no longer at the site of her assassination attempt.

She made another face while she arched her back. If she knew what he was, she wasn't showing the usual attitude of the magekind toward the kin. She did, however, block his psychic connection into her head. Rather neatly. As if she'd had practice. "Well," she said, affecting a perky smile. "I guess we're not in Kansas anymore."

"Interesting," he said. "Were you ever?" He picked a speck of lint off his sleeve before he returned his attention to her. He held her gaze, but stayed out of her head. For the moment.

"No." She wasn't trying to use her magic. Not any of it. Her right forearm and a quarter-sized area at her right temple were marked with a delicate green tracery that could have been mistaken for tattoos if the lines weren't swirling under her skin. "Just trying to make a little conversation, that's all."

"I am curious," he said in a low voice, "to know how you got within inches of making today Christophe's last on Earth. He's not usually so careless."

Sitting, she scooted back until she could lean against the base of the column. "Inches, huh?" Durian didn't answer, and she exhaled. She patted the ground around her, then looked around as if she'd lost something.

"I disposed of your gun."

"That cost me good money." Emotion flashed across her face, gone too quickly for him to identify without a link into her head. "Where is the rat bastard now?"

"I am not at liberty to disclose that information." Knowing dit Menart was out there and pissed off didn't do much to improve Durian's mood.

"Why not?"

He took his time studying the woman. Like most

fiends, he was not adept at interpreting the nuances of human expression without a psychic link. Her psychic blocks were quite effective. She looked serious enough, but he couldn't be confident he was right. He said, "Who are you?"

The woman took her time looking him up and down. "I'm not at liberty to disclose that information."

He leaned toward her; just a tip of his shoulders in her direction, really, but enough to make his point. "I can get the information without your cooperation."

Her eyes widened, and for the first time since she'd stopped pretending to be unconscious, he locked onto her emotions without having to try. Uncertainty. Then, terror. Quickly suppressed by bravado. Her block clicked back in place. "Fuck you," she said.

Durian shrugged. "This will go much better for us both if you answer my questions." He glanced down, saw that one of his trousers' legs wasn't falling in line with his knee, and reached to straighten the crease. "Now. Who are you?"

"Gray."

He arched an eyebrow.

"All right. Gray*son*."

"What am I to make of that response, pray tell?"

The merest beat passed before she answered. Durian was inclined to think she was about to lie to him.

"Grayson," she said. "That's my name." She rested the back of her head against the pedestal and stared at the rotunda ceiling. He'd dampened a perimeter around them so that no human wandering by would see them. The precaution also meant she couldn't see out. She was mildly claustrophobic but hiding it well. "Fine. Grayson

Spencer." She lifted a hand and let it fall to her lap. Her mouth curved but the result wasn't much of a smile. "You can call me Gray."

Interesting attitude. She was a good deal braver than he would have expected from someone in her predicament, confronted, as she was, with someone like him. He had no doubt now that she knew exactly what he was.

Gray brought up one knee. Pale knee cap showed through a frayed rip in her jeans. "Since we're getting all familiar here, your name is?"

He tipped his head to one side. They had not reached a point where he was going to even things by telling her his name. "Why did you try to shoot Christophe? Were you unable to use your magic against him?"

She snorted. "As if."

Durian waited for something more to leak from her thoughts but nothing did. She had impressive control. Practiced, one might say. Curious. That sort of control generally indicated a far more powerful witch than she was.

"Okay if I stand up?"

"Be my guest."

She did, and he got his first thorough look at her. Chronologically, she appeared to be in her late twenties, maybe early thirties. You never knew with one of the magekind how old or how powerful they were. Not from just looking at them. Dit Menart, for example, could pass for twenty-seven or -eight, and he'd been living in Paris before Columbus sailed the ocean blue. There was no way to guess her true age.

Gray Spencer was tall for a human woman. Five seven or eight, he estimated. Her face was an odd combination

of pretty and cute. She was too skinny and dressed like—
he had no idea what to call it. Christ, it hurt his eyes to
look at her.

A man could go blind from looking at her shoes, high-
top canvas sneakers painted in interlocking puzzle shapes
of neon orange, blue, and purple that extended from the
rubber trim at the soles to the aglets. With the exception
of one lace that was nothing but shredded string at the
end. Then there was the rest of her clothes.

Surely, no one dressed like this on purpose. Ragged
black jeans faded to charcoal, a too-small orange and
green striped T-shirt that didn't reach the waist of her tight
jeans and short, spiky, improbably red hair that looked
like she cut it herself. Without looking. Streaks of pink
amid the red added to the virulent effect. In contrast to
her hair, her eyebrows were dead black. The combination
of all that wrongness made her face seem less pretty than
in fact it was. A silver skull the size of his thumbnail dangled from a metal bar that pierced her navel. Not a ruby
anywhere, and rubies were a gemstone known to enhance
magic and therefore prized by the magekind. Very curious
that she had none.

He started a slow walk around the woman.

She tracked him so that she stayed facing him. The
traceries on her arm and temple moved faster. "What else
do you want to know?"

"How long were you apprenticed to dit Menart?"

Her eyebrows drew together in what appeared to be
genuine confusion. "Apprenticed?" Her puzzlement came
through clearly just from the arrangement of her face. "To
Christophe?" She laughed. A wild bitterness edged the
sound. "Oh, God, that's rich."

"If you weren't his apprentice, how did you come by the magic that makes you one of the kin?" A smudge on her cheek that he had taken for dirt was, in fact, a fading bruise. Another bruise purpled the back of her other arm, the one without the markings. Durian focused on her traceries. The color deepened as he watched. The magic was reacting to him. To what he was.

"Admiring my tats?" She lifted her arm. He saw another bruise on its underside.

"Hardly."

"They're not really tattoos." She tipped her head. "Seems like you know that. I don't know what they are. When they showed up, there wasn't anyone around I could ask." She sounded lost, unbelievable though that was. He jerked his gaze from her arm and studied her face and the bruises. He thought about going into her head and just taking the information he wanted, but didn't. Not yet. "I take it you know what these are?" she said.

"Yes."

"Mind sharing?"

Durian was struck by the plaintive note in that simple request. "There is one obvious way for you to have come by those."

She kept her arms loose as she moved with him. The bruise on the back of her arm continued upward and disappeared underneath her sleeve.

"And, alas for you, not many others."

"I didn't *do* anything." She lifted her arms and let them drop. "They just showed up."

He came close enough to take her right hand in his. She flinched at the contact. A flash of her fear came at him with the force of a freight train before she shut him out.

Emphatically. That brief contact was enough to confirm what was already obvious to him; psychically, she was a desperate mess. Durian pulled her hand toward him so her arm stretched between them. His finger hovered over the inside of her forearm, but he did not touch her. Cold blue eyes stayed on him and for a moment, a moment only, she connected with him.

She's done this before, he thought. He cut her off immediately.

Gray took a step back. He didn't let go of her hand so she didn't get far.

"These so very delicate colorings appeared underneath your skin in the forty-eight to seventy-two hours following your murder of the fiend whose magic you now hold."

Her eyes, huge and arctic blue, widened. The paleness of her irises made her pupils seem unnaturally dark.

"I hope the ritual was painful for you, especially after you lost control." He pushed her hand away. He was guessing about that, of course. "You deserve every agonizing moment you've experienced since then."

"I didn't perform any ritual, and I didn't kill anyone." Her eyes blanked out long enough for Durian to notice but not long enough to figure out what that meant. Not that there was any great mystery about that. Magically speaking, she was stressed out and it was taking a physical toll. Chances were high she was self-medicated.

"What drugs did you take before you went after Christophe?"

"None." She shoved her hands in her back pockets. She shivered. Just once.

She didn't look like she was coming off a copa-induced high. Copa would have turned her eyes from pale blue to turquoise. It would, however, make sense for a witch who had damaged her access to her magic by calling on too much too soon, to resort to copa in the hope that the drug would restore her abilities. She wouldn't be the first. Or the last. He had no use for witches.

"I know what you are," she whispered. He didn't need to be in her head to know she was afraid. Which, again, was interesting. Not many of the magekind were afraid.

He wanted to give her a chance before they did this the hard way, though he had no expectation of hearing the truth. "If it wasn't a ritual that burned you out, what did? A talisman?"

A talisman was an object that contained the spirit of a ritually murdered fiend. The magekind used them to enhance their magical abilities. It was possible for, say, a witch, to crack one open and take on the magic inside. The procedure was risky, but success conferred longer life and more power. Most mages of sufficient ambition considered it worth the risk, despite the danger. If failure didn't kill them outright, they died after a degenerative period, not unlike the woman's current condition.

Her eyebrows drew together. "What? No. It wasn't a talisman."

"Then we are back at the ritual, which you deny."

"I didn't perform any ritual." She shook her head. "I couldn't have."

He stared into her wide blue eyes and saw the lie there. "I ought to obtain a sanction on you right now."

"I don't know what that means. Obtain a sanction on me."

"Request permission to terminate you." How could one of the magekind, possessed of enough power for a killing ritual, be so bloody ignorant? He tipped his head to one side. "I would receive it, I assure you."

"So, what, you're an assassin?"

He didn't answer.

She wasn't stupid. She knew what his silence meant. The human ground her back teeth so hard he could see her jaw muscles contracting. "There wasn't any talisman. And I wasn't the one performing a ritual. It was Christophe."

She looked around the rotunda again, trying, he supposed, to penetrate the darkness beyond the perimeter he'd established around them. Her magic flared up—the magic she'd killed for, not the magic she'd been born with—but it was unfocused, as if she could pull, but didn't know what to do next. She'd murdered for that magic but couldn't use it.

Durian smiled. There was justice in the world because sooner or later that stolen magic was going to kill her. He let his mind connect with hers until he felt the chaos of her mostly human reactions. Getting past her psychic block wasn't easy.

"Stop," she said.

Sensations came at him too fast to examine in the careful manner he preferred with a potential sanction. She felt human. She felt magekind. Most of all, she felt like one of the kin. What he didn't get from her was evidence that she was a liar. Yet she must be.

She clapped her hands to the sides of her head. "I said, stop it."

Something wasn't right, and he disliked not knowing what. He didn't pull out of her mind, but he stopped looking around. The intensity of her panic unnerved him. "Start talking."

Her hands fisted at her sides. Her breathing was shallow, her heartbeat a rapid *thub-dub* in the back of his head. She was seconds from some sort of psychic meltdown.

He took a step closer. She smelled like someone in need of a bath. "Go on."

She raised her eyes to his, so full of anger and resentment that was not directed at him, that he cocked his head, far more interested in her now than he had been moments before. "Christophe killed one of his magehelds."

"And Christophe dit Menart"—he gave the name a subtle emphasis—"did not complete the ritual? Forgive me, but that is difficult to believe."

Her physical state stabilized, and, with that, her panic receded. She shrugged, her bravado back in place. "He didn't."

"You," he said, "have the dead fiend's magic, and that makes it next to impossible you didn't do the deed yourself."

She shifted her weight from one foot to the other. Her eyes got big and a bit too focused. "I didn't kill Tigran."

Christ. Her vocalization of the fiend's name came with a whole host of conflicting emotions. He didn't say anything for half a breath. Outside the barrier he'd erected around them the chill night air penetrated like the memory of cold. Cold but not cold. The fog was coming in.

She wasn't lying. Impossible as that was, Durian was sure of it. He was less interested in her denial than the way her voice sounded thick with emotion, how her mouth thinned with, if her body language was to be believed, her effort to keep back tears. You'd think she'd been the victim herself.

"If not you, then who?"

"Christophe," she said in a choked voice. Her hands clenched and unclenched at her sides, and her eyes stared blankly forward. At nothing. Her shoulders slumped. "I saw it happen."

"The ritual in question isn't a trivial piece of magic." Even the late, great and unlamented mage Álvaro Magellan had been known to have help on hand for that sort of thing, and Magellan had been considered by most to be the most powerful mage ever to have lived.

"No kidding." She ran a fingertip along her right eyebrow and then rubbed the whorl near her temple. Her hand trembled. Curious. Very curious. She was the color of chalk and that made the traceries stand out even more.

"Presumably, you were assisting dit Menart."

"Me?" Her gaze snapped to him and it was laser sharp. Whatever emotional low she'd hit earlier was over. Her expression hardened to ice. "I want to kill Christophe. So, no, I wasn't helping. I didn't want to be there."

"Then why were you?"

"Christophe had a point to prove."

"Which would be?"

She shivered again, but it didn't last long. She had a hold of herself now. "Don't disobey. Ever."

"And why would he need to prove that to one of his own kind?"

"His own kind. Is that what I am?" She walked to him and didn't stop until mere inches separated them. "I don't know what the hell I am anymore." Her eyes were an uncanny blue. "Have another look. I'll let you just this once." One corner of her mouth quirked like she thought she was amusing. "If you find out what I am you let me know."

Durian gazed into her eyes. Her lashes were long and black as sin. He wondered if she was insane.

"Go ahead," she whispered. "You have my permission."

He touched the bottom curve of her eye sockets, pressing that tender skin to feel the shape of the bone itself. First the left, then the right. Humans were fixed to just one form. She had nothing but this so easily damaged, corporeal existence.

He stroked his fingers along the lower rim of her eye. "Gray," he said, and he heard in his voice the soft silk of a lover. "You understand, don't you, that if I find you've lied, that if you did kill Tigran, things will not go well for you?"

She held his gaze.

"Do you have a different story to tell me?"

"Nope." Her eyes, a lighter blue than the sky, met his without fear. This was not insolence from her. She'd made peace with death some time ago. Most of his sanctions never saw him coming, but this woman, she looked into the abyss of what he was with full awareness of the consequences. She was either stupid, insane, or telling him the truth. He wasn't sure which would be worse.

She stopped shielding herself at all. Not even the minimal protection the kin used as a matter of course. He eased into her head and found anguish. Such overwhelming anguish it was at first impossible to get anything from her but that. She swallowed, blinked twice and managed to pull herself together. Given the state of her emotions, he was impressed she could. Then more impressed when she focused on the events he wanted to know about.

The terror she'd felt that night flowed back to him. Sharp as a knife. Defiance, too. Hopelessness. An image came at him. Christophe standing over a body that was familiar to her. Tigran. The mage's arms were bare, and her memories were detailed enough for him to see the words tattooed on Christophe's skin.

Intimate. A lover. But not Christophe's.

Tigran.

The words the mage had said that night carried power that resonated in her still. She'd known what was happening. She'd known Tigran would die and that she could do nothing to stop it. Other images cut in, but they weren't from the night Tigran died. Her alone with Tigran. Touching. Bodies sliding together. A terrible, keening grief. She'd cut herself off from her emotions and lived when others hadn't. A room. Bodies entwined. Horror and a cold, deep rage. Christophe's knife descending. Such pain and anger. Everything mixed up, out of order.

She was breaking down before his eyes. She gripped his wrists as he withdrew from his link to her.

"Gray." She wasn't lying about what Christophe had done or about her lack of participation. She had been as much a prisoner as Tigran. Durian didn't force their mental connection any deeper. Her mind might completely shut down if he did, leaving her no way back to sanity.

CHAPTER 2

Gray's legs were wobbly, and she was feeling light-headed with the aftereffects of the fiend's tromp through her head. As a consequence, she held onto the demon's upper arms so she wouldn't fall over. She was aware, too, that her stomach was sore where his arm had been clenched around her right after she'd shot at, and missed, Christophe. Her head was sore, too, but that was from having the guy look around the way he had.

She focused on the demon because it helped pull her away from the memories he'd been after. A more satanically lovely man she'd never seen, if you liked a face that was all angles and no charity. Definitely smoking hot. Not that she wanted to sleep with him or anything. Hell no. She just couldn't help noticing his looks. He oozed charisma without even trying.

The fiend cocked his head and lifted one eyebrow. Even his expression of irritated curiosity was lovely. Not in a pretty boy way, either. She liked that in a man. Or whatever. As she recovered from their psychic link, her brain started to process more than the demon across from her. Like where she was, as in *not* with Christophe. Not under Christophe's control. Not a prisoner anymore.

"You tried to kill Christophe because he murdered Tigran." He sounded like he was having trouble believing it.

"That's one of the reasons, yes." Her back was about four feet from one of the rotunda columns to the water side of one of the most photographed landmarks in the City, short of the Golden Gate Bridge and the painted Victorians. Splashes from the fountain in the middle of the pond landed on the water with musical tones. Under different circumstances the sound might have been soothing, except that she could only hear the fountain, not see it. She couldn't penetrate the veil of shadow he'd drawn around them.

"The other reasons? If you don't mind sharing."

She had to block herself off so she could speak without breaking down. This wasn't someone who was going to take pity on the human woman. "Tigran. Like I said." She was still a bit shaky, but it occurred to her that she might be safer not holding on to him. His arms were hard with muscle. He could break her in half if he wanted to. "And the fact that Christophe kidnapped me."

"Revenge, then." He nodded, like that made perfect sense. It did in her world. If it made sense in his, they had something in common.

"Partly. Maybe mostly. One of the benefits to killing him was supposed to be getting his magehelds off my back. They've been looking for me. But that wasn't Tigran's idea. To kill Christophe." She shrugged. "I thought of that on my own." Her throat got thick again.

"After." She swallowed hard and gestured with one hand. "You know."

"What were you supposed to be doing instead?"

She studied him without caring that it was rude. Her heart beat faster as she considered the risks of telling him. His hair wasn't black the way she'd thought at first. It was dark, dark brown and barely skimmed his shoulders. His clothes were straight out of *GQ*: expensive black trousers, expensive black pullover sweater, and expensive shiny black shoes. "According to Tigran," she said, "there are free fiends in the city." By which she meant demons who weren't enslaved by a mage the way Tigran had been.

"Really?" he said.

She absolutely could not read his expression. "Supposedly, they're headed by a warlord calling himself Nikodemus. I was supposed to try to find him. Or someone who knows where I can find him."

"For what purpose?"

"To ask for refuge. And for help with what I am now. Because, you know, I'm not what I used to be. And Tigran...um...Right. He isn't around to help me." A bus rumbled along one of the surrounding streets. Even at this hour, the city was alive with noise. She doubted anyone could see them. In an arc that extended maybe six feet past the man's shoulder, the rotunda lighting was out, smothered by the same kind of magic that was giving her chills. The way these things worked, anyone looking in would see and hear nothing of whatever went on inside. "Do you know where I can find Nikodemus?"

The demon didn't answer, and she got the sinking feeling that she'd just done something more dangerous than failing to kill Christophe. His dark eyes flickered as if there were something moving behind them; a whole other world, maybe. Tigran's eyes used to do that, too. "Perhaps," he said, "you ought to come with me."

She wasn't necessarily opposed to that. But she wasn't an idiot, either. "Where?"

His scowl deepened. "Wherever I tell you to go."

A thought occurred to her. "Are you Nikodemus?"

He laughed. "Hardly."

"I guess that would have been too much of a coincidence."

"Not too much more," he said, with that lovely wry expression of his.

"Do you know him?"

All he did was lift his eyebrows.

"Have you met him?" Still no answer. "Do you know of him?" More silence. "You heard the name once? Someone told you about him? Jesus, what is your problem?"

"You ask too many questions."

"You aren't very good at answering them."

"No. I'm not." He took a step back with the result that her hands slid off his arms. "Shall we go?"

Her hands felt cold now that she wasn't touching him. "The last thing you're supposed to do is go anywhere with someone you think might be a killer."

"I'll take my chances."

This time, she was the one who laughed.

The demon gave her a sideways look, part irritated, part amused. "I'll take you someplace where you can bathe before we discuss your situation and what might be done about it."

"That's not very specific."

"I'm sure you understand the need for discretion."

"A shower would be really nice."

He gave her what was almost a bow, like he thought it was a hundred years ago when women were pampered. Unless they were poor, of course. Then they worked like horses and no one bowed or opened doors for them. "Come along, then."

"Well." She shoved her hands in her back pockets. "I'm not so sure that's a good idea. I don't even know who you are. Or who you know. If you know anybody."

"You know what I am. I should think that is sufficient."

She tapped her sneakered foot on the ground. "You stopped me from killing Christophe."

"I am bound, at present, to see that no harm comes to any of the magekind currently in this territory." His fathomless gaze gave her chills. "That means, much to my regret, Christophe. And you, Gray," he said softly. "Since you are also magekind."

She snorted. "Magekind? Me? Not hardly."

"Enough that it matters." He picked a speck of something off the sleeve of his sweater. She wondered if he was doing that to hide the flickering change of his eyes. "This is not the place for us to discuss your future. Or who I might or might not know."

Her stomach roiled as she had another thought. "Are you mageheld?"

His gaze shot up to meet hers.

"At least answer that question."

He smiled, and it was a killer of a smile. He touched the center of his chest and for a second there she was convinced he was in pain. His mouth quirked. "What if I've been instructed to lie if asked that question?"

"Exactly."

"I am bound—" His voice just missed being a growl. Gray's heart kicked up.

"—by my free choice."

"Free choice? Bullshit." She stared at him, a chill crawling down her spine. "Magehelds are slaves, pure and simple."

Tigran had told her that once she had his magic, she wouldn't be able to feel a mageheld, only the free kin. Except there'd been a hiccup with that. Her best guess was that she'd ended up with a little of Christophe's magic because a lot of things weren't working the way Tigran had said they would. Was she sensing what this demon was because he was free—which he'd just said he wasn't—or because of the magic she'd accidentally stolen from Christophe?

"Bound, yes," the demon said. "But not bound to a mage, human. To a warlord." He continued without letting her object. His eyes weren't brown anymore. They were purple. "I am no one's slave." He wouldn't look away, and she wasn't going to be the one who blinked even though he scared the hell out of her. "I am one of the free kin."

"I'm not anyone's slave either," she said. "Not anymore. Not ever again."

The demon went completely still. If he was breathing, she sure couldn't tell. Then he nodded, touching his fingertips to his sternum again and then to his forehead. She had the weird idea that he made the second motion out of respect. He said, "Shall we go, Gray?"

She nodded, and the blackness around them slowly faded. City noises got louder. The smell of exhaust turned the air acrid. A foggy mist curled off the water behind the

Rotunda. She heard, saw, and felt the rumble of traffic on the street.

They walked in complete silence the couple of blocks to Baker Street. They were near Bay Street when he pulled out a key fob and pushed the button. A few feet away, a pair of headlights flickered on. She looked over at him. "A Volvo?"

"As you can see."

"Not what I expected someone like you would drive."

"Is that so?"

"A Porsche seems more your style. Or..." Her knowledge of high-performance cars started and stopped with Porsche, so she just waved her hand as if she knew more but couldn't be bothered with an extensive list. "Something less soccer-momish than that thing."

"You'll have to bear up under the disappointment." He smiled, and boy, the things that did for his face.

As he opened the passenger door for her, Gray had a weird displaced flash that he was her date and making major points for gallantry. He was all dressed up, for one thing. Like he wanted to look good and make an impression. And he'd opened the door for her.

While she stepped around him to get in, he said, "What now?" under his breath.

A burst of heat zinged through her chest and set off a rush of adrenaline. She would have run as fast as her weightless body would take her except he put a hand on the back of her neck and murmured, "Stay calm."

So she stood there like a complete dunce while Christophe dit Menart came around the nearest corner and walked toward them, his seven mageheld bodyguards in tow.

CHAPTER 3

Shit," Gray whispered.

Christophe and his bodyguards sauntered toward the car like Christophe was king and everyone was supposed to be on their knees before him. The mage was working his magic for maximum effect, so she wasn't surprised that her pulse raced until she could hardly breathe.

One of the bodyguards growled. The sound made the hair on the back of her neck stand up. Christophe liked it when people were afraid of him, and his magehelds were good at being mean and nasty.

The mage didn't dress like royalty. He dressed like a professional slacker. He wore the same clothes he'd had on when she'd gotten to him earlier in the evening: black zip-up hoodie, unzipped, black jeans, sneakers, and a T-shirt. He was slender, just shy of six feet tall. With his head of curly dark hair and his boyish face, he was a good-looking man. A row of piercings lined the outer edge of one ear. In one form or another—stud, bead, cabochon, or faceted gem—each earring contained a ruby.

One of Christophe's favorite tricks was cranking up the desperation in the people around him, enhancing feelings of hopelessness, amplifying insecurities. She'd always thought of it as the emotional equivalent of pulling the wings off insects. Usually, she wasn't susceptible. She'd learned the hard way how to shield herself. Right now, none of her defenses were in place. With Christophe's magic pulling at her like an undertow, she fought to stay free.

"All will be well," the demon said in a low voice. He released her and stood on the sidewalk like he didn't have a worry in the world. Cold air swept over her skin where his fingers had been. Despite the lack of physical contact, a spot at the base of her skull tingled with an awareness of him. She did her best to shut it out, but she didn't have much luck.

Christophe and his magehelds kept walking toward them. The demon slipped his key into his trouser pocket and left that hand hanging free at his side. She didn't realize she'd backed up until her legs hit the side of the car. The minute she came in contact with the cold metal, an unpleasant realization slammed into her.

The demon had been messing with her mind. Soothing her. Eroding her natural suspicions. Christophe's appearance here wasn't any coincidence. He'd lied to her about not being mageheld, and right now he was relaxed because he'd known all along this would happen. He was going to give her back to Christophe.

She said, "Screw you."

He turned his head to get a look at her, eyebrows lifted. "I beg your pardon?"

"Your word, my ass. I never should have listened to

you. Never. You planned this." She shot a glance in Christophe's direction. "Meeting up with him."

His eyes narrowed at her. "No."

"I won't go back." She looked around the darkened street. There wasn't much chance she could escape. The demon had planted himself in front of her, ostensibly to put himself between her and Christophe, but the fact was, his position blocked her in. She didn't think that was a coincidence. Even if she managed to slide from behind him and run for it, Christophe would just send one of his magehelds after her.

Whoever he sent would catch her. If she knew Christophe at all, he'd have given the magaheld wide latitude about what he could do to her when he caught up.

She'd rather die.

"Christophe," the fiend said in a voice that was nothing but reason and patience. "What is this?"

She took long, slow breaths to calm herself. Her chest hollowed out and the magic she had got all tangled up inside her in one big painful knot of tension that she had no idea how to release. Her right arm twitched as whatever the hell those markings were curled and slid underneath her skin.

The mage stopped walking. "Fiend."

"Good evening." The demon's voice was calm, but he managed to sound annoyed. The back of her head crackled with electricity. He walked forward like Christophe had no power to harm him.

Christophe had come to a stop in the dip of a driveway. Behind him was a white stucco house with a wooden gate to one side that would lead to the rear of the house. If she got close enough while they were distracted with each other, she could jump the gate and take off, one backyard after another.

That was *if* her first strike made it through Christophe's heart. She wasn't going to delude herself there was any way she could get free without killing the mage. If he didn't die, she was as good as caught. And then she was as good as dead. If she was lucky.

She was counting on the likelihood that the magehelds would fight the compulsion to save Christophe once he was dying because when it was over, they'd be free. They wouldn't come after her, or else they'd stop if they were in pursuit when he died. The only one she needed to escape from after that was the freak in black, and that meant she had to be fast. An adrenaline rush would propel her once the mage was down and hopefully she could vault over that gate while the magehelds were disoriented from the dissolving bond to their mage.

Or, things could go terribly wrong and she'd die. Or the demon could stop her and she'd die. Either one was better than ending up back with Christophe. She scanned the area again, trying to pick out where he might have stashed more magehelds.

Some ten feet past the mage, an elm tree shadowed the sidewalk and street. She could just barely make out the mageheld lurking in the dark. She felt him more than she saw him. His magic drew her notice and, in some bizarre way she didn't yet understand, she saw the mageheld more clearly because of that.

Two of the mageheld bodyguards split off from Christophe. One of them walked a few paces into the street, blocking off the most obvious escape route. The other one took up a position at the opposite corner of the block.

The one lurking by the tree was probably too far away to stop her. That left the three who kept themselves glued to Christophe. And the demon she wasn't entirely sure about. Maybe he wouldn't care once Christophe was dead.

She stuck her hand in her back pocket to palm the metal pick there. With the side of her thumb, she worked off the wad of tape that blunted the sharp end. Duct tape wound around the other end provided her with a grip. The demon hadn't looked around her head quite thoroughly enough to find out she had it. Shooting Christophe hadn't been her only option. Just the easiest.

She poked a finger on the business end of her makeshift weapon and yes, the tip was damned sharp. If she was going to die tonight, she was sure as heck going to do her best to take Christophe with her.

The buzzing in her chest from all the magic she couldn't do anything with had settled into a constant, low-grade vibration. The back of her head, however, wouldn't stop tingling. In fact, the sensation got worse. For half a second, she considered stabbing the demon before she went after Christophe, but there was no way she'd do him fatal injury even if it turned out she was fast enough. Christophe needed to go down. Anyone else was a waste of time.

The moment her decision clicked into place, she was just as calm as the demon appeared to be. Earlier in the day, when she'd ambushed Christophe with her black-market Magnum—she'd bought the biggest gun she could afford— she'd had a similar reaction. All her fear just slid away, leaving her in a state of hyper-awareness. No emotions to get in the way. She saw better, her mind worked faster. Just like now. She knew exactly how she was going to do this.

The freak in black turned his back on Christophe. From experience Gray knew that wasn't wise; turning your back on a mage. She admired his balls for doing it, though. The fiend got close enough to her to touch her if he wanted. The tingle in the back of her head flashed hot.

He outranks me.

He can crush me without trying.

She felt like a goddamned dog being forced to acknowledge the alpha wolf.

"Try anything with the mage," he said in a low voice, "and I will terminate you, whether you are a witch or not."

She gripped her pick, keeping her hand behind her back. Her stomach tied itself into one monstrous knot, but she didn't acknowledge the reaction. "Stay out of my head, you freak. And while you're at it, take your fancy clothes and your bad attitude and go to hell."

"I did not lie to you, Gray."

She made a point of looking around his shoulder at Christophe. "Oh, look, there's Christophe. And seven of his biggest, meanest magehelds." She tipped her chin up to look into his face. "I don't give a shit what you want."

She didn't. She really didn't. All she wanted was her chance to take down Christophe for what he'd done to Tigran, and to her, and her sister, and make sure he didn't ever do it to anyone else.

A smile curved the assassin's austere mouth. For some reason that made her awareness of him feel like a living thing, echoing there in the back of her head. "Then you will be dead, and Christophe will still be alive."

Gray stared into eyes so dark they were nearly black. His lashes were insanely long. If he were human, she'd be thinking his eyes were pretty. But he wasn't. All he was right now was in her way.

"Tell me, Grayson Spencer, is that the revenge you planned? To leave him alive and Tigran unavenged?"

He didn't wait for her answer. He turned his back on her and faced the mage. She had the unsettling feeling he knew all about her makeshift pick but didn't consider it enough of a threat to bother with. She glared at his back and thought, as hard and as intensely as she could: *bastard*.

If he picked up on her epithet, he gave no sign of it.

Christophe and the three magehelds who'd stayed close to him took up the entire sidewalk and then some. If this broke into a fight, how the hell were they going to keep mundane humans from seeing something they shouldn't? From what she'd seen and heard from Tigran, that was one rule the magekind took seriously: Never let the vanillas know there was any such thing as magic.

At this time of night there wasn't much traffic, but there wasn't none, either. They were on a residential side street so there was less chance someone would come along. Less, but not none. In her experience, though, people didn't like it when you stood under their windows in the dark morning hours and carried on a conversation. Idiots on the street late at night were never as quiet as they thought.

"Is there something you need, Christophe?" the fiend asked.

"You have her in custody." He rubbed his hands together. "Excellent."

His English was accented, but the accent tended to come and go. Most of the time he sounded British. Every so often, particularly if he was angry, he lapsed into French-accented English or, even, outright French.

The fiend lifted his hands. "She is here, as you can see. As to custody? I'm not sure what you mean."

The air took on an electric buzz that sizzled along her arms and down her spine. Underneath her skin, the whorls of green slithered and twisted more and more quickly. Sweat trickled down her back. The fiend became a blazing awareness in her head.

At last, Christophe's attention settled on her. The vibration in her chest kicked up. Her heart skipped a beat and then another and another. He could do things no ordinary mageborn person could. With no effort at all, he could pull magic that would kill her in horrific fashion.

The fiend moved, and she had a clear shot to Christophe dit Menart.

She gripped her metal pick hard.

Now or never.

CHAPTER 4

Durian's awareness of the woman deepened. He moved until he was blocking her line of sight to the mage. If she'd had any idea what she was, Christophe would have died this afternoon. The murdered fiend Tigran had been quite strong. He had to have been to manage what he'd done to her. Her survival spoke volumes to her own resources and fortitude. Few humans could have survived.

He doubted dit Menart fully understood what Tigran had accomplished. The mage did, however, understand quite well that Gray now possessed what he'd intended to take for himself. The power and the extension of life that went with the taking of a fiend's life was now Gray's, and Christophe dit Menart was furious. So furious he wasn't blocking his emotions. And perhaps not thinking clearly, either.

"What have you done to yourself, Anna?"

"I don't answer to Anna anymore."

"Whatever you're calling yourself now, I hardly recognize you." He took five long paces toward her, his three nearest magehelds keeping pace. He affected a look of considered appraisal as he gazed past Durian to where she stood. Indeed, the mage was not thinking clearly. There was more than fury in the emotions Durian was getting from the mage.

The woman had walled herself off psychically. The source of her expertise in mental blocks was appallingly clear. The defense was a skill even vanilla humans quickly learned if they spent much time around the kin, mageheld or free. Right now, he got nothing from her, and that concerned him. Certain humans became abnormally calm in a crisis, quick, clear thinkers when most others were not. Just his luck. Gray, it appeared, was one of those.

He was afraid she intended something rash or unfortunate. Probably both. And that her current mental state meant she would be able to carry out whatever attack she intended. Durian very much wanted to learn how she had survived both Tigran and Christophe. If he had to kill her tonight, he'd never find out. "Send your magehelds away so that we may discuss matters peacefully, Christophe. They needn't go far." He pointed to the street corner. "Just there is sufficient."

"I think not."

"The situation with the human is well in hand," he said. "You are safe now." Durian might as well have called him a coward outright and Christophe knew it, because his mouth thinned. Durian kept back a grin. One took one's pleasures where possible.

So far, Gray was keeping herself under control, but he didn't expect that would last. She still intended to kill Christophe. If he were in her place, he'd feel the same. He admired her commitment, if not the trouble she was causing him.

The mage's smile hardened. "Need I remind you," he said, "that Nikodemus gave me his word? In his territory, the magekind are to be safe from harm by those of your ilk."

Durian nodded and studiously ignored Gray's startlement. "I am not in need of any reminders of my duty, mage."

She shot him a poisonous look. Durian ignored that, too.

"I intend to lodge a complaint over the events of tonight."

Gray inched closer to Durian, but only because she was trying to get close to Christophe. One of the magehelds swung around, spearing her with a savage look.

She had a weapon of some sort. He'd felt her burst of satisfaction when she eased whatever it was from her pocket. In his opinion, Gray had the right idea. Christophe dit Menart needed to die. If it weren't for his oaths to Nikodemus, he'd let her try again.

He was inclined to think her experience with Christophe and his magehelds meant she didn't understand the free kin at all. She had, therefore, both over- and underestimated what Durian could and would do. Killing her would be a shame.

"You came to no harm this evening, mage." He understood the politics of Nikodemus's agreement. Hell, he'd helped forge the agreement himself. But there were times when the worthy goal of creating a peace in which the centuries of enmity between magekind and demonkind were, if not forgotten, then set aside, seemed unobtainable. Such as now.

"Malfeasants must be punished." Christophe hooked

his thumbs in the belt loops of his jeans, leaving his fingers to curve around his pockets. The sleeves of his hoodie hid the tattoos that ran up his arm—real ones old enough to have faded to pale blue-black, but there were several more words inked on the undersides of his fingers. "I'll take the woman, if you please."

"No," Durian said. He had ideas of his own about what to do with Gray Spencer.

"As a courtesy to me," the mage said. "For my inconvenience tonight."

Gray pushed past him, her shoulder brushing Durian's arm as she did. Her mental control was far too tidy. "Sure," she said. "Let's go right now."

She was lying, of course. He knew she had no intention of going anywhere with Christophe. Her lie would get her close enough to try to kill the mage.

With a sigh of regret, Durian grabbed her shoulder and stopped her half a second before she lunged. The magehelds couldn't tell he was using magic to keep her still, but Christophe surely could. "I must warn you, mage. She is determined to do you fatal harm. If she were to go with you, I cannot guarantee your safety."

"She's a woman." The mage waved a hand, flashing the tattoos on his palm and fingers.

She jabbed backward with an elbow, but Durian evaded her. "Let go."

Christophe walked closer but stopped just out of her reach. And his. The three magehelds nearest to him shadowed his movements. Durian's fingers tightened over her shoulder. The mage looked at her, but she didn't flinch. "Still so lovely," he said in a low voice. "Despite the alterations."

He felt the burn of Christophe's magic along his skin. The magic wasn't directed at him. The mage was attacking her, going after her magic in an attempt to take her mageheld. She doubled over and without thinking, Durian dropped his block of the natural connection between the kin. The agony of what Christophe was doing to her ripped through him like a blade. He slipped into her head to do what he could to help her. There was only so much of the pain he could divert to himself before his own status was compromised.

Durian said, "It is not wise to use your magic here, Christophe. Or in this manner."

The mage kept walking a perimeter around them, turning his head to watch Gray. As a human, he might easily be taken for a slacker one paycheck away from being on the street. "If I choose to take her, fiend, do you think you can stop me?" His smile didn't reach his eyes. "More to the point, once I've formally lodged my protest, do you think Nikodemus will allow you to keep her?"

Under the terms of the agreement, no more kin were to be enslaved. There were exceptions of course, on both sides, but the bald fact—the controversial result—was that the powerful mages were being allowed to keep the magehelds they had. Durian understood the conditions handed down had been necessary. This was the hallmark of diplomacy; no one liked the way things were, but everyone was willing to see the other side accept unpalatable conditions. Most of them recognized this perverted situation was better than war.

"You merely delay the inevitable," the mage said. Christophe planned to argue that the woman had been his at the time of the agreement, that given her attempt to kill him, he was entitled to have her back. There was a chance Nikodemus would agree.

His connection with Gray thinned. She dropped to her knees, clutching her head between her hands as Christophe worked the magic that would bind her to him as his mageheld. It was an ugly, soul-stealing magic, and every atom of his being objected.

Durian took a step past Christophe and with quicksilver speed, touched each of the three magehelds in turn. He held back enough that he didn't kill them, but his anger made it a near thing.

Two were immediately inert. The other hit the sidewalk and convulsed. At the end of the movements that got him his three touches, Durian grabbed a handful of the mage's shirt and cotton jacket and pulled hard enough to bring Christophe to his toes. The remaining four magehelds sprinted toward their mage, but he'd counted on the natural hesitation of a mageheld. He had the seconds he needed.

"She wasn't mageheld before." How easy it would be to kill Christophe. Oh, how he wanted to. "Therefore, under the terms of our agreement, you cannot take her now."

"She's mine."

"No longer, mage."

"She stole from me."

"I do not give a damn." He glared at Christophe and got the distinct sense that Christophe had not been talking about Tigran's magic. "Do not break your promise to Nikodemus. Release her. Now."

Christophe flicked a hand in Gray's direction and the magehelds stopped their dash to protect the man who enslaved them. They retreated to their original places. What pain Durian had been able to divert from Gray vanished from his body. His chest ached with familiar pain. One of the fallen magehelds groaned. The other two didn't move. He pushed Christophe away.

On the ground, the woman's arched back flattened out. She squeezed a hand into a fist and pressed it to the ground. She hadn't screamed. She hadn't made a sound despite what Durian knew to be shattering pain.

Christophe straightened his hoodie. Two of his three downed magehelds got to their feet. The third wasn't moving yet. Gray breathed slowly, getting her mind back under her control. Durian buried his anger, taking refuge in the darkest parts of his magic.

"Tonight, with no provocation whatever, she tried to kill me."

"You think she won't try again?" Durian's attention stayed on Christophe and his magehelds, but he was aware Gray had recovered her wits. He stuck out a hand and helped her to her feet. She stumbled once, but Durian didn't change his grip on her. She was now within striking distance of the mage with three of his magehelds compromised by what he'd done.

Well played.

Christophe pointed at her but he looked at Durian. "Return her, and all is forgotten, fiend."

Her decision flashed into Durian's consciousness.

Now.

She was faster than he expected. She lunged, a thin metal rod clenched in her left hand because Christophe and his magehelds would expect her to attack from the right. What a shame he was required to stop her. Durian didn't move. He didn't need to. Besides, he took a vicious pleasure in watching the fear in Christophe's eyes as he saw Gray charge at him. He waited a hair too long. Or perhaps not long enough.

As before, things happened quickly.

The human shouted, not in pain, but frustration. Her fingers popped open and the metal rod fell from her grasp. That was Durian's doing. Not a compulsion but the far simpler solution of superheating the metal. His act saved the mage's life. Such a shame.

Two of the magehelds lunged for her, but they hadn't recovered from Durian's touch and weren't as quick as they should have been. Christophe attacked as well. He tangled his fingers in her hair and made a fist, muttering to himself. She reared back, but Christophe yanked her toward him, forcing her head back so she had to look at him.

The hatred pouring from her was a match for anything a mageheld ever felt for a mage. He could practically touch it.

Christophe bent over her. "You're an animal, Anna Grayson Spencer. One of them now."

A mageheld emerged from the shadow of a tree and leapt an inhumanly far distance to the mage's side. When he landed, hands stretched toward the woman, Durian put out an arm and shoved him away. He put enough magic into the contact for the mageheld to shriek in pain.

"You belong to me, Anna." Christophe's accent was heavily French now. He said something in French so old Durian couldn't make sense of it. Not that it mattered. The mage was finishing what he'd started.

It would be interesting to let him do it and see how

Nikodemus reacted to a blatant violation of the agreement. He wasn't callous enough to leave her to that fate.

Gray brought up her hands and punched the heels of her palms into the mage's face. He staggered back, ripping out some of her hair when his hold slipped. She would have launched herself at him except Durian caught her around the waist and hauled her back in an unsettling moment of déjà vu.

"That, Christophe," Durian said, "is perilously close to breaking your word." He held up a hand. "You will take no one mageheld. That was your promise. Your bounden promise to Nikodemus. Break it, and he will give me your sanction and you will die."

Christophe's cheeks flushed red. His nose and the side of his face were a deeper red where Gray's palms had struck him. Durian hoped she'd broken something. "She attacked me."

"She's one of us," Durian said. "An *animal*. Did you expect more from an animal?"

She lunged again, but Durian tightened his arm around her. She didn't say a word. Not a sound escaped her as she fought to free herself. He outweighed her by nearly a hundred pounds, and he was using magic on her, too, slowing her movements until her limbs must have felt to her like they were moving through cement. She could have kicked and clawed until she puked, and it wouldn't have done any good.

"Calm yourself," he said. The words were low and soft and pitched to penetrate her psychic blocks. And still, he wasn't sure he could get through to her.

"He killed my sister." The words tore from her throat. Durian had both arms around her now. "He didn't even have the courage to do it himself. He had to send Tigran to do it for him."

Christophe bent to pick up the metal pick. "She is a liar. A delusional, burnt-out copa-addicted witch. You cannot trust anything you find in her head."

"Thank me, mage," Durian said with a calm he didn't feel. "For taking her off your hands."

"I want her returned to me."

She took a step forward, or would have if he hadn't prevented her. "Fuck you, Christophe."

Durian suppressed his smile while he carefully kept his attention on the mage. "We have nothing further to discuss."

"I will bring a formal complaint to Nikodemus."

"By all means." He was furious with the mage for trying to take her mageheld. That was so near a violation of their agreement that he wondered why Christophe had risked it. At least now he understood exactly why she wanted to kill the mage. In her place, he wouldn't have felt any different. "Good evening, Christophe."

"This is not over."

Durian smiled, and it felt uncharacteristically good. "I imagine not. But in the meantime, she is under our protection."

Even as the words left his mouth they felt oddly prophetic.

CHAPTER 5

Gray's awareness of the demon didn't change even when she tried to block him out. It was like he was permanently lodged in the back of her head. She wasn't sure if that was cause for panic yet. She surveyed the now empty street while she worked to regulate her breathing and her emotions. Life lesson number one: never give a fiend a way into your head. Especially when you were otherwise defenseless. You might never get him out once he was there. She was still alive, though, and that was something.

"Christophe's not going to let you get away with this, you know," she said to him.

The fiend strolled to his car and opened the passenger door again. He held it for her. His expression was impossible to dissect. "I am well acquainted with his dislike of losing. Particularly to someone like me."

"Yeah." She shoved her hands into her back pockets. "You animal."

His gaze was steady. Opaque. No sense of humor. Gorgeous man, but honestly, she liked a guy who smiled more than once a century.

She held his gaze. "How long have you known Nikodemus?"

He tugged on the top of the car door.

"You're good buddies, though. Right?"

"Buddies?" He put a hand to his chest and looked appalled.

"Don't go having heart failure over it. Pals? Amigos? Chums, acquaintances only in passing?"

"Please get in the car."

She sighed. "It's not like I have anywhere else to go. I need a new plan for killing Christophe anyway." She walked to the car. "Mind if I pick your brain on that one?"

"Gray."

She shrugged and got in. Most cars had something of their owners about them. Papers. Gadget chargers. Gum, mints, spare change, or a travel mug. There wasn't anything like that here. The interior was pristine.

"Where we going?" she asked when he was in the driver's seat.

"Someplace we can talk without interruption," he said in a voice as sterile as the inside of his car.

"Can't wait to hear all about you and your BFF Nikodemus."

After ten, maybe fifteen minutes of silence while the guy drove like an old lady on her way to church, he pulled into the garage of a house on Broadway up near the Presidio, a rarified neighborhood of mansions with views that hurt your heart to look at. It was still dark, so there wasn't much to see right now. He walked her through the side door of a large house. A very large house.

She looked around and didn't see anyone. The house wasn't empty, and she couldn't figure out why she thought that, given how quiet things were. There was an awareness in her head, a sense of someone else. Whoever it was, he outranked her, whatever that meant. The worst part, the creepy part, was that she didn't know why she felt that way. The markings on her arm were going crazy again. Her skin ached as if she had a bad sunburn where the green markings had shown up. They were moving again, shifting into new patterns. She gritted her teeth while she tried to ignore the feeling that something was alive underneath her skin.

Most of the lights were off and she didn't hear noises like you'd expect to hear when someone was home. No TV. No hey-I-live-here sounds. The kin, she knew, didn't sleep. When they were passing as human, they faked it when they had to. As she and the demon walked through the silent house, she had no problem making out high ceilings, carved moldings, and museum-quality furniture. He knew his way around, that was clear.

They ended up in a twenty-by-twenty room on the first floor, an office of some sort with a glass desk and some crazily curved bookshelves. There were a few books on the shelves, a pair of jade Foo Dogs and several blown glass vases in neon colors and warped shapes. All the vases were empty. There was a sound system with an iPod dock. Against one wall was a smallish couch of crimson leather. A set of tall windows in the wall opposite the desk looked onto darkness. The wood floor was laid out in strips that formed a broad arrowhead pattern.

She looked down at her ragged pants and shoes, then at the fiend in his ensemble of meticulously tailored black and more black, then around the room again. She thought about her sense that someone else was here. Wherever she was, this wasn't his house. Just why she thought that wasn't clear to her, but she did think so. "Is this where Nikodemus lives?"

He stood by the door, hands loose at his sides. The guy was scary just standing there. "No. Nikodemus does not live here. The owner is attending to business outside the country."

"Does he know you're here?"

After a brief hesitation, he said, "Yes." He closed the door and motioned to the couch. All business.

"Can I assume I've found the free kin Tigran told me about?" Maybe she hadn't found Nikodemus himself, but this might just be close enough.

"Yes. Do please sit down, Gray."

She sat at one end of the couch. The far end. The demon sat at the other. There might as well have been an ocean between them. He didn't say anything. She settled her foot across her knee and wrapped her fingers around her ankle. Upstairs, someone walked a short distance, then settled down again.

"So. Whatever your name is. What are we going to talk about?"

He inclined his head. "Durian."

"Durian." She nodded.

"Some background is in order." He plucked at the crease of his pants leg until it ran straight down to the top of his shoe.

"All ears."

"As perhaps you have guessed already, I am sworn to the demon warlord Nikodemus."

"What does that mean?" She leaned forward. "Is it anything like being mageheld?"

He had a way of looking at her that made her think about creatures that hid in shadows and that you never knew were there until it was too late. He was looking at her that way right now. "I have free will, Gray."

"You're not footloose and fancy free, either, though."

"No." His dark, dark eyes watched her. Scoured her, actually. "Are not all of us bound by constraints of some sort? We agree to conventions of behavior and, most of us, to the rule of law."

She forced herself not to move, to keep her expression as blank as his. Inside, she was a mass of conflicting emotions. "Part of me wants to walk out."

"You are free to do so."

"I'd be safer on my own, far away from the kind of creatures that can take over my mind. Force me to do things I don't want to." She held up a hand to stop his interruption. "For as long as I could survive without anyone to show me how to manage Tigran's magic."

"You understand your situation, then."

She nodded. "Can you help me?" Colors flickered in his eyes, mostly shades of purple, but other colors, too. That didn't startle her. She'd seen that effect before, after all. His silence, however, freaked her out. "Can you at least tell me who might help me?" Filled with a nervous and desperate energy, she jumped to her feet. "I haven't got any money, but I can get a job and pay my own way." She paced a few steps. "All I need is to know how to deal with this. With having Tigran's magic. It's not—not what I thought it would be like."

"I might be of assistance."

"Might?" She shook her head in a tight negative as she paced. "I'm no good at subtext. Not when my life is at stake. How about you explain that *might*?"

"Tell me what happened, and I'll be in a position to know if I can help you. Clear enough?"

She stopped pacing. She'd found the free kin, just like Tigran had wanted her to. She wasn't going to throw away his sacrifice because she was afraid. "Okay. Here's the thing. We figured Christophe was eventually going to find out what we were doing—I'll explain that better in a bit—and that he might kill Tigran when that happened. We knew that was a risk. He taught me what to do in order to take his magic if it came to that, and when it did...I did. Only, somehow I think I ended up with some of Christophe's magic, too."

"Did you have magic before this?"

"My sister was the witch. Never me."

"I'm sorry for your loss." His gaze stayed steady.

"Me, too." She sucked in a breath. It hurt to think of her sister. The loss was as sharp as ever. "Look. I don't know what you're like. Right now, you're scaring the hell out of me."

"I can see that."

"It's like I spent all this time with a tame panther and you're a wild one. What I know might be completely wrong. Enough to get me killed."

"What is it you know?"

"Magehelds like Tigran are cut off from the normal psychic links with the free kin. You can't sense each other the way you should."

"Go on."

"The more powerful the demon, the better looking their

human form tends to be." She laughed, but she sounded nervous because she was. "Well. I mean look at you. Jeez." That got her what she was starting to think of as the glare of doom. "Tigran said that's because there's more magic to create and hold the human manifestation. You have alternate forms, some more than one, and you reproduce with human women. You aren't fertile unless you're in your alternate form."

"So far that's not inaccurate."

"A mageheld is a slave to his mage." She swallowed. "There are ways for them to resist, but an order is an order. Nikodemus is a warlord and he's organizing a resistance against the magekind. Tigran wanted me to join up, but I would have wanted to anyway."

"Please sit down, Gray."

"Right." She sat on the couch again. "Sure."

"I am interested in hearing about what happened between you and Tigran such that you ended up here. Asking to join a resistence movement."

"Is it true?" All that got her was silence. She stared at the ceiling. Words flew around in her head but none of them seemed adequate to shape any kind of reply about what she and Tigran had done. Or, more specifically, what Christophe had ordered him to do to her, and what she and Tigran had done about that.

"It is remarkable you were able to thwart Christophe in any respect."

She realized she was tapping her heel against the floor. Faster and faster. She stopped. The room with its crazily tilted bookcase and vases that looked like they'd been left in the oven too long was getting to her. Her entire life was getting to her. "Right. So, okay." She rubbed her hands over her face. "I understand completely that Tigran was not acting from his own choice. There were probably things he couldn't tell me that he should have. All right?"

"Understood."

"It's like this. Christophe had my sister killed and me brought back to his house. I thought Tigran was some psycho killer at first. But he sat me down and he explained what he was and what he had been ordered to do and what that meant for us both." She shook her head. "That very first day he told me he was willing to die." She had to wait a bit before she could continue. God, all that just seemed unreal now. "It took a while before I believed him and then we needed time to . . . get things to a point where there was a chance it would work."

"Where what would work?"

She couldn't answer right away. "Right." She stared at a spot on the floor and gathered herself. "Tigran was supposed to reproduce with me." She could feel her cheeks burning hot. She did her best to separate herself from her emotions. "Christophe wanted children he could take mageheld from pretty much the start. So he wouldn't have to go out and find free kin."

Durian drew in a long breath and let it out just as slowly.

"The wiggle room was in me staying pregnant. My idea, actually." Gray stared out the window even though there wasn't anything to see. "If I ever have kids," she said, "if I still can, they won't be born for any reason but me wanting them or knowingly taking the risk of having one. I'm not a fucking baby factory for Christophe or anyone else." She glanced away from the window. He was watching her too carefully, she thought. She held his gaze. "I don't care what you think about that."

She rocked forward, realized she was giving away her turmoil, and stopped. She got up and went to the window, talking to the darkness. She could see his reflection in the window. "We knew he'd figure it out eventually, since, obviously, there would never be any children, and that Tigran would probably pay with his life. But what that bought us was time for him to make sure I could take his magic when the time came." She dropped her voice to a whisper. "Because that way, you see, Tigran wouldn't die for nothing. It was awful." She turned around. "It worked. Just the way he said it would."

On the surface, Durian didn't react to anything she'd said. He stayed exactly where he was with exactly the same unreadable expression on his face. Except something did change. Her sense of him opened up. She dropped into his head, and there was a world there so foreign, so breathtakingly dark she went stock still.

He had killed. Many, many times. Swiftly. Without mercy. Without emotion. And he would do so again when it was required of him. Isolation. Anticipation of the hunt for his next target. Rage. Control so complete she might never find what lay beneath the surface he allowed her to see. She tried.

He blocked her. Her awareness of him went nova, and it freaking hurt. The markings on her arm and temple turned to fire underneath her skin. She didn't know he'd gotten up or that she was going to fall on her ass until his arm shot out and stabilized her. He let her go when she was sitting on the couch again. She blinked a few times while her stomach threatened to turn inside out.

"None of the kin would fault you for surviving."

She blinked at him, half expecting him to change

forms. She fought her panic. Durian stayed human. Thank God. He leaned toward her, his eyes swirling with purple. He continued in the same smooth tones as before. "I am, at this moment, open to you. As you are to me. And that, Gray, is not something I often permit."

"Are you going to help me?"

"Yes."

She nodded. "Thank you."

He extended one arm along the top of the couch. His eyes were brown again, that dark, dark brown that was almost black. "There are things you must understand before we proceed."

"Such as?"

"Though I have a number of responsibilities to Nikodemus, there are two that need concern you now. The first is his safety. The second is my work as his assassin." His upper back relaxed against the couch. "If you imagine those two things are closely related, you would be correct."

"Makes sense."

He flicked something off his trousers. His habit of lapsing into impenetrable silence was starting to irritate her. His irises had flecks of purple in them again. He was pulling, she realized, bringing his magic up from its source to a place where he could use it. Her skin prickled.

"Nikodemus is a warlord. As you know." He considered her. "This means he leads by dint of power, which he gains through the bonds he forms with others of the kin. Kin swear fealty to him in return for his protection and leadership." He spoke calmly, in deliberate tones. "Other warlords have sworn fealty to Nikodemus, and that is not a circumstance to be dismissed lightly."

Her sense of Durian deepened. She felt as if she knew him better than she did, and that was a dangerous thing to let happen. He definitely wasn't tame. "You don't like him, do you?"

His eyebrows lifted. "It is not necessary that I like him. It is only necessary that I keep my oaths to him unless or until he gives me cause to break them." He hesitated, and her skin went goose pimply from head to toe. "The same is true for any of the kin who swears fealty to another."

Durian pressed his hands together, almost as if he was praying. He stared at her from over the tops of his fingers. "If you wish to remain safe, you should ally yourself with someone, Gray. A fiend who does not forge such a relationship is likely to soon find himself mageheld or dead."

She was going to give herself a headache trying to figure out where he was going with all this. "So, I should align myself with Nikodemus."

The edge of Durian's mouth quirked. "Not necessarily. Not directly, at any rate."

She licked her bottom lip. He waited in that annoying way of his. Her stomach got queasy. But there was exhilaration, too.

"There are decisions to be made, Gray. What is yours?"

"You want me to swear fealty to Nikodemus?"

"No." His smile made her feel like she'd walked straight into a trap. In a way, she guessed she had. "Not Nikodemus."

She took a breath. "Make it crystal clear, if you don't mind."

"If I'm to help you, I want you to swear fealty to me."

CHAPTER 6

Jackson Street, San Francisco

Three blocks from the condo that was his destination, Christophe dit Menart got out of the back seat of his parked car. In Paris he never drove except on those infrequent occasions when he left the city. In Paris, people came to see him, not the other way around. Here, he was not feared or esteemed to the degree he had been in Europe. Naturally, that would change. When he had been here long enough to make himself known.

In the New World doing without a car for even the meanest tasks proved nearly impossible. This was something few Europeans understood until they'd been here. One could sit in a café in sight of the Eiffel Tower, smoking a Gauloise, the bitter perfection of an espresso at one's hand, the scent of a freshly baked croissant inhaled with every breath—a croissant of the sort almost impossible to find in this country—and say, *Those Americans, driving everywhere in their SUVs. Feh*.

Only when a man had traveled thousands of miles to alight in this most Parisian of American cities, only when he had done this and learned he could drive eight hours and find himself still in California—only then could a man begin to understand the American mind. The sheer size of this country oppressed.

And so. One required a car. Though he owned the condo to which he was headed just now, he refused to park in the communal garage. The underground lot was too confined. He preferred to park far enough away, on a different block each time, that during the walk to his destination, he had time to assess possible threats. From humans. From the magekind. From any of the demonkind who lived here with such offensive impunity.

Californie. The new frontier.

San Francisco was rotten with demonkind. Centuries of vigilance in Europe, Russia, and lands in between had reduced their numbers to the point where they rarely caused serious trouble. They'd been killed, controlled, or simply driven out.

The demonkind had fled here like the disease-carrying rats they were and had integrated themselves into society. They passed for human with frightening accuracy. Nikodemus was the worst of them. The most dangerous. The fiend had so often said he and his kind were no danger to anyone that Christophe now thought the demon warlord might actually believe it. As if Nikodemus or any other fiend could resist his nature forever.

If Nikodemus were right, how then did Álvaro Magellan die at the hands of a fiend? It was only a matter of time before one of them snapped, perhaps Nikodemus himself, and innocent lives would be lost.

He intended to one day have the warlord under his control and Magellan's former dominion acknowledged as his. To have such a one as Nikodemus free among humans; that was a danger none of the magekind could afford to ignore. When the warlord fell to him, as inevitably he would, his minions would fall, too. Humans would find the world a vastly safer place.

He paid no attention to his magehelds as he walked to the condo. They kept up because they had to, because it was no challenge for them to do so. Even if he were to run, they would stay with him. He possessed not even a quarter of their physical strength or stamina. The least of his magehelds could crush him with a single blow. If they weren't under his control, they could take over his mind. Ruin his life. Three hundred years ago, one of them had tried just that. Sheth, a monster who would never harm another human again. The demon now paid for his sins in service to Christophe.

Six paces from the entrance to the condo, one of his magehelds hurried forward to open the door. He swept through. The same thing happened when they reached the door to his destination. This was a dance by now. A familiar one, well choreographed.

Erin knew he was coming before he arrived. Naturally. Being what she was. A self-trained witch who had not lost her powers despite her lack of a mentor. She had no idea the rarity she was.

She stood in the middle of the living room, wearing an ankle-length silk robe. Her hair was loose, a river of black down past her shoulders. She ravished him with her smile. "Christophe."

Her beauty took his breath as it did the first time he saw her and every time since. He unzipped his jacket, shrugged it off and dropped it on a chair. The runes and Latin wards inked onto his skin flashed in his peripheral vision. He had only to see her, and he wanted to touch her. Caress her. Hear her moan as he sunk into her welcoming body.

He signaled to his magehelds. All but one of them left the room. The one remaining, his companion of the last three hundred years, retreated to a shadowed corner. Christophe walked to Erin and put his hands on her shoulders. He breathed in and checked that his spells were in place. She was still his. He lived in a state of almost constant fear that he would one day find she was no longer his.

"My love." Even now, with the evidence of her adoration of him, his heart pinched with the fear that one day he would find a crack that could not be repaired. He put his hands on the knot that fastened her sash and leaned in to kiss her. Softly. Gently. As if he would die if he could never kiss her again. He drew back. "How are you tonight?"

"Good," she said, keeping her voice low. Her eyes darted sideways, in the direction of his remaining mageheld. "You?"

He kissed her again, fingers loosening the silken knot of her sash, which, at last, parted. Either she understood the futility of her discomfort or she gave into their mutual desire, because she did desire him. For which he almost daily gave thanks. She leaned into his embrace. Her mouth was soft under his. It was miraculous to him that after so many years of living he could feel any degree of lust without a magical enhancement of his senses or experience. He kept his hands around her rib cage, where they'd wandered while he kissed her. The knowledge that he loved this woman frightened him because all of it was built on a lie.

"What did you do today?" he asked. One hand wandered to the curve of her belly. Three more months. So short a time and yet an eternity, too, before the child was born.

"I picked out colors for the baby's room today." She leaned against him, catching his fingers in hers for a moment. Such a sweet gesture. "Will you come see?"

He cradled her face between his hands. "In a moment." He kissed her forehead and pushed her robe off her shoulders. The material fell down to catch in the crooks of her elbows. "Do you remember how we met?"

"On holiday. In Paris," she said automatically. She had, of course, never been to Paris, but the memories were there and Christophe liked to make sure they stayed vivid. Her arms slid around his waist, too. He feasted on the sight of her naked breasts. "I wanted chicken for lunch, but the waiter refused to understand me." She laughed at her memory. "You rescued me."

"Yes. I rescued you." He glanced over her shoulder and saw the bottle of wine and glasses on the table by the couch. For her, only water. He moved them to the couch, and she curled up next to him, leaning against his side. His mageheld was a bright presence in the corner of his mind, enhancing the desire he felt on his own. Christophe draped an arm around her shoulder. "I almost didn't go to that café. Imagine, my love, if I had not."

A fiend felt lust with such a visceral intensity that Christophe wondered how they ever restrained themselves. His mageheld's lust for Erin burned in him to the point where he considered making love to her right now. Before she was ready.

"But you did, Christophe. And you showed me Paris." Erin was tall and as slender as could be thought healthy for a woman expecting a baby. She leaned in and kissed his cheek. "I would have stayed there for you. You know that, darling."

"I know," he said. He touched her pointed chin. She was beautiful and so far pregnancy agreed very much with her looks. "But I was happy to move here."

She smiled and Christophe's heart lurched. What would become of him if Erin stopped loving him?

"I'm glad you came after me." She reached for the wine to pour him a glass. While she did that, Christophe looked at his mageheld. Sheth's attention was fixed on Erin's nearly naked body. Christophe reached to cup her breast. "You're much later than I thought you'd be tonight. Is everything all right?" As she poured, she looked at him from under her lashes. "Or don't you want to talk about it?"

"Another time, perhaps." He took his wine from her, drank much too fast, until the glass was empty. If she'd served him swill, he'd never know. "I have a favor to ask of you."

Her eyebrows arched.

"A very large favor, I'm afraid."

"Go on."

"A friend of mine is dying. Someone I have known for a very long time."

She rested a hand on his arm. "Oh, Christophe. I'm so sorry."

"He is the only remaining parent for his son." He turned his wine glass in a slow circle. She knew about his magic, but not the extent of his power. He dabbled, he told her, but his money came from an Internet application he'd created and then sold to a much larger company. "The boy, he has no other family, I'm afraid, and my friend has asked me if I would raise his boy should the worst happen."

She sat up straight, rearranging her robe more modestly. "You told him yes, I hope?"

Christophe smiled. He didn't even have to use his magic to achieve the desired result. "I told him I must speak to you first."

"Tell him yes. Yes of course!" Her eyes glittered with tears. "Is he very young, the boy?" Christophe nodded. "Oh. How tragic for them both. Does he know his father is ill?"

"Three years old." He caressed the top of her shoulder, baring her skin once again. "I can't say when he'll come to live with us. My friend might survive after all. If not—" He grimaced. "There are always legal formalities."

"He can use the room across from the baby's, don't you think? I'll have it painted. New curtains. We'll want to bring as much of his own things with him as we can."

"Find a bed and a dresser at least. When the time comes—" He crossed himself. A habit for him. Christophe had been alive too long not to understand the power of habit and ritual. "—I'll bring what I can."

"That poor, poor child. To lose his family like that. Is there really no other family?"

"No one. Your heart is so tender." He brought Erin in close and kissed her and he hardly needed Sheth's intervention to feel a sexual reaction. He would have a son from Erin. A miracle, the child was. She hadn't gotten pregnant right away, but that had only given them time alone. Time for him to fortify the memories he'd given her and bury the others. Time for him to become more than a little fond of her.

Her sentimentality ought to annoy him, but it didn't. He was touched by her concern for the soon-to-be-orphaned boy. Christophe was confident his own son would be magekind. With two parents of power, how could the child not be? Nor would he mind more children. Erin answered a part of his soul that had been deaf and blind for too long. He pulled away from her and poured himself a second glass of wine.

"Your day *was* bad, wasn't it?"

Christophe sighed. "Worse than you can imagine."

"Your friend?"

He let her think that was it. What choice did he have? He could hardly tell Erin the truth, which was that he needed a young witch or mage whose magic he could siphon off to augment his own. The great Magellan himself was rumored to have done so himself, and on more than one occasion. Though most frowned on the practice, Christophe could feel the hole left behind by Anna's theft.

Anna, or Gray as she seemed to be calling herself now, and that damned fiend of Nikodemus's, that's what had him in such a vile mood. She was to have conceived by Tigran, producing demonborn offspring whose power, Christophe was certain, could be taken before they were ever a threat to humans. If Magellan could take power from young magekind, then surely, one could do the same with young demonkind.

All those weeks and weeks Tigran had been dutifully fucking Gray. God knows how many times his mageheld must have impregnated her before Christophe found out what was really happening. Though it was impossible to fathom how a mageheld could have defied him like that, Tigran had somehow learned how to end each and every one of her conceptions. The fiend had deserved to die for his defiance. Cutting out his heart was too kind a death for such a betrayal.

He downed his second glass of wine as quickly as the first, and then he took Erin in his arms again. She responded to the heat of his anger. She was an excellent lover. Her magic made her sensitive to his moods. As ever, tonight she understood what he needed. Hard. Rough. Fast. He opened himself to Sheth. *Dieu.* The fiend wanted her more than he did. His cock was rock hard. Aching for her.

She accepted his passion, never suspecting that Sheth was responsible for his ability to perform. Already she had his shirt off and was tracing the blue inking that wound around his upper body in a combination of words and phrases in French and Latin. Runes in an even older language. Erin read none of the languages. With a glance in the direction of his mageheld, she resisted him removing her robe.

He pulled back, his fingers underneath the fabric, stroking her skin. "He's nothing, Erin." He kissed her earlobe, nipped her softly there and inhaled her perfume. "He looks human but he isn't. You know that."

"Christophe."

"I adore the way you say my name." Her American accent lacked the softness of French, but when she said his name with such longing he forgave her every syllable. Her magic resonated in him, and he reached out and drew from that pool of unused ability. She felt that, and sucked in a breath. Christophe kissed his way down the side of her neck and in return got a moan of arousal from her. He slid a hand between them and onto the fly of his jeans. "Erin. You are so very beautiful."

She didn't relax, although she let him slide his other hand down the center of her naked body to linger over her belly. "Can't we go to the bedroom?"

Their bedroom was arranged so that unless one knew where to look, his magehelds weren't visible. Their task was to be alert to intruders who, after all, were unlikely to spring from under the bed once the room had been inspected. Unbeknownst to Erin, they were also to be mindful of the possibility that she would attempt to do him harm. Something could happen to restore her memory, and she might turn on him, too. As Gray had done.

No one was exempt from suspicion. No one at all.

He had not survived hundreds of years by taking foolish chances.

"It's no different than having a guard dog in the room. His presence is required for my safety. And yours. You know that. He would only come with us into the bedroom, my treasure."

His hand delved into the folds of her body, and, well. Erin responded to that as he had known she would. Christophe shivered with the sexual response he shared with Sheth. He dropped her robe to the floor and proceeded to stroke her with both hands. From the corner of his eye, Christophe saw his mageheld stir.

He leaned in and kissed her mouth while he allowed

his mageheld to seat himself more fully in his head. As he did this, she opened his jeans and slid a hand over him. Christophe was, after a fashion, addicted to the rush of a mageheld's lust for a human woman, and Sheth was by now whipped into a frenzy. For Sheth, it was as if she was stroking his cock instead of Christophe's.

He felt his mageheld's arousal, touched through his skin, tasting with his mouth, all with a richness of sensation that had vanished from Christophe's life hundreds of years ago. He shoved away his jeans and underwear to slide into Erin's body, drawing from her magic, supplementing his own and letting his thoughts slip away. He knew what it felt like to take a human woman when his body was not. More than once he had lived an experience no human man ever knew, a pleasure beyond anything he'd felt on his own.

Though his body was human, he had made contact with the internal fire that kept Erin alive. Even though it wasn't possible for him to live in another's head, he had done so through monstrous abilities shared by Sheth and others like him, including Tigran. Sex with Erin through Sheth was like nothing he could experience as a man. Oh, yes. He was addicted to this, but he had long ago come to terms with his weakness.

Christophe adjusted himself and Erin to sink deeper into her body, and she accepted him. She accepted the scaring eyes of the mageheld with whom Christophe was sharing his physical experience. She gave back what he needed, which was her complete adoration. He looked into her blue eyes, knowing that his mageheld saw and felt what he did, and said, "I love you."

He felt the slight diminution in his power that was the

result of whatever had gone wrong the night he killed Tigran. He had not understood then what had happened, which was that Anna, or Gray, or whatever she was calling herself now, had managed to damage him when she took Tigran's magic. The woman now possessed part of his magic. Not much, but any part was too much. That magic might mean the difference between keeping Erin and losing her forever.

For that, Christophe decided, Anna Spencer had to die.

CHAPTER 7

Broadway near Baker Street, San Francisco

The first step to treason was easier than he'd expected.

Durian walked to the mini-fridge tucked under the desk. He wondered if he was mad to be doing this. Binding Gray to him with an oath of fealty was not without precedent. Nikodemus himself had bound a witch to him. There was no practical reason why he could not do the same. There were, however, myriad political reasons why he shouldn't.

He took a bottle of water from the fridge and gave it to Gray. He had himself under tight control. He always did. There was little chance she'd see more than he intended if they did happen to link again, as would be natural, given that she was kin. The kin had long followed strict customs about what degree of psychic contact was acceptable between each other and with humans. Since the first trouble with the mage-kind, many of those customs now gained the force of law.

Gray twisted off the cap and drained half the bottle without taking a breath. She looked at him so steadily he wondered if she'd guessed after all the enormity of the step he proposed. He wasn't sure it would matter to her, whether or not she had picked up on that. Certain humans were highly intuitive—or nascently gifted that way. She might be one of those. If her sister had been a witch, perhaps the ability ran in the family.

"I'll teach you what you need to know." With that, he leapt off the cliff into free fall. He *was* going to do this. There was no taking back an offer he should have run by Nikodemus first.

"I'm listening." Her hair, he noted with a shudder, was almost precisely the same color as the couch.

"There is one condition," he said.

She lifted her chin. Suspicious thing, wasn't she? "Yeah?"

"It is crucial that you fully understand what I'm asking of you." She frowned, and he said, "Perhaps more so for you than anyone else I might ask this of, given your history."

She narrowed her eyes at him. "Meaning?"

"Your oath of fealty to me will be more binding than any physical tie you can imagine, Gray. Understandably, you have strong feelings about your personal agency, if you will. If you do this, there is no walking away because you decide it's inconvenient or that you don't care for the responsibilities imposed on you."

"What responsibilities?"

"You will be obliged to support me. You cannot act against my interests without consequences you will find most unpleasant."

"Right." Her mouth tightened while she thought about

what he'd said. "You've sworn fealty to Nikodemus?" When he nodded, she continued. "It's common for the free kin to swear fealty to each other?"

"It is how our society operates."

"All right then. I'm in."

This was exactly what he'd feared would happen; agreement without due consideration. "Gray—"

"I get it. Fuck you over and it's pain and suffering for me." She laughed to herself but it wasn't out of amusement. There was a hardness in her that made him sad, despite his disinclination to pathos. "I know all about pain and suffering, trust me."

He nodded because she did.

She pointed at him. "I get it. Really, I do. You teach me how to deal with what I am now and in return I'm your good little soldier. Am I right?"

"There are obligations on my part as well."

She cocked her head, water bottle halfway to her mouth. "Like what?"

"So long as you uphold your oath, I can do nothing unjust where you are concerned. I cannot be capricious or malicious in any requests I might make of you. If I were to be so, you would reach a point where you would cease to be bound by the oath."

"Sounds fair."

He let her surprise pass unremarked. "You won't be without protection. None of the kin can harm you without repercussions from me. I assure you, there aren't many who would care to have me seeking revenge against them."

She looked at him sideways. "What if I kill Christophe? Hypothetically speaking."

"I can't be sure, but if you were to succeed, I believe your oath of fealty would prevent me from killing you." He straightened his sleeves until they were even. "Which is not to say that Nikodemus would not later decide to punish you."

"All due respect to your warlord, sir, but if I manage to off Christophe, I don't care what he does to me." She sat up and raised a hand, palm out. "I, Anna Grayson Spencer, do solemnly swear to be your loyal minion under penalty of perjury and pain of a gruesome death. So help me God."

"Sarcasm is neither appreciated nor helpful."

She shrugged and kept her emotions blocked from him. Gray Spencer was, in some ways, more damaged than he was. "It's been a long day. I'm low on good manners."

He let the silence close in on them. "You must be certain. You must freely accept."

She let her head fall back against the couch. Her fingers curled around the half-empty water bottle. She whispered *Jesus* under her breath and then looked at him. "Define *free*."

"Don't be tiresome. You know full well what I mean."

Still slumped down, she crossed her arms over her head and rolled her eyes, then she cocked her head and looked him up and down. Her shirt rode up, exposing a wide strip of her belly. "I bet you go for the educated girls. Doctors or lawyers. The ones with PhDs. A woman who can talk about science, history, and world politics and give you her opinion on the Impressionists versus the Modernists. Not some punk like me." She laughed softly, then drained the bottle in one long drink. "You'll make yourself want me, though. Eventually."

She was astonishingly accurate in that, by and large, he did prefer the sort of woman she described. "To be clear," he said, "I am not asking for a sexual relationship with you."

Her gaze flicked to his. He was struck once again by the intensity of her eyes and the bleakness that lived there. She lifted her water bottle in his direction. "I'm not your type."

The water bottle collapsed under the force of her fingers around it. She stared at the broken plastic. Durian got another water from the mini-fridge. The bottle was cold and wet against his fingers. He handed it to her.

"Thanks." She drained that one quickly, too. When she finished, she picked at the label until she had a strip of plastic loosened. She sat with one foot on the couch, her elbow on her upraised knee, the rest of her body relaxed. Durian stood in front of her, feet apart, arms crossed over his chest. He stayed out of her head.

She ripped off the rest of the water bottle label and let it fall to the floor along with the empty, after which she leaned forward with her arms down, hands clasped between her shaking legs. The position made her look submissive, but she was anything but submissive. Nor was she as collected as she appeared. Her magic was all over the place. Burning hot one minute, cold the next. The traceries on her arm moved faster, a reaction to her unsettled state and proof of how desperately she needed to learn to control that magic before ignorance killed her.

Still bent over, she lifted her head and gave him a smile that made him think she was wrong about what kind of woman was his type. "Christophe killed my sister. He took away my life. What I used to be. The life I loved.

And then he killed Tigran. And nothing happened to him. He has the same cushy life as ever. Where's the justice for my sister and Tigran? Or me?" She sat up, back straight. Her gaze had no bottom, and he was, in all honesty, taken aback by such savage intensity in a human. "What matters is that I promised Tigran."

"Then you accept the risk?"

She met his gaze straight on. Unblinking. She had extraordinary courage and that was always an asset. Her focus stayed on him with such intensity the skin along his arms prickled with heat. "You're damn right I do."

"Come here."

She walked to him with a loose-jointed flow, perfectly aligned and centered. She had an athlete's body. Slender. Long legged. With the kind of poise that came with knowing how her body worked. He wondered what she'd been before Christophe got his hands on her. Not the academic sort.

Durian pulled enough magic to be prepared for anything that might go wrong. "I'm curious to learn what limitations you have. Aside from your permanent physical ones."

"You mean because I can't change?"

"Yes." He took a steadying breath. She was right about him. His type or not, he could easily persuade himself into sex with her. He touched her cheek with the tip of a finger. She quirked her eyebrows at him and gave him a smile hot enough to boil water.

Her taste in clothes was execrable, and he doubted she knew a Monet from a Manet, but she was still a damn good-looking woman.

Durian opened himself to her until he felt the beat of

her heart, the pulse of her blood. The level of magic in the room increased, flowing over his skin and bringing his instincts into focus. Sight, sound, smell. Touch. Taste. Magic. Everything was more intense. More real. More everything.

Her eyes jittered and then went still. Her pupils contracted to pinpoints of black until her eyes were almost nothing but white and the arctic blue of her irises. The traceries on her arm and temple shifted into new whorls and curlicues. Tigran had been a fiend of significant power, and, he suspected, possessed of a magic very similar to Durian's own.

He pulled hard at the same time he veiled the part of his magic he'd need if things went wrong. He was reasonably certain he would be able to terminate her even without an explicit sanction from Nikodemus since he would likely be acting in self-defense. "Closer, if you please," he said.

She moved in.

If he lifted a hand he could touch her, but he hesitated. For all her size and permanently human form, she was dangerous because of her lack of control over her magic, not to mention the magic she had taken from Christophe. If he had to terminate her, he wasn't sure there was anything he could do to save Tigran's magic from oblivion. That might be lost to the kin forever.

Eyes closed, she lifted her chin. Now that he was looking past the mismatch between her hair and her complexion he could see that before she'd destroyed her appearance, she might have been more than a little attractive.

"Ready?" he said.

She nodded.

He rested the tips of his fingers on the bare skin showing above the collar of her shirt. He leaned forward, closing the space between them, breathing in the scent of her body; stale sweat and fear. A chemical scent rose from her hair, the lingering result of whatever process had altered her natural color. His fingers slid up the side of her neck, more slowly than he should have done, over her tense jaw, upward past her temple and then, at last, to her forehead. Her skin was quite soft.

He let his eyes drift closed as he pressed the pads of his first and second fingers to her forehead. He heard her quick inhale, felt her stiffen as he pulled his magic through him. Beneath his fingertips, her skin warmed his, and a trickle of her magic flowed into him.

Indistinguishable from one of his kind.

He was directly in her head and so close to an indwell he would be hard-pressed to explain to anyone why it wasn't. He slid his hand up her left arm until his palm cupped her shoulder. He didn't want to make contact with the traceries on her right arm, not when he was so closely linked with her. Not with the unstable state she was in.

"Gray," he said. He waited until she opened her eyes. She did so slowly. Languidly. He stared into her eyes, recognizing the faint glow of magic in them. How strange to see the signs of her kinship while feeling, so viscerally, her humanity.

She stepped back, but he didn't let go of her. He was still in her head and the truth was, he was aroused. She knew it, too. An understandable, perhaps inevitable, reaction. She was cautious now. Afraid of him. Her mouth went white around the edges; she had her teeth clenched so hard he could hear them grinding. He could feel her drawing in on herself. Protecting herself out of habit.

He squeezed her shoulders gently. Enough to get her to look at him. "No. You must be open to me." He maintained his connection, though drawn down now to a thin and reedy flow between them. "When you're ready."

Seconds ticked by while she accepted that he was going to keep his word about not hurting or forcing her. Her head bowed, and he no longer needed the physical contact.

Anticipation made his limbs light and jittery. His body recognized the high and prepared for what this always meant; a sanctioned kill. The magic required was similar to what he was about to do.

He tipped her face to one side so her throat was exposed to him. She ran hot for a human. Arousal, he told himself, was normal under the circumstances. Every creature on earth had a set of instincts that ran so deep not even sentience suppressed the reaction. She was too much kin for him not to feel the desire to touch and connect, and too human for him not to feel the desire to possess. And quite female enough, thank you.

Nothing would come of this except that by the end, he would have a sworn fiend who was not directly bound to Nikodemus, and a promise to her he'd have to keep. He released a trickle of magic, just enough to allow his fingers to change. She sucked in a breath, and beneath his fingertips he felt the ripple of goose pimples along her skin. Her magic was a touch of ice across his nerves.

He nicked her throat. Blood scent rose sharp, hot and sweet. So sweet. He gave Gray the words to say. They weren't precisely necessary, but they helped. In her case, they probably were required. She'd not otherwise absorb what they were doing. Words spoken in ritual and shaped with magic took on power beyond the surface meaning.

She repeated them in a low, steady voice. He knew she would keep her oath. She'd been loyal to Tigran, after all.

Durian was in command of his connection with her, an excellent thing since she didn't have good control of her magic and her mental state just now was labile, to say the least. Her magic ebbed and surged. Despite her limitations, the fealty oath took effect. He pushed away his triumph.

Not yet done. Not yet complete. But taking hold in them both.

His awareness of her changed and settled in him, became a part of him. His fingers tightened on her face. He heard the rasp of her breath, took in the scent of her blood before he bent his head and tasted.

Their minds touched, the pull between them stronger than before. She was human, but what came back to him along their link was the magic of his kind. Magic that was very much like his own. She could have been a warlord herself. If she learned to master her magic, she would be an asset to the kin.

He pulled back and made a cut over his throat, too. She anticipated what came next and went up on her toes. Though he accommodated the difference in their heights, she still had to put her hands on his shoulders and stretch toward him. The embrace was too intimate, primed as he was by all that had gone before. She was right that she wasn't the kind of woman he liked to have sex with, but his body reacted. In predictable fashion. She noticed his response and froze.

"If you're going to back out, now's the time," Durian said. He would not act on his instincts. Would not. He slid a hand around her waist, holding her close, fighting for every ounce of control he possessed. "Otherwise, finish this."

Was that his voice, so low and inviting? He sounded like he wanted to have sex with her.

He did.

Indeed.

He tightened his hands on her but did nothing even when instinct roared at him to finish this with her whether she wanted it or not. She needed to be willing for this oath to take hold with the necessary strength. There should be no words to influence her acceptance, no compulsion from him, nothing that would tip her over the edge into compliance without her full acceptance of the bond between them.

She pushed up on the balls of her feet, and her mouth settled over the cut he'd made in the side of his neck. He damn near went out of his mind.

The minute his blood hit her tongue, the closure of the fealty bond shot through him. The sensation unsteadied him enough that, if only for a moment, he opened himself to her without reservation—his entire being was hers to take. Enslave. Destroy, if she wished.

He cut that off just in time. By then the oath between them had taken hold. A part of her became indelibly linked to him; a part of him linked to her.

Just like that, Gray Spencer's loyalty belonged to him. If required by circumstance, she would lay down her life for him. And he would, in return for this, keep her safe. God knows she was going to need that.

Her mouth on his throat was soft. Her tongue slid along the cut he'd made. Her touch answered a need for contact with his own kind that he'd hardly known he still had.

His.

The single thought belonged to him but echoed from Gray.

His. One of them. Kin.

Like him.

CHAPTER 8

Several Hours Later

Durian, Gray thought, was the kind of person who would get the door for a woman. When they got to the big glass doors of the Nordstrom San Francisco Shopping Center, as expected, he took a quick step forward. He held the door for her to walk through ahead of him. She didn't mind that he was polite that way. In a way, it was kind of sweet of him. Two young women behind her giggled as they went through. She had to wait for Durian to finish holding the door for them, so she got a good look at them batting their eyes at him.

He watched them through and let go of the door to join her, which was when the reaction hit her. As if someone had flipped a switch, her head was too full, the way everything clogs up right before the whammy of an insanely bad cold hits. Damn. The sensation was more than a little disorienting, but nothing she couldn't tough out. In the initial days after Tigran had died, she'd felt a hell of a lot worse than this.

She grinned as the two girls passed, still ogling Durian. They were way too young for him. She said, "You going to ask for their numbers?"

"No." Durian put a hand to her elbow. Her head felt better. Not back to normal, but better.

"Why not? They're cute." That earned her the stare of doom, and she decided to let the subject go. They walked out of the entryway and into the center atrium where he dropped his hand from her elbow.

The pressure in her head came back, a thousand times worse; the hammering of hundreds of voices in an enclosed space, all of them demanding to be heard. She came to a full stop. She met an elderly man's eyes and his thoughts blasted into her head with the force of a blow. There weren't really discreet words, but she knew his hip hurt, that he was pleased with his purchase and that he agreed with Durian on the subject of her hair color. The old man moved on and the hundreds of other consciousnesses rushed back until she wanted to scream.

Outside, this hadn't been a problem. People hadn't pressed in on her the way they did now. She tried blocking them out, but her usual methods did no good here. Either vanilla humans weren't the same as fiends or she was having some kind of breakdown that was going to shatter her mind into pieces.

At her side, Durian took her elbow. Immediately, things improved, but not enough. She resisted Durian's attempt to move forward, afraid to move, with her eyes squeezed closed. There were still thoughts and emotions, swear to God, being broadcast directly into her head.

"Gray? Are you all right?"

She worked up the nerve to move her head and crack her eyes open enough to see Durian. A whole new set of psychic noise yammered at her from the people beyond him. "No."

"What is it?"

"So many people."

He frowned, but then understanding dawned in his expression. He slipped into her head, and the voices dampened to almost nothing. She slumped against him, glad to feel his hand on her back. Relief washed over her at the blessed quiet. He settled his other hand on her shoulder blade and rubbed slowly. "Do the same, Gray," he said with his mouth close to her ear. Jesus, his voice was sexy. "Come into my head. I'll show you how to block them."

She nodded.

"Concentrate. And reach for me."

She took a breath and did, feeling like a complete fool until it worked. At the psychic level, he came alive for her. His hand slid to the small of her back and pressed her to him. Part of her recognized him as kindred, and it soothed her.

"Good," he said in that same low voice that made her stomach sizzle. "I'm going to stop, then start blocking. Ready?" She nodded. She trembled when the pressure of the voices came back, too much. Too many. She clutched his arm.

"Like this." He pulled his magic but she didn't catch on to what he was doing. He had to show her a second time before she was able to block the way he did—at a different frequency, if that was even the right word, for what she needed to do. "We'll stay here while you practice."

It didn't take her long, though she had to concentrate to

keep the voices and emotions out. *Thank God*. Echoes of the pain lingered still, but now she could open her eyes and look around without making herself vulnerable to an unexpected ride in someone's head, or just ending up crushed by the cacophony. She kept her hand on his arm because she needed the contact. Durian didn't seem to mind.

"Better?" he asked.

"Much. Thank you."

"Forgive me," he said. "I assumed you knew how to block out humans. It's amplified, as you discovered, in an enclosed space."

"How do you stand it?"

"Soon enough you'll block them without thinking about it." He left his arm around her shoulder as they walked toward the escalators. "What did you do after you left Christophe? Surely you encountered that effect?"

"I was outside most of the time. Or not where I was around this many people. That I remember." She shuddered just thinking of those disorienting first hours after Tigran was killed. "I lost a couple of days, to be honest." She glanced at him, trying to guess what he was thinking. She had the feeling he wasn't someone who tolerated much weakness. "I woke up in a shelter for battered women. Pretty messed up. They didn't ask any questions. Just told me I didn't deserve to be hit."

"Christophe struck you?" His voice hardened. "Or did one of his magehelds do that?"

They were on the escalator, and she ducked the question by walking up the left side. Durian grabbed her elbow again and dragged her to the right with the other standees. He pitched his voice so no one else would hear.

"Christophe struck you?"

Gray looked around. The shoppers around them had their own business to attend to, although more than a few of the women were checking out Durian. And why the hell not? He was hot, if you liked the stuffy-shirt type of Adonis. "Why wouldn't he? Considering he didn't see anything wrong with turning me over to Tigran?"

"Point taken."

She stood close to him so she could keep her voice low. "Christophe was pretty pissed off when Tigran was dead and he didn't have his magic. He took it out on me. As it turned out, that got me into the shelter." She shrugged. She didn't want to think about Christophe or Tigran. "There's not much else to say."

They rode to the third floor and a few minutes later they were in Nordstrom. He took out a thin black wallet and held out a credit card. "Please buy everything you need."

She looked down at herself then back at Durian. All right. So she wasn't going to make a best dressed list any time soon. "Throwing money at a problem to make it go away?"

"It is my duty, Gray, to see that you have what you need until you are self-sufficient. Buy clothes you can work out in as well. You'll need a great deal of physical training just to get you to a point where you're not a danger to yourself."

"Indoor training or out?"

"Both. Running gear. You needn't buy a gi, but get something suitable for the martial arts."

She took the card between her thumb and forefinger. He had a point. One set of clothes wasn't enough. "This place is pretty expensive, Durian. What's the limit?"

"Twenty thousand would not be an issue."

She figured he couldn't possibly mean that. "I can never tell if you're serious. When you make a joke, smile so I know, okay?"

"When have I not been serious?"

"You have got to be kidding. I can't spend that much money on clothes." She shoved the card back in his hand.

He looked her up and down and winced. "Please try."

"I hate shopping."

"Please, Gray." He wasn't exactly ordering her but it was close enough to give her a twinge, and wasn't that a strange feeling? "Buy enough of what you need."

She made a face at him, but all he did was give her the patented Durian silence. She took back the credit card and studied it. A corporate card. "If you say so."

"If you need me, text me." He handed her a slim phone in a black clip-on case.

"Sure."

"My number is programmed in, along with other numbers you should have. If there's trouble and you cannot reach me, call one of them."

She shoved the credit card in her front pocket and opened the case. An iPhone. She opened up the messaging app and selected Durian's name. "Right. Text you. That should subdue any trouble makers."

"Gray." He sounded put upon. "Among so many vanilla humans, we are unlikely to encounter mages or magehelds intent on trouble. Not even Christophe would be so foolish."

"Where are you going to be?" She didn't like sounding as if she needed to be around him. He was a big boy and he could take care of himself, dammit. Except she couldn't shake the conviction that she needed to be with him in case there was trouble. Walking off with or without his plastic didn't feel right. Besides, she came from a long line of cheapskates and cheapskates never shopped at Nordstrom's.

"I will be safe here, Gray, shopping." His expression didn't change. "I won't be far. Buy yourself suitable clothes."

"This is cruel. I won't forget this."

"I would be happy to buy clothes for you." He held out his hand for the credit card and she handed it over. "Be aware that I have a fondness for women in frills and impractical shoes."

"You would." She shuddered at the parade of frou-frou dresses and shirts that marched through her head.

"I hope you like pastels."

She held back a laugh in case he wasn't joking. "Not too much, actually." She plucked the credit card from his fingers. "All right, boss. I'll be picking my own clothes. On your dime."

"Excellent."

When he walked off, she waited a minute or two for her anxiety to settle, then went to the messaging app on her spiffy new phone and typed *I am in UR base spending UR $$* and sent it to Durian. If it didn't mean shopping, she'd rise to the challenge of maxing out his damn card.

A few minutes later, she was in the ladies department staring with horror at row after row of clothes. Jesus God. What a nightmare. Her phone dinged.

xlnt.

Yeah, right. Excellent.

She really did need everything. If she had any idea

anymore of what kind of person she was, it would be easier to know what to buy. Best to keep it simple, she decided. She gritted her teeth and shopped until the credit card should have been smoking.

Along the way she picked up Joy, a personal shopper who was just now standing by the bags she'd amassed so far, having set out a selection of leather jackets for Gray's consideration.

She was studying them when some guy who looked like he was lost wandered near and smiled at her. Cute. Better than cute, but not her type. She didn't know what her type was, but he wasn't it. Her head was throbbing from the effort of keeping herself blocked so she wasn't in the best mood. Not his fault, of course.

At first, when she noticed him staring, she nodded and went back to looking for a jacket that would hide blood. Not a requirement she felt she ought to mention to Joy, but Durian *was* Nikodemus's assassin. She might end up doing some wet work one of these days. She already had what she called her mini-Durian clothes; everything black, only not fancy. She had workout gear, underwear, and lots of jeans, T-shirts, shirts, and sweaters. It turned out she favored bright colors and strong patterns. She was looking for a black leather jacket because spending someone else's money turned out to be addictive.

"Hey," the lost-looking guy said when she made the mistake of making eye contact with him the second time she noticed him. He was about her age. Maybe a little older. Very corporate looking.

She smiled and went back to the jackets. She tried on a couple more but she wasn't feeling the love.

"We meet again."

Gray looked up at the guy talking to her. He was standing right next to her now. She didn't like that she hadn't known he'd moved so close. He looked like an Italian lawyer, with the suit and tie and shiny shoes to go with the Mediterranean complexion. She knew from what Durian had told her so far that the kin couldn't feel magehelds. If he was one, she wouldn't be able to tell from Tigran's magic. Christophe's, though, that might work. If she knew shit about it.

His black hair was long enough that she was pretty sure he wasn't mageheld. Mages, Christophe included, shaved the heads of their magehelds. "Come here often?"

The guy's eyes flicked down to her left hand. She smiled in relief. Nothing nefarious here. He was just a normal guy making sure he wasn't about to try his lame moves on a married lady. "First time here," she said.

He held her gaze and smiled. He actually looked a little shy when he did. That settled her nerves down. "A virgin, huh?"

"Yeah." She slipped off the jacket she'd tried on.

"The other one was better on you. Not that my opinion matters."

"Thanks." She hadn't been hit on in so long, she could hardly remember how to make him go away with no hard feelings.

He flashed her another smile, but something got inside her blocks. She didn't like the way it felt, but she didn't know enough yet to figure out if he was just some sociopathic human or something she ought to be afraid of. He pointed at one of the jackets. "How about that one?"

Something about him wasn't right. While she pretended to look, she took out the phone Durian had given to her. "Nah."

"Listen." He tugged on his tie. "You're going to think I'm coming on too strong, but I think you're just..." His cheeks flushed. "Can I buy you a coffee?"

"Oh, hey. That's really nice of you to ask." If he was a normal human, she didn't want to hurt his feelings, but no way was she going anywhere with a stranger. "I have a boyfriend."

"It's just a coffee." He smiled a little too hard. "What's the harm in that? Come on. Just to talk."

Gray backed away and got out her phone. She navigated to Durian's contact entry. "Let me ask my boyfriend. If he's done, sure. We'll have coffee."

His smile froze in place. "That sounds like fun."

The phone on the other end stopped ringing. "Durian here."

"Hey, sweetie," she said, trying to play it real for the benefit of whoever this guy was. "Can you come find me? I'm over by the leather jackets. There's someone here who wants to have coffee with us."

He didn't say anything for a bit. "On my way."

She kept the phone in her hand. "He'll be right here."

"Great," Italian lawyer said. "I can't wait to meet him."

Durian must have been close because before she expected him, he was sliding himself beside her, a hand around her waist. He had a shopping bag in the other hand. He bent to kiss her cheek. And then he went for her mouth. "Darling. Mm." Short as kisses go, but he managed to rock her world.

She froze at the contact. His mouth was soft and warm. At the last minute, it occurred to her she needed to act like she kissed Durian all the time. She plastered herself against his chest and reciprocated. And damned if she didn't get turned on. When he drew back—tactical error there, she realized—she should have been the one to pull away—he stared into her eyes.

Like an idiot, she stared right back. His eyes were just beautiful. "God, you smell good."

He blinked. "Your favorite, of course."

If she was going to make of fool of herself by behaving like a teenager with a bad case of puppy love, she might as well make it worth the humiliation afterward. She snaked an arm around his neck and pulled his head back to her. She gave him a short, hard kiss, but open-mouthed, and she lingered at it afterward.

"Remind me," Durian said when she moved away, "to be sure I have an ample supply of that cologne."

"Durian." The guy stuck out his hand for Durian to shake, and for no reason at all, Gray stepped forward until she was between Durian and the man. Durian pulled her back to his side. She gave in and leaned against him. "It's been a long time. Nice to see you again."

Durian kept his arm around her waist, but his hand angled toward her hip. The tips of his fingers brushed the bare skin between her shirt and her jeans. Warm skin, his was. "You're a long way from home, Leonidas."

"This is my first trip to America." Leonidas pulled back his hand. She looked between the two, trying to figure out if they were friends, enemies, or something else. "Will you and your young lady join me for coffee?"

"I regret we cannot."

"I am sorry to hear that." His voice changed from easygoing to tense. "I would have enjoyed your company."

"You two know each other?" she asked. She let herself lean against Durian's torso. Since her left arm was dangling awkwardly between them, she hooked her arm around his waist. Under his expensive clothes was a well-muscled body. My. Wasn't that nice?

Leonidas examined her a little too closely for her peace of mind. "Let's say we know of each other."

Durian gave him a brisk nod and addressed Gray. "Where are your bags?"

She pointed to where Joy stood and the next thing she knew, they were loaded down with shopping bags and walking out. They were on the street before Gray dared to speak. "So. Who was that?"

"A mage, as you must have guessed by now."

"I got that."

"He is one of the more powerful mages. He's from Greece. Sparta, most particularly."

"More powerful than Christophe?"

"Yes." He looked at her as they headed onto the street. "It's no accident that he found you. There will be others, Gray, and chances are they won't be as polite or circumspect as Leonidas."

She didn't like the idea of more mages. At all. "If Nikodemus won't let you kill Christophe, then I'm guessing he won't let you kill Leonidas either."

"No."

"Bummer."

"We'll start your training immediately."

CHAPTER 9

A Few Days Later

Watch me first," Durian told Gray.

She locked gazes with him and like that, he was in her head. Her magic was there, drawing him deeper than he expected. Since they'd begun working together, she'd improved beyond his expectations. She now had more than decent control of her magic, for example. There were other effects, too, mostly as a result of her fealty oath. The part of his soul that had been so long isolated didn't seem quite so vast anymore.

Her smile slowly disappeared. "You don't think I can do this, do you?"

"In respect of your magic, I have no doubts about your ability."

Her disappointment was a flash of heat that transferred to him, too. "Liar."

"No doubts that matter, I assure you. Your physical limitations are what concern me."

"We just ran three miles in fifteen minutes." She rolled her eyes. "That's twice as far as I've ever run in my life."

"All things considered, you did well. You aren't out of shape, and that is a benefit."

She looked down at herself, in her snug black leggings and a neon green T-shirt that made him wish he'd done the shopping for her clothes. He looked at her, too, since the opportunity presented. She was more sleekly muscled than he'd expected. She hadn't been sedentary in her previous life, that was plain.

"Gee, thanks," she said.

Best, he thought, to keep this businesslike. "Over the next few weeks, your magic will continue to contribute to your endurance in much the same way that it reduces your need for sleep and increases your strength and quickness."

"You think I'm going to be hopeless at fighting, don't you?"

He looked around the upstairs room he'd cleared of furniture so they would have a place to train. "You have decent control of your magic." He'd spent the better part of the last few days working on nothing but that. "That mastery does not mean you could hope to physically prevail against any but the least powerful of the kin."

"I'm still using training wheels; is that what you're saying?"

He felt the corner of his mouth twitch. "You will outrank a good many of the kin, Gray. But we've only begun. For you to learn everything you need, to integrate the physical and the magical, that could take weeks. Months."

Leaning over with her hands propped on her knees, she dropped into a deep side lunge. At least her limbs were flexible. "Maybe."

He didn't trust her too carefully blank expression. If she was annoyed with him so be it. "I'll go slowly," he said. "So you get a sense of what you need to learn." He saw the glitter of a challenge in her eyes, and his heart sank. "I admire your spirit, but pride will only be a barrier to what you need to learn."

"I'm a quick study."

He walked to the middle of the floor and set himself. "Ready?"

She nodded.

Taking care not to move at anything near top speed, he moved through one of the simpler forms he'd devised for the training that made him feared among the kin and magekind alike. He had, over the years, created a highly personal hybridization of several of the warrior arts. Humans were clever about turning disadvantages into advantages. Even used against a creature an order of magnitude faster and stronger, the martial arts could be quite effective. When someone like him used them against a sanction, the results were always lethal.

The series he'd elected to start with was simple enough but the various steps would reveal which weaknesses he would have to work on with her. Balance. Coordination. Strength. All things that came naturally to the kin, but that in humans required dedicated training.

He relaxed into the movements. At the end, he finished an explosive upward kick with a controlled return to center. He was always more psychically balanced when he worked through his forms, and now was no different. He reset himself into a waiting stance and met her gaze. "This time, you follow along."

"No need," she said. "I got it."

He didn't hide his skepticism. He'd developed his style of fighting over centuries, borrowing and adapting from any system that contained something useful to him. He had spent years adapting movements to his magic, until he arrived at the deadly blend he used today. "This is not a game."

"I didn't say it was." She stretched her arms. "You're good with your body, and that means you make it look easy. I get that it's not."

"I would be happy to show you once more."

She didn't blink. "I have it."

He stepped aside and added overconfidence to his list of required remediations. "Then do show me."

Gray nodded at him. She shook out her arms and legs, finished off with an oddly controlled roll of her head and shoulders and took up his starting position. Before his eyes, she transformed herself. Not the shift from human to a true manifestation of one of the kin, but a transformation nonetheless.

She executed his form without a single error.

Perfect. Better than perfect. She took the physicality of his form and made it lyrical. Breathtaking grace and power. He saw flashes of himself in her movements, but they became hers. Her magic had already made her stronger and faster than she had been, so some facility was to be expected, but her adaptation to the change in her physical state was astonishing. Not just perfect but sublime.

Gray brought the form to the ritual conclusion he'd

devised on his own, and it was heartbreakingly lovely to watch. She released the finish pose, and cocked her head at him, deadly serious.

He took a step back, half in love with her simply for her sheer physical ability. He felt he'd been deceived, too, though he knew it was mostly pride that made him feel that way. Quite stupidly, he'd thought she would be... anything but what he had just seen.

He said, "What were you before Christophe?"

Some of the light went out of her eyes. "Does it matter?"

"Yes."

"Why?"

"You aren't just good, Gray. That was—" He flicked a hand. The thought of what she could do with that kind of command over her body made him think it was Christophe who had been lucky to survive. "—brilliant."

Something flashed behind her eyes and was quickly suppressed. "You're angry?"

"I made a fool of myself, telling you it might take years to teach you."

Her mouth twitched. "Maybe you had it coming. A little."

He gazed down at her and had to relent. "Perhaps."

"You do need to teach me." She put her hands on her hips, and he was put in mind of Degas and his bronze ballerinas. "I don't understand the magic. What you do, Durian, what you are, comes out in the way you move. Physically, sure. No problem. Bring the whole mind thing into it?" She swept a hand around his makeshift do-jang. "This gets more complicated than what you showed me. I know that."

He walked toward and around her, letting his magic build up to match what he felt from her. "How old are you? Twenty-seven? Twenty-eight?"

She opened her mouth to make what he was sure would be some acid retort, but then didn't. "Twenty-eight."

"Thirty years ago, Gray Spencer, before you were conceived, I was already three millennia old."

One corner of the room was piled with rugs so there'd be a place for them to sit comfortably if they so desired. She walked to the rugs now and reached for one of the water bottles stacked there. He held up two hands in an I'm-going-to-catch-it motion. Gray tossed hers to him and picked up another. She cracked the top and took a long drink. "I danced."

"What kind of dance?" For some reason he imagined her doing the tango with some dark-haired tuxedo-wearing partner.

She shrugged and stared into her now empty water bottle. "A bunch of stuff, really." She tossed the bottle into the corner. One thing he'd learned about her was how stubbornly she protected her previous life. "Nothing that matters."

"You were good at it. Obviously."

She stood up, her weight on her back leg, her front leg turned out. "Do you mind if we don't talk about what I used to be?" Her face was too carefully neutral. She was keeping him away from anything but a surface connection with her. "That's over with."

He should have guessed much sooner. "A professional," he said.

She didn't answer, and Durian's chest pinched. Someone with her physical gifts, and he had no doubt she had been gifted, had to have suffered when it was taken away. Christophe had much to answer for.

He nodded curtly. He hadn't shared any more of his past with her than was necessary. No matter how deep his curiosity, he wasn't going to insist that she share anything with him. She was right. "Does this bother you? The reminder?"

However badly he'd put it, she got what he meant. He saw and felt the catch in her emotions. "Thanks, Durian."

In a rare moment of acknowledgment, they stood silent, both of them, he thought, aware their lives had just changed course. They were more to each other than they had been just moments ago. If they were to become lovers, something he'd begun to think of as a rather enticing inevitability, the result would now be more than just a pleasing sexual union. She would scour his soul when it happened.

What, he wondered, would happen to her?

She cleared her throat. "It'd be easier not to think about what I used to be, but it's there. A part of me." She looked away. "Besides," she said in a quiet voice. "I won't deny there's joy. Even if it hurts."

Durian forced himself to stay where he was. He wasn't ready to confront what had just happened to them, and he didn't think she was either. "Shall we continue?"

Within twenty minutes of him working with her she'd picked apart his physical tics. Every dip of a shoulder that betrayed him, every quirk of a muscle. She saw, absorbed it in some way he could not reconcile with her human limitations. She nearly always flawlessly reproduced what he'd done. Usually better.

He moved them quickly past the simpler forms.

Ninety-nine percent of the time she put herself precisely where she needed to be. She rarely made a mistake twice, and if she did, she recovered quickly. Once or twice she made him show her some move or combination until she was sure she understood—whatever it was she thought she needed to understand. On those occasions, she'd crouch down and watch him with a laser focus until something clicked for her. After which she was perfect in her execution. Her only difficulty lay in integrating her magic. She did struggle with that. He was confident, however, that she would overcome her present difficulties.

Every now and then, they stopped their work to eat one of the energy bars he'd brought along, or rest quietly, each lost in their personal thoughts. Sometimes when she thought he wasn't looking, she'd do some movement on her own, and each and every one of them sparked his hunger for the beauty of her movement and the command she had over her body.

Her endurance was already well beyond what any normal human possessed; they'd been working for several hours at nearly top effort. They stopped for another break. Durian loosened his hold on his magic and watched the tracings on her arm and temple react while he had her eat another energy bar. They were close and without thinking he drew a finger around the edges of the traceries on her temple.

She shivered. He dipped his head toward her, and after an infinitesimal hesitation, she lifted her chin. His fingers moved over her, and her magic sparked underneath his fingers. He wanted her with a vicious ache. He was afraid to take her too far, too fast, yet curious to know how much she could do.

He allowed her magic to seep into him, to permeate him. His oath to her shimmered between them. She sucked in a breath. With her head clasped between his hands, he said. "What you could do if you stopped fighting your magic." Too much. He wanted this too much. He released her and forced himself to step back. "You might take Christophe without even trying."

Her eyes opened wide, and he stared into those chilly blue depths and thought she saw far too much. She said, "Teach me how. If I'm not doing something right, tell me. Show me what I'm doing wrong. I'll learn. I swear."

"You must learn to connect your magic to your body."

She nodded. "How?"

"If I am to teach you about what I am, you won't be able to go back to something safer."

Her eyes caught his and when her mouth curved, he touched her there, with the edge of his thumb sweeping along that arc of her lower lip. She said, "Safety is way overrated."

"You move...exquisitely." He opened himself to her so that she could reach, if she cared to, for the darkness he'd been keeping from her, that dark and dangerous edge to his magic that made him what he was. "Let your magic fill you when you do. Trust it. What Tigran was belongs to you now." He touched the tracery at her temple. "Don't be afraid of what you are, Gray. I'm here. If you get into trouble, I'll help you."

"All right, then."

He pulled without hiding from her what he did or how this magic took shape. He reset and after a moment, she did the same. While she watched, to one side of them, the air quivered, darkened and took form. A darkness formed out of the air and took shape as a humanoid creature, not flesh and blood, but shadow and magic. Durian directed himself to the entity he'd called up.

"What is that?"

"A form of imp," he told her. "Created from my magic and possessed of a limited though self-sustaining consciousness."

She looked suitably impressed. As she ought to be.

"In short, this is the perfect sparring partner." As a conjured creature it lacked heft or weight, but when he moved to show Gray what he meant, it countered him as if it had both. "We'll work together at first." He tapped his head and relaxed his usual hold on his magic. It was freeing to hold so little back from her. "We'll be linked, and, if you'll permit me, I'll draw on your magic for you." He cupped the side of her face for a moment, and he flashed onto the moment, yet in the future, when he would touch her like this as a prelude to sex. "You'll see and feel what I mean about using your magic with your body."

She nodded.

He returned the gesture then passed a hand through the creature's body. Shadows separated then closed after him. "Don't make the mistake of thinking that because it isn't physically substantial that it cannot harm you."

"How, if it's not real?"

"I did not say it isn't real." He allowed himself a smile. "When I give the word, and it becomes conscious, if it touches you, it'll hurt like hell. Or worse."

Her eyes widened. "Ah. All right, then."

They began. He opened himself to her, aware that he was trusting her with a great deal. Her oath of fealty ensured her loyalty and bound her to protect his physical safety. Emotional safety was another matter entirely. He had not connected with any of the kin at this level in too many years to count. The psychic connection between them tightened. Once he'd surrendered his usual psychic blocks, he could feel her absorbing the physical knowledge of his centuries of work. It was exhilarating.

They moved even more quickly through the defensive moves he'd shown her. When he began the offense, he used moves that, with the proper magic behind them, could kill at a touch. He showed her the magic, too, something he had never allowed anyone else. Until it was too late.

When he drew on her magic, shaping his pull as he had with his own, her traceries deepened in color. They extended farther along her arm and around the side of her face. The magic came alive between them to the point where it was difficult to tell which one of them he was pulling from. They moved as one. Sinuously. She slid in close to his construct, and Durian knew that had the construct been physically alive, she would have had her first kill.

They stopped, on an unspoken and mutual agreement, and for a time they just looked at each other. Magic rocketed through them both. For a split second, he was in her head completely and the sensation was better than anything he'd felt in his life.

He pulled back, shaken that he had succumbed for even a moment.

Gray stood less than two feet away, with her hands on her hips, her fingers curled around her pelvic bones, sweat dripping down her face, her arms, her hair damp with it.

"Jesus, Durian," she whispered. "You are one hell of a

demon." A grin curved her mouth. "That was good. Really good."

He nodded. Her pounding heart and racing pulse echoed in his head. And something far more elemental. His hand settled on her shoulder and she stepped toward him because he was pulling her forward, and she knew exactly what was happening to him. His lips peeled back from his teeth, and he growled, low and soft.

He was reacting according to an ancient instinct he wasn't sure he wanted to resist any longer. As a species the kin were hardwired for psychic connection with a human. Gray knew that. Just as she knew it was normal, perfectly normal, for him to crave physical contact to go with the psychic.

He wanted to touch her and feel the rush of arousal, his need for the pleasure of human skin beneath his hands, under his mouth, in contact with his body. He wanted to caress her, put his mouth on her, kiss her, taste her blood. The side of his thumb slid over her skin and the next minute he felt her flinch at the cut he made along her throat. He drew her closer yet and lowered his head to that place. Her inhalation was a soft sound.

His mouth touched her skin, his tongue swept away the welling blood. He slid a hand over the back of her head, threading his fingers through her hair. Her torso tipped toward him. She was willing. Compliant. He wanted to strip off her clothes and put her flat on her back. He could. She wouldn't resist him.

He bowed his head and steadied himself. "This is not safe," he said. "Not now."

CHAPTER 10

One Week Later

Christophe dit Menart sat with his back to the computer desk built along his office wall. Behind him three monitors winked to black. His MacBook was on his lap with one of his less sensitive e-mail accounts open on the screen. He ignored the mage sitting on the couch opposite him in favor of making his point about where the other man ranked in Christophe's estimation: not very high.

While Kessler waited in silence, Christophe tapped away on *MacMage*, the nickname he'd given his twenty-first century aluminum beast, doing nothing more exciting than deleting unwanted e-mails and sending offers to enlarge his penis to the spam folder.

A year ago, he would have considered Rasmus Kessler a mage who needed to be killed before he took control of the local magekind in this, his adopted homeland. Ironically and rather wonderfully, Nikodemus and his band of hell-spawn had made that unnecessary. He deleted several more e-mails. Not until he was certain Kessler must be seething with resentment did he close MacMage. He turned on his chair to set MacMage on the counter behind him, speaking as he did. "Thank you for coming."

Kessler made the interesting choice of going on the offensive. "Are you certain we are safe here?"

With an expansive gesture at the room and a smile intended to hide only minimally the degree to which the question offended him, Christophe said, "This room alone cost me five million euros."

The other mage kept one hand in his lap, attempting, Christophe knew, but failing, to hide the tremor of his thumb and first two fingers. The extent of Kessler's injuries had been the subject of much speculation among the magekind. A vulnerable mage or witch was at risk of losing his magehelds and with the loss of magehelds came a loss of power. Indeed, Rasmus Kessler had suffered just such depredations from other magekind. He had not been able to maintain his ranking.

Christophe had to presume his injuries were permanent since he hadn't been able to heal himself by now.

"Forgive me," Kessler said. "I am unclear how that expense keeps us safe from intruders."

Us. *Us?*

The hubris, Kessler lumping himself in with Christophe as if he were an equal.

He resisted the urge to grind his teeth. What was Kessler but some pissant mage unable to retain control of his own magehelds or replace the ones he had lost? By all accounts, Kessler had come within inches of burning out his magic, and not so long ago, either. The Dane ought to be on his knees begging for help, not doling out insults.

"Five million euros is perhaps a small sum for you. It is not for me." He heard the French cadences creeping into his voice as happened when he was under the grip of strong emotion. "Even with my limited need for skilled human labor." He pointed. "That door is custom built to my own design, *cher* Rasmus, so that a seal may be achieved at every conceivable angle and plane. That is wood paneling over a steel shell which itself contains a layer of crushed rubies."

"Where did you acquire the rubies?"

Rubies, encapsulated in this manner, prevented outside magic from coming in and inside magic from going out. The result was a shield that permitted a mage to use magic in formidable amounts without drawing unwanted attention to the effort. Such a carefully prepared room was all but impregnable and Kessler knew it.

"Burma, naturally. Why do you think the cost was five million?" Lab-grown gems could be used, but there was a marked diminution in efficacy. The better the stone, the better the result. He smiled again. "The walls and ceiling as well contain pulverized ruby. Even the insulation is made with a slurry of ruby dust." He gestured. "This marble floor across which we have walked was reformed with rubies. I spared no expense and cut no corners."

"Yes, I feel the effect." Kessler shook his long blond braids behind his shoulders. There were dozens of tiny braids, each of them with ruby beads worked in that lent him a piratical air. He looked older than he ought to given his reputation. Still young looking, still an attractive man, but at the farther edge of maturity now. "With all respect, Christophe, I have seen a similar room breached."

He waved a hand. "Perhaps you were careless."

Kessler gazed at Christophe. "The room I saw breached as if it were butter instead of six layers of steel and ruby was in Álvaro Magellan's house. And that mage was never careless."

By design there were no windows. From floor to ceiling, the walls were painted with stylized runes and sigils, some of which had been drawn in blood. His personal work, made with his blood and the blood of one or two of his magehelds. Others were drawn in ink or painted in oils; those too in his own hand. The smell of linseed oil and turpentine lingered still. The effect of his ruby-fortified walls was at once colorful and disorienting. Hallucination was a risk of staring too long at certain of the patterns.

"By the end," Kessler said with his attention downward rather than at the wall behind Christophe, "Magellan was dead."

The unspoken fact was that Magellan, the greatest mage ever to have lived, had not survived. And Kessler had. That was something, indeed. If Christophe's information was accurate, the Dane's injuries had come some months after Magellan's death, in an entirely separate incident. Offended as he was, Christophe decided he would be unwise to dismiss Kessler out of hand.

"Perhaps Magellan was not as good or careful as we were led to believe." He let his smile slip. "Whatever happened that night, or on any other, Rasmus, I attest that here you and I may speak safely."

Christophe leaned back in his chair, hands clasped

behind his head. A disturbing pulse of magic came from the other mage, stronger than he would have expected from one so severely damaged. "Seven of my magehelds stand guard outside the door. If this room were to be breached, unlikely as that is, those seven will die saving my life. In this room, we are as safe from harm as is possible. For men like us."

"If your magehelds are severed?" Kessler's gaze was unblinking. "What then?"

"You jest."

"No, mage, I do not." Despite his damaged hand, Kessler no longer looked quite so ineffectual.

Christophe's stomach clenched. The thought of someone with both the will and the ability to sever a mageheld demon put the whole of the human race within sight of their doom. If such were true, mankind needed more mages, not fewer. "Stories," he said, feeling sick. "Stories parents tell to frighten their children into behaving. This is not a skill anyone today possesses."

"Not stories."

"Has this happened?" He speared Kessler with his gaze. "Of your personal knowledge?"

"Yes."

"*Merde.*"

"My question stands. Are we safe here?"

Christophe jumped up from his chair and paced the length of his computer desk. He kept his hands clasped tightly behind his back. "If what you suggest were to happen, then no." He was not pleased at this conversation. "In such a case, no one is safe."

The other mage nodded.

Christophe stopped pacing. "Given the unlikelihood

of such an occurrence, I represent to you that here you and I are as safe as it is possible to be." Kessler had been there the night Magellan breathed his last. Damaged Rasmus Kessler was the only one who knew what had happened. Therefore, whatever he thought of the mage now, it behooved him to listen and to believe. He kept his attention on the Dane. "I was in Paris at the time, as you know," Christophe said. "We heard a great many rumors in Europe. Each more fantastical than the other."

"Kynan Aijan killed Magellan."

He had to steel himself not to react. That rumor had been one he had dismissed as impossible. "His own mageheld?"

Kessler remained impassive, too. "By then, he was no longer mageheld."

"How?"

"A witch severed him."

"Who among us would do such a thing?" Christophe wanted to sit down but didn't because that could be taken as a sign of weakness. "Who would free a creature such as that? To let him loose among the innocent?"

"Nikodemus found a way to bind a witch to him." Kessler leaned forward, releasing his hands. Both of his hands, the damaged and the undamaged, remained still. For now. "She was Magellan's witch. From a very young age. He would not have been able to use her for much longer. She got away somehow, survived and now does the warlord's bidding."

Christophe's breath left him. A captive witch? Worse, one who was now enslaved to a warlord. In his mind, he saw Erin, his lovely, beautiful Erin, in thrall to a creature like Kynan Aijan or Durian. His heart turned to ash at the horror of thinking she could be lost to a demon. Turned against her own race, the people she loved. Turned against him. Even her own child. He crossed himself, muttering familiar Latin under his breath.

The Dane didn't relax.

"What more?" Christophe asked.

"I think," Kessler said, "that if I am to tell you anything beyond what I have already, we should have a firm understanding between us."

"Go on."

For the first time since the mage had walked in, Rasmus Kessler smiled. "You cannot act against Nikodemus. Not directly."

Christophe understood what Kessler meant. The Dane did not live in the warlord's territory. Therefore, Kessler was not bound to the agreement with Nikodemus. He gestured at Kessler's hand. "Forgive me, my dear Rasmus, but what can you do?"

"As I am now? Nothing." His smile widened. Once again Christophe felt the pulse of magic in the other mage. He was damaged, yes, but not without power. "If I had thirty magehelds there would be a great deal I could do on your behalf."

"Five."

"That's not enough, mage, and you know it." He leaned against the couch and crossed one leg over the other. "Fifty is a better number, but I understand the scarcity of the resource and can make do with thirty."

Thirty was not an outrageous number. But he wasn't about to give Kessler the resources to fully restore the standing he'd lost. Not unless there was no choice. "Ten."

"Thirty, Christophe." The mage's eyes were steady.

Ah, Christophe thought. There was a reason for the dozens of ruby beads in his hair. "I'll even throw you a bone. There is another demonbound witch."

"Who?"

He held up his hand, with the useless digits trembling. "Thirty of your magehelds, Christophe, and I will tell you the rest. I might even be persuaded to eliminate the demonbound witches for you."

Christophe stared at the runes painted into the wall behind Kessler. Two witches bound to a warlord. Inconceivable. Had he underestimated Nikodemus so badly? He tore his gaze from the written symbols. "Do you require assistance with the ritual?"

The mage inclined his head, but not before he saw the rage in the white-lipped set of Kessler's mouth. Not directed at him, but at the humiliation of having to admit he needed help with what must once have been easily mastered magic for him. "Yes."

"Twenty-five, then. Including the ones you kill tonight. And you will assist me exactly as I ask, until you have replaced the magehelds I give you."

Kessler blinked. "Very well. Twenty-five."

"Who is the other witch?"

"My daughter, Alexandrine." At Christophe's shock, Kessler made a dismissive motion. "She did not pass her initial tests so she was fostered out. As it happens, she had magic after all and survived the onset."

Dieu. "And is now demonbound."

"To another of Nikodemus's sworn fiends." He held up his hand again. "She is responsible for this."

Two demonbound witches. Worse than he had imagined. Far worse, if there was more than one fiend capable of that kind of magic. "You understand that both your daughter and Nikodemus's witch must die, yes? This cannot be allowed."

"Agreed." Kessler tipped his head to one side. "There is another witch. Not demonbound yet, but a danger nonetheless."

This, at least, was not news. "I assume you mean Maddy Winters."

"I do."

Christophe hid his smile. "Eliminate her and I'll send you ten more magehelds."

"Since my resources will be limited, I make no promises about when or where."

"Easier to kill her than get to the demonbound witches." Christophe walked to the door and released the lock. He pointed to two of the magehelds on guard outside. "You. And you. Come in. And you." He pointed again. "Bring down two to replace them." Whether the magehelds he'd selected understood their lives were required was no concern of Christophe's. They came inside. When the door was closed and resealed, he said to Kessler, "There is another task for you. Another witch."

"You have but to ask, mage."

He let out a breath. "She betrayed me, and I fear may already be demonbound."

"Who?"

"Her name is Anna Spencer, but she's calling herself Gray these days. I want her brought to me alive."

CHAPTER 11

A few days later. Muir Woods National Park,
Marin County, California

Durian parked but left the keys in the ignition. He
tapped a finger on the steering wheel. Even here in the
parking lot, this island away from concrete and glass
soothed him.

From the passenger seat, Gray looked out her window.
"Why here?" She still had the horrific red hair, now with
fading pink streaks and black roots showing. Despite the
money she'd spent, her choice of clothing was—the best
he could come up with was *eccentric*. Jeans and an electric blue shirt worked with an intricate white pattern that
looked like paisley in outline. The shirt underneath that one
was mustard yellow. He wondered if she was color blind.

If he could tell anyone what this place meant to him,
it would be her. "Sometimes, it's good to get away from
the city."

His fealty to Nikodemus had not been given lightly. He had served the warlord well and loyally. Perhaps no longer. Two other kin sworn to Nikodemus had come by the house: Kynan Aijan, a warlord in his own right, though he did not at present have sworn fiends of his own, and Iskander, a former blood twin who continued to struggle without the woman whose magic had once been intimately bound with his.

Both Kynan and Iskander behaved themselves as best as they could while attempting to find out with varying degrees of subtlety what was going on with Nikodemus's assassin. The plain fact was, Durian wasn't prepared to deal with questions about him and Gray. Kynan had given him a hard look and told him Nikodemus was starting to worry. Iskander had told him he looked like he needed to get laid.

Gray interrupted his mental lapse when she reached out and grabbed his hand, stilling the tattoo he'd been beating on the steering wheel. "Hey." She gave his hand a gentle squeeze. "What's up, Durian?"

"Let's walk. If you don't mind." He turned his head to look at her. He ought to be appalled by her appearance. He wasn't.

"Sure."

Before he had time to go around to her door, she got out. When he joined her, she looked around, head craned up. "I've never been here before, and I grew up less than an hour away. Crazy, isn't it?" She turned in a circle. "You see pictures and they don't really convey what it's like."

Durian relaxed. "Shall we?"

He paid the park entrance fee and they walked into the shade and cool of the coastal redwood rainforest. As always, he immediately felt better being out of sight of what passed for civilization. Gray stayed close to his side. Though he set a quick pace, she didn't have trouble keeping up. Each day brought her more strength, better endurance. Better control of her magic. One day she would make a fine assassin.

As they walked, their psychic connection strengthened, not from intent but from familiarity and habit. The fact that he was comfortable with anyone maintaining that sort of link with him was extraordinary, but then he trusted Gray as he trusted few others.

They left the groomed trails for a rougher path through trees that had been old long before he came to the continent. Eventually, they emerged from the redwoods onto an open hillside where, after the shade of the redwoods, the sun felt all the more delicious for the shock of heat.

Fifty feet above them a road cut into the hillside; out of their direct sight but occasional traffic noise dispelled the sense that they were far from the city. At their backs was the forest. Downslope, oak trees made their own dense forest, a deeper, dustier green against the fading green of the late spring grass. Already there was more brown here than green. The pure blue of the Pacific shimmered at the horizon.

The path curved sharply behind a boulder. Durian veered off the trail to the front of the massive rock and leaned against the sunbaked surface. Gray stood next to him and after a moment's hesitation, he put his arm around her shoulder.

Their link deepened. And then a bit more, yet he remained content with that, when he had never been before with any of the kin. He wished, even, that matters between them would go further. Her life had been in turmoil for too long. She, too, needed the emotional quiet a place like this offered. She leaned into him.

He turned so that he faced her, his palms on the boulder, just above her shoulders.

"It's pretty here," she said. She tipped her chin up, closing her eyes while she basked in the sun. "Very restful."

"Then I'm glad I brought you here." He was aware that his chest was inches from hers.

Their gazes met when she opened her eyes again. He didn't look away, or do anything but enjoy the first shiver of arousal that zinged along the connection between them. "Come here a lot?" she said.

"Not often enough." He slid the fingers of one hand along the side of her neck, then along her jaw, the outside of her face. The heat of the sun felt good against his back. He glanced between them and dropped his hand to the skull charm that dangled from her navel. Horrible thing, that, and yet it suited her. He even liked the fact that he didn't like the piercing. He flattened his hand on her belly, and she didn't move away. "Would it be disastrous for us if I kissed you?"

She smiled. A soft, slow smile full of inappropriate challenge. "Probably."

His slipped his first and second fingers through the belt loop at the side of her jeans. This was safe, he thought. They could explore what was happening between them without things getting out of hand—whatever that might turn out to be. "No doubt you're right."

She grabbed him by the shirt and pulled him toward her. He let it happen, and it turned him on more than he expected. Her smile was too cheeky by far. "There's only one way to find out, Assassin."

"Only one?" His magic sparked, and he let that happen, too.

Gray angled her head toward his as she slowly brought him closer. The wait was delicious. Would they? Their bodies were close. So close. Then closer. He curved his fingers around the side of her hip and savored the moment. Her breath flashed warm between them. "You're supposed to kiss me," she said against his mouth.

"Excellent point." He leaned in hard and opened his mouth over hers with an aggression that was not usual for him. The women he took to bed weren't anything like Gray. None of them had ever challenged his control. None of them had mattered to him.

Her tongue swept into his mouth and he reciprocated with a kiss that wasn't polite or controlled or any of the things that it should have been. The intimacy burned through him and he reveled in it. She answered his demand and he didn't have to worry that he would do something that would give away something about what he was.

Her body was lovely, and he wanted to strip her naked right here and do the same himself and get inside her.

She tasted good. She smelled like his soap. His.

Here in the open air was not the place to take this where he needed to go.

He drew back and for a while he gazed into her eyes, struggling to keep himself from deciding if he should just take his chances on them not being interrupted. With some effort, he stepped back and straightened his clothes. She'd just done the same when a flurry of pebbles rained onto the path from above them. He and Gray turned and looked up at the same time. Durian expected to see some animal, a feral cat perhaps, or a deer for some reason startled out of its daytime hiding place. But that wasn't it.

Two men careened down the hillside from the road. From this distance they might be taken for college students using a dangerous shortcut into the redwoods in order to save the entry fee. In their sloppy jeans and T-shirts, they slipped in the slick grass as gravity propelled them down the hillside. They fought for balance during their mad, barely controlled run to the path.

"Idiots," Gray said. "They're going to break their necks."

They moved swiftly. Too swiftly. Too sure of themselves. He pulled to have his magic at hand. She keyed off his magic and pulled, too. Moments before the two reached the path, Durian knew what they were. Or, more precisely, what they were not.

They weren't human. He felt nothing, of course, but their eyes didn't reflect normally in the sunlight, and there was only one reason for that catlike effect in broad daylight: magehelds with a hell of a lot of magic on tap. Beside him, Gray stiffened as she reached the same conclusion he had.

The two magehelds jumped the last ten feet, landing on the narrow path with a spray of dirt and gravel. With hardly a pause, they sprinted toward Gray. There was no way to retreat. He and Gray would have to fight.

The ferocity of Gray's response when her oath triggered took him aback. She lunged in front of him and dropped into a crouch as the two magehelds reached them. In a flash, she had more magic at hand than he'd ever felt from her before, focused and laser sharp, that sent ripples through him. The traceries underneath the skin of her right arm made her forearm glow like a beacon. Underneath all that was the tickle of her other magic, no longer quiescent.

Interesting, he thought, that the magic that ought to be antithetical to what he was seemed to have been triggered in his defense.

She darted to one side, stuck out a leg and tripped the first mageheld. Sparring with a construct was different from fighting a living creature, but she executed the move perfectly. In the same motion she sent a bolt of heat into the creature that slammed it down hard. The backwash of her strike sparked through the air. The mageheld didn't die, though, because her magic was off. For obvious reasons, she'd never used a lethal strike before. Durian moved in closer, ready to intervene if Gray ran into trouble.

The downed mageheld didn't stop. Instead, it lurched to its feet and attacked Gray again. It should have known it was outmatched and beat a retreat until its situation could be remedied or reinforcements called. The other mageheld closed the distance to them, heading for Durian.

With a sound straight out of a Bruce Lee movie, Gray shot forward before Durian could do anything. She grabbed either side of the other mageheld's head, braced her shoulder against its chest and twisted her arms. When she released the other mageheld fell dead at her feet.

While this was happening, Durian slid in closer to the first mageheld and stretched for his touch just as it reached for Gray. The enslaved fiend went down and stayed down. Beside him Gray's chest heaved, but she hadn't taxed herself. Her pupils, however, were huge, with only a narrow rim of color around the black.

Durian stood over the mageheld Gray had killed.

"Brash," he said, like her, no doubt, feeling the effects of having survived the attack. "Not as elegant as I would have liked for your first kill."

"Fuck you," she said, but she was grinning. He grinned back as she said, "It's dead, and you're not, right?"

"I don't argue with the outcome. This was well done," he said.

"There's something wrong with them, though." She shook her head. "They didn't feel normal."

"No, they did not."

She wasn't looking at him, but rather to the side. Her head whipped around. Her other reaction sizzled through him. "More coming."

Durian turned toward the forest. Too fast for normal humans, two more men tore out of the woods heading directly for them. Faces misshapen, their bodies lost coherence while they transitioned from human to something else.

Caught up in the surge of Gray's magic, his own physical state snapped from the dampened senses of his human body to the hyper-awareness of his other form. This close to changing, all his senses were exquisitely responsive.

On the road above them, a car door opened. The vibration that shot through him meant a mage of significant power was nearby. He looked up and saw that their encounter with the magehelds had been observed. A man in a dark suit stood at the edge of the pavement, a car with the rear passenger-side door open just behind him. His blond hair was long and braided. Sunlight glinted off the beads worked into the braids. Rubies, every single one. Then, Durian had more immediate worries.

The two new attackers came on with a frenzy that obliterated the cunning that marked a mageheld fiend. It was as if all intention had been stripped from their minds, leaving only the barest sanity to maintain their functions. For these two, nothing remained between thought and action.

Gray's strike at the first reverberated in Durian's bones, a psychic blow focused enough and deadly enough to be worthy of Kynan Aijan. She got better every time. The mageheld she hit slowed, stumbled, but didn't go down and, damn, it ought to have. The second one continued on a trajectory straight at Gray. Neither one gave him the slightest look. As with the first two, they were after her. Had she realized that yet?

The nearest one went for her back, the other careened off the path to get at her from the other side, but it slipped on the slick grass and that gained Gray and him precious seconds.

As if in slow motion, Durian saw the first mageheld's extended claws, the color of old blood and a thousand times more deadly. Those talons arced through the air, ripping apart the very molecules of oxygen, reaching for Durian because he was physically blocking the way to Gray. Her magic arced through the air. She whirled with one arm extended, fingers curved into hooks, as if she, too, had talons. Durian forced a connection to the mageheld's mind and found nothing but a mad intention to take Gray alive.

Durian launched himself and stretched for his touch. The mageheld nearest him died before it landed. Durian hit the path and rolled, ignoring the scrape of gravel along his arm and ribs. He got his legs underneath him and leapt to his feet, pulling more magic then he'd ever needed for a sanction. The other mageheld wasn't close enough for him to touch. Gray darted in, a reckless, dangerous move that would have ended badly had she missed. But she didn't. The second mageheld died, too.

Movement on the road above them distracted Durian. Rasmus Kessler stood unmoving. He moved a hand in a ritual signal.

Durian charged up the hill, holding nothing back, knowing he was going too fast for Gray to catch up and that her oath compelled her to try. At half the distance, he heard the mage muttering, saw the movements of his hands and knew in his heart that Kessler was sending more of those damaged magehelds after Gray. Durian dug his hands and feet into the ground, just soft enough for him to gain purchase. He exploded up the hillside.

He hauled himself closer, nearly blind with the desire to see the life fading from the mage's eyes. Durian scrambled toward the road, intent on reaching Kessler before he finished whatever spell he was casting.

The mage spoke, raising his voice just enough to be heard. "You have two choices, fiend."

Durian knew that voice, and he had to bury his reaction fathoms deep. After he'd regained his freedom, he'd spent months imagining all the ways he would kill the mage when he had the chance.

"Come after me." Durian heard the smile in Kessler's voice. "Or return to the witch. But not both. Which will you choose?"

He looked downhill and saw three more magehelds burst from the redwoods, racing along the path. Gray was below him, a quarter of the way up the hillside. She wasn't fast enough to escape them. If he went after

Kessler, those three would catch her, and he already knew they didn't intend to kill her. Gray was capable, but this was her first encounter outside the do-jang. The smallest mistake would be deadly. Worse, these were not normal magehelds. Kessler had done some something profoundly and horribly wrong to their minds. Durian wasn't even sure he could deal with them.

He leapt toward Gray and the magehelds speeding toward her.

Above him, the car door slammed over the churn of wheels against the pavement edge.

Gray reversed herself when Durian launched himself past her to intercept the first of new magehelds. He killed two with the same strike, but she got to him in time to take down the third with a clean touch that exploded the mageheld's heart.

Durian's chest bellowed in and out as he hovered between human and something else. He ignored the pain that ripped through him, furious in a way that he hadn't felt in far too long. Not at Gray, but at mages who thought his kind were no better than animals to be killed.

"Durian?"

He reached for his control and found it. At last. "Yes?"

"You have blood here." She touched the side of her forehead and made a face. "Is it yours?"

It was his blood, because his skin stung when he touched the spot she meant. His fingers came away smeared with red. His back, too, was scraped, and both knees. Nothing that wouldn't heal before they made it back to the car. Gray wrapped her hand around his wrist.

Durian stilled.

She brought his fingers to her mouth. He shivered when she licked away the blood. His lips peeled back from his teeth, and the sound that came from him wasn't human in any sense. Durian found it in him to take a step back. He didn't like the way he felt right now—his rising sexual response, the burn of his oath to protect her, his desire to connect and fall into the shared mental space with her.

The inevitable aftermath of what they'd done here would hit them both, soon. "We need to get out of here."

She released his wrist.

He did what was necessary with respect to the corpses of the magehelds they'd killed, though in any event without the magic that sustained them, their physical bodies would not last long. But the kin had learned from bitter experience never to take the chance that someone would steal such magic before it, too, was gone. Not ever. That lesson his kind had learned too well.

He and Gray began a lope through the woods. They could talk about what it meant that she could feel magehelds later. When he was sure they were both safe.

Right now, they weren't. Not with Rasmus Kessler one of the mages intending to find out exactly who and what Gray was.

CHAPTER 12

Broadway near Baker Street, San Francisco

Are you hungry?"

Gray yawned even though she was still jumpy from the fighting. Her need to protect Durian hadn't yet receded, despite the danger being more or less past. He hadn't been joking about the obligations of her oath. A human's oath relied on honor and, she supposed, the punishment of a guilty conscience. Both could be powerful forces. She felt elements of both with Durian, but as she now understood, the moment Durian was in danger, she could no more have failed to attempt to protect him than she could have failed to breathe. Both were reflexes over which she had no control.

In her head, she continually replayed her touches as if her brain were stuck in an infinite loop. How she'd missed at first, what she could have done better. What would have happened if she'd failed.

The experience wasn't anything she'd been prepared for. She'd *killed* to protect Durian. Compelled or not, those magehelds would have killed him. The very thought kept her edgy. The sound and feeling of the mageheld's neck breaking wouldn't go away. When she wasn't getting flashbacks about that, she got them about the magehelds she'd killed with a touch of her magic. Killing shouldn't be that easy. The fighting, that was hard, but once she pulled her magic the way Durian had so painstakingly taught her, killing was easy.

She knew she'd do it again, too, if required.

Durian put his arm around her shoulder. "Gray?"

She yawned again. His arm tightened around her, and she got another shot of adrenaline because she remembered what they'd been doing before the magehelds came after them. She got shivers in the pit of her stomach just thinking about the way he'd kissed her. Who'd have thought the original stuffed shirt could turn on the sexual heat like that?

"Ah," he said. They were at the bottom of the stairs, not far from the doorway to the living room. His arm remained draped around her. "You are tired."

Unlike humans and the magekind, demons did not sleep. "I still need a few hours."

"A downside of your fealty to me." His low voice reminded her of sex. Hot and wild sex. "There is a cost to everything."

"At least I haven't turned into some Renfro-like creature snacking on flies and saying 'Yes, Master'."

They looked at each other. With exhaustion pulling on her, she mentally checked out and stood there thinking his eyes were too pretty for words and that his mouth was drop-dead sexy. He blinked, and she came back with a shake of her head. She sighed. "Those magehelds were after me."

"Yes."

"You recognized the mage, didn't you."

"His name is Rasmus Kessler."

"I thought for sure it was Christophe. Huh. Do you think he's working with Christophe? Or was this just another day in the life of an assassin, and this Kessler person was just trying something?"

"Almost certainly he was working with Christophe."

"Damn. Those mages get around, don't they?"

Durian crossed his arms over his chest. "We have avoided the issue of the magic you took from Christophe."

"Yes. Yes, we have."

"That magic has been quiescent, and I allowed myself to think it was nothing we need be concerned with." He fell silent again, and she had no idea what to make of the quiet. He was blocking himself, but he did that a lot. "It seems there is an unexpected benefit."

"Am I in trouble?"

"Of course not." His eyebrows drew together. "Quite the opposite. You felt the magehelds when I could not. That is a useful gift."

She yawned again.

"If you are tired, you should sleep."

"Or down six or seven shots of espresso."

"There is an espresso machine in the kitchen."

"Kidding about the coffee, Durian. All that would do is make me crash even harder."

"How long since you last slept?"

She almost didn't answer him. "A few days. I'm fine."

He tilted his head slightly. "We'll talk, Gray, after you've slept."

"About what?"

"Killing." He stopped and swung around so he faced her. His eyes raked her head to toe. "And other things."

Gray swallowed. "Okay."

He headed up the stairs. Since it was daytime, on the way she could see the jaw-dropping views from just about anywhere the house faced away from the street. The bay was impossibly blue today. They kept walking until they reached a door near the end of the hall. He touched a round, carved medallion on the wall by the doorjamb. A thread of magic leaked from it.

Gray's eyes drooped closed, and she stood there thinking that when they got to the room she'd been crashing in next door to the do-jang, she'd just pass out on the bed with all her clothes on because she was too tired to change or even shower first.

"Gray?" He touched her shoulder.

"What?" She'd actually fallen asleep on her feet. Durian held the door open for her. She blinked a couple of times but couldn't make the room look like the room she was expecting. "This isn't my room."

"No." He touched her waist, and they walked inside.

The room turned out to be a suite. Her new sneakers, scuffed up from the hike and the fighting, looked shabby against the Persian rug that covered most of the floor. "Where is this?"

"My quarters." He stayed close to her. "When I wish to be private."

"Oh." She thought about her old place, the one she'd

never go back to. Her apartment had been full of second-hand furniture culled from flea markets and Craig's List giveaways. In here, a hardwood floor shone wherever the rug wasn't. A small but colorful abstract painting hung on the wall. Original and expensive, was her bet. Durian didn't seem like the kind of guy to have a reproduction.

In this first room, the desk against the far wall was the antique kind with cubby holes and tiny drawers. Real wood. Not veneered particle board. No sidetables covered with a kicky shawl to hide the warped top. A leather jacket slung over the chair in front of the desk probably cost more than she used to spend on clothes in a year. To her right, an interior door opened into another room, but the lights were off in there.

Durian hung his keys on a brass hook by the door and closed the door behind them. He touched another wooden medallion small enough to fit on the door frame near the lock. The face carved in the center looked eerily real. For a minute, she was sure she saw it blink. She really needed some sleep. Durian, of course, didn't need to sleep. None of the kin did.

Above the door frame were three more wooden medallions the size of her palm. The faces painted on them looked real, too. They must have something to do with magic because she was getting a vibration from them that reminded her of Durian.

"You can sleep in here," he said after he'd walked to the desk and put his wallet on the polished surface. "For the time being."

"Where?" She took in the room. She meant it as a joke, but she was too tired to make it come out right. "On the floor?"

Durian looked her up and down.

"Are you checking me out?"

She thought about what she must look like to him. Scrawny. Disaster-red hair chopped off without the aid of a mirror. Dirty and sweaty. Her jeans were a mess, and her new shirt had blood on it. If they ever ended up in bed, she was going to have to remind herself that she wasn't his type or she'd end up hurt. Still, she liked the idea of having hot and sweaty sex with big, dangerous Durian.

"The shower is this way." He walked past her to the open far door and reached in to turn on the light.

She went in after him. The walls here were a dark, dark matte red with crown molding shiny enough to be gold leaf. Lights glowed from recessed areas near the molding. More painted medallions were spaced every three or four feet on the molding. There was enough magic in them that she felt a ripple in the air when she came close.

She pointed at one, eerily convinced they were watching her when she wasn't looking directly at them. "What are they?"

"An alarm system of sorts." He'd been up there fighting, too. How did he manage to look like he'd just stepped off a modeling job for insanely hot men? What if he'd changed his mind about starting something physical with her? She knew for a fact that sex with a demon had its dangers for someone like her. He might not want that. Except, there was that scorching hot kiss... "They will prevent entry by almost anyone not authorized by me, or else make them wish they had not attempted. And inform me of an intruder's presence."

"Oh."

He gazed at her. "They are a magical construct that can

be defeated by anyone with sufficient power or motivation. But not without cost." He thought about that. "So I like to flatter myself."

"I love it when you get all paranoid on me." She examined the wooden disks.

"The nature of my work for Nikodemus warrants caution."

"True."

"Gray."

"What?" She went back to examining the medallions. She touched one with her fingertip. The surface felt hot. Inside the circle of wood, the carved face hissed, baring a tiny pair of fangs. "Mean little buggers, aren't they?"

"They protect me."

"You'd think they'd know I'm doing the same thing."

"If they didn't, Gray, you would have lost your finger just now."

She turned around. "Whoa. You could have warned me."

"The medallions pose no danger to you."

"Is that so?" she asked.

He started to speak, then changed his mind. He lapsed into one of his infuriating silences. While he stood there, silent and brooding, he didn't take his eyes off her. Silence got to be a habit after a while, and Durian, she was certain, had been in the habit of being silent for a long time.

"You're not my type, either, you know, but if I was clean and even halfway awake, I'd jump your bones in a heartbeat."

More silence. Except eventually he said, "Then we ought to remedy your situation, don't you agree?"

"Right now, I'd agree to just about anything." She

pushed off the wall and jammed her hands into her back pockets. This time, the silence wasn't uncomfortable. Their eyes met and she didn't look away. Another shiver of arousal washed through her.

She walked into the room and took her time looking around. A wide stone table pressed up against one wall. A king-sized futon on a series of Japanese tatami mats was against the opposite wall. The floor in here was a bluish gray slate, which was rough under the soles of her sneakers. There was a gold duvet over the futon, but no pillows. Besides the door they'd come in, there were two more doors. Both closed. Her whole apartment would fit in just this one room.

She was definitely in the bat cave; the place to which Durian retreated when he wanted privacy. Like now. Privacy for two people.

He crossed to one of the interior doors and opened it to reach around and come back with a thick terrycloth robe. Even with the dim light, she could see that he'd opened a bathroom door. "If you'll give me your clothes, I'll have them washed while you are sleeping." He took a step back. Then another, but he was looking at her with a hungry gaze that was melting her inside. "I'll wait."

She stuck her head in the bathroom and took a look around. Sandstone floor and walls, ochre-tiled sunken bathtub big enough for a couple of men Durian's size, if you decided to soak instead of shower. The sink was a copper bowl atop a narrow bronze pedestal. The toilet was white. Back in the doorway, she said, "I could take a really quick shower."

"The thought appeals, Gray. A great deal. However, my ego would never recover if you fell asleep while we were…"

"Getting to know each other?"

"Precisely." He smiled and boy. Talk about heat. "I'll wait for you, Gray."

"You better."

She went in and peeled off her clothes. Dirt cascaded from her jeans and from her shoes. The silence in here got to her. She felt as stripped away inside as she was physically. Her legs trembled and in her head she heard that mageheld's neck breaking, felt the echo in her hands and arms.

The robe Durian had given her was several sizes too large for her, but she wrapped it around her as best she could and tied the sash before she brought out the bundle of her soiled clothes. She handed over her shoes, too, laces tied together.

After he took them from her, with one of his old-fashioned bows, he brushed a finger across her cheek. The tingle went straight to her belly. "You could take a shower with me."

"Tempting." His mouth curved. She closed her eyes and had to forcibly make them open again. He was still looking at her. "If I did that, Gray, you would not get the sleep you need." He cocked his head. "Another time, perhaps?"

"Promise?"

He gave her a gentle push toward the bathroom door. "Go, before I change my mind."

She needed a few minutes to figure out how to start the shower, but she managed it. It was much nicer than the one she'd been using and that one was pretty *chichi*. The hot water felt like heaven. She took her time getting clean. A few of her scrapes stung, but she healed quickly these days. None of the cuts and bruises would bother her for long.

When done, she stepped out, toweled off and put on Durian's robe—it was so soft and thick she started plotting ways she could manage to never give it back. She wandered back to the bedroom. The stone floor was cool underneath her bare feet.

Despite the drag of exhaustion, she'd gone beyond tired and was now wide awake. There wasn't much here. No television. No radio. No stereo that she could see. No clock. No gadgets that would link Durian to the twenty-first century. The walk-in closet didn't have many clothes: just a suit, two pairs of trousers on hangers, some shirts, all in a palette of gray, black, brown, and dark blue. At least ten pairs of shoes were lined up in the closet, most of them dress shoes. Now that felt like pure Durian.

She wandered back to the bedroom and ended up in front of the photograph hanging over the stone table. The Icelandic poppy looked too large for its spindly stem but you could see how the sun streamed through the petals and made them glow brilliant orange. A color she would have worn in the old days. What, she wondered, had made him choose this photo over all others he could have hung here?

The sounds and events of the fighting kept replaying in her head and there wasn't anything to distract her. She gripped the edge of the table, overwhelmed by the need to cry. They had been slaves to that mage Rasmus Kessler, and he had sent them to their deaths.

She was still in front of the photograph thinking about what the sun must have been like on the day the photograph was taken when the back of her head buzzed. She faced the door but kept an eye on the medallions until she was sure it was Durian. A few minutes later, he walked in from the anteroom, two dark bottles dangling from the fingers of one hand.

"Hey," she said, shoving her hands as deep as she could into the pockets of her robe. His robe. The sexual tension between them came back full force.

"Since you are not sleeping." He lifted the bottles.

"You knew?"

Once again she got the fathoms-deep stare. "I will always know such things."

He'd showered somewhere else, because his hair was damp and slicked back in a look that completely worked for him. He wore clean clothes, more casual than before; black trousers, a heavyweight black T-shirt, and shiny black loafers. He looked damned good. He held up the two bottles again. Beer.

"You drink beer?"

"I do not drink bad beer, Gray." He walked to her, and she took the one he held out.

The label featured a leering horned demon. At the top were the words *Oaked Arrogant Bastard Ale*. At the bottom, the label read *You're Not Worthy*. "Thanks," she said, smiling.

She took a pull of the ale. The alcohol hit her stomach hard, but it tasted good. She hadn't had a beer this fine, well, ever. Back before Tigran, she almost never drank. Maybe a glass of wine if she was celebrating something. Couldn't afford the calories. She took another sip from her ale.

He took a drink of his beer, too, and she wondered if drinking straight from the bottle was his idea of loosening up. He put it down on the table. There was a strange energy in the room she didn't completely understand.

He sipped his beer. "I am not like other kin. At this point, I think it's safe to say that you are not like other kin, either. There is seldom opportunity to connect with my own kind. I find that after a sanction, I prefer to contemplate my oaths, and the consequences of them." His fingers tightened around his beer. "You might find the same is a help to you."

"Thanks. Maybe I'll do that." Silence rose up between them. She was thinking she was all over the possibilities with Durian. "Can we maybe sit down or something?" The only place to sit in here was the futon. How convenient was that? Unless he'd changed his mind. Had he? "Or not."

He moved in close and touched the side of her throat. Not in a sexual way, which she thought was a shame, because she was certainly thinking about sex. As she watched his face, the tension around his mouth and eyes eased. They connected, that surface link that she had come to find so restful. His eyes slowly drifted closed, and her sense of him expanded. The sensation was different than having him in her head. This was just so...peaceful.

"I am unused to having someone so close to me." She looked into his dark eyes and found she couldn't look away. "You have been more tolerant of me than I deserve." He smiled and her stomach took flight. "I have been isolated a very long time."

She blinked and at the other end of that blink she saw through Durian's eyes even though she was aware of the boundaries of her body and his, and the place where his palm touched her cheek. The darkness in him, the desolation, his magic, resonated in her. She blinked again and was back in her own body. They remained in the psychic connection, sharing not thoughts or intentions but a heightened awareness of the other and the oaths that bound them.

They stood there like that, separated by inches, his hand on her cheek, looking at each other. Durian took her right hand in his. He pushed up the sleeve of her robe until her forearm was exposed.

A flicker of arousal started up in her. She considered pretending she wasn't thinking about sex, except, you know, why bother with a deception like that? Her chest felt funny. Like something inside was breaking apart, and she didn't know if that came from her or from him.

With his other hand now warm around her wrist, his index finger brushed the tracery on her arm. A shot of heat raced up to her shoulder. He kept touching her and she didn't want to do anything that would make him stop even though he didn't mean it that way. Not the way she wanted him to.

He slid the side of his thumb over the mark at her temple. He closed his eyes and breathed in and her magic reacted to him. She ignored the resulting sexual heat. Or tried to. If he could control himself, so could she. He raised her arm between them, turning the inside toward him and bringing her forearm to his mouth. Gray held her breath as he pressed his lips to her skin.

The bottom dropped from her stomach when his mouth opened. His breath warmed her skin. A lock of his hair fell forward, brushing over her. She knew what was coming, and she braced herself. His teeth scraped her skin. A zing of pain traveled up her arm. The backs of her knees quivered, and then he pulled, and she got dizzy.

A trickle of blood slid toward her elbow, a crimson trail, so bright. The scent rose between them sharp and pungent. She felt Durian's reaction as he drew her blood into his mouth, the sharp inhale, the tightening of his muscles. The taste echoed in her, too, as did the roar of his magic moving through her.

He followed the line of blood, taking in every drop.

She knew what he was doing, but not why. She and Tigran had made blood exchanges in order to cement the links he'd forged between them, to make sure she was ready for the changes he intended to make in her and so she'd be stronger when he did. Some of what he'd done had been so painful that, when she slept, she still had nightmares about it. Sometimes, though, the blood exchange enhanced the sex.

When he released her, she was bereft. She shivered, and didn't know how to release the pressure in her head. He extended his arm and with the side of a fingernail that briefly flashed into a talon, he opened a cut near his elbow. The smell of his blood rolled through her and sparked a familiar hunger in her. She knew about this. The taste of a fiend's blood, the rush of power that came with it. Her hand shook as she reached for his arm, cupping his elbow and wrist in her hands. She bent her head and breathed in, anticipating the tang against her tongue just from the scent.

Durian hooked his other arm around the back of her neck and pulled her close until her side rested against his torso.

She could swear she tasted his magic in his blood as her psychic connection to him deepened. Her oath to him remained quiescent, something that existed but was not currently in play. She felt his bonds with Nikodemus, too, and other bonds she couldn't identify. She caught an image from his thoughts; bodies intertwining. The curve of a woman's breast.

At last, she lifted her head. He smiled, and her desire was an ache. The longer they looked at each other, the more the connection between them intensified. She was turned on. So was Durian. She knew that. They both knew.

"This is only unusual—" he said in slow, deliberate words. He kept his arm around her neck, kept her close to him. The tip of his tongue darted out to pull in a tiny drop of blood on his lower lip. "Unusual, in that you are a human female. With everything that means for one of the kin." His eyes were half-closed. The kin reproduced with humans, so of course Durian was thinking about more than normal sex. "We will find a way to manage that."

Her head jangled with a sense of another fiend. One who outranked her considerably. In fact, whoever it was also outranked Durian, and that was a bit scary. "Damn," she whispered.

"It's all right," he said. Durian cupped the side of her face, and she turned toward the contact. His fingers stroked down her neck, then along the collar of her robe in a soft caress. The thing was too big on her. Of course it was. The outside was wrapped halfway around her body just to keep it closed. His fingers swept up to touch her temple.

She let her head fall back against his supporting arm. His hand moved up the side of her throat, pausing over the pulse point there. She stretched toward him because the contact felt so good.

The door opened, and another fiend walked in. Durian had already turned around and said, "Kynan Aijan."

CHAPTER 13

The Berkeley Hills, Berkeley, California

Maddy Winters stood hands on her hips at the side of her pool. She was barefoot and wearing a bikini top with an orange and green sarong tied low around her waist and hips. The shade of an enormous oak tree kept her out of the direct sun. She'd stopped about a quarter of the way down the long side of the pool, nearer the shallow end than the deep end, and was shamelessly staring.

Pitcher of lemonade in hand, she tried to deny her little pull of arousal. Hopeless, really. He ought to be declared illegal. Seriously. But she did so appreciate the sight, even if she felt pervy for staring. If there was any fiend more of a psychological mess than Kynan Aijan, it was this one.

Iskander reached the deep end and hauled himself out of the water. Muscle rippled all along his back. When he was out and on his feet, he slicked his dark hair out of his face and lifted his face toward the sun. Five blue stripes of

varying widths ran down the left side of his torso, disappeared into the waistband of his boxer-style swim trunks
and continued down the back of his leg.

She happened to know that if he turned around, she'd
still see five stripes down the left side of his body, including his face. If she were to look she would see that the
blue coloration affected his hair, too. Water dripped off
him, spattering on the concrete as he walked to one of
her lounge chairs, shucked his trunks and draped himself,
gloriously naked, on the chair.

Iskander had no inhibitions about his body. He was comfortable in his skin. Considering what he looked like, no
wonder. He had a perfect body. Not a flaw in sight. Really.
Not even one. No man should be that beautiful. It wasn't
fair. Well, though, the more powerful the fiend, the more
perfect the physical form. She shook herself and headed
toward him.

Of all the kin Nikodemus could have sent to work
with her and her group of mages and witches, he'd sent
Iskander, the least well-adjusted and most mercurial of all
of them. The psycho who couldn't go five minutes without saying something inappropriate. He was a destabiliz-
ing influence. If he weren't so damned good at this, she'd
have told Nikodemus to forget it and send someone else.
Almost anyone would do.

By now, Iskander had propositioned all of her witches
and two of the three mages. He was discreet and, unbelievable as it seemed, must be charming at some level,
because none of the ones who'd said yes to him—she
believed that was most of them—were hurt or bothered
when he moved on. Moving on was, apparently, inevitable with him. Sooner rather than later.

She'd never seen the love 'em and leave 'em type leave so little damage behind. He must really be gifted.

"Lemonade?" she said when she reached the patio furniture. Over the course of his time here, Maddy had learned how to avert her gaze to avoid overt leering, but still. He'd caught her ogling him more than once, and he'd never come on to her. Most of the time she was relieved. But sometimes not.

"Please," he said.

She poured them both a glass and handed one to him, making sure she kept her eyes at his chin level or higher. As with so many of the kin, as she was learning to refer to them, his eyes were just this side of abnormally colored. Sometimes, of course, they were unnatural. At present, his irises were cobalt blue. Not human. While he drank, she wandered over to the grill and flipped his steak and her chicken. Another part of the routine. When he was done working for her, she let him swim and then she'd feed him.

"Practice went well today," she said. She turned over the vegetables she had grilling, too, and then basted everything again.

"Think so?"

"Yes." She glanced at him over her shoulder. His blue eyes were on her ass. On Nikodemus's orders, he worked with her and her group three days a week, helping her teach her misfits what to expect from a fiend, how to forge a mutually beneficial link, and even defend against a psychic attack. He could also, they discovered by accident, spark magic in a latent human. Behaving wasn't easy for him. God, no. But he did just about everything she asked without complaint. He worked hard, and he never lost patience with her newbies.

From the lounge chair, he said, "I was at the Tiburon house the other night. Kynan Aijan was there. He asked about you." He meant the Marin County enclave the warlord Nikodemus had made his primary residence.

Maddy hoped to hell she managed to hide her start. Thank God she wasn't facing him because there was no telling what he'd figure out from seeing her reaction. Sometimes he was remarkably dense about reading human emotions and other times, he saw far too much. And he was unpredictable about which way he'd be at any given time. "Oh?" she said.

"Yeah."

"What was he asking about?" She brushed the chicken with more marinade. She was used to him being naked like this after the others had left. She didn't care for the discomfort on her end, but that didn't mean she didn't appreciate what she saw. In a way, she regretted that she didn't want to get involved with him.

"The point," Iskander said, "isn't what he said but what he meant."

Since he liked his meat rare, she grabbed a plate and some silverware from the supply on top of the grill, flipped his steak onto the plate, added some of the veggies and walked it over to him. Her heart beat faster than it should and Iskander, being Iskander, probably noticed. Hopefully, he was in one of his unintuitive states. "What did he mean?"

"He wants you so bad his nuts hurt." He took the plate from her and sat up, legs spread wide so he could put his steak on the chair.

"Oh, for God's sake." She stood there like an idiot, befuddled at the sight, holding on to her spatula. Nothing like regressing to her thirteen-year-old self all over again. It wasn't as if her previous encounters with Kynan Aijan were the stuff of girlish fantasies. Hardly that. They had been, to understate the case, intense. And not particularly safe, either. She knew what Iskander was. And wasn't. Unfortunately, intense seemed to push a button or two for her. "How can you even tell what he wants?"

He swallowed his first bite of steak. "Excellent as always." Then he pointed his fork at her. "He's still messed up over his whole deal with Carson, but he wants you."

Carson being the witch Nikodemus was permanently linked with. Kynan had been responsible, to the extent a mageheld was responsible for anything he did, for a great many wrongs against Carson. "Kynan Aijan is insane."

He got a thoughtful look on his face and there was just something so subtly un-human about his expression that she couldn't help a chill. Kynan wasn't human, either. So what the hell was her excuse, thinking about sex with either of them?

"People say that about me, too." He ate a few veggies and then cocked his head in the direction of the grill. "Your chicken's going to burn."

"Oh, rats!" She dashed back to the grill. The chicken wasn't burning, though. She turned it over again and brushed more marinade over everything because it gave her a reason not to look at him. Eventually, though, the meat was done.

While she was plating her food, Iskander said, "If you like insane, why not hook up with me?"

Maddy turned, plate in hand. "What?"

"I never asked you before because I figured you and Kynan—"

"Kynan?" Her chill wasn't unpleasant. "And me?"

"Well, then." He looked her up and down. Twice. "If there's no Kynan and you, what about you and me?" He stretched out on the lounge chair, catlike, and grinned. His empty plate was on the ground beside him. He crossed his arms behind his head and the things that did to his torso. My God. "Come on, it'd be fun."

"Fun."

"Sit down and eat, Maddy. We can talk about this." He polished off his lemonade and stared into the empty plastic cup with puppy dog longing.

"There's nothing to talk about." Oh, but he was just insanely beautiful. All meanings of that intended. She sat on another of the chairs, sideways and with her knees firmly together.

Iskander looked her up and down, smiling. "It's okay if you don't like to talk during sex."

"Stop it." She lifted a forkful of chicken to her mouth and then froze.

"I'm a talker." His grin widened. "I hope that doesn't—"

"*Hsst!*" She slashed her hand through the air. Fear rolled through her, and disbelief. "You don't feel that?"

"What?" He was relaxed, unable, she was afraid, to see that she'd shifted into a whole new set of emotions that had nothing to do with going to bed with him. Or not. Against her better judgment either way. Half the time she thought she was crazy not to. The rest of the time she thought she'd be crazy if she did.

Maddy stood and the chill in her head got bigger. The sensation rolled over her with a measure of anger. "Magehelds."

Iskander got to his feet with leisurely grace. He wasn't smiling anymore, but he also didn't look concerned. He should be. He really should be. "How many?"

She concentrated. The stink of the perverted magic that kept a fiend enslaved nauseated her. Iskander, she knew, could not feel them. None of the free kin could feel a mageheld. "At least four."

Who the hell was sending magehelds after her? She'd left that world years ago. She doubted many of her former colleagues knew she was still alive, let alone what she was doing here or that she had associated herself with Nikodemus. No one. No one knew there was any reason to retaliate. To be honest, even if her fellow magekind did know, they'd think she was wasting her time. The arrogance of her kind was chilling at times.

The wooden fence between her yard and the uphill neighbor's bowed inward with a groaning screech of nails sliding against dry wood.

What if the magehelds were here for Iskander?

She pulled her magic because she was damned if she let her negative feelings about the use of magic against living creatures stop her from saving her life or Iskander's, if it came to that. Judging from the way he stood there, stark naked and smiling like this was the greatest day ever, she was going to be saving his life as well.

Five feet from where she and Iskander stood, the fence popped back into place, snapping two of the boards in half.

"Why don't you go inside?" Iskander said. So far he hadn't turned a hair. But then, he couldn't feel what she did; that massive wrongness that permeated the air. Wrong even for a mageheld fiend.

"Oh," she said as the first mageheld ducked through the break in the fence. A second came through right behind him. Both of them were large. Whoever sent them wasn't messing around. She had time to notice there was something off about them before the other two came through the fence from the downhill neighbor's side. She stayed focused on the nearest threat. "Two more behind us."

She gathered herself. An instant before she would have released her magic at the magehelds who'd trespassed in her backyard, Iskander moved past her. She cut off just in time.

His magic flashed hotter than she would have believed possible. He met the two magehelds at the edge of the concrete and after that, everything was a blur and over before she finished exhaling. She saw a flash of red and the first mageheld fell to the ground in an uncoordinated heap. The second hit a moment later in the same boneless manner. She had time to register that she no longer felt their magic and that both had gaping holes in their chests before the other two fiends were too close to ignore.

Again, Iskander moved past her without a sound. He grabbed the first mageheld to reach him and then his hands and body were a blur. A sound of pure joy ripped free from him. Seconds later, the last mageheld was on the ground too. None of them were moving.

Maddy blinked. It couldn't have been even thirty seconds since the fence broke, and the attack was over. She didn't feel any more magehelds, just a fading perception of something gone terribly wrong.

While she stared at the bodies, trying to make sense of what she'd seen and what she was seeing now, Iskander knelt over each one in turn. His lips moved, though she heard nothing. At the edges of her ability to sense magic, she caught a faint bluish mist in the air above the dead magehelds. Iskander's magic flashed hot again. The bodies collapsed in on themselves and then vanished. But not before she put together the visual puzzle; the bodies didn't look right because Iskander had ripped out their hearts.

There was blood on the concrete, but Iskander was turning his attention to that too.

"What the hell did you do to them?" she whispered.

He shot her a quick glance. "Killed them."

"I've never seen anything like that. Ever."

When she looked up from where the bodies had been, Iskander stood motionless. His body tattoos rippled with an interior, glowing cobalt blue. His eyes were the same brilliant blue as his tats. That amount of magic coming from one fiend was almost impossible to imagine. A ripple of fear shimmered up her spine and lingered at the back of her neck. Any sensible person would be afraid.

Iskander hadn't been mentally stable for very long. She knew that. Nikodemus had warned him about what would happen if he lost control, and had insisted that she'd be safe and that Iskander was safe to be around. A guarantee given, she sometimes thought, with the confidence of knowing he wouldn't be there if he happened to be wrong.

Blood dripped down Iskander's arms and fell onto the cement where it vanished in a sizzle of red mist. He wasn't even breathing hard. He reached out to flick something glistening off his forearm but left behind a smear of blood. He grinned at her. "Mind if I take a shower?"

CHAPTER 14

Gray heard several soft pops from the other room. The medallions, she realized. The sound rocketed around inside her head. Every nerve in her body sizzled. Every muscle tensed. Durian remained completely calm. She forced herself to relax. Whoever had come in wasn't kidding, and he wasn't welcome, either. In the bedroom, the faces in the medallions along the walls shifted, and unless she was losing her mind, the colors intensified. Most of the ones she could see from where she stood contorted, as if the faces inside the circles of carved wood were shrieking.

Durian muttered something under his breath and the magic icing up her back and spine melted away, but did not vanish. Not by any means. The tracings on her arm and temple whipped into a frenzy of motion. This time, she didn't ignore it. Durian might not care, but she was bound to protect him. She pulled.

The fiend who walked into the bedroom looked like a college student. He probably got carded a lot, Gray thought. The way he dressed didn't help much. He had on faded jeans that hit low on his hips, a ratty T-shirt and a pair of leather flip-flops. His light brown eyes were, at the moment, focused entirely on her. Because she had put herself in front of Durian.

She was ready to kill the guy if she had to. More likely she'd die trying.

The fiend gave her a good long up and down, without once looking at her face. With his hands turned palm up at either side of his waist and a predatory grin in Durian's direction, he said, "What the hell?"

"Gray," Durian said. Was he ever anything but cool and collected? His fingers curled tightly around the top of her shoulder, sliding over to the nape of her neck. "Allow me to introduce Kynan Aijan. Kynan, this is Gray Spencer. She is—"

"I know what she is." He stalked toward them. He stopped about a foot from her and looked her up and down again. Twice. Like she was naked. Gray had a lot of practice hiding her emotions, and she hid hers now. There wasn't anything for him to get from her.

He was too close, but with Durian behind her, she couldn't back up, not that she would have given him the satisfaction. A trickle of fear slid down her spine, but she cut that off. The guy was trying his damnedest to provoke a response. "Like I said, Big Dog, what the hell? Have you taken her to Nikodemus yet?"

Durian's fingers stroked over the back of her neck. Kynan's attention focused on that with a gaze that looked like it could melt stone. Pressure built up in her head. It was a light touch, but if it weren't for Durian's hands on her, she'd have said something very rude about keeping the hell out of her head.

The fiend let out breath and at last turned his attention fully to Durian. His lip curled. "Assassin. I didn't think you had it in you."

"Back off." Gray put a finger on his shoulder and pushed. Not very hard. She didn't have a hope of getting him to move if he didn't want to. Then again, she had a lot of magic at hand right now. Kynan took a deliberate step back. She wasn't dumb enough to think he was worried at all.

"Human." He said the word like it tasted bad in his mouth.

Kynan Aijan had the kind of power that reached out and grabbed you by the throat. The kind that could control you before you knew it was happening. "You're a warlord, aren't you."

The fiend gazed into her face. "Mind if I ask whose heart you took?"

"It wasn't me," she said. "I didn't kill anyone," she said. Except she had. Just today. "Not for the magic."

Durian's fingers tightened on her. That was the only sign she got that he was tense. Psychically, his state was unchanged. "If she had done such a thing, Kynan, I would have killed her. You know that."

"That's a real comfort," he said. He didn't mean it.

Kynan looked her straight in the eye and just like that, he was a part of the connection between her and Durian. The impact took her breath away. Durian was cool and dark, fathomless. Kynan Aijan rocked her like he was nothing but heat. The initial flare up settled into something less than a bonfire, and it was just the three of them sharing the same top-level consciousness. She knew without any doubt that if he wanted anything more he could make it happen. At the moment she didn't get any sense that he intended harm. Not immediately anyway. Durian's hand on her shoulder relaxed.

Durian's reaction helped her settle down. A little.

The warlord's mouth twitched into a smile. "Look who you're hanging with, human. He touch you with those hands of his? He kills with them, honey."

"Kynan—" Durian said.

"You sure you want him touching you with his killing hands?"

"There is no need to be offensive."

"The way I see it, Big Dog, it's my only virtue." The warlord walked over to the table and picked up one of the beers. He examined the label. "Someone needs the balls to tell it like it is."

"Kindly put that down."

He stared at Durian over the top of the bottle. "What for?"

"That is Gray's."

Kynan stopped with the bottle half way to his mouth. "Arrogant Bastard."

Silence fell. The connection between them remained open. Kynan wasn't even trying to hide that he was thinking about her body, him and rough sex. About Durian, too. In the same way.

"Nevertheless, warlord," Durian said.

"I'm sure as hell not going to drink yours. No offense." Kynan smiled. He looked adorably boyish when he smiled. He lowered the bottle and stroked the neck. "You were all over her. If I'd been five minutes later, I'd have walked in on you two doing the nasty. How's she going to save your sorry ass after you get her knocked up and she's seven or eight months along?"

"You misunderstand," Durian said.

"I don't think so. I felt your reactions from all the way downstairs. I get here and she's this far from naked." With one hand, he held his thumb and index finger a quarter inch apart. "Your hands were heading for her ass. What's to misunderstand?"

Gray walked to Kynan. He stared down at her the whole time. The color of his eyes changed from light brown to bronze, and with that came a stronger rush of his magic. Her pulse thudded in her ears, but she didn't back away. Neither did he. His level of sexual interest ratcheted up. Without saying a word, she held out a hand. He handed over the beer, and she took a slow drink from it. She played it for all it was worth. Savoring the taste, indulging herself in the sensations and making sure he felt them all.

She handed the bottle back with her awareness of Durian and Kynan crackling around her. "You can have that, Kynan. But that's all you're getting."

Behind her, Durian laughed.

Kynan put down the beer. For half a second she thought he wanted both hands free for physical retaliation. She braced herself. But he faced them both again and moved way too close to her. He tipped his head to one side, exposing the side of his neck. Then he reached up with one hand and drew a finger down the side of his throat. A thin crimson line appeared on his skin.

Bright, bright crimson. Despite herself, she breathed in. The scent made her hungry deep in her belly.

The tension in the room went through the ceiling. Kynan reached out psychically as he snaked an arm around her waist and pulled her toward him. She pushed up on her toes and curled her palm on the opposite side of his neck to bring them closer at that point of contact between them. Behind her, Durian came close enough that his torso pressed against her back. His hand brushed over her neck and then she felt cool air on her shoulders, her torso exposed, the sharp coldness of Durian's teeth sliding through her upper layer of skin. There. Just there. Her thoughts wrapped around his, following the darkness.

One of Kynan's hands slipped between them and the next thing she knew her robe parted and his fingers were gliding down her body. The odd thing was, the warlord wasn't thinking about sex as much as he was about the physical contact. He stroked her with both hands now, along the sides of her rib cage, her hips. She took in a long, slow, breath, drugged with the sense that she belonged here. At last. Home. Her hand fell away from Kynan's neck.

Durian lifted his head, too, and warmed the tops of her shoulders with his palms. The touch sent her further into a catlike pleasure. With a quick motion, Durian grabbed the back of Kynan's wrist and bit hard on the tender inside surface. Gray smelled blood.

A growl rumbled up from the warlord's chest, but he didn't move. The arm he had around Gray's waist tightened. The image of another woman came to her. Petite with dark brown hair and skin darker than his golden brown. A witch. Sexual desire, but something else, too, that was at one and the same time twisted up with a longing to lash out and hurt and the need to be touched without violence.

When Durian lifted his head, Kynan said, "I'm too fucked up for her."

This time it was Durian who pressed a palm to Kynan's cheek. "She doesn't hate you."

Kynan pushed away from them both and dropped out of the connection without warning. He didn't say anything for too long. Too long. "Not yet."

He turned on his heel and headed for the door. He stopped before he got there. "Take my advice." Kynan looked over his shoulder at them. "Go see Nikodemus before he calls you in."

Durian nodded, pressing his fingertips to his forehead. "Thank you."

The warlord nodded and left.

In the quiet afterward, Durian dropped his head to her shoulders. His lips moved softly across her skin. He, too, dropped out of their connection. "I am no longer in control of myself tonight."

He left her there, standing in the bedroom with her robe untied, alone. She wondered if she would be able to sleep.

CHAPTER 15

*About 1:00 P.M. A few days later. Octavia
near Jackson Street*

Tracking, Durian had told her, was an art consisting of
equal parts instinct, experience, and deduction. Oh, and
luck. Which he claimed came only after mastery of the
first three. He seemed to be right. The easy assignment of
the moment was tracking Christophe since she was familiar with both the mage and his magehelds.

Tracking involved getting herself into a meditative
state and then following remnants of stale magic from
Point A to wherever the end point might be. The specific
task Durian had put to Gray was straightforward enough.
Find all the places frequented by Christophe dit Menart
without anyone knowing what she was doing. So far, she
sucked at this. Durian had to help her a lot.

It was hard. Really hard. She kept losing the trail
and picking up some other set of magical remains. She

was getting better at reaching the state of mind-altered consciousness that let her find the wisps of magic, but only because she lost her way so often and had to reset herself. She was getting a lot of practice.

They weren't going to do anything if she managed to find the mage. Too bad. She suspected, and hoped, that Durian wanted to know all the places Christophe holed up so they'd be prepared if they ever got authorization to take him down.

Meanwhile she was stuck learning something she wasn't good at. It had, for example, taken her three days to end up at Octavia Street where Christophe, if she had guessed right, and probably she hadn't, owned a condo. Somewhere around here. Or knew someone who owned or rented out here and liked to visit. Her first thought was that if he owned or rented here, then, what with the parking nightmare of most San Francisco neighborhoods, he'd have parking in the building. So. Her brilliant idea was to find him by checking the parking garages of the various buildings on the street.

So far, not one single trail led to the garage of any of the buildings on the section of Octavia Street she thought was most likely. Or, rather, not one single garage entrance yielded even the faintest evidence of Christophe. Not one single building entrance either.

Durian wasn't helping her. Not that he should be. But still. She was frustrated by her lack of progress.

At the moment, she and Durian were standing near the corner of Jackson and Octavia. He was leaning against a large tree, arms crossed over his chest, the sole of one shiny loafer against the trunk. "What does this tell you?"

"That I'm wrong about him coming to Octavia Street, wrong about where he'd park if he did come here, or just heinously unable to pick out the evidence." She blew out a breath. "Or all of the above."

His mouth twitched, and she was so frustrated by her lack of success that she narrowed her eyes at him and glared. "You're correct. Christophe has been here."

Gray circled her index finger in the air. "Whoop de doo. We knew that. It's a long street."

"You've ended up here, though. Not several blocks away. Consider that."

She scuffed her shoe on the sidewalk, knocking aside bits of debris shed from the tree. "Christophe is paranoid. Knowing him, he parks someplace different every time. There's a limited area for him to park." She looked up and met Durian's steady gaze. "In which case," she said, "I am an idiot."

"I wouldn't say that."

"Because I've only succeeded in finding one of the places he parked. He walked to wherever he was headed."

"Ah."

"He'd hide his trail. Take a different way every time. There has to be overlap." She speared Durian with another glare. "If you call me 'grasshopper,' I'll stab you, I swear."

He laughed, and when she got over her shock, she still had time to see it did great things to his face.

"Oh, all right," she said. "Let's go trolling again. Find the perimeter and work our way inward."

Durian pushed off the tree while she struggled to get herself into the meditative state required for her to pick up traces of old magic. This time, of course, she would also be looking for magic a trained mage had been deliberately obscuring. Fun.

Someone came out of one of the buildings about half-way down Jackson Street from where they stood, and that distracted her. The door banged closed behind the woman and the tall man with her. Not that it was so surprising that someone would come outside. It was a nice day. Not everyone had a day job at a remote office, after all. There were lots of parents around here and two parks within walking distance.

"Concentrate, Gray—"

Durian reacted first. He went vanilla and gestured for Gray to do the same. If he thought he needed to pass for human, then so did she, no questions asked. The woman walking toward them was a witch; Gray felt the shiver of reaction only shortly after Durian. The man with her didn't resonate the same way. He reminded her of the magehelds who had attacked them at Muir Woods. "That's a mageheld with her," she said softly.

Gray stared as the woman continued down the sidewalk. She was close enough now that you could tell she was pregnant, but also beautiful, with long, straight black hair.

Durian leaned over to speak in her ear. "We should not stay."

Her heart pounded so hard she couldn't breathe. Gray took a step toward the woman. She was familiar, but that had to be impossible.

She didn't recognize the mageheld with the woman. He had a hand to the back of the woman's elbow, as if he were a boyfriend, not a bodyguard. Gray didn't doubt for a minute that he was mageheld. She felt it. His eyes were aware, scanning the environment the way a good mageheld would do for the mage he was bound to protect. Besides the short hair, he was tall and good-looking. Strikingly so, and that meant power. He wore jeans, a blue button-down shirt, and a casual jacket, but then not all mages insisted their magehelds adhere to a dress code.

The witch's black hair, fastened into a ponytail, hung over one shoulder, and when Gray looked into her face, her pounding heart drowned out everything except her disbelief about what she was seeing. She trembled. "No. It can't be."

"What?" Durian asked.

"Tigran lied to me." *Emily.* "That's my sister. She's alive." She shook off Durian's hand and headed for the woman. She wanted to run, but she had just enough sense not to do that. Though she was vaguely aware Durian was following her, she paid no attention. "He told me she was dead."

"Gray?" That was Durian's voice. His magic was in her head again, but she shut him out.

Emily was as breathtakingly beautiful as ever. She slowed as Gray approached, and then stopped, watching her with a puzzled expression in her light blue eyes. Gray stared, trying to find a way for this to be real. Emily was alive. And she was pregnant.

So far, her sister hadn't given any sign she recognized her but maybe she wasn't close enough yet. And then her hair was red, for Christ's sake. The last time they'd seen each other, Gray's hair had been black and almost as long as Emily's was now. The magcheld leaned in to whisper something to Emily.

Durian grabbed Gray's arm, but she shook him off and kept going. In the back of her head she felt Durian using his magic to hide what they were. Good. Good, she thought, because Emily didn't know what had happened to her. She stopped about five feet from her sister, wary, for the moment, of the mageheld.

"Emily?"

Gray's sister cocked her head, a puzzled look on her face. The mageheld took a step forward, keeping himself enough in front of Emily that he could quickly act if needed. Even Gray, in her current overwrought state, knew better than to get too close.

"It's really you." She extended her arms but then let them fall to her sides. Durian took Gray's hand and physically prevented her from getting any closer. Her voice shook but she didn't care. "I thought you were dead, Emily. Oh my God, I thought you were dead. They told me you were dead."

"I'm sorry," her sister said, her smile slowly fading. "Do I know you?"

"It's me. Anna." For a moment, she was baffled by Emily's lack of reaction. She touched her hair. "God, I know, I've done a number on myself, haven't I?"

Emily's smile returned, but it was tentative. Her fingers tightened around the orange leather bag on her shoulder. A diamond flashed on the fourth finger of her left hand, along with a matching gold band. She was married. The sister she'd thought brutally murdered was married and about to have a baby.

"I guess you never thought I'd ever be a redhead." What the hell was wrong with Emily?

"I'm so sorry." Emily took a step back, closer to her mageheld. "Anna, did you say your name was?"

"It's me." She searched Emily's face. There wasn't any doubt that this was her sister. "So much has happened. I hardly know where to start."

"Obviously, you know me." She shook her head,

frowning. "But I'm afraid I'm drawing a blank. Where did we meet?"

"Where did we meet. What do you mean?" The past rushed back, rolling over her, drowning her in memories she'd kept locked away over the last year and a half of her life. Durian tugged on her arm, but Gray ignored him. "Emily?" Was she faking? Pretending she didn't know her own sister? "I don't look that different, do I? How can you not recognize your own sister?"

Emily put a restraining hand on the mageheld's arm. "It's all right." The mageheld relaxed, but kept his attention on Durian and her. "I'm so sorry, Anna. But you've mistaken me for someone else. My name is Erin, not Emily, and I haven't got a sister."

Durian was holding a lot of magic, and he'd linked with her without holding back much. The markings on her arm and temple burned until Gray managed to shut down again. "Dammit, Gray," Durian murmured.

The mageheld's eyes widened, and Emily frowned. He pulled a phone from his jacket pocket and started pushing buttons.

"Put that away," Emily said. She covered the mageheld's phone with her hand, gently pushing down. "That's not necessary."

Gray's heart shriveled to ash. She wracked her mind for an explanation that made sense. Emily had survived an horrific attack that day. Was it possible she didn't remember who she was? "There was an . . ." Durian's hand tightened on her. "An accident. We were both hurt and I had to . . . go away to . . . recover. Don't you remember?"

Durian squeezed her hand hard enough to hurt. "I beg your pardon," he said to Emily. "It's a misunderstanding."

"Your name is Emily Spencer," Gray said. "We grew up across the Bay in Piedmont. Our mother's a judge. Dad teaches medieval history at Cal." She held out her arms again. "I'm your baby sister, Anna."

Emily gave a breathtaking smile. "No," she said. "I'm sorry, but that's just not right." Her eyes, worried, darted to Durian, who by now had an arm around Gray and was holding her tight. "I was born in Boston. I'm afraid my parents are dead, and I never had any siblings. I'm sorry."

"Emmy." Gray used the nickname she'd had for her sister. "Emmy, what's happened to you?"

Emily touched her temple and grimaced. "I'm sorry." She shook her head. "What did you call me?"

"I'm Andres," Durian said before Gray could answer. "Andres Aguirre. So sorry for the misunderstanding." He gave Emily's belly a significant look. "My wife, it's been hard for her."

He squeezed her tighter when Gray twisted to look at him. His wife? Who the hell was Andres Aguirre supposed to be?

"Oh." Emily darted a glance at Gray. "Yes. I see. I understand. I'm so sorry for your loss."

"Thank you." Durian kept a firm grip on Gray as he stuck out his free hand. He was doing a damned good imitation of a human.

"I'm Erin...well—" She gave another of her breathtaking smiles as she and Durian briefly clasped hands. The mageheld was a shade too late to stop the contact. Not that he would necessarily have dared. "I suppose you know that. It's Erin dit Menart."

Durian's hand clamped down hard on Gray's shoulder. He was fully in her head now, preventing her from saying anything. She had just enough of her wits left to understand the enormity of the blunder she'd made. She let Durian draw her away. He restored his psychic hold on her. God. Emily thought she was married to Christophe. She stared at her sister's belly, and then the mageheld and felt sick.

Worse, she knew she'd endangered her sister's life. This was going to get back to Christophe, if not from Emily then when the mageheld told him.

"You must think I'm crazy," she said. "It's just...the resemblance is just uncanny. You look so much like her. I can see now that you're not."

Emily's shoulders relaxed, and she smiled again. The familiar sight broke Gray's heart. "It's quite all right."

The mageheld still had his phone out, and he was watching Durian very carefully. If he called someone, Gray realized, it was going to be either one of Christophe's bodyguards, all of which knew her on sight, or Christophe himself. Her mouth went dry at the thought of what that might mean for Emily.

"Let's go, honey," Gray said. She was cold inside.

Durian gave her a squeeze. "Sorry to have bothered you, Mrs. dit Menart."

"It's quite all right."

They walked away, continuing past the building Emily had exited. At the next street, they walked toward downtown for several blocks before Durian hailed a cab. He pushed her inside and slid in next to her while he gave the driver an address in Tiburon. Tiburon was a city on the other side of the Golden Gate Bridge from where they were now.

"I'm sorry," she said as the taxi pulled into traffic.

He pulled her against him. At first, she was shocked

he'd do something so...humane, but the contact felt good and she decided not to question it. "I understand it was a shock."

"I thought she was dead. All this time." She looked at him and actually took comfort in his stern face. "Tigran lied to me." Tears burned hot in her eyes. She swiped at her face. No breaking down. She wouldn't. "He told me she was dead, Durian, and I believed him."

"Christophe surely told him to lie."

"Of course he did." She grabbed Durian's wrist. She'd known all along she could never completely trust Tigran. She didn't blame him for that. That day, she'd seen Emily lying in a pool of blood, and she'd assumed the worst. "She wasn't pretending. She really doesn't know who I am."

"I touched her only for a moment, but it was enough. You are correct. She wasn't whole in her mind. There are...anomalies. Christophe, or someone like him, has altered her memories."

"He's going to find out. He'll know I saw her."

"Gray," he said softly. "It's unlikely he'll harm her."

"You don't know Christophe. What if he's doing to her what he couldn't do to me? What if he goes after my parents? What if he's already done that?"

Durian grabbed her by the shoulders and turned her to face him. She didn't want to feel this kind of emotional pain but she couldn't seem to turn off her feelings this time. "Is your family still in the East Bay?"

She nodded. "I can't see them."

"Why not?"

"Because my father will know what I am. He isn't going to be okay with that."

"Your father is a mage?" She felt Durian stiffen when

she nodded. She moved away from him. He drew her back. "Given your sister's abilities, it stands to reason one of your parents is magekind."

"He doesn't practice anymore, but he helped Emily when it turned out she had magic. He was disappointed I wasn't talented, too. He thinks I don't know, but I heard him talking to Emily about it. Not to mention she told me anyway. He's going to think I've gone over to the enemy. It was just as well I was dancing." She glanced at him. "I moved to New York when I was fifteen. So I wasn't around much anyway." She licked her lower lip. "Emily never shut me out, though."

Durian took her hand in his and slowly unclenched her fist so he could twine his fingers with hers. "Your sister said she was Christophe's wife."

"Maybe he just told her that."

"She was with a mageheld." He lowered his voice. "You know as well as I do that he was not insignificant. Christophe has one of his more powerful magehelds protecting her. He would not do that for just anyone."

She leaned against him, and he kept his arms around her. Emily was alive, and no matter the circumstances that was better than believing she'd died. Gray watched the ocean as they crossed the Golden Gate Bridge. "Where are we going?"

"To see Nikodemus."

CHAPTER 16

About an hour later. Tiburon, California. Primary residence of the Warlord Nikodemus

Even before she entered the house, Gray's head started buzzing. She stubbed her toe on the first step and stopped, one hand pressed to her temple. Her arm hurt, too.

"What is it?" Durian asked.

She looked up, scanning the windows. Dread unfurled in her chest, shadows of uncertainty about whether Durian would be safe going inside. One of the things in there—creatures, monsters, fiends—weighed her down, as if he was deliberately making the air heavier. There was another one inside the house that was almost as bad. "How many are in there?"

"Fifteen. Including Nikodemus." Durian didn't seem to be affected. Not the way she was.

The awareness of so many separate minds buzzed in her head and made her dizzy even without making a connection to them. Durian put a hand to her back, but her feet refused to move.

"I don't want to go in there."

He kept his hand on her back, but didn't urge her forward. "What you're feeling is how we know our standing with respect to other kin. It's normal. You will become accustomed to it." His mouth twitched. "It's useful to know when you're outranked and when you are not."

"Jesus." She rubbed the outside of her arms.

"You may be assured, Gray, that you outrank more than a few of the kin inside."

"Not Nikodemus." And not all of them.

"No," he said. His palm pressed into the small of her back, pushing her forward.

They climbed the rest of the stairs without her sense of dread going away in the slightest. Any minute, she thought, they'd be attacked. Ripped to shreds and what was left of their bodies strewn about to rot in the sun. At the door, she slapped away Durian's hand before he could open it. "Me first."

For half a second, Durian looked like he was going to tell her to get out of his way, but he didn't. She stayed in front of the door, driven by a compulsion she didn't understand. No way was she letting Durian go inside before she knew it was safe. "Sorry," she said.

She didn't mean it, and he knew it. He leaned a shoulder against the side of the house. Perfectly calm. Like this sort of thing was an everyday occurrence for him. Maybe it was. For him. "With respect to your magic, trust your instincts. You will do fine in that case."

"I don't know shit, and you know it." Hell. She'd

completely messed up with Emily. Now she was going to meet Nikodemus and what if she messed that up, too?

"You are inexperienced. If, when we are inside, something should go awry, allow me to act as I see fit."

"Does that mean you think something will go wrong?"

He actually smiled, and it did a lot to relieve his stern looks. He reached for the doorknob. "It means Nikodemus is a warlord and is not pleased with me."

"Because of me." He didn't say anything in response. "Kynan is a warlord, and he doesn't feel like this."

"Kynan does not yet choose to exercise his abilities. When he does—"

She stuck a hand on the doorjamb, blocking his way. "Maybe we should leave."

Durian's expression didn't change. "That would be unwise. Nikodemus knows we are here. We cannot leave now. Not without paying our respects."

She kept her hand across the doorway. "And you getting your head taken off because of me."

"Please move, Gray."

The compulsion in his words tugged at her. "Against my advice, assassin."

"Duly noted." When she moved, he opened the door but held back so she could go in first. She did. Looking for threats in every corner, too. There weren't any. That she could tell. The other kin in the house didn't come downstairs, but she knew they were there and aware of her and Durian.

They found Nikodemus in the living room. He was alone, sitting on a black couch wearing jeans and a green T-shirt that said *Without me it's just Aweso*.

This was a warlord? Given the way his magic shook

her, she'd expected fangs. Bodies heaped about him and eyes like fire. Kynan Aijan looked scarier than him.

Durian walked to within five feet of Nikodemus and touched his fingers to his bowed forehead, "Warlord."

She followed him. She didn't have any choice. Electricity zipped through her. Nikodemus looked like the boy next door who grew up into the hot man you wished you'd paid more attention to before he was out of your league. Bronzed brown hair, a bit shaggy, and piercing blue-gray eyes. Gorgeous man with an open, inviting smile. Except his magic flat out scared her silly.

Like Durian, she pressed her fingertips to her forehead. It seemed like the thing to do.

Nikodemus made an impatient gesture with one hand. "What the eff, Durian? Seriously." He wasn't smiling. "What the effing eff?"

Gray stayed where she was. The impact of his magic at such close range made her knees wobble. Durian rose and started walking toward him. She forced herself to match Durian's stride, heart in her mouth the whole way.

Without more, Durian told Nikodemus who she was and what had happened with Tigran and Christophe. He gave a broad-strokes picture that left out a lot. When he got to the part about the mage's intention that Gray be forced to conceive and how she and Tigran had found a way to circumvent the commands, Nikodemus bared his teeth at them in one of the scariest smiles she'd ever seen. Her skin rippled with gooseflesh. He gave an evil smile when Durian got to the part of her ending up with some of Christophe's magic, but then Durian started in on her taking her oath of fealty, and the warlord lost all hint of his previous amusement.

The warlord slouched on his chair looking more and

more pissed off. Her head vibrated with the growing conviction that this encounter was going to end badly. She didn't like the way the warlord watched Durian; looking at him from under half-lidded eyes. The markings on her arm swirled and buzzed underneath her skin. She moved closer to Durian until her left shoulder was in front of his chest.

By the time Durian finished with the part about meeting Emily, the warlord looked ready to spit nails. At her.

"What's your story?" The warlord looked at her without a drop of friendliness. A star ruby in his ear caught the light and she caught a glimpse of a perfect star in the cabochon.

"Pretty much what he said."

Nikodemus gave her a searing glare. The back of her knees jellied, but she was damned if she was going to let on. She clamped down on her thoughts. The warlord could go to hell. He wasn't going to get so much as a hint to her thoughts or mental state.

"There's a few things that didn't get mentioned in that little recitation."

"Like what?" She hoped her phony surprise was enough to fool him.

The warlord reached out to her psychically, and she blocked herself in self-defense. "Not wise," Nikodemus said, and not in a nice voice. "Makes me think you have something to hide."

"Spoken like a tyrant, warlord."

Nikodemus got up and strode toward her, but Durian made a low sound and that made him pull up, barely. The mood turned distinctly menacing. "Nikodemus. She did not know her sister was alive."

Nikodemus pointed at Gray without taking his eyes from Durian. Her tracings zipped around enough to make her skin burn. He had enough magic on tap to fry her to a crisp. "So? The fact is," he said in a black voice, "her sister not only lives with Christophe dit Menart, she's fucking married to him."

She took a step forward. "Less than an hour ago, I thought my sister was dead."

"I know every mage or witch in my territory." Nikodemus stalked to her. He came to a halt much too close to her but she refused to give him the satisfaction of backing up. "Out of the blue, this self-trained witch marries Christophe dit Menart. About a year and a half ago. No mage helds of her own but not without some power."

"You knew?"

"What the fuck do I care if some mage gets married? I didn't know she was anybody's sister." He looked at Durian. "If this one hadn't been hiding you from me, I might have put two and two together. I've met your sister. Making sure she understood the agreement we have going here."

"I saw her die." She struggled to regulate her breathing, but everything was jamming up in her throat, and she was shaking again. She clenched her hands into fists. Durian touched her shoulder. "There was so much blood."

"You look a lot like her." He tilted his head to one side. "If you didn't have red hair. She's not as skinny as you, and, no offense, even better looking. A little more up top, too, but then she's about to have a kid. You're not bad, honey, but she got the looks. No wonder Christophe got the hots for her."

"What if he kills her?"

"Why would he kill his wife?" the warlord shot back.

"Oh, come on. We're talking about Christophe dit Menart here."

Nikodemus's eyes turned solid black, which was scary even if she didn't have a dose of his even scarier magic. She didn't doubt for a minute that he would take her down with a smile on his face. He put his hands on his hips and stared down at her. "Shit. You really didn't know, did you?"

"I don't think the baby's even his."

His features softened in a way she was in no condition to analyze. "He wouldn't have married her otherwise."

"She doesn't remember me. Or who she is."

The warlord nodded. "You think she'd be happy and healthy the way you said she is if she knew the truth? There's no way Christophe is going to let her remember what happened." The warlord plopped down in an upholstered leather chair. "Durian, we have a problem."

"Warlord?"

"It won't be any surprise to either of you if I tell you Christophe has made a formal request to have Gray returned to his custody."

"She isn't going anywhere," Durian said.

"I don't give kin to mages." He lifted a hand. In Durian's direction, not hers. "I told him to fuck off." He gave a quick grin to them both. "I was polite about it."

"She isn't sworn to you, Nikodemus."

Nikodemus stretched out his legs and crossed them at the ankles. He didn't say anything for a while. He just gazed at Durian. "We need to have a talk about that."

"No."

The tracings under her skin started moving faster. She watched the green lines on her arm form intricate loops and swirls and shivered when Durian's magic seemed to practically dance into her head, down her spine and then under her skin.

The warlord's eyes stayed on her face. "So, Gray, how loyal are you to my assassin? When the shit gets real, are you going to put him first?"

"Yes."

"You better," Nikodemus said. His eyes flashed from silver to black. "I need him."

She straightened, not liking the way the magic was building up.

"You think I didn't know the minute he took your oath?" He glanced at Durian then back to her. "He's been through a lot lately, and I've been making allowances. The truth is I need him. I need him strong and focused. I need mages like Christophe dit Menart worried I might send my assassin after them. What I don't need is dit Menart thinking he has something he can use against me. Like your sister. If they're not afraid, no mage is going to so much as daydream about stopping anything. And my kin and the warlords sworn to me, they aren't going to take me seriously if I don't have Durian around to scare their fucking pants off."

"You still have that," she said.

"Do I?" He left his chair and strolled to her. "He has your fealty. Does he tell me what he did? Ask my permission? No. I get silence. He comes to see me, and the first thing I know before he's even through the door, is that his loyalty is divided. When things get dire, and I promise you they will, who's he going to attend to first? Me or you?"

Gray lifted her right arm and held it out, palm up. The markings underneath her skin writhed, reacting to the magic in the room. "He's teaching me." She touched her right temple. Her fingertips burned. "I think that's to your advantage, don't you?"

Nikodemus crossed his arms over his chest. "So?"

"You can't trust Christophe," Gray said.

"Hell, no."

"Warlord, I think—"

"Stay out of this, Durian. This is between me and your girl, here." His gaze burned into her. "You better be sure you understand the consequences of crossing me."

The room went unnaturally silent and the quiet sent icy fingers skittering down her spine.

She thought about that. Her concern right now was keeping Durian out of trouble, and she was willing, she realized, to say anything that would solve the problems now. The hell with later on. They had to make it through this. "Maybe I don't."

"You screw me over, you screw him over." He waited while she worked that out. It didn't take long. She nodded. "I get that."

The warlord's mood settled down. "You watch out for him like you swore you would, and maybe we'll be fine. Set him up, betray him in any way, and I will come after you when I'm done with him." He smiled. "I promise *you* a painful death."

"Understood."

Nikodemus frowned, and Gray couldn't tell if she'd averted disaster or not. "Tell me, Big Dog, is she any good at what you do?"

The warlord's command to Durian was subtle, but she felt the imperative tug at her chest.

"Yes."

"How good? As good as you?"

Durian's face was absolutely unreadable. "Not yet."

"But close. Am I right?"

He nodded.

"She needs to be bound over."

When nobody said anything, Gray looked at them both. "What does that mean?"

"I won't permit it," Durian said.

Nikodemus's reaction was far too calm. Gray didn't trust it at all. "No?" he said.

Gray coughed. The fake kind. "Excuse me, Durian, but I think I can make up my own mind about this, if you don't mind." She met Nikodemus's gaze without flinching. "I've already sworn fealty to him. Can I do that again? To someone else?"

"Not an oath of fealty, Gray," Durian said. "He means to bind you with a different kind of oath. One that will prevent you from taking a life without a sanction except in defense of your own or another's life. If you were bound by this oath, Nikodemus and only Nikodemus could give you a sanction. And if he did so, you would be required to carry it out."

She looked to Nikodemus. "That accurate?"

"More or less."

This time she looked to Durian. "I take it you're already bound over like that?"

"Yes."

"I'm not sure I see the problem, Durian." She tapped the side of her leg, trying to figure the downside. He could have been a rock, for all the emotion he showed. In her head, it was a different matter. Durian was close to breaking with Nikodemus and she knew she couldn't let that happen.

"It's necessary, Big Dog, and you know it."

"It's dangerous." Durian and Nikodemus practically spit sparks at each other. "And you know it."

"What happens if I don't get bound over?"

"Nothing," Durian said.

Nikodemus was pulling again. "You aren't a warlord yet, Big Dog."

"That was never my intent."

The stress between the two climbed again.

"What was your intent?" Nikodemus's voice got very soft. "Were you looking for a way to break your oath? Is there something going on I need to know about?"

Durian went down on one knee, fingers of one hand pressed to his forehead. "No, warlord."

"Get up."

Durian rose, but nothing was resolved yet. He said, "You have a bigger problem than Gray, warlord. Christophe dit Menart meant to take our children and raise them to slavery. She will testify to that."

Nikodemus was silent. "He took her before the agreement went into effect. What he did was before she was kin. So far, he's keeping his word, Big Dog. No new magehelds. No attacks on my sworn kin. I don't like it any better than you, but he's not in breach of our agreement. Which, you might recall, you helped forge."

"He is breaching the agreement."

"Proof." He leaned forward. "We need proof."

"He's using Rasmus Kessler, who, as you are aware, is not bound by any agreement. Kessler's found a way to overcome the damage done to him, warlord, and he is now working against you, with Christophe's help."

His eyebrows lifted. "Proof?"

Durian continued. "Kessler attacked Gray and me using magehelds whose minds had been destroyed. We saw this. I saw Kessler with my own eyes."

"You saw Kessler with Christophe?"

Durian made a cutting motion with the side of his hand. "If you wait until there is no doubt, it will be too late. Give me dit Menart's sanction."

"You know I can't do that."

"Then give me Kessler's. That's no breach."

"Rasmus Kessler and I are negotiating. Obviously, I wasn't going to ask you to do the honors and you've been making yourself scarce lately." Nikodemus cocked his head. "We can't go back to the way things were. We can't. You listen to me, Big Dog. I understand your feelings about Kessler, but I'd fucking talk to Álvaro Magellan if he were still alive."

The tension bore down on Gray like a weight. The two were at the breaking point, and she didn't know what to do to stop it from happening. The warlord glanced at her and she shook her head.

"I'm sorry, warlord. I won't go back to Christophe."

Nikodemus scowled so hard she took an involuntary step back. "You're kin. I don't turn kin over to the magekind. Not for any reason." He sighed. "If you're not bonded to me, I don't have direct authority over you. Christophe knows that. You know that. You're working with my assassin and, sweetheart, what he's teaching you to do makes you too dangerous not to have that power bound over to a warlord." He raised his hands. "If not me, fine. But it'll have to be Kynan instead."

Gray snorted. "Hell no."

The warlord laughed. "Still having trouble making nice, is he?"

Durian stayed intent on the warlord. "Since she is not bound over, under the right circumstances, she can kill Christophe without breaking the agreement."

The air crackled as Durian's bonds to Nikodemus stretched to the limit. She knew it. She could feel it. "Don't do this," Nikodemus said.

She walked between the two of them and faced Nikodemus. Tigran had taught her that kin social structure was based on a combination of power and the bonds that conferred rank. A fiend with no bonds was almost certainly weak and definitely at risk of existing outside the social structure of a highly social people. The kin didn't enter into such bonds lightly. As Durian had already pointed out to her, they carried consequences, but they were also a fact of their existence.

"If I'm bound over to you, what does that mean?"

"It means you won't be able to kill except on my order, in self-defense, or, in your case, in defense of Durian."

"Gray—"

She ignored Durian for now. "My decision, right? Not yours. Not Durian's."

Nikodemus nodded.

Her decision meant giving up the revenge she'd promised herself after Christophe murdered Tigran, but if doing so meant keeping Durian from breaking with Nikodemus, well, it felt like the right thing to do. "I say bind me over."

CHAPTER 17

While Durian waited for this ill-begotten situation to be anything but what it was, Nikodemus faced the door and flicked a hand. The locks clicked shut. The rest of the room sealed off, too. Then he looked at Gray over his shoulder and winked at her. "Don't want anyone walking in on us."

"I guess not." She shoved her hands in her back pockets, trying not to be obvious about watching them. Not that it mattered. Durian had shut himself off from her the minute she agreed to be bound over, and it was bothering her. Gray, on the other hand, wasn't blocking herself so he and Nikodemus both knew she was worried. Nervous. Uncertain. Afraid. As well she should be.

She was choosing him over killing Christophe, and if it weren't for the fact that her decision had prevented disaster between him and Nikodemus, Durian would have been angrier than he was. He might not like her decision, but he could not, in conscience, judge it a betrayal.

"Don't be an ass, Durian." Nikodemus went to him. He

put a hand on Durian's shoulder. Durian could not help but react. Though the contact soothed him, the effect should have been more immediate. More intense. He wondered how badly his bonds to the warlord were weakened or whether it was his oath to Gray that interfered.

He inclined his head. "Warlord."

"Durian," Nikodemus said softly. "I know this isn't what you want. I understand what you were after." His hand tightened on Durian's shoulder. "If I were in your place, I might have done the same. This has to be done. She doesn't want it to be Kynan and I'm guessing you don't want that, either. Do you want me to ask one of the others? Huijan maybe?"

"No." He didn't want Gray bound to Nikodemus or to anyone else. For any reason. The reaction was irrational, he knew that. Just as this aspect of his power needed to be bound to a warlord, so did hers.

"Let's get this done." Nikodemus took a step back and toe-heeled off his boots. He stripped off his shirt next, then his socks and jeans. Naked, he tossed his clothes onto his chair, oblivious to Gray quickly turning her back.

Nikodemus took on his true form.

The room got warmer, the air thicker. The skin down Durian's back rippled with the magical resonance.

Gray peeked at Durian. Her pupils were huge and her cheeks were bright red. He wanted to reach out to her, but that would only cause problems. "Please tell me I don't have to take off my clothes for this."

"Sorry, but yes," Nikodemus said. Gray's head whipped around, her eyes wide.

"You don't." Durian put a hand on the back of her neck. "He's being an ass." He brought her in close.

"You're no fun," Nikodemus said. He gave them both an easy grin. "Keep your clothes on, sweetheart."

Durian slipped off his shoes. As he, too, stripped down, he folded his clothes and placed them on the seat of another chair, out of the way. He kept his one-way link with Gray.

Changing forms wasn't entirely comfortable. The urge to be naked tended to be overwhelming, and Nikodemus was right. It was much easier, much more natural to be unconfined by human clothing.

Durian stayed where he was, and let his body shift. His surroundings seemed to shift, too, though he knew they hadn't. In this form, his experience of the world changed. Magic flowed along his skin and through his body without the need to pull for it. Colors were more intense, more vibrant. All his senses sharpened. He no longer had a core of magic encased in a human form. His emotions were bigger. More elemental. More raw.

In this form, Gray's humanity called to him irresistibly. She was ancient prey. She was female. The object of his intense sexual desire. By extension, Nikodemus would have the same reaction to her. To any human female. Regardless of his bonds to Carson. Gray knew it and was afraid.

Nikodemus walked toward her and Durian immediately found himself holding back from an attack.

He crouched, one hand touching the floor. He growled, twitching with the urge to keep Nikodemus from getting anywhere near her. But he managed himself and stayed where he was.

Light altered and bent around the warlord so that at times his body glittered brilliant black or slid into shadow so he was hardly visible at all. Durian's oaths to

Nikodemus burned hot and collided with his obligations to Gray. He held steady when Nikodemus touched her. She was his sworn fiend. What Nikodemus was about to do would not change that.

This must be done.

Gray's eyes opened wide at the warlord's touch to her forehead and upper chest. At the contact, the surge of magic from her made for a potent mix of power tinged with her very human fear. She wasn't going to break because of her emotions, Durian did not doubt that for a moment. She was kin, after all.

He widened his connection with Nikodemus and Gray.

Along his skin, inside him, through the core of what he was, his oaths shifted in weight and realigned. The sensation was odd, disorienting even. For years, he had never wavered in loyalty to Nikodemus, even when they disagreed. Nikodemus had been right to worry about Durian's allegiance. Now, at this moment, his need to protect Gray took precedence over his oath of fealty to Nikodemus.

He moved closer, concentrating on what Nikodemus was doing while keeping himself in Gray's head. Enough to be certain she was safe, not enough to interfere with Nikodemus.

The binding required a deft use of power. As Nikodemus shaped his magic, the air around him shattered into prisms that reflected color throughout the room. Nikodemus formed the threads that created the oath that would prevent her from using her killing magic without justified cause. He worked quickly. Deftly and with a precision that made what he did look simple.

When it was done, Gray pressed her hands to her chest and stood motionless, head bowed.

There was no sound in the room but for their breathing.

Nikodemus remained standing over Gray, his head thrown back, his body vanishing into shadows. His chest expanded with his breath. Then, without a word, he turned on his heel and walked out.

Gray lifted her head. Her eyes were wide, icy blue in her pale face, not in reaction to her bond with Nikodemus, but to seeing him in his true form. Her dark lashes and eyebrows made the color of her hair all the more brilliant and unnatural. Her hands remained touching her chest. Their gazes locked and Durian felt his control thin. He didn't dare move.

Slowly, Gray walked to where Durian stood. He quivered with all the instincts of his kind; the desire to possess, to increase the mental connection they already had, perhaps even to disappear into her. She knew it, too, and knelt in front of him anyway. The magic in the room continued to spread through them both. He curled his taloned fingers toward his palms, resisting the urge to touch her.

She studied him, taking in what he was. "We'll find another way to take down Christophe, all right?"

CHAPTER 18

A few days later. Broadway near Baker, San Francisco

Durian crooked his fingers at Iskander. "Come after her. And mean it, fiend."

Iskander stood there, a smile spreading over his face. "You sure?"

There was only so much a construct offered. Gray needed to go up against the unpredictability of an independent consciousness. Physically, she was far beyond any of the lesser kin, which was why he'd tapped Iskander.

She tapped Iskander's shin with the toe of one foot. She was much better than Iskander realized, and Durian was looking forward to him finding out just what he was facing. "Do it, big boy."

Iskander wasted no time. Except he didn't come after her. He came at Durian hard and fast. Durian centered himself just in time.

Gray's oath to him required nothing less of her than to lay down her life to protect him, and she went after Iskander with a ferocity that echoed in his bones. Despite everything, there was nothing wrong with her oath. She shouted, and his connection with her flashed through his body. Hot. Intense. Immediate. For a moment, while he was fully in her head, Durian couldn't see anything at all. The next, he felt Iskander and Gray both with a precision that startled him. His vision returned.

She rolled, turned, grabbed, and had Iskander on his back and one hand around his throat, going for his heart. Iskander laughed and blocked her easily. The tats down his face lit with an inner glow. He damn near took off her head.

Her body bowed backward but she reached for his chest, her fingers inches from a touch. Just when he thought Iskander had forgotten himself, the other fiend released his magic, and she flew off him, sliding several feet on the floor.

"I forgot about her oath," Iskander said. His eyes stayed a brilliant, unworldly blue.

Gray was on her feet, her mouth pressed closed so tight her lips were white at the edges. Her hands, too, were clenched at her sides. She stood and momentarily towered over Iskander like Godzilla over a fallen Rodin. "This isn't a game, Iskander. Play it the way Durian said."

Durian absorbed what she was, how she looked—her svelte body, lean and yet so undeniably female—and Iskander hooked in. Iskander's reaction to Gray's humanity and her magic was predictable and entirely normal. The sizzle between the three of them grew insistent.

"Why?" Iskander got to his feet in one motion. He slid

a glance at Durian but addressed Gray. "The world out there will not play by your rules. What are you going to do when Nikodemus sends you on your first sanction, little one? Ask him to please hold still while you kill him?"

She closed the distance between them until she was toe-to-toe with Iskander. "Are you trying to be an asshole?"

"I don't have to try." He grinned. "It comes naturally."

Gray looked at Durian. "How the hell do you stand him?"

"We all have our burdens to bear. He is mine."

"What have you been doing to the Big Dog?" Iskander put one hand on Gray's shoulder and the other over his heart. Durian held back a growl of protest. "Did you go out and steal him a personality?"

"Lay off, will you?" She poked Iskander in the chest. The tension receded.

Iskander met Durian's gaze over the top of her head. "My friend. Do you deserve such loyalty?"

"Can we get back to work?" Gray took a step back.

"Anything you want." Iskander's smile slowly faded. He cut off his connection with Gray, and Durian did the same because he didn't want to incidentally help her. She needed to know how to fight alone.

Durian lifted a hand in Iskander's direction and gave the signal to start. And then Iskander pulled. Hard. His eyes cycled from plain blue to cobalt. The tats down his face deepened in color. A wave of air solidified and shot straight at Gray.

She deflected the attack just in time. Considering who she was up against—there was a reason Nikodemus kept Iskander around—she acquitted herself well. Iskander needed fifteen minutes before he had her immobilized.

When she was down, Durian found himself locked out of Iskander's head. He did not, at first, think much of it. The practice bout was over.

Iskander's hand gripped her throat, and the sound he made rippled through the air like something that had walked in straight off the savannah. The hint of cobalt in his hair shimmered until there was no mistaking the color for anything natural. He locked gazes with Gray and leaned over her. He released her throat, but still touched her. "You want an animal?" he said softly, his mouth just inches from her face. "Say the word and I'll do you however you want it. Whatever he won't."

"Fuck you," Gray whispered.

Iskander grinned happily. "That's the idea."

"Iskander." Durian didn't like the way they were looking at each other. "Behave please."

"Why?" His hands were wandering. "That isn't what she wants. Is it?"

She pushed him away, rolled to her feet and without looking at Durian, reset. "Again." She stared at Iskander. "No link this time."

The air took on an electricity that rippled along Durian's skin. The stripes down Iskander's body glowed. Gray's eyes did that odd jitter, as her vision changed, but her focus was laser sharp.

They began.

Gray quickly slipped beside Iskander, but he whirled, blocked her as she came at him from the side. Iskander brought a hand down so fast she almost didn't duck soon enough. Even Durian standing where he was felt the disturbance in the air as Iskander's hand skimmed past the back of her neck.

Her best hope was getting in behind him; failing that, coming in dangerously close. Durian didn't doubt that was her intention. Recklessness was a part of who she was now.

And then Iskander dampened his magic.

Durian lost all sense of him magically.

The air around Iskander shimmered, and he vanished.

Gray didn't react in the slightest. He felt like he was watching his own personal performance. From watching her he could guess where Iskander was or what he might be doing. Twenty minutes later she was still untouched.

His student was brilliant.

Without warning, Gray stopped dead. At first, Durian suspected a ruse, but she didn't move and that wasn't like her. Her hands rose to her throat and her eyes opened wide. Her magic lost focus, and the whorls on her arm and temple went from green to cobalt blue.

Iskander, who could never really be trusted, had taken possession of Gray's physical body, and she was panicking. His heart thudded against his ribs and without conscious thought his magic was at his fingertips.

"Iskander."

The fiend reappeared. His tats glowed searing blue as he dropped to one knee, swept her feet beneath her and that was it. She went down hard.

Iskander touched her shoulder. "You're dead, human."

Gray lay on her back, panting. The traceries on her arm faded as she lost contact with her magic. Her eyes went blank.

"Enough," Durian said.

Iskander put his face close to hers, his hair falling forward, and growled. But the sound wasn't meant to intimidate as it had been before. She pushed him away, except Iskander didn't budge. He kept his hand on her.

She glared up at him. "You going to kill me now?"

"I'd rather kill Durian." He released her, though, and very deliberately snarled at Durian. She shot up like she was on fire. The next thing Durian knew, Iskander was on his back and Gray was straddling him, her hands pressed hard to his chest. Her upper arms trembled.

She leaned over him. "The hell you will, fiend."

"It's not Durian I want." He smiled at her. "But remember, Gray," he said softly. He cupped the side of her face. "If I wanted to kill you, you'd already be dead."

"More practice then." She remained straddling him, her breathing more normal. But now her magic was disorganized. Something had happened when Iskander took possession, and she hadn't shaken it off yet. Still she looked over her shoulder at Durian. "Again?"

"No," he said. He let go of his psychic blocks, though. Gray and Iskander resonated with magic. The connection between her and Iskander went deeper than the normal casual link, though.

One hand still on Iskander's chest, she dipped her head to her other arm to wipe sweat off her forehead. "He's right. I'm still not ready."

"Babycakes," Iskander said, "was that as good for you as it was for me?"

"Shut up."

Even with Durian's superficial link with her, her response to Iskander was unmistakably normal for the kin. Perhaps not lust but not nothing, either. Iskander had relaxed enough that Durian was aware of his state of arousal, too, and that *was* lust.

Gray set her palms on Iskander's chest. "You're a freak, you know that, don't you?"

"Oh, yeah."

They were all three of them on edge, and the three-way connection was back, flowing between them. Durian considered dropping out of the link, but found he did not wish to cede anything to Iskander. Doing so was the same as telling Iskander he felt no claim on her but that of her oath.

"Do you do social media?" Iskander said. He put a palm on the middle of her back, turned his hand and slid his fingers down the back of her workout pants. "What's your Twitter id? We'll follow each other and I'll DM you my home address so you can come over. Whenever you want. You can do whatever you want to me." His hand delved and he waggled his eyebrows. "Tonight?"

Durian clenched his teeth. The asshole was coming on to her.

"Perv." But she was laughing.

"Oh, yeah, Gray." Iskander's voice fell a notch. "Oh, yeah."

Durian, willing or not, was pulled along with the two of them. Iskander was sparking off her humanity—and he could not blame the fiend for it.

She got off him and extended a hand. He took it and she helped him up. He straightened his shirt and adjusted his jeans while she turned around to face Durian.

From behind her, Iskander's fingers tightened on her shoulder, and then he dropped his chin to her shoulder. She closed her eyes, and Durian was pulled along. He let it happen even though he knew it was foolish.

The heat between the three of them racheted up.

Iskander circled an arm around Gray and with a swipe of a now taloned fingertip, opened a cut along the side of her throat. He drew in a deep breath. "Sweet," he whispered.

Durian took her hand in his and from nowhere, Iskander's fingers wrapped around their joined hands. The three of them might well have ended up on the damn floor, except that the magic turned ugly on them.

An explosion from downstairs shook the floor and rattled the windows.

They didn't make it two steps toward the stairs when something screeched like a dying beast. They shoved on their shoes and raced down the stairs with the smell of ozone wafting toward them.

Magic burned around them when they reached the center of the magic. They were under attack from a mage.

Durian watched the entire bank of windows along the far wall bow inward and shatter.

Shards of glass flew through the air.

CHAPTER 19

Durian reached the living room ahead of Iskander and Gray. Within seconds magehelds swarmed through the broken window frames on the left side of the room. The sound of breaking wood and glass falling to the floor filled the air, along with the grunts and shouts of the invaders fighting for entry. Kynan was already here, having come down from another part of the house. He was fighting magehelds near a bank of windows by an entrance that led to a back hallway.

Information clicked into Durian's mind, flowing in from Kynan, Iskander, and Gray. These magehelds were mindless brutes, just like the ones who'd attacked Gray and him at Muir Woods. Time slowed. So much happened all at once, stimuli hit all his senses; sight, smell, sound, touch, taste, and magic. Iskander moved past him to take on the magehelds flooding in at the windows. Kynan continued his battle. Gray tucked in beside him, a welcome presence.

A mass of squirming, seething bodies pressed against

the broken windows, the individuals behind so frantic to get in they crushed the ones in front. What kept them out so far was the remnants of the proofing, and that had to be near to breaking point. The faces contained in the medallions along the molding contorted in silent screams of rage. Above the shattered windows, the medallions were charred black.

The proofing around the windows near Kynan gave way with a nerve-shivering buzz. A single mageheld vaulted in as the other two windows gave out. He died as the forces constrained in the medallions broke free. Behind him, more magehelds came.

None of the free kin could sense a mageheld's magic, and fighting magic you couldn't feel was dangerous. It wasn't easy to defend against what you didn't know was coming at you. Not when you were used to the advantage of knowing.

Durian had enough time to realize that the frenzy and the number of magehelds trying to get in had probably saved their lives. They fought each other for ingress rather than attacking. Had the magehelds been more coordinated, Kynan would have been overwhelmed before they made it down from the do-jang. Enough low-ranking fiends could take down even a warlord. More magehelds made it inside, many with wounds from the broken glass and wood. With Gray at his side, Durian prepared to meet the ones who made it past Iskander and Kynan.

As he and Gray moved to intercept the first wave, he knew this didn't make sense. Magehelds were compelled to do as ordered, but they were rarely stupid about it. A mageheld fiend was a cunning and dangerous creature, and none of these monsters demonstrated the slightest awareness of their surroundings. As far as Durian could tell there was no leader. No one coordinating and directing the attack. No mageheld leader anyway.

Now that they'd lost the edge the ambush had given them, they weren't retreating. No regrouping. There was just this mindless press for destruction of whatever stood in their way.

Durian pulled more magic than was safe. Iskander and Kynan were already doing the same. So was Gray. He opened himself to her, locking in on her, and she flowed along his senses. They worked well together. They gave each other opportunities and created openings.

Kynan's magic flashed through the room and the vanguard swarming from the windows fell to the ground before they got a quarter of the way inside. Those who didn't die were either fully or partially immobilized. Few of the survivors maintained their human forms. More pushed through the windows, stepping on the bodies of their fallen comrades, tripping, stumbling forward without apparent thought or plan.

Perhaps a minute had passed since they'd come downstairs, but it felt like forever. His sense of wrongness increased. Driven by compulsion and whatever else was wrong with them, the creatures who'd been outside the limits of Kynan's magic and thus survived his attack, swarmed forward, crawling until they could lurch upright. They paid no heed to the glass that sliced into them. Blood dripped from their gaping cuts yet they kept coming on. Kynan let loose with a cry that echoed off the walls. He showed no mercy. As was fit.

Despite the disparity in numbers, the magehelds were so disorganized and bunched up that from time to time Iskander shoved a knot of them to the ground and moments later a red mist danced around them. By the time the mist cleared, the magehelds were dead.

Durian killed the first three magehelds to come within his reach. Quickly. Without reflection or preparation. His chest ached and before long he was sure his ribs would crack apart. He didn't stop. This was about survival, not the elegance of his kill.

On the far side of the room, Kynan shifted to one of his alternate forms. The warlord planted himself between the magehelds and the side of the room where Iskander had more magehelds backed up against the wall. The two of them trapped the magehelds behind a magical wall. Passing through that barrier ought to have been too painful to bear, but they were trying, and it was a horrific sight. A grinning Kynan killed the ones who came through alive.

Durian and Gray had their hands full with the interior of the room. She plucked a leg from the ruins of a table and used it as a cudgel. She was faster than a normal human, but not faster than a mageheld. She was stronger, too, but he didn't know if, like other kin, Gray would heal from wounds that would kill a vanilla human. There wasn't time to think about what was going on with her because there were more magehelds to deal with. She was capable of keeping herself alive. Chances were high that her oath would keep her near him.

The first time magehelds ended up between them, he killed them and any others who'd made it past Iskander and Kynan. The second time, he understood the magehelds were trying to separate them. The one and only glimmer of intelligence from them. Durian circled back to her but was cut off again. Once more he regained her side and twice more magehelds separated them.

Again, they were after Gray.

The moment he had an opening he shot toward her. He came at her sideways, in low and from her left, taking down as many of the magehelds around her as he could touch.

She clubbed one and it reeled back, tripping another one, which fell face down on Durian. The thing clawed at Durian's belly with extended talons. Before he could shatter the mageheld's heart, though, Gray killed it with a two-handed swing of the table leg and followed up with magic to ensure it was dead. She shoved the body away with her foot. She whirled to face another mageheld and dispatched it, too.

He rolled to his feet. So much was happening at the same time: Kynan Aijan fighting, Iskander's defense, Durian's own trajectory toward Gray, and her deliberate stride toward the door. More of them worked their way toward her.

Durian's heart banged against his ribs when he saw her surrounded. She maintained a bent-kneed posture, gripping her weapon with white-knuckled hands. The stance was not a defensive one, and outnumbered as she was, it should be. He didn't know how long Kynan and Iskander would be able to continue with magic that struck so broadly. It was draining and dangerous. A miscalculation might easily injure or kill any one of them by mistake.

He opened himself to Kynan and Iskander, bringing them into his link with Gray, knowing it was dangerous but risking it just the same. Kynan was a warlord, Iskander practically so. They could deal with unblocked exposure to Durian's magic. Psychically, all four of them locked in on each other. If they didn't work together they weren't going to come out of this alive.

Durian bulled his way through to Gray, touching

magehelds when he could—they had no instinct for self-preservation. The challenge lay in the frenzy that made them fast and unpredictable. The smell of bodies and magic choked the air. Somewhere out there, a mage was controlling this.

He watched her swing her table leg at three magehelds. The first went down, the other two lunged, and she got her touch, one, two. Then others went down. She was using the edge her ability to sense magehelds gave her, anticipating where they would be before she struck.

More magehelds swarmed through the side door like they were going over a hurdle. One peeled off and went for him, clawed hands outstretched. Durian killed it with a touch and as the others passed him, he spun and more died. While he was engaged, she killed two more. One of the bodies bounced unnaturally as it landed and hit Gray a glancing blow to her side that knocked her on her back.

This level of carnage and sustained attack was insanity, yet the surviving magehelds were trying harder. All of them worked toward Gray. She moved faster than he anticipated given the limitations of her physical form. So quick on her feet. He was seeing—because he recognized it—a near perfect imitation of his technique augmented by the magic she had taken from Christophe.

God, he could love a woman like her, he really could. She caught his eye for a moment and he grinned at her. She smiled back, and they both went back to work.

A hole appeared in the space between the double main door and the jamb. The wood collapsed against itself as if it were being squeezed by an invisible hand. And she kept moving toward whatever was on the other side. The living room door disintegrated from its midpoint outward.

"Get down, get down!" Durian threw himself at her, covering her with his body as the sound of the door vaporizing boomed in his ears. Her table leg went flying. She fought to crawl from underneath him and nearly did. He tightened his hold and pushed her head to the floor. The disintegration of the proofing that protected the house from magical intruders carried a lethal blowback. By design. "Head down, fiend."

Uttered like that, she had no choice. He'd given her a command both verbal and psychic. The last of the proofing gave way. His ears popped and then, every mageheld he could see between here and the door died. When it was over, he rolled off her, keeping low to the ground as he cast about for status.

The room fell silent. For a moment, Gray was utterly still in a position that reminded him more than a little of himself. She looked at him with eyes that did not focus as they ought. "Is it over?"

Durian looked around and saw Kynan Aijan at the far side of the room and Iskander, who, as Durian watched, released the mageheld he'd just killed. Blood dripped from his other hand. The body tumbled to the floor.

Iskander shook his arms; they were bloody up to his elbows. Crimson droplets flew through the air. He backed away from the dead around him, stepping over bodies as necessary. He looked as sick as Durian felt. "There's nothing there," he said. His eyes were wide, his pupils black discs amid the surrounding blue. "Not for any of them." He touched a finger to his temple. "Gone."

Kynan made an inhuman sound. His eyes blazed gold. His fingernails were too sharp to be normal. Though he was human in appearance, he was not human in fact. The warlord teetered at the edge of his control. Gray shivered in reaction to the warlord's magical state. Durian saw the ripple of goose bumps down her arms. He held his breath. If Kynan lost control, they were all in trouble.

"My friend." Iskander spoke softly. He headed for Kynan, which was either suicidal or courageous. "My friend."

For a moment Kynan stood with his taloned hands raised to the ceiling, head back while he brought himself under control. He shifted back to his human form but there wasn't any mistaking him for a twenty-something human male. Not any more. His magic burned through the room. The warlord's attention fixed on Gray.

Iskander caught Durian's eye and motioned to Gray. "Get her out of here, Assassin."

CHAPTER 20

Gray held her breath. The way Kynan was looking at her, with his magic boiling hot, she was surprised he didn't come after her. She knew he wanted to because he was letting her see what was in his head. And it wasn't pretty. He had a link to her. They all had during the fighting. Kynan was the only one who hadn't released. She tried to dislodge him but nothing worked.

It was the magic she'd taken from Christophe that triggered his reaction to her. In a room full of magehelds that magic had flared to life, and she'd used what she could in anyway she could.

Having Kynan in her head was like getting hit by a train. In no time he found her memories of Tigran, all those images and conflicting emotions about what had happened to her. She'd made a bargain with the devil where Tigran was concerned. Kynan Aijan had been through something similar, which she knew not because he let her see but because she recognized his emotions.

"I did what I had to." She nodded to the warlord. "I

think you probably did the same thing." He was still super nova, but he wasn't after her. Not anymore. "Fuck the mages, warlord. All of them who do shit like that."

Kynan stayed locked up in her head, burning with a crackle of electricity that robbed her of the ability to tell whether she was standing or flat on the ground. Impossible as it seemed, what she got from Kynan wasn't pity or blame, but a profound shock of recognition.

She snapped back to the room feeling like the inside of her head had been set on fire. She couldn't see normally, just the blazing presence of Durian. Kynan was across from her, staring at her with eyes that shone brilliant gold.

The warlord took a step toward her and the other two fiends interpreted his actions completely wrong. Iskander hauled him back while Durian got a broad shoulder between her and Kynan. He wasn't going to attack her. She knew that. He was just shocked as hell to find out they had a lot in common. So was she. She held Kynan's gaze. "It's cool," she said, waving a hand. "Let him go."

Awkwardly, because Iskander still held him up, Kynan pressed three fingers to his forehead and bowed his head to her. That was big. Warlords didn't acknowledge a fiend of lower rank first. Ever. Unless something extraordinary had happened. Their eyes stayed locked, and even though he was hyped up from the fighting, she knew he meant it. He nodded at her again. "You're on the other side now, human."

He let her see something of himself. Enough for her to understand that he'd been mageheld once and had done things that had killed something in him. She said, "Does it get any easier?"

Kynan didn't answer right away. "Yeah," he said at last. "If you have the right people around you, it does."

"Thank you." She replicated his bow as best she could.

"Take her upstairs, Assassin," Kynan said. "Make sure she's all right."

"Warlord." Durian tightened his arm around her, and she allowed herself to relax against him. With Kynan's magic tugging at her like a riptide, he walked her out of the room. They headed for the back of the house. She was rapidly feeling better after that electric contact with Kynan Aijan, but the lights made her eyes water. Whenever they passed a switch, she turned the lights off. He stopped in a now dim hallway. "How are you feeling?"

She blinked a few times. A burnt stench floated on the air, particularly pungent here, for some reason. "Better."

They reached a side door with a frosted glass window at the top and a mesh curtain stretched over it. Even with the lights off, she could make out the lumpy shapes of the recycling and garbage through the curtain. Durian stayed close to her.

"Why are we here?" She could make out the outline of his face, the shape of his lower lip, the dark shadow of his hair.

His hands stayed on her, and she didn't move. "There is a mage out there." His eyes glowed faintly purple.

"That means there'll be more magehelds out there."

"We cannot accuse Christophe without proof." He lowered his head. Not to kiss her, but so she could hear his soft words. His hands settled around her waist. Her heart skipped a few beats. "If he is behind this attack, I intend to get that proof. Tonight."

She grinned at him. "Excellent." Durian ran a hand through her hair, and she tipped her head back. "Sorry. Still red."

"I'm starting to like it."

"Yeah?"

He smiled. "Whoever is out there needs magehelds with their minds intact. We can find the mage easily enough, but his magehelds are another matter." His fingers tightened around her. "With your particular gift, you could find them easily. They can be disabled before the mage understands what's happened."

"Got it."

He rested his forehead against hers. "This is not without risk," he said softly.

"What?" She pretended to be shocked. "You mean we'll be in danger?"

Durian's hand slid to the nape of her neck. "Point made."

"Let's go."

"A little planning is in order." He gestured. "The goal is to find and neutralize the magehelds without the mage knowing something has happened."

"I take care of the magehelds while you go after the mage." She lifted her hands, palm up. "See? I get it."

"No. We should approach the mage together." Durian gave a smile so fierce she got chills. "When he understands that his magehelds have been removed without his knowing what happened to them, he will feel motivated to speak frankly with us."

"How's that going to work?" She frowned, trying to think this through. "The magehelds aren't going to feel yours or Tigran's magic, but the mage will. And what about my other magic? Magehelds will feel that, won't they?"

"I'll dampen us."

"What does that mean?"

He brushed a hand across her cheek. "It means I can hide us both for a time. Long enough to do what we need to once you've located the magehelds for us."

She looked around the little anteroom and snatched a dark hooded sweatshirt off a hook by the door. Her skin was too pale for the stealth they needed. Any mageheld halfway paying attention would see her. The sweatshirt was several sizes too large and hung past her butt. She rolled up the sleeves enough to keep them from interfering with her hands. To do this right, she needed gloves, but there wasn't time.

She held up a hand and started counting off on her fingers. "First task: locate the magehelds. Second task: we figure out which order to take them in. Third task: scare the living hell out of a mage."

"Sounds about right," he said.

"Ready when you are."

He nodded. Her skin prickled when Durian's magic flared. Jesus, he was heinously strong. They got a link going, strong enough that they wouldn't need to talk much. She took a few deep breaths, then she opened the door and the two of them slipped into the night. The pull of Kynan's and Iskander's magic on her eased, which was a relief. She was glad to be away from the stench of death, too.

The back of the house was clear. From Durian, she got the distinct idea that he would have been surprised to find anything different. Kynan and Iskander were in the living room. This close to the two, Gray could feel their magic. She rubbed her arms as she and Durian moved on.

The house and grounds were alarmed both electronically and magically. Out back, the perimeter proofing remained intact. The house's wired alarm had been disabled. Durian demonstrated for her how it had been done and how to undo the effect. "Neat," she whispered as the unit glowed back to life and Durian re-entered the arming codes.

Several charred and blackened medallions were scattered on the ground along the side of the house. Following the trail of destroyed medallions was easy enough. Even with her mediocre tracking skills, she could tell that one set of magehelds had gone through the garage outlet to the house while the bulk of them had poured in through the now shattered windows after having come from the front of the house.

Just as Durian said, locating the mage was easy. Even before they were around the front of the house, she felt his magic. In the back of her head she felt a tickle of awareness. Oh, yes. There were magehelds around. With Durian behind her, she inched forward, keeping to the shadows.

The mage was leaning against the side of a dark Mercedes sedan, watching the house from across the street and about twenty feet down the block. Four magehelds loitered by the open driveway gate, not even trying to hide. She didn't need magic to find them. They'd been placed where they would be most likely to be of assistance to the other magehelds—back before their brethren were decimated. Across the street, two more stood with the mage. They weren't trying to hide either, and at any rate, she wasn't worried about those two.

Five others were spread out at various locations up and down the block. These guys were taking pains not to be seen. Without the way they resonated in her head, she'd probably never have found them.

Getting past the four at the gate was easier than she thought. The dampening Durian was doing worked. Another neat trick, she thought. When this was over, she was going to have to try that on her own. With silent agreement, they moved past these four. If they went down, the mage would see they were no longer there. Their quarry were the five who were still hiding, starting with the nearest of the five, and working their way out.

As she moved within striking distance of the first two mages they were to take down, her nerves vanished. The world narrowed to just the details she needed to accomplish her task. Her hearing was acute enough to take in distant sounds, but she filtered them out as soon as she knew they were not relevant. Traffic on other streets. A far away siren. The only noises that mattered were the ones contained in the perimeter around her targets.

She crept close and made her two touches; not killing touches, but enough to make their eyes roll back in their heads. Durian caught each mageheld as it fell, senseless, to the ground. She went on to the next two. She knew with Durian dampening them they wouldn't sense her magically, but they also never heard her coming. Done. Five minutes later, they were done again.

There were more, but they were far enough away not to be a threat to her and Durian getting to the mage. If it had been necessary, though, she would have taken them down, too.

Easy.

She and Durian, with him continuing to dampen them, walked down the middle of the street. They headed straight for the mage who didn't have any idea what had happened to his magehelds.

CHAPTER 21

The mage came off the car with a start when Durian undampened them and crossed the street with Gray at his side. She, of course, had been magnificent. Focused. Calm. Intent on their goal. With no reason to worry she'd need assistance, he'd been able to concentrate on keeping their magic ramped down to a point too low for all but a rare gifted few to sense their presence. He and Gray worked well together.

The magic that kept the mage hidden in shadows that were darker and quieter than normal floated around the car like smoke. A ripple of awareness of the mage slid down his back. A few more steps and they were close enough to identify the mage.

Gray's disappointment that it wasn't Christophe was palpable.

Nor was it Rasmus Kessler.

Leonidas.

How disappointing, and for any number of reasons. Still in the street, he and Gray came to a stop, close enough for Durian to see the mage's eyes go wide. Leonidas didn't quite manage to suppress his leap of fear. The mage knew what Durian was, after all. There weren't many reasons for an assassin to appear as if from nowhere.

"Shall we have that coffee now, Leonidas?"

Leonidas muttered something under his breath that moved through Durian like a whisper of fell air across his soul. Within seconds, the magehelds he and Gray had left alone loped toward them, coming from both ends of the street. Too little. Too late. In any event, they weren't moving fast enough to have been ordered to attack.

Never trust a mage.

Durian kept his magic at the ready. Leonidas frowned, realizing, Durian supposed, that not all of his magehelds had responded to his summons.

"I'll take that as a no," Durian said. "Well. I'd invite you in." He tilted his head in the direction of the house. "But I'm afraid we have some work to do before we have guests again."

"Where are the rest?" The mage gestured toward the opposite side of the street where his other magehelds had been standing watch. The two magehelds who had stayed with him took up positions at the trunk and hood of his car, a placement more defensive than threatening.

Durian slung an arm around Gray's shoulders but twisted his upper body to look behind him. When he looked back, Leonidas was watching Gray. Intently watching. Durian kept his arm around her and said in a deliberately easy tone, "The ones you sent inside will not return. The others are . . . not currently at your command. Give them a few minutes to recover."

"Thank you." He inclined his head. "It would have been

a pity to lose them." Leonidas straightened the sleeves of his double-breasted suit jacket. A pair of faceted square-cut rubies glittered from his cuffs. Absolutely perfectly made suit. His trousers fell with exactly the right drape.

"Custom or bespoke?"

The mage looked insulted. "Made to my precise measurements, fiend." He didn't put a mage's usual insulting tone behind his words. "I use a tailor in London. Bond Street." The magehelds he'd called in reached him, but he lifted a hand. The fiends stopped. They arranged themselves on the sidewalk near the trunk of the car. Not so close that they represented a danger, but not so far that they would not be of assistance. Durian did not feel more magic from the mage.

"I prefer the Italian style," Durian said.

"Is that so?"

He did not begrudge the mage his superior smile. He still had on the dark sweat pants and shirt he wore for training with Gray. "Perhaps you've changed my mind," Durian said. "I don't suppose you'd give me your tailor's name?" Gray jabbed him in the side with a sharp elbow. He covered his reaction by drawing her closer to him and smiling.

"No."

"He tried to kill us. Is there some reason you're making nice?"

"Kill you?" Leonidas looked offended. "Hardly."

"My dearest love," he said. "That suit was made by someone who knows his way around a pair of scissors. I had to ask."

She rolled her eyes. "He's hot for your clothes, mage. Don't you find that a little disturbing between enemies?"

Leonidas's attention moved from Durian to Gray and back. "Perhaps I am not your enemy."

Gray's look of astonished disbelief made Durian smile. "You attacked us. I think that qualifies us as enemies."

The mage studied Gray for much longer than was polite. He, too, stood in the street, though he kept his back to the car. The chances of a fight in the street were low but not non-existent. This was not a neighborhood where one could get away with conversations that disturbed people in their rest, and the kind of magic Leonidas was using to mask their presence only went so far. They kept their voices deliberately low.

"I find," the mage said, "that some enemies are more worthy than certain allies." He reached into an inside pocket of his jacket. When Gray went on point, he slowly extracted a pack of rolling papers at the same time he gave Durian a questioning look.

He shrugged.

"Circumstances change," Leonidas said. "I have been alive long enough to watch allies become enemies and enemies become one's closest allies." With the same deliberation, he took a small paper packet from an outside pocket which he unfolded. He proceeded to roll himself a cigarette from the substance inside. From the color and texture, the contents were likely copa-laced tobacco. Mages used the drug when they were magically exhausted or when they needed to call more magic than they comfortably possessed. Leonidas did not have the latter problem.

The mage's dose of the drug looked to be too small to give him much of a boost, but then Leonidas would be well aware of the dangers. For his kind, copa was addictive, and addiction led, inevitably, to magical burn-out. When he was done rolling his cigarette with practiced hands he replaced everything and took out a square silver lighter. "The ones inside were not mine."

"No?" He didn't like the way the mage continued to stare at Gray over the top of his copa cigarette.

"No." The lighter flared. The paper caught and hissed as the mage inhaled. A moment later, the scent of some rich blend of copa-infused tobacco wafted into the air around them. His hands shook as he inhaled and returned his lighter to his pocket.

"If not you," Durian said, "then who?"

"Forgive me," Leonidas said to Gray. "Do I know you?"

Durian tensed. Leonidas was one of the older mages. Possibly the oldest of Durian's acquaintance. He was, among the magekind, one of the few whose opinion had any effect on the more powerful mages. He distrusted and disliked his interest in Gray. "I doubt it."

At the same time, Gray said, "Sure. You were hitting on me at Nordstrom."

"That isn't it." He took a step forward, his free hand extended with the obvious intent of taking her chin between his fingers.

Durian grabbed the mage's wrist in a motion too fast for a human to track. Gray recoiled. One of Leonidas's mage-helds growled and took a step into the street. The mage shook his head, and the mageheld backed away. Durian locked gazes with the mage, his magic banked but ready should Leonidas strike or order his magehelds to do so.

"Try to touch me again, mage," Gray said, "and you'll lose the hand."

Leonidas spread the fingers of the arm Durian gripped, a response meant to indicate he intended no harm. If Leonidas were anything but a mage, Durian might even believe it. "The old days are gone, Durian," he said in a soft voice. "When humans worshiped at your temples and our women came to you willingly."

"Long gone," he agreed. "We have adapted."

"Yes." He looked at Gray. "Yes, you have."

"If the other magehelds weren't yours," Durian said, "who sent them?"

Leonidas took a long drag on his cigarette and didn't answer until he'd exhaled the smoke. "If we're enemies after all, of what benefit is it to me if you know the answer?"

Durian kept Gray close. "The benefit? I won't need to assume it was you who attacked here, despite your presence here. Nikodemus, I'm sure you understand, won't be pleased if I tell him you tried to kill us." He allowed his private outrage to show in his voice. "Nor will he appreciate what was done to those magehelds. If it was not you, then I assure you it's to your benefit that Nikodemus know that."

"That was an abomination, fiend." The set of his mouth hardened. "Abomination." He cocked his chin in Gray's direction. "As bad or worse than what Christophe did to her."

"Agreed."

He took another drag, holding his breath for a moment before he exhaled. "I had nothing to do with that."

"Yet here you stand. Smoking copa to regain your strength."

Leonidas stared at his hand-rolled as if he didn't know

what it was. "Not for that," he said in a low voice. "That is an unwise use of the drug. By the time I arrived, it was done. There was nothing I could do." His eyes took on a faraway look. "I stayed behind to make sure none of them escaped to the general population." He shivered and reached up to rub the outside of his arms. His cigarette glowed between his index and second fingers. "He destroyed their minds."

"Who?"

"I don't want to imagine what could happen if even one of them had gotten free."

"Careful," Gray said. "Next you'll be agreeing fiends are people, too."

The Spartan frowned. "I presume, Durian, that none of them did survive."

"No."

"Thank the gods in heaven for that." Tension bled out of his shoulders. "I've heard rumors about dit Menart," the mage said. He glanced over his shoulder at his magehelds and lowered his voice. "Unpleasant ones. Are they true?"

"Most rumors about the magekind are unpleasant." Durian returned his steady look.

Leonidas flushed and avoided looking at Gray. "That he intended to breed his magehelds. With human women."

"If you want to know the answer to that question," Gray said, "why don't you ask me?"

Durian slid his hand to the back of her neck and softly stroked there, as much for his own calm as for hers. He steeled himself against a too familiar rage. Dit Menart deserved to die. For what he had done to Gray and more. Nikodemus was a fool to think there was a greater good in keeping that mage alive than there was in killing him. "I think this is not the time for such a disturbing discussion, Leonidas."

"She's human. You should release her." He took another drag of his cigarette and offered it, butt end, to Durian.

"No, thank you." He kept his magic hot. At his side, Gray's traceries reacted to his pulling and holding his magic, and that got another stare from the mage. Leonidas twisted his wrist, and, after a moment to prove he didn't have to let the mage go, Durian let him go.

"Not entirely human, I'll grant you that." Leonidas blew smoke over his head. Another whisper of magic came at him. Leonidas had always been a subtle user.

"Whatever you're doing," Gray said, "stop it."

"No wonder dit Menart is so desperate to have you back. He can't be happy knowing you came away with some of his magic. How on earth did you manage to escape with your life? "

"He underestimated me."

"No doubt he did." He cocked his head, his copa cigarette momentarily forgotten, though his eyes were turning from brown to a brassy gold. For a mage of his longevity, he was remarkably sensitive to copa. Most mages who'd been alive as long as he had either never touched copa or needed more than he'd had to experience any effect.

"Fascinating. I wouldn't have thought it possible for anyone to integrate the two sources of magic as you have."

A taxi came down Broadway going at least twenty miles over the speed limit. All three of them retreated to the edge of the street. Durian felt a flare of magic from the mage, but it was defensive only, a push outward. Away from them. Aided by the copa he'd taken.

The driver stayed intent on the road. His passenger stared out the window, a cell phone to her ear. If she noticed any of them standing there on a street of mansions, she gave no sign of it. When the taxi had disappeared toward its downtown destination Durian took Gray's hand in his and pulled her out of the mage's reach.

"I should very much like to study how it was done. The implications are enormous."

Slowly, she shook her head. "Christophe likes to go on about how dangerous fiends are." She took a step closer. "If you ask me, the magekind are just as dangerous. More, because you seem to think you have some kind of holy call that makes it all right to do whatever you want." She gestured at his magehelds with a movement of such ineffable grace that even Durian was arrested. "Slaves, Leonidas? What's just or right about that?" Her quiet voice gave her words power. "How long have you been alive? How many lives have you taken so you could live another year? How long since the kin were more of a threat to you than humans are to themselves?"

"Passionate, isn't she?"

"I don't much care for mages," Gray said.

"Understandable." Leonidas looked to Durian. "If Nikodemus is interested in an alliance, tell him I'll meet with him. Christophe needs to be stopped, and I expect I am in a position to help make that happen. Provided you, Assassin, do not carry out a sanction on me for doing so."

"I'll see Nikodemus gets the word. Anything else is between you and the warlord."

"I'm relieved to hear you say so." He smiled. "Are you

sure," he said to Gray, "that you won't let me study you? I could make it worth your while."

"Like how?"

Leonidas grinned. "I'll give Durian the name of my tailor."

Gray smiled back. And then she said, "Give up your magehelds and maybe we'll talk."

CHAPTER 22

Gray shook her head when Durian held the back door for her. There was just no changing some habits. His were growing on her. When the door closed behind them, she stripped off her borrowed jacket. She got a whiff of herself and shuddered. "Don't get too close. I need a shower."

"Thank you for the warning." His expression stayed as serious as ever, but there was a hint of a smile on his mouth.

She headed upstairs to her room next to the do-jang because that's where her clothes were. She turned the water on as hot as she could stand it and soaped off what felt like ten layers of sweat and grime. She changed into fresh clothes: faded jeans, a lime green shirt over white, and a pair of sandals. Her hair was still short enough that she didn't have to do anything to it but give it a good toweling off before she headed downstairs. She found Durian, once again dressed in meticulous black and more black, standing in the ruined doorway to the living room.

What had once been a living room worthy of a decorator's envy was now a disaster. Ruined furniture littered the floor. Her vision wasn't completely normal yet, but she could make out bodies, some in grotesque positions. The remaining corpses were harder to see, and the smell of magic lingered like burnt air. Fog-tinged air came in through the shattered windows, carrying the smell of blood and viscera through the room, cloying and sharp.

From her experience with Christophe, she knew a house in a non-magical neighborhood had to be warded to prevent the transmission of the sounds, odors, and other effects that were bound to occur. Despite the battle that had raged here, if she was right about the warding, and she knew she was, it was just about impossible for the neighbors to have heard anything. If they were to come look at the house right now, they'd see a damn convincing illusion of an undamaged structure. No broken windows. No smell of death.

The inside of the house held no illusions. Behind where she and Durian stood, a large armoire had tipped over near the opposite wall and now lay partially front-side down with one door broken underneath. She steadied herself and turned her attention back to Durian as an intense desire that she not be alone in her thoughts shot through her. "How did any of us survive this?"

He reached for her hand and held it and it was exactly the right thing to do. "Kynan and Iskander are not kin to be trifled with. Nor am I. Nor," he added, squeezing her hand, "are you. You acquitted yourself well, Gray."

"Did we really fight like that? It seems like a dream. Or something I imagined." She leaned into him without thinking of anything except how much she needed the comfort of touch. Their contact, not even skin-to-skin but for their hands, intensified their low-level psychic connection. She put a hand on his cheek, and he tipped his head into her palm.

"Not a dream," he said.

He was just too lovely for words. Facing him, she slid her palm along the side of his face. In answer, the tips of his fingers danced along the top of her arm. The contact wasn't sexual but it was sensual in the way of the kin. They took comfort from touch and she was learning to do the same. Amid the calm, she thought about holding him closer, her fingers sliding along the length of his spine, as far as she could reach while his hips flexed forward. Naked skin touching. He knew that about her now, and she was counting on his reaction being as unconcerned as was the case with other kin.

She set her other hand on his waist and her hand ended up underneath his shirt, and the touching felt good. Necessary. Her fingertips found the dent of his spine and moved upward. He didn't draw away or close her out of his head. They needed this. Both of them. She didn't push the connection between them; she just let herself fall into his magic. So much. So dark.

Durian bent his head and pressed his mouth to the tracery at her temple, and it was like feeling her body coming awake. He parted his lips, and his tongue touched her skin, and she was appallingly aroused. She wanted to bury her fingers in his hair and bring his hard naked body over hers and feel him push inside her. If he didn't do something about that in the next five minutes, she would.

And right then, right when she was about to pull Durian's head down to hers and to hell with waiting for the right time, someone came down the stairs and Durian pulled away, though at least he kept his arms around her.

"Kynan Aijan," Durian said softly.

Kynan stopped in front of the ruined armoire. He had a lot of magic on tap, and his eyes still weren't completely normal. The armoire lay tilted to one side, partially propped up by a table that had been near it. One broken door sagged open. "What happened outside?" Kynan asked. "You find Christophe?"

"Not him," Durian said.

"Is he dead?"

"No."

"Why the fuck not?" He turned his head to her, smiling. He looked younger than she did. "Honey." His voice was wry and a bit annoyed. "Chill. I'm not going to do anything to your assassin."

Iskander came down the stairs at a trot. The blue markings on his face glowed brighter than usual. He slowed when he saw them. He didn't release his magic either, which only made things worse for her. They were both setting off her oath to Durian. "Did you find the mage?"

"Not Christophe," Kynan said. He held out a hand in Iskander's direction and wriggled his fingers. "Pay up."

Iskander came the rest of the way down the stairs. He pulled a crumpled bill from his front pocket and dropped it onto Kynan's palm. "Damn. I bet on Christophe."

"You should have kept your money, Iskander," Durian said. "The mage we found denies responsibility for the attack."

Kynan snorted and shoved the money into his front pocket. "The bet wasn't about who did it. A fucking mage did it. That's all we need to know."

"That seems a rather fine point, if you ask me." Durian, she realized, was still holding her hand. "And probably not in the spirit of the wager."

"Give me back my money."

The warlord glared at Iskander. "No."

Gray cleared her throat. "What was the exact wording of the bet? Iskander?"

"I bet him a hundred dollars you'd find Christophe out there."

"Who did you bet on?" she asked Kynan.

"Anyone but Christophe. This has Rasmus Kessler's stink all over it." Kynan pointed at Gray. "Not that it matters. What mage did you find?"

Iskander dug in his pockets again. "I'll give you a hundred dollars to say it was Christophe."

"Sorry," she said over Durian's laughter. "I can't lie when you suck so bad at bribery. We saw Leonidas."

"I always hated the Spartans."

Kynan said, "You ever get tired of her, Big Dog, you let me know."

CHAPTER 23

Did Kynan hurt you earlier?" Durian leaned against the bathroom door while Gray splashed water on her face.

The lights were out in his room; they'd probably blown a fuse when the proofing gave out. The lighting was limited to the dim glow from the constructs Durian had conjured. Even here an acrid scent of death and magic hung in the air. The medallions remained in place but several were nothing but misshapen lumps and most were blackened to some degree or another. A few were charred to nothing.

Gray looked a little pale, and he couldn't help worrying about the aftereffects of her incident with Kynan Aijan. The warlord had not been under very good control at the time. She stood leaning over, one hand on the edge of the sink, and took a deep breath. He snatched a towel from the rack and handed it to her. He made a note to make sure her things were moved down here.

"Thanks." She dried her face, folded the towel in half lengthwise and hung it up. "No," she said. "He didn't."

"It did not look or feel that way."

"No question, Kynan's really something," she said. "But no."

"Can I ask what happened?"

Gray propped her hands on the edge of the pedestal sink. "He was mageheld once."

Durian nodded. "To Álvaro Magellan."

"I don't know how much I should say." Her gaze focused on the sink, then slid to him.

"It's no secret Magellan abused Kynan." Durian touched his chest then dropped his hand. "He had a weapon in Kynan. Magellan did not hesitate to use it."

"It was worse than that," she said in a soft voice. "Bastard mage." In the dimness, her hair looked black instead of bright red, and he wondered if he was seeing her as she had once been. Before.

"You're certain you're well?"

"Yes." She pushed off the sink, and he followed her out of the bathroom. He was feeling a little lost. He considered himself an experienced lover. He'd certainly taken his share of women to bed, but he didn't know what to do about Gray. No relationship he'd had in the past put him at risk of anything but the possibility of bad sex. "What's the deal with Leonidas?"

"In what sense?"

"Is he very powerful?"

"Yes."

She stood in the middle of the room, hands on her hips, facing him. "Nikodemus is going to want a deal with him."

"Nikodemus is creating a new history for us." Durian could remember, now, all the reasons he'd once believed so passionately in Nikodemus. And perhaps still did. "He's right. The killing must stop."

"I'll second that."

"There is another of the kin, his name is Harsh, who has been traveling on his behalf, talking to the other warlords and mages. I imagine Harsh is probably why Leonidas is here. From what I hear, the situation in Europe is rapidly disintegrating. A good many of the surviving free kin came here or to other locations where the magekind were not so aggressive. It's also rumored, and I've heard this from multiple sources, that there are fewer magekind being born. Even here. Fewer magekind. Fewer of the free kin."

"You think Leonidas will be the same as Christophe?"

"That is uncertain."

"Can he be trusted?"

"He's a mage, Gray." He walked closer to her, now deeply suspicious of her intentions. "What are you thinking?"

She shrugged. "It's stupid I guess. Just whether he meant that about studying me."

"I can assure you, he did mean it." He put his hands on either side of her face. She wasn't closing down their link, and he didn't back off. Not from what he was feeling and not from touching her as if she had been born to the kin. "Don't get caught up in anything Nikodemus wants. It's enough that you're bound over to him as you are. Leave well enough alone."

"You don't."

"I have obligations to him that you do not."

"Because you don't leave well enough alone."

He tightened his hands on her and lost his struggle not to smile. She was right, after all. "Gray."

"I can't help even if there's a way? Even if he agrees to give up his magehelds? You can't be serious."

"I didn't say that." She was right. Hell, she was right about that.

"You meant it." She looked determined. Like the warrior she was. She jabbed a finger at him. "This has nothing to do with my loyalty to you. If you don't have the guts to accept my help, too bad. I'll do it on my own. You aren't my boss, my father or godfather, or anything else. You can't stop me, Durian."

He nodded. "No, I can't. However, I am permitted to express my concern for your safety. Leonidas is a very powerful mage, and unlike most of the other kin sworn to Nikodemus, you have no protection against being taken mageheld."

"I appreciate the warning. Thank you." They stood there, inches apart, staring at each other. "I'll try not to do anything stupid, okay?"

His hands slid to her shoulders. "You are an honorable woman, Grayson Spencer."

"Isn't this much better?" she said. "When we agree like two civilized people?"

"I haven't agreed to anything."

Her smile was so heart-stoppingly tender he knew he was in trouble. "You don't really need to, do you?" She closed the distance between them.

"I suppose not." He didn't back away. When she kissed him, he did nothing to discourage her. In fact, he kissed her back with the thought *at last* echoing in his head. At last, he was kissing her where they would be private. At last. At last.

She pushed up on her toes because he was taller than she was, and there she was, pressed against him the way he'd been thinking of all too often. His body reacted with a surge of pure lust, and he was unable to think of anything except her. She kept kissing him, her mouth was soft and gentle on his. Her breasts pressed against him, her hips, and he wanted this.

Gray pulled back, her eyes searching his face. "Wow," she said.

After a very long time, when he was reasonably sure he had himself under control, he said, "I promised I would not require sex of you. This is not required, Gray. You can say no to this."

"You did promise me that." She cocked her head and gave him a smile that belonged in the bedroom. "But I didn't promise that."

"True." His fingers tightened on her, and he brought her back to him. "You didn't."

This time he held back so little that holding her, kissing her, was as blistering hot as he'd ever imagined. He wasn't even in her head and this was still hotter than anything he could remember.

There must be a reason, Durian thought, that he should not do this. But he couldn't think of one that outweighed her acceptance of him. Gray had her arms wound around his shoulders, and she had already taken him to task for deciding without consulting her, so he didn't stop her. She could certainly push him away if she didn't want the intimacy.

He pulled back, not far but far enough to realize his hands were low on her hips, keeping her hard against him. "What we have just been through—" His hands stayed on her hips, almost to her backside—hell, he had his hands on her ass "—The fighting. It makes the need for contact more intense."

"Got it."

"You're certain?"

"I know what I want, Durian."

He drew a breath and said, "Good."

"Very."

He slid a hand along her throat and up to cradle the back of her head and press her mouth to his neck, silently demanding that she do more than kiss him. She did. She bit him, not as hard as he might have liked, but hard enough. He lowered his head to hers, allowing her plenty of time to pull away. She didn't. She stepped forward and while her head tipped up and to the side, one of her hands cupped the nape of his neck.

So he kissed her again. Gently to start, familiarizing himself with the softness of her mouth. He ended up holding her head between his hands. The edge of his left palm rested partially at her temple; at the point of contact, his skin twitched whenever any of her traceries moved underneath.

Her lips were soft. So soft. For him, the world dropped away. Gray in his arms was heaven. One of her hands moved to his waist then down, around his hip to his ass, pulling him against her while he broke apart inside. He didn't want her to think about the last time she'd had sex or any of the things Tigran had done to her, and yet he was not certain he could be as gentle as she needed.

His other hand moved downward from her shoulder, along her ribs, slipping, skidding, fumbling a little, then sliding underneath her shirt so he could spread his fingers over her bare skin. His skin to hers. A low growl came from the back of his throat.

This need for her, he knew, was not usual. Touching was common among the kin. They craved such contact almost as a matter of course, but this sexual response, his need to possess her because she was female, that was not an impulse he should indulge. But he was going to do it anyway.

His fingertip brushed over the piercing in her navel, and when he felt the echo of her response to that touch, he went back and brushed over the metal again, swept down the skin beneath and around, then tugged on the charm, lightly, but it was enough to make her press against him. She had a firm, muscled body, and he already knew how precisely she commanded her physical form.

He was nearly out of his mind with wanting her, slipping away into territory far from a safe return. He drew back, though his arms stayed around her. Her upper body bowed against him, bridging what little space there was between them. She opened her mouth beneath his, kissing him harder, and he struggled not to respond in kind. *Not too rough.* He had to keep himself under control.

Except her fingers tightened over his shoulders, and she bit his lip. Not hard, but enough, and that was not the response of a woman who was remembering past trauma.

He drew away and met her gaze and his hands went on moving despite his better intentions. He cradled her head, tangling his fingers in her hair, and angling her head for another kiss. She opened herself to him so that her physical state was absolutely unmistakable. The moment threatened to incinerate them both.

"Gray . . ."

She said, "You're holding back. Stop it."

"I don't want to hurt you."

"I know what you are. You won't frighten me." She slid her hands down his back until her palms rested in the small of his back. Her eyes were half lidded so he got only a glimpse of her pale blue eyes. "I'll tell you if I'm not okay with something you do, all right?"

"As you wish."

"Oh, yes." Her voice was low and sultry. "I wish."

He kissed her with a great deal less delicacy than before. Much less. God knows, she was strong. Resilient. And she was right. If he crossed a line she didn't want crossed, she'd tell him. Gray leaned into him and held on tight, giving back as good as she got.

She put her hands on his chest, just below his shoulders and pushed him backward to the futon, following with him so they remained touching the entire time they walked; him backward, her forward. She was in his head, and at first he welcomed the contact because it meant he felt her arousal even more intensely. They ended up with him on the mattress and her straddling his hips. He went still. She gave him a look that smoldered and pressed him down.

On instinct, he resisted, then realized she must be interpreting his reluctance as stemming from some lack of desire on his part. He lay back.

When he was stretched out, with him carefully controlling his reaction, she propped her hands on either side of his head and leaned over him. It helped that he wanted her so badly he hurt. And it helped, too, that he was moving his hands up and down her spine, sliding around to her breasts, and yes. Hell yes. He wanted her like this, moaning for him. Because of him. Once he had his hands full of her softness, passing a finger over her nipples, he acknowledged there wasn't any going back. Whatever happened, she would never harm him. That wisp of magekind magic would never be used against him

She gave him a questioning look. "You okay?"

"Come here."

"Maybe not quite yet."

He watched a wicked smile appear on her mouth when she reached down and covered his sex with her hand. Her head bent to watch what she was doing. The urge to put her on her back and strip her naked was just about irresistible. Until he caught a glimpse of her pale blue eyes before her lids lowered. The heat there sent a thrill of arousal through him. He stayed right the hell where he was. He was outrageously aroused.

Her fingers closed around him and stroked up through the material of his pants. He caught his lower lip between his teeth and lifted his pelvis toward her hand. Her lashes fluttered, and he saw glimpses of that icy blue that, right now, were about a million miles from cold.

"Jesus, Durian," she said in a voice so full of frank appreciation that he had to laugh. She unfastened the buttons at his waist and drew down the zipper. Slowly. Lithe creature that she was, she got his pants off him with a minimum of fuss. He had on a pair of close-fitting cotton boxers and those were next. She hooked her fingers in the waist of his boxers and pulled down, careful but quick about it. Before he closed his eyes, he got a glimpse of her red hair and thought it was the most erotic thing he'd seen in his life. He opened his eyes to watch her again.

She addressed his pelvis with a heartening reverence. "God, you're beautiful."

His breath hissed when her hand touched his naked cock. She was already bending over him when he put his hands on her head. Her fingers angled down and she cupped his balls in her palm. "Your mouth," he said in a voice that rumbled from deep in his chest. "Please."

He lifted his hips toward her as she obliged him. The heat and pressure of her fingers, her mouth, and her tongue rocketed him toward orgasm. His fingers touched her lips, feeling her around him, and it wrung him out. As the crest hit him, he shouted.

When it was over and he could think again, he got his hands around her waist and with a twist of his hips and thigh, put her on her back. She stretched out beneath him, in no different a state than he was, shoving herself back just enough to sit up. He leaned in and stripped off her shirt, and while her arms were still in the air—her abs were damned ripped—he reached in and divested her of her bra. Up and up, and her arms raised up. There.

There were no niceties between them. This wasn't a moment for sweet words or slow caresses. He was caught in the raw heat of her need for him. She shook her arms and her shirt and bra fell to the floor and while he was getting a riveting eyeful of her naked torso, she reached for the waist of her jeans. With his weight on one elbow, he helped her get them off, but mostly he was touching her and looking his fill.

Her body was sleek and lush all at the same time. She'd shaved her pubic hair at the sides, nothing extreme, just a trim neatly done. She was more slender than his usual taste in women, but she wasn't merely skinny. Her body was lean and muscled, her breasts lovely, her skin pale, nipples pale brown, more than enough to fill his cupped palms.

He put her naked back to the mattress. While he covered one breast with his mouth and sucked, his hands were busy everywhere else. He trailed his mouth down the midline of her body to that ridiculous barbell through her navel and took the thing in his mouth with gratifying results. She squirmed under his touch, and let out a gasp.

"God, Durian. That feels good." She buried her fingers in his hair and arched toward him while she brought one of his hands back to her breast. "More."

Oh, yes.

He threw a thigh over her which was when they both came to the realization that he still had on his shirt. She put a hand to his cheek and said, smiling impishly, "You have on too many clothes."

He froze.

He'd forgotten.

Gray's hands slid underneath his shirt, pushing up. He resisted until she let out a frustrated cry and got her hands far enough up that she felt his scar. Their eyes met. Hers cautious, wondering. And his? He could only imagine what she saw in his eyes.

If the scar repulsed her, then there was nothing he could do or would do about that. When she pulled up his shirt again he ducked his head and let her drag it off him. She didn't say anything for long enough that he thought he had his answer.

And a bitter one it was. He cut off her contact with him.

"No," she said. "Don't do that." She sat up and, eyes on his chest, set her palm to him. He didn't move.

He knew what she saw. A still-healing wound ran from the top of his sternum to just above his diaphragm in an irregular line. The scarring there twisted through and faded into, out of and across the interior edges where his skin still burned deep crimson. From her face, he surmised she understood what she was looking at.

"You were mageheld?"

He took command of himself. Buried himself far from anyone. Far from her. "Yes."

"And this mage—"

He ought to be dead. He shouldn't have lived once he'd been cut open. When he spoke, this voice came from far, far away. "Not Christophe. Álvaro Magellan."

"—he tried to kill you." She touched his chest and glanced at his face. "The way Christophe killed Tigran."

"Yes." He closed his eyes. His memories were not pleasant ones, and though he didn't want her to pick up any part of them, she did. "Nikodemus and his witch, Carson, prevented that."

She cradled the side of his face. "No wonder you're loyal to him."

He shouldn't let her see what had been done to him. "After Magellan died that night, I was unlucky. Another mage, Rasmus Kessler, took control of me." He leaned away from her touch, but she followed him, touching, and he wanted that from her and knew he would never recover if she rejected him. "Later, another fiend and his witch severed me. Xia and Alexandrine." He cast around for his shirt and grabbed it, except she was faster. She snatched the shirt and threw it as far as she could.

He watched her, eyebrows raised in question.

"This matters to me, Durian," she said. "But not the way you seem to think." She touched his chest and followed him when he flinched away from her. Her fingertip slipped along the edges of his still-healing wound. "This means you understand what happened to me. What it was like for me."

The tightness in his chest eased.

"This wasn't long ago, was it?" She touched him gently.

"Longer than you think. It is healing slowly. But," he said because this was not the time for anything but plain truth, "not so long ago."

She pressed her mouth to one side of that twisting scar then moved to his nipple. The tip of her tongue flicked over him, and he felt that all the way to his balls. He hadn't been touched like that since long before Magellan. Far too long ago. The sensation was entirely pleasant. More than pleasant. She was putting him in a fair way of forgetting about all but where else she might use her tongue. He lay back, open to her in every way possible. His breath caught when she got a hand between them and found his sex. She had a way with her fingers, too. Hell. Oh, hell.

A growl rumbling in his chest, he grabbed her by the hips and pulled her underneath him. Her scent was musky with sweat and desire, her skin salty when he kissed her shoulder, the edge of her mind tinged with a darkness that echoed in him.

Durian re-established eye contact and took their desire and kicked it higher. Because he could. Because he could make this even better for them both.

She gasped, but he was running his hands up her athlete's body, spreading her legs as the heat between them continued to build, with her magic and his cranking them both into this state of frantic desire. He kissed her there, between her legs, and she groaned and the next thing he knew he had his mouth between her legs as he worked her toward an orgasm, which was easy because he knew when she was close. She wasn't the least shy about telling or showing him what she needed to get her there, either.

She came, with him racheting her to the point of no return. Then her release. Her giving in to her body. Gray untangled her fingers from his hair and slid from underneath him. Once again he ended up on his back with her straddling him.

"I want you inside me." She threw her head back when he levered himself up to kiss the tip of her breast. Her nipple contracted in his mouth. "Jesus," she breathed. "That's good. Do that more."

He grabbed her right wrist and brought her arm to his mouth and then he touched the traceries with his tongue and perhaps nipped at her skin. The magic so close to the surface of her skin set off a buzz in his head that made him open to her wider than he had to anyone else. Even Nikodemus. Made sense, that they so easily reached that kind of closeness. She was his sworn fiend. Not that he cared much about anything but where this was headed.

Her breath hissed in, and he didn't care if it was because of his mouth on her arm or because of the tactile contact with her magic. The sizzle had them both holding their breath. They were right back where they'd been before his scar. He slid a finger along her arm and then did the same at the tracery at her temple. The anticipation of being inside her was turning him inside out. And she knew it. They both knew it. She smiled at him, dared and invited him to touch her more.

More.

"Come on," she whispered. "It's time."

Her voice was low and smokey and she was in close and at the light brush of her fingers along his penis, he was out of control. He didn't object when she guided him into her. One thrust. His or hers?

Her body was ready for him. Hot and soft and tight. He put her on her back, his body over hers, and pushed farther inside her and then he bit her again until there was blood he could lick away, to taste and savor and, there was that faint shivering of the magekind about her, and hell, yes. Their connection pulled on them both and he didn't do anything to stop it. He knew what she wanted. He'd seen it. Felt it.

She came apart again. He wasn't far from finishing himself, but they were belly to belly and he was driving inside her.

The skin down his back quivered and that was new for him, too. She wouldn't be the first human woman he'd taken in his other form, but the last time he'd been this close to an unintended change during sex, the rules had been different. In those days there hadn't been any. There were rules now. Even as far gone as he was, he knew he had neither requested nor obtained permission to have sex with her in his altered form.

The sound he made wasn't human. At all. He concentrated on keeping his human shape while he thrust into her body, wanting more and more and more of her, and she arched against him and bit him while he felt the convulsions of his orgasm begin in his balls and a tightening in his low spine, and he stopped thinking about anything but the woman beneath him.

CHAPTER 24

Two days later. Café Demonde, downtown
San Francisco

Gray resisted the urge to stand up when Leonidas walked in. She hadn't been sure the mage would actually show. Now that he was here, with his magic setting off a tickle of recognition in her, she was nervous about the meeting. After some discussion, she and Durian had agreed that though Durian would not be far, she would meet Leonidas alone at first. He might watch his words more closely when speaking in front of Nikodemus's assassin. The location had been Durian's suggestion since a café full of humans would force Leonidas to behave.

The mage wore a suit similar to the one he'd worn the night they found him outside the house on Broadway. Black this time instead of gray with a metallic green tie and another stark white shirt. Shiny black shoes. Even this near the financial district where so many of the men wore suits despite the trend to casual, Leonidas stood out as a splendidly dressed male in his prime. She reminded herself that his apparent youth came at a terrible price.

He walked straight toward her. As of course he would. A mage would know what she was even before he saw her. Leonidas acknowledged her with a nod and a smile. "May I get you something?"

She lifted her coffee. "I'm fine."

The wait for him to get to the barista gave her time to assess him and the number of eyes on him. There were many. The café was filled with the lunchtime crowd, people who'd come down from the high-rises; lawyers, financiers, executives, and their support staff. Durian was right. She was safe here. There were too many normal people around for Leonidas to consider trying anything. When he had his drink, he brought it to her table and sat on the chair opposite her.

"Thanks for coming," she said. "And for leaving your magehelds outside."

"Gray." He glanced over his shoulder to where his magehelds were clearly visible through the plate glass window. They were waiting because they had been ordered to and had no choice but to comply. "A promise is a promise, after all."

She sipped her macchiato. The espresso was hitting her hard. She hadn't had coffee this strong in weeks. She liked the edge. He was handsome, no denying that, but she preferred Durian's looks to his.

He'd ordered straight espresso, and he proceeded to empty three packets of sugar into his demitasse. "A pity, in my opinion. Someone with your unique gifts—" he lifted a hand heavenward, his fingers pinched together before a quick release, "—a kiss from the gods."

Her heart contracted, but she held Leonidas's eye. "Is that how you see it? Because I'll tell you, what Christophe did to me wasn't a gift."

"My apologies." When she didn't reply, he said, "I had hoped that you and I would not meet as enemies."

"We're not friends."

He nodded acknowledgment of that. "If I was not prepared to come to you as a friend would, I would not have accepted your invitation."

"So you say. But mages lie all the time."

He looked at her from under his lashes while he stirred his coffee. "It must be very useful to Durian to have a witch under his control."

Gray curled her hands around the handleless bowl the café used to serve its coffee. "You think this was his idea?"

He placed his spoon on the table, aligning it so the handle was perfectly vertical. "No. But I am aware of the synergies that can result when a fiend of power and one of the magekind are bound." His gaze flicked over her, and she didn't like the sexual appraisal. "Durian would want that."

She took another sip of her coffee and thought about getting another one to keep the caffeine buzz going. "Maybe you have him all wrong."

He sat back, holding his demitasse. "Do I?"

"Yeah, you do."

The physical appraisal of her started up again. "I presume Durian is having sex with you."

"Not your business."

His eyes were intent on her. "But you understand—"

"Listen up." She leaned over the table, angry beyond words. "I choose." She tapped her chest. "Me. My decision and only my decision about who I have sex with and whether we do it straight or kinky or upside down. My decision whether I want to get pregnant and stay that way, and that's only if Durian agrees he wants to be a father."

"I'm sure there are other—"

"Don't even go there, mage." She lowered her voice. "If I do have sex with Durian like that, not that it's any of your goddamned business, there won't be a mage sitting around thinking he's got a ready-made slave on the way." Her hands clenched into fists. "Christophe tried to take that choice away from me. A mage. Durian, on the other hand, won't force me one way or the other."

She felt him probe her. Even his slight push at her brought back the panic of the last eighteen months of her life. Her hand shot out and she grabbed his wrist, pinning his hand to the table at the same time she blocked him. She had to work at not snarling at him. "Not without my permission."

He flushed. "I apologize."

"But you're not sorry."

He smiled and for a moment he looked just like the young man she'd first taken him for. It seemed like a hundred years ago now. "Forgive me, then."

"You know what? Durian knows he hasn't done anything to me that I didn't agree to from the start. That's more than I can say for you." She grabbed his espresso, lifted it in a mock toast, and downed it in one swallow. The empty cup clinked against the saucer. "How's it feel?"

He leaned back and tapped his fingers on the table. "Would you care for another?"

She dug a crumpled five from her pocket and dropped it on the table.

"Allow me," the mage said, leaving her money where it was. "It's the least I can do."

Several women watched him walk back to the line and order again. She wondered why Durian didn't hate Leonidas the way he did other magekind. From what she'd seen so far, he wasn't any different. He returned with two more espressos, straight up. She watched him put sugars in his with the same fastidious attention as before.

"What the hell are you after, Leonidas? Why are you all worked up about me? Was that talk about a deal with Nikodemus bullshit while you really get in tight with Christophe? Because I can tell you right now, I won't let any harm come to Durian. Or Nikodemus."

He sipped his espresso. "I admire your loyalty to the warlord and his assassin."

Gray rolled her eyes. "You think I don't know what he is?"

He put down his demitasse. "I've known him and known of him for longer than you've been alive. He's dangerous." He held her gaze. "As I'm sure you know."

"And you're not?"

"I promise you I am." He leaned back in his chair, one hand on the table, the other on his lap. His ruby cufflink glittered in its gold setting. "You were not born magekind."

"No."

"And yet you have both kinds of magic. That would be fascinating even if you hadn't taken both. To my knowledge, that's never been done. By anyone."

She pushed away her coffee. "Nikodemus does

something about his lawbreakers." She looked at Leonidas straight on. "What are you doing about mages like Christophe?"

He put down his demitasse and spread his hands. "We have oaths of our own, you know. We protect humans. It's our purpose." He swept a hand around the café. "We keep them safe. If demonkind are present and do no harm, I see no reason to kill them. There can be a balance."

"Sounds like heresy to me."

"I mean it."

She cocked her chin in the direction of Leonidas's mageholds. "You think you're not killing them right now?"

"They aren't dead."

"You forget that I know what it's like for them."

"You're human." He stopped with his demitasse halfway to his mouth. "Not one of them. You belong with your own kind."

"I lived like they did." She touched her demitasse. "Christophe didn't give his mageholds a choice about what happened to me." She turned over her arm and examined the traceries there. They didn't creep her out anymore. "Considering how much you magekind like to talk about protecting humans, it wasn't one of you who got me away from Christophe. A magehold died to save my life."

Leonidas gestured. "And made you into this."

"If he hadn't, I'd be dead." She leaned toward him. "Christophe did this to me. His orders. I'm free because of Tigran." She sat back. She was angry, not for herself but for the kin. "How about you tell me what holding slaves and killing them when you feel like you need a few extra years has to do with protecting humans?"

Leonidas lapsed into a silence worthy of Durian. "We need our power. We need to be strong."

"You are so full of it. You don't need their magic to be strong. You're killing them so you can live longer than you deserve."

People at neighboring tables were giving them worried glances. Gray looked at the closest to them and gave a reassuring grin. "We're rehearsing for a play."

One of the women at the table laughed, but she was all over Leonidas. "I was waiting for one of you to pull a knife."

"No knives here." Gray returned her attention to Leonidas. "Your line now."

He stared into his demitasse for a while. As she watched, she could see the play of emotions over his face. Guilt was one of them. "I am here, far from my home, because the warlord promises another way."

"You don't need me for that."

Leonidas looked up and frowned. "What if I could augment your magic?"

"Give up your magehelds and I'll let you try."

"I'm not that curious."

She picked up her espresso and downed the whole thing. A familiar shiver ran down her spine, and she glanced over to see Durian outside. He walked past the magehelds and into the café.

Leonidas reacted a moment later with a twitch of his hands. If he hadn't been holding his coffee, she might not have noticed. "Your master has arrived."

She snorted. Durian wore black again, and damn, he looked good. His pullover fit close enough that there was just no hiding the perfection of his body. "Hardly."

Durian strolled to their table and, taking an empty chair from another table, sat down catercorner to Gray. He leaned over and kissed her cheek. "Gray." He nodded to the mage. "Leonidas."

The mage nodded in return. "A timely appearance."

"Is it?"

Leonidas stood up. "I was just leaving."

"I'm sorry I missed you." He sat next to Gray and looped an arm around her shoulder.

"Tell Nikodemus I wish to discuss an alliance. Have him call me if he'd like to discuss the particulars."

Gray looked up at him, astonished. "What made you change your mind?"

"We cannot go on as we are." He nodded at Durian. "What world do we live in when the demonkind have begun to protect humans from the magekind? The time for change is long past." The mage took a business card from his pocket and slid it across the table to her. "If you need my help, I will do what I can. It is the least I can do."

"Thanks." She took the card and stuck it in her pocket.

"I look forward to hearing from Nikodemus, Assassin."

"I'll let him know."

They watched Leonidas walk out. Through the window, he said nothing to his magehelds as he passed them. But they followed him all the same. Because they had no choice.

A few minutes later, she grabbed her jacket and walked out. Durian followed. They didn't speak until they were on Kearney Street and long out of sight of the café.

"We can continue to walk, if you wish."

Gray came to a halt. "Do you think he meant that?"

"I don't know." He pulled her into his arms, and she stayed against him when he moved them out of the way of most of the pedestrian traffic. He stroked her hair. "I hope that he does. And yet, if he does, there will be chaos."

"We need to get my sister away from Christophe."

"I think," he said slowly, "the sooner we do that, the better."

CHAPTER 25

The next day. Piedmont, California

They don't know I'm alive." Gray folded her arms around her waist when she and Durian stood outside her parents' house. Their target wasn't the main house but the granny unit in back where Emily had lived and where her own life had come to an end. She shivered even though she wasn't cold. Her old life stared back at her, dredging up memories she'd rather not face.

"They must continue to think so," he said. "For a while longer. Until we know what happened."

He was right. Until then they wouldn't be safe. "I came over to meet Emily's new boyfriend."

"Christophe, I presume."

She nodded, shoved her hands into her front pockets and hunched her shoulders against the bite of the wind she didn't feel. "There were bodies," she said. "Afterward. Including one that was supposed to be me. Christophe showed me the articles about it. It had our pictures in it. Emily's and mine."

"A mage as powerful as Christophe could easily have done the magic that would transform a human's physical appearance." Durian, too, gazed across the street. She didn't get much from their link except a sense that he was thinking things over. "We know the woman you saw killed was not your sister."

"Good enough to get through an autopsy?"

He looked at her. "The kin have been living among humans for a very long time. We have learned a great deal about how to pass without revealing ourselves. The mage-kind have been no less resourceful."

Gray shook her head. She hardly knew what to think anymore. She didn't want to go inside the house where everything had ended, just like she didn't want to be standing here, confronting the past. "Everything looks the same. Like a movie I've seen. Not anything that really happened. Familiar. And not familiar."

The elms shading the street grew large, with thick, gnarled branches. A few oaks grew here, but not young ones. These oaks had been growing before the area was ever settled and now had trunks too large to get arms around. In a few places, the roads had been diverted around the massive trees.

"I don't belong here. Not anymore."

"Perhaps not," he said in a low voice.

"You could." She pointed behind them to where his Volvo was parked. "That car belongs here. Look at you. If you had a briefcase, anyone who saw you would think you're some white collar worker pulling down six figures."

He reached to realign the crease along the front of his trousers. "You grew up here. Not I."

Had she really once walked this sidewalk, barely old enough to be out without supervision? "No one could look at me and think I belong anywhere near a million-dollar home." She scrubbed her hands through her hair. "The neighbors are probably looking out the window thinking you're some hottie from three blocks over. Parking out of sight so no one knows you're bringing home the skanky girlfriend to do nasty things to you during your lunch hour."

His expression was inscrutable. "Very nasty."

He stepped off the sidewalk and Gray followed him. Did the Witmarks still live next door? Did they even talk to her parents anymore after what had happened? A neighbor's misfortunes brought a community together or tore it apart. Which one had happened here?

He paused on the sidewalk in front of her old house. With a look at her, he said, "Consider this another lesson."

She squinted because a ray of sun through the trees was in her face. His mouth quirked, but he wasn't smiling. "What?"

"It's crucial that we make no mistakes once we are inside. Maintain your calm no matter what memories may come to you. Observing me will help keep you focused." He touched just behind her ear. Such light contact, but the gentleness of it rocked her. "I will understand if that is not possible."

Gray nodded. Her stomach clenched with tension, though. Everyone thought she'd died here. In a way, she had.

"If there is trouble of any kind, please expect me to

take over. By which I mean, take control." He tapped her forehead and their link deepened. "Not an indwell, unless it's for some reason necessary."

In her head, she made sure her memories were too far away for her to get to.

He put a hand on her waist. "I may have no choice."

She wheeled to face him, and this time emotion did flare sharper than expected. Not the kind of control Durian wanted to see from her. "Whatever you need to do to find out what happened, you do it. Don't ask permission. Don't worry if I'm going to get all upset." She met his gaze. "Just do what needs to be done."

He nodded. "I'll mask our presence when we go in. Do the same if you can. Unless we are unlucky, there is little chance we will be disturbed. Inside, I'll need to concentrate on my magic. We will not have the same protections, is that clear?"

"Yes."

"Very well, then." He touched her forehead. All business. She thought he was sexy as hell like this. His fingertip was warm against her skin. The connection between them came alive in her head. There was a sensation of bringing the energy toward him to be shaped according to his need. She felt the burn of him drawing his magic, the specific twisting of the air around them that prevented others—human or otherwise—from taking notice of them.

Her mother, a Superior Court Judge in nearby Oakland, was unlikely to be home, but her father might be. Depending on his class schedule. When they crossed the street her sense of detachment increased. That came from Durian and it was useful to take up some of his calm. She remembered even though she didn't want to. Bringing in the mail after school, her mom or dad driving her to ballet classes and piano lessons or years later, visiting for the holidays, and later still coming here to see Emily. She remembered her sister opening the door to her knock.

They approached the house. From the silence, she guessed they were lucky. No one was home. Durian did something to the alarm system that she didn't catch—his use of magic was over practically before he started. Then Gray led the way around the back. Her old self on that last day walked beside her like a ghost made of the memories she'd kept locked for so long. Why hadn't she known something was wrong?

The latch on the gate shone with new metal on old wood. This door was alarmed, too. Durian let her take care of this one. It turned out to be easier than she thought. The granny unit was attached to the house, but you had to be outside to get to it. There wasn't any interior connecting door between the two buildings. Almost nothing had changed in the backyard. There was a birdbath she didn't recognize. The Witmarks' cat was sunning itself underneath it. The same gravel path was lined with miniature roses.

Durian did his thing with the separate alarm on the unit. He didn't need a key to open the door because with a quick pull of his magic, the tumblers in the locking mechanism aligned and clicked into place.

All the breath in Gray's lungs vanished when they stood inside the apartment where her sister had lived. The place was spotless. But for the eerie neatness, she could imagine Emily still lived there. All her things were still here. The television, the stereo. Her furniture. The wall she kept between old and new disintegrated.

The past rushed at her in a maelstrom of memories and emotions that were breaking her apart. In this room, Emily—or someone she thought was Emily—had put her arms around her and told her how much she loved her baby sister. As kids they used to fight all the time, but as adults, that changed. They got to be friends. Gray had kept Emily's secret when her sister admitted she was practicing magic, and Emily had never, ever belittled Gray for being the less talented of the two. No matter how much she remembered, or how vivid the recollections, she couldn't reach back into the past and bring her sister safely to her.

Durian touched her elbow and the storm eased. Some of his darkness seeped into her. She welcomed the separation he gave her, the numbness. She followed his circuit around the apartment. He wasn't using any magic yet that she could tell. Getting the layout, she guessed, since all he did was look into the rooms. Bedroom, kitchen. Living room. He stopped at the wall of pictures between the kitchen and living room and after a bit, she joined him because she was safely without emotion.

"That's Emily," she said, pointing to one of the pictures. "The two of us at the beach when we were kids. She was gorgeous then, too. My mom and dad there. Her graduating from college. She did her undergrad at Mills. Grad school at Berkeley."

"And this one?"

"Emily backstage at the Met." She touched the frame, remembering that night and how proud Emily had been of her. She didn't dare look at Durian. She didn't want to know what he thought, but she kept explaining anyway. "That's me at the Opera House not long after I came home from New York. I was in Lausanne the year before. With Béjart."

Her two lives pushed against each other, crushing her.

"And the gentleman with his arm around you is?"

The man in the picture was a stranger to Gray Spencer. And not. "Val."

He wrinkled his forehead. "Val."

"Emily took that picture of the two of us."

"And this?" he said at last. "This is you, Gray?" And of course he meant the framed cover of *Dance Magazine*.

She nodded. "The year I made soloist at New York City Ballet. I was twenty years old. It's how Val and I met. We did *Billy The Kid* the next year, but he also staged something of his that season. Marakova was his principal dancer, but I had a solo."

"I should have known," Durian whispered. He stared at the picture as if the dancer on the cover was the President of the United States in pink tights and toe shoes. "This," he said. "I did not expect this."

She couldn't have said anything if she'd wanted to. Her throat closed off.

"Not just good, but gifted."

"That was then." She couldn't deal with the admiration. He made it too real. "Who cares what I used to be?" She stared at the picture of the smiling ballerina and it didn't even look like her anymore. She remembered the day of the shoot. She'd hit that arabesque dead on and could have held it all day.

"Gray." His finger brushed along the line of her jaw. "It explains a great deal about you." He kept touching her, and she kept wondering what would happen if she smashed the picture. "I did not understand how much you lost. Not truly."

"Would it have been all right if I was just some regular person with a regular job?" She grabbed the framed cover and yanked hard enough to rip the fastener halfway out of the wall. "Why does it matter what she used to be?" Rage and agony boiled in her, white hot with the futility of wishing she could have it all back. She raised the picture over her head and hurled it downward.

Somehow Durian caught the picture in the millisecond after it left her hands. He returned the frame to the wall and slowly turned to her. His presence in her head got bigger and darker. Panic welled up because she knew what came next. Tigran would push her into a corner of her mind, and she couldn't even pretend her life was her own. Air whooshed out of her lungs and refused to come back in. Her vision completely cut out.

"Gray."

Someone touched her, and it was warm and not angry. Not looking to hurt.

Her mind was still her own.

Durian. Not Tigran. Durian's arms were around her. Gentle. Holding her, and she wasn't being made so small or insignificant that she didn't matter. Durian pressed his lips to the top of her head. "Hush, love. Hush."

She got herself under control, and by the time she stepped away from his embrace, she was almost normal. Durian didn't look angry. He almost never did, but his magic wasn't telling her any different. He waited, as if he had unlimited time and patience.

"Better?" he asked.

"Yes."

He continued watching her and she had the strange feeling that he was seeing her for the first time. Whatever he was seeing, it wasn't really her. "Val." He said the name with puzzled emphasis. He closed his eyes for a moment and cut off her psychic link with him. She was alone. So alone. When he opened them again, his irises swirled with streaks of purple. "That man in the picture with you is Valantis Antoniu."

"You've heard of him." Of course he had. He liked opera and ballet and fine art. And women like Emily, with beauty and brains.

"I saw Antoniu dance when he was a young man. Before he retired and turned to choreography."

She willed her tears gone. "That was a long time ago."

He nodded. "He was a great deal older than you."

"So?" Her eyes burned hot. She didn't dare blink again because she didn't want to look like any more of a fool. He needed her to be calm. She would be calm.

He was quiet for so long, she gave up trying to understand what was going on with him. He wasn't letting her see much now anyway. "We will discuss this another time."

Her pulse got going hard. "Understood."

"Nikodemus is right. You and your sister do look alike." He turned from the photographs.

She didn't move right away. No dust clung to the corners or muted the color of any of the frames. She touched the picture of Emily and wanted her sister to be safe and happy. What if that meant being married to Christophe dit Menart? What if it meant Emily hated what Gray was now?

"We do not have much time, Gray."

She did a slow turn and looked around. "Someone's been in to clean, obviously, but that's all. This is pretty much how it looked when Emily lived here."

He inhaled, long and slow, and she felt the quiver of

his magic flow over her from that dark pool inside him. "Yes, that's so."

Durian knelt in the center of the living room and closed his eyes. She stayed to one side. "This is not unlike tracking."

"Great. I'll suck at this, too."

He opened one purple eye. "Pay attention, please."

She saluted and then, slowly, the air around him became charged until the hair on her arms prickled and her hair crackled with static electricity.

He let out his breath. "Did you see how I did that?"

"Not really." Not enough to try by herself.

"This is as good a time as any for you to learn." He opened his eyes. They weren't purple. They were the color of new pennies. She caught her breath because she knew that color meant he was close to changing.

"Change if you need to, Durian."

His eyes flickered, and she had never thought he looked less human than he did right now. "That is not necessary."

He repeated what he'd done before, and she tracked his magic as best she could. This time she was prepared for the eerie sensation of the air tight with tension. After a few minutes of that, he rose from his kneeling position to move through the house. Every so often, he'd stand immobile, breathing deeply, and the air around him sizzled with expectation. Once or twice she caught an echo of something, a glimpse of energy that had lain dormant until Durian's magic raised it. So, he was right. What he was doing was similar to tracking. The way jogging was similar to running.

Because she was in his head, she worked out some of what he was getting from his examination of the apartment. Psychic residue clung everywhere. It drifted from the ceiling and swirled around their feet. She fell deeper into her link with Durian.

She shivered when she felt Tigran, an echo of him, far away and yet, it was him. Undeniably Tigran. Things got stranger still. She swore she heard the faint whisper of conversation. *Anna, you look great.* A beating heart. The distant scent of blood. Fear rippled down her back, but it was distant, a memory of fear, of being certain she would die. Emotions that didn't belong to her. *You, too, Emily.* A scream that didn't end and wasn't her or Emily.

Hey, Val.

She knew Durian was blunting her emotions. There was more here, but he knew she couldn't relive the final day of her old life without the scream that was building in her head getting free and endangering them both. He was hiding other details from her, too, and frankly, she was grateful. After a second painstaking circuit of the apartment, Durian put a hand on her shoulder, sliding his palm to the nape of her neck. "A few moments more and we're done."

They began again, following an odd pattern from the back door through the room, to a niche by the front door where Emily had stashed an umbrella and a pair of sneakers. When they reached the place where Val had been taken down, Durian cut their connection to a trickle. His eyes burned copper-red. Her skin felt slick with the residue of the magic he'd been pulling and shaping and letting fall onto everything in the house.

"This, I will do on my own, Gray."

She could barely move her mouth. "Please."

Durian crouched at the spot where Tigran had brought her down to the floor, kicking and screaming. He'd muffled the sounds while he did something to her that had burned like fire through her head and chest. By then Val and Emily had already been dead. Durian stayed where he was for what seemed like forever but wasn't any more than five or ten minutes.

He rose and resumed his pattern through the house. The unit was small but he made it seem microscopic. Kitchen, bathroom, laundry area, bedroom. The wall of pictures from a life that wasn't hers anymore.

"Well?" she said when he released the magic he held and stood motionless. Her entire body tensed, but the memories, the sounds, scents, and emotions faded with his magic.

He opened his eyes. "Understand, Gray, that I cannot yet be sure."

"Of what?"

"Three deaths happened here. I did not know Valentis or Emily before this happened so I cannot say that it was them who died. Given what we know, probably it was Valentis who died. Christophe had no reason to keep him alive if he was human and even less if he was magekind."

"The other two?" Gray covered her mouth with both hands, afraid to ask the questions that roared through her yet desperate to know the answers. She tried to swallow the lump in her throat.

Here, exactly where she stood, was where Val had kissed her cheek that day and told her how rehearsals had gone and that he was sorry to be late. He was having trouble with his principal dancer for his newest work and not only that, the understudy was better. She'd been standing there with flour all over her hands, helping with dinner. Emily, still in the kitchen, had called out *Hey, Val.*

Through the window, she could see the stepping stone path to the house. The day Christophe had come for them, she'd stood there waving at Val through the window before she'd let him in to be killed by a monster.

As she stared past the reflection in the glass, Gray was half-convinced she would see Val just as she had that last day, him smiling and pantomiming a big air-kiss for her, his white hair mussed as if he'd been running his hands through it. A permanent condition, he liked to say, so he could frighten the corps de ballet.

A bone-white face appeared in her line of sight.

She screamed because for a moment she actually thought it was Val, but with pewter hair instead of white and ashen skin too loose on his skull. Durian whirled and the moment he saw what she did, he touched her shoulder, and then she didn't feel anything at all.

A key slid into the exterior door. The mechanism turned and clicked, and whoever it was came inside. "Who's there?"

She didn't move. Neither did Durian. They didn't make a sound.

Gray's mother stared into the house, standing there in her low-heeled pumps, her cheeks pink now instead of the ashen white she'd seen through the window. Her breath was loud. She walked across the living room. Her head turned this way and that, eyes darting toward the shadows.

The framed cover of *Dance Magazine* hung lopsided on the wall.

Her mother's hair was gray now, instead of the platinum she remembered. More lines creased her face, and she was thinner than ever. Her heels clicked on the wooden floor, echoing as she walked, and the curious thing was, she followed a pattern similar to the one Durian had taken. She went into the bedroom and stayed there a little longer than it would take to be sure no one was there.

On her way out, her mother stopped in front of the cluster of photos that had so drawn Durian. She reached out and touched the framed cover of *Dance Magazine* and then straightened it.

The silence suffocated her, plugged up her ears, stole all the air in the room. Thank God she could not feel.

Her mother turned around and whispered, "Anna Grayson?"

There wasn't any answer.

Gray thought her heart would break. She took a step forward only to have Durian check her. He was right. She knew that, but she wanted to have her mother's arms around her. To breathe in her scent and believe that everything would be all right. If she gave in to the impulse, she might endanger her entire family. She knew for dead certain that Christophe would retaliate with lethal force if she made any contact with them.

Her mother waited before she sighed and walked out. The door clicked closed after her, leaving a breath of air to ripple through the room and die. After a bit, the key turned in the lock again with a hollow echo.

She steeled herself. "Now what?"

"We plan."

CHAPTER 26

Durian let himself into the granny unit where Gray's sister had once lived. He'd come prepared and didn't need to turn on any lights. His clothes were across the street in his car. In his altered form, his vision was more than acute enough to see even if the room were pitch dark. But it wasn't. In a city, there were too many lights for any place with windows to be dark.

Floodlights from the main house shone into the apartment windows, casting a sickly light on the floors. Despite no one living here, gadgets and appliances glowed with red or green lights.

Gray's fragile state had meant he hadn't done everything he wanted or needed to do. He made a slow pass around the rooms he'd been through earlier. The small area was an advantage to balance against the difficulty of the age of the evidence trail. He'd analyzed much older scenes before, locations where the residue was more contaminated and attenuated than was the case here. Here, the challenge was in overcoming his preconceptions. He believed he knew what had happened and those convictions might warp his interpretation of what he found tonight.

There was the additional problem of him recognizing and then separating the physical and psychic residue from Gray's presence here in both the distant and recent past. Even before Tigran, she'd left traces of an insistent presence. Despite the passage of time and the changes Tigran had forced on her, Durian recognized Gray's psychic patterns.

Familiar to him. Intimate. Disturbing. All the more disturbing because of what had happened to her here. What Tigran had done. The magic required for one of the kin to bind a human to him was dark enough by itself, but the terror and horror experienced by the victim left behind a multiplying effect. Then later, what Christophe had done to cover the truth.

He went still. He needed to be in a state that cut off sensory input of all but what was necessary to analyze Christophe and Tigran's attack here. If someone came in, human or anything else, he might not know until it was too late. He closed his eyes and breathed deep, opening himself to what had been destroyed here. Her sister's magic carried a distinct enough quality that he could easily filter that out. That left two humans without magic and Gray.

Gray's aura clung to things she'd been emotionally attached to or had frequently touched. He filtered out the more recent signals, what Gray was now, her mother, and other signifiers too old or too new to interest him until at last he was down to the remnants that were relevant.

A great many humans had been here, as was usually the case when a human death was involved: police, emergency medical personnel, detectives, the personnel required to remove the physical traces of death. Dozens of signals were present to examine for signs of magic and to exclude from further consideration if there were none or if the magic was from a human who didn't know he or she wasn't completely normal.

Eventually, he filtered out the extraneous lives and touches and was left with a base set from the day that interested him. Gray, her sister Emily, and three vanilla humans. One of the dead humans he believed was Val Antoniu. The other was the woman he believed Christophe had transformed to look like Gray. Last was the woman whose body had taken the place of Emily Spencer's. All Christophe would have needed was some hair and a drop or two of blood. And, of course, an alternate body.

In his state of heightened senses he could smell the blood. The deaths, unnatural as they were, formed an unsettling void in the normal psychic detritus of any space where humans, the kin, or magekind had been. Here, in the living room, quite near the door, was where Tigran had killed the human male. Val Antoniu. Emily had been the next to fall. Then Gray herself, with all the nerve-slivering horror of Tigran's binding of her. Christophe had known exactly what he wanted to achieve here.

Tigran, as a mageheld kin, was a complete nullity to him. That void could be a trail to follow, but one had to take care that an absence of resonance wasn't mistaken for evidence of a mageheld. On occasion, though, Tigran's presence could be extrapolated where the nullity of his magic intersected with the other traces in the room. And, naturally, the effect of Tigran's magic on Gray had left behind its own terrible pattern.

He pushed himself off the floor where he'd been seated and worked his way through the rest of the house. He could extrapolate now. Antoniu dead first. Emily incapacitated. Gray taken down and bound over to Tigran. Then Christophe with, no doubt, the assistance of his mage-helds, killed the two women whose bodies he required.

He thought it likely Christophe had begun his magicking of Emily's memories long before the mage met Gray. He wondered now if it would ever be possible to return Emily Spencer's memories. There was no telling how badly she might be damaged from what Christophe had done to her.

Durian ended up by the wall of pictures—an accident that he should stop here? He studied the *Dance Magazine*. Her hair was black as ink, her smile brilliant and joyful. Durian wanted to kill Christophe for robbing the world of her talent. Almost more than he hated the mage for destroying her life. In the picture of her and Val Antoniu, they were both smiling. A happy couple. Would she have married Antoniu? He couldn't imagine any man not wanting to.

There was another, smaller snapshot of Gray in a studio. She wore tights and a sloppy, short-waisted gray sweater over her leotard. She was *en pointe* in a breathtaking attitude, making a funny face for the camera. The flash had gone off and the glare in the mirror behind her had obliterated the reflection of whoever took the picture.

If not for Tigran, she would be dancing still. Perhaps coming to the end of her career, but married to Antoniu. He might even have gone to see her perform, never knowing more about her but her talent and the beauty of her dance. Chances were he would have sat in his orchestra section seats at the War Memorial Opera House and known only that this dancer was human. Nothing more. He would never have known the breathtaking sensation of sliding inside her body or heard the sound she made when he kissed her breasts or when she came or when her mouth was on him and he was thinking of things better not explored. He would never even have spoken to her.

The door to the granny unit opened.

Whoever came in meant to be stealthy. If Durian hadn't come out of his trance-like state, it was doubtful he would have heard. He stilled himself and his magic. And waited.

"I don't mean harm." That was not a young man's voice wavering in the silent air around Durian. Outside cars passed by on the street. "Please. Show yourself."

The interloper turned on the light. Magekind, with that odd reverberation of aborted power that came when a mage had burned himself out. But this wasn't Rasmus Kessler. This man who came in had never been anywhere near Kessler's level of magic.

Durian watched him walk in, from all appearances an older human man with a full head of salt and pepper hair. He wore steel-rimmed glasses, but behind the lenses his eyes were the same pale blue as Gray's.

The mage walked to a sidetable and switched on the lamp. "Forgive me. My vision isn't what it once was." He returned to the center of the room where he stayed, looking around him. He slid his hands from the pockets of his cardigan sweater. A wedding ring glinted on his finger. He looked harmless. A human man nearing the last years of his life, yet Durian knew he was looking at a trained mage. "I know you are here," he said softly. "Fiend."

Durian didn't move.

Gray's father held out his hands, palms up. They trembled in the air. "I burned out my magic," he said. "Years before Anna was born. I will not attack you. There's almost nothing left of what I used to be. As I am sure you have ascertained by now." The tremor of his hands increased. He laughed. "At this point, I doubt I could do you harm even if I wanted to."

Durian kept a firm hold on his magic, but he let himself be seen; in his non-human form lest there be any mistake about what the mage faced if he were lying. "Tonight," he said, "is a good night to kill a mage."

"No doubt you are correct." He cocked his head and the light flickered off his glasses so that Durian could no longer see his eyes. "These days, I'm known as Richard Spencer." Slowly, he lowered his hands. The tremor didn't stop. "I'm Anna's father, in case there is any question."

"I know who you are."

Spencer frowned. "That was you here before, I presume. My wife said she felt our daughter."

Durian didn't reply.

"Curious," Spencer said. He tipped his head to one side. "Unless I am mistaken, you are not mageheld. Am I wrong about that?"

"No."

"Who are you?"

He reacted to the man's magic, trivial though it was now, and he had to be cautious lest the thrill of that magic seduce him into a mistake. Durian gave him not a name, but the title that would mean the most to a mage. "I am Nikodemus's assassin."

Oh, yes, Richard Spencer knew that name, though he tried to hide his reaction.

"Nikodemus?" He smoothed the sides of his sweater. His hair was a bit wild. He must have gotten out of bed and come here without doing anything but throwing on a change of clothes. "Did he send you to kill me? After all this time?"

"No."

"If he has, it's too late." He seemed old and frail. Experience and the natural process of aging unslowed by ritual murder had etched deep lines in his face. "Is Anna alive?"

Durian bared his teeth. Like hell was he going to tell a mage anything about Gray.

"She's my daughter." The mage took a step toward Durian. "Is she with you? Is she all right?"

He didn't answer.

"Losing the girls almost killed my wife. The violence of it. What those animals did to them—It's beyond comprehension even for me. And my wife? She's human, you see. No magic in her. She doesn't know what I am." He checked himself. "What I used to be. Nor did Anna. Emily knew, of course. She had to be told once she came into her power. Things would have been easier if they'd both been talented." He slid two fingers under his glasses and pressed them against his eyes for a while. "I teach Medieval History. A bit eccentric. Absorbed in my studies. Publish or perish. Nothing more. In declining health now." He lifted a trembling hand into the air. "My physician suspects Parkinsons' but as I'm sure you've guessed it's the copa that's done this to me."

"Yes."

"I was once a young and foolish mage." He pushed his glasses higher up on the bridge of his nose. "Well.

No more." He gave a dry, mirthless laugh. "Anna had no magic, but then she was always crazy about dancing. It's all she ever wanted. Emily was different. I thought she had escaped notice. I trained her myself, as far as I could. I didn't want—well. I'm sure you can imagine. Though she would have done quite well, I think. I thought that would keep us all safe. Whoever did this—" He swept a trembling hand around the room. "Whoever it was used magehelds, so please. I know it was not you." He took another step closer to Durian. He squeezed the bottom of his sweater. "Please. Tell me. Is she well? Safe?"

"You are aware Emily is alive?"

Spencer paled. "I know Christophe dit Menart has her."

Durian regarded the man. He was working a minor spell to make himself seem less threatening.

"If I contact her he'll kill them. Emily and my wife. He told me that quite specifically." The man rubbed his face with a hand, briefly dislodging his glasses. "I was the one who found the bodies." He expression hardened. "The place stank of magic. When I confronted Christophe, that's when he threatened me. My wife and Emily. He made it quite clear he had the power to carry out his threats. To whom could I turn for help in such a case? The police?" He drew a slow breath. "All this time, I've assumed Christophe had no interest in Anna. That she was dead."

"Gray is alive," he said at last. "Anna."

The old man bowed his head. "Thank God." When he lifted his head, tears glistened in his eyes. "Where is she now? Is she all right? Can I see her? Will you take me to her?"

"It would not be safe. Not for either of you." He

stretched out his fingers, making no effort to hide the talons.

Spencer took off his glasses to wipe at his eyes with the sleeve of his sweater. "How is it that you, a free fiend, are here? In this house? How do you know anything at all about my daughters?"

"That is a long story, mage."

"Has Emily bound you somehow?" His lips moved in a silent series of words, but the result was a trivial spurt of magic. "Have you been compelled to come here?" Whatever magic Spencer had been trying to work ended with—nothing.

"No." Durian didn't bother moving. "Tell me about your daughters."

"And in return, you'll tell me what?"

Durian wondered how old Spencer was if he knew the traditional way of dealing with the free kin. Always an exchange. Tit for tat. "In return," Durian said, "I will tell you what I can about the daughter you thought was dead."

"I warned Emily against Christophe. She was quite strong in her magic but so young. Compared to Christophe, she was almost completely untrained. I didn't care for dit Menart showing up, I'll tell you that."

"But not Anna."

Spencer ran his fingers through his hair. "What possible interest could a mage have in her? Naturally, I assumed he was here sniffing around Emily. I was right, too. All that beauty, and the magic. Of course Christophe wanted her."

"Did you ask anyone for help? Another mage?"

"You've no idea how difficult it is for someone like

me to gain access to the practicing magekind. The kind who would have had the power to help." He gripped the bottom of his sweater and pulled. "They don't care to be reminded of what might happen to them. We magekind do not help our rivals or those less fortunate."

"My heart bleeds," Durian said.

He focused on Durian, and he bared his teeth. "I've told you all I'm going to. Tell me about Anna." His voice softened. "Please."

Durian laughed and the sound made Spencer take a step back. "Your daughter, mage, belongs to me."

CHAPTER 27

10:20 P.M. *Cow Hollow, San Francisco*

Iskander was downstairs in the Vallejo Street home he hardly ever stayed at because he still had trouble being alone. But he was making headway with his issues. In the last few weeks he'd found himself coming here more often and staying longer than he used to. He even had furniture and a few other things he liked. Some Japanese wood-block prints on the walls, a stylized carving of a giraffe in one corner. A Wii.

His bare feet were up on the coffee table and he was drinking root beer and watching an episode of some vampire show on his plasma TV, looking forward to someone getting bitten when his doorbell rang.

Scared the hell out of him because he didn't get many visitors. He knew it wasn't any of the kin because he didn't feel anyone, and he would have if it was one of the kin out there. A mageheld, he figured, wouldn't bother knocking. Magehelds would already be in the house try-ing to kill him. The only person who ever knocked on his door without trying to sell him candy bars or magazines was his tenant. One hundred percent human vanilla. She was a recluse, too. Had to like that in a tenant.

Still, who else would be ringing his doorbell? Must be her. He got a kick out of vampires on television and didn't want to be interrupted now that he was all set to watch. But he had these pesky legal responsibilities toward his tenant. He paused the show and got up, though not with-out pulling enough magic to kill a dozen attackers if he had to. There might be times when his mind didn't deal well with the loss of Fen, his blood twin, but he wasn't stupid.

He was finally learning to cope with not having access to his twin. The connection between blood twins was complete. They shared their magic, their thoughts and their emotions. For years he hadn't needed anyone but Fen. Her betrayal of him had nearly destroyed him.

He opened the door to the cool night. Most of the time he spent alone here, the city felt like it was wearing him away. But not tonight. Tonight he was liking the traffic sound and glare of the street lamps. He even liked that he was sane enough to help his tenant out of whatever housing-related jam she was in.

He looked down. "You're not her." Which was one of the stupidest things to come out of his mouth in some time. The thoughts in his head started whirling around like there was a tornado in there.

He had a few favorite fantasies about why Maddy Win-ters would bother to find out where he lived and then show up on his doorstep looking good enough to eat. Unfortunately, he was enough in command of himself that he recognized the stupidity of thinking she'd come here for that.

"Oh." Maddy closed her eyes. Her lashes weren't long but they were thick and inky black. When she opened them a second later, she said, "I'm sorry. You're expecting someone. A date. I shouldn't have bothered you."

She could have called instead of just dropping by. Interesting that she hadn't. "I thought you were the woman who rents the unit above my garage. Her garbage disposal is always breaking down. Or some damn thing anyway. Why the hell are you masking, Maddy? You thought I wouldn't answer if I knew it was you?"

She blinked at him. "You have a tenant?"

Iskander leaned against the doorway. He took his time looking at her. She was wearing jeans that flared toward the tips of her high-heeled, pointy-toed shoes. Her button-down shirt fit close and had just enough buttons undone that he got a little distracted thinking about her cleavage.

"Yeah, I have a tenant. Helps me pass." He ran a hand through his hair. "Who the hell thinks their landlord isn't human?"

"Oh, I don't know about that." Maddy smiled, and his heart did a little flutter. She kind of took his breath away when she smiled. Brunettes weren't his thing, but hell, she was gorgeous no matter what color her hair was. She also never gave him the time of day, so he tried to get his mind out of the gutter. Not hard enough, though. "You'd be surprised." She kept smiling. "Is anyone else here?"

"No." He stared at her for a while until she rolled her eyes and pushed him out of her way. Since he turned to watch her, he got a great view of her ass when she walked inside. She was too short for him. Too small. Nothing like the kind of woman he went for but, damn. He knew what she looked like in a bikini. She was smoking hot.

He followed her inside and almost didn't remember to close his own front door. He sure as hell didn't forget to reset his proofing, though, and she waited while he did. When he was done, he felt her magic, and that got him worked up. He was used to being around the magekind now, and he'd gotten good at controlling that particular instinct.

She dropped her purse by the door and faced him, that smile on her mouth again. He wasn't used to her smiling at him quite that way. Right. When someone you knew came to your house, you were supposed to ask them in and give them food and beverages. Before he could offer, she said, "I'm not sure it was Christophe dit Menart who sent those magehelds after us."

"No?"

"I'm not the first witch to be attacked, either. In the last two days, three other mages, lesser ones, are dead. Here and in the East Bay. I don't think it was Rasmus Kessler, either." She adjusted her purse on her shoulder. "Does Nikodemus know some mage or witch is trying to remove the competition? Because I can see him getting blamed for this. Not keeping the magekind safe."

"That's outside his territory. Come on in." As he led the way to his living room, he said, "Why come here? You could have talked to Nikodemus yourself."

"I suppose." She looked away. "But I'd rather not."

"Oh."

"I'd rather talk to you." She hesitated and Iskander wasn't sure why, exactly. "You can tell Nikodemus what he needs to know."

"You don't like him, do you?"

She lifted her eyes to his. "I think he's unpredictable." She sat on his couch and slipped off her pumps. She was barefoot. She had tiny feet and high arches. Her toenails were a glittery pink. He tried to think what he had in the house to offer her. There hadn't been much to eat when he got here, and he hadn't felt like shopping. The cheese doodles were gone. "You want some toast?"

"Toast?"

He shrugged. "I have bread in the fridge. And root beer. Want some?"

"Root beer."

"Organic." He lifted his bottle so she could see.

Her mouth twitched. "Yes, thank you. I would love toast and root beer."

In the kitchen he discovered he was out of butter, which was bad but not a disaster. But when he opened the bread to take out a couple of slices, a cloud of green dust wafted out of the plastic. The rest of the fridge was empty except for the root beer, which he happened to know was still drinkable. He brought her a bottle and when she took it from him, he said, "I decided it would be better if I ordered a pizza or something. Unless you want Chinese."

She looked down the mouth of her bottle of root beer. "Pizza's good."

"Or Indian. I know a good place that delivers."

"Pizza is fine."

Iskander ran his fingers through his hair again. He pulled out his phone, but didn't call out. Did she expect him to sit here in his own house being polite and good and sane when she knew he wanted her flat on her back with him on top? To start.

He needed to get a grip, and it wasn't easy when he

was thinking that if he were normal or Kynan Aijan, he'd know what she was here for and it wouldn't be for any goddamned pizza.

"I guess I should call Nikodemus."

She gazed at him and didn't say a word and the silence and the fact that he didn't know what she was thinking got him seriously bent. "Christophe has located a boy." She frowned. "Not his own, but I'm sure this one passed his test. He can't be any older than four or five."

That about took the planet out from under his feet. "Shit."

"I don't know whose child it is. He's hiding him someplace in the city for now, I don't know where yet. From what my sources tell me, he's getting his documents in order so there are no legal questions."

He grimaced but opened his phone and punched one of his speed dials. The assassin answered the phone on the second ring. Iskander resisted the temptation to tell Durian he was an asshole and instead gave him Maddy's news.

On the other end of the conversation, Durian cursed softly, and Iskander got the feeling his information wasn't unexpected and that pissed him off. That was something the magekind did that he just didn't understand. Take a kid before his magic sets in and over time, block off the magic so the child could never use it. The mage could, though. The kids never lived much past twenty-five or -six. The drugs needed to block off the magic were eventually fatal. Magellan had done that to Carson. And now Christophe was going to do the same to some other human child.

He disconnected the call when there wasn't anything more to say, and there he was. Staring at Maddy again.

"Maddy." He forced himself to let go of his hair and take a step toward the couch. "Why are you here?"

"I told you." She blinked at him with her big black eyes. Her shirt was white with skinny green stripes and he couldn't stop thinking about unfastening all the rest of those little buttons. She had a body to make a man cry, and he was fully grown, damn it all.

"You want to talk about dit Menart and some sick plan to kill all the magekind around here until he's the only one left?"

"Mm." Some of her black, black hair fell over her shoulder when she shook her head. "Is Harsh coming back anytime soon?" At one time, Harsh had been Fen's lover and so, of course, his too. When Fen betrayed him to the mage Rasmus Kessler, she'd betrayed them both. Until Nikodemus and Carson came along, Harsh had been Kessler's mageheld. Iskander had just been insane. Now Harsh, like Iskander, was sworn to Nikodemus. Harsh was traveling the world for Nikodemus, contacting the remaining warlords and even, if you listened to rumor, some of the magekind. He didn't envy Harsh that job.

"Still in Mexico." He didn't know what the fuck to do. The small talk was killing him.

Maddy looked up. "You know what?"

"What?" He looked down. She'd given him the cold shoulder or just plain misunderstood him so many times he wasn't going to assume a damn thing.

"I don't want to talk about magehelds right now," she said.

"Football?"

"Iskander," she said. "Really." She put down her root beer and walked over to him. Without her high-heeled pumps on she was a lot shorter than he was. She stopped about six inches from him, past the point where a normal person would have stopped.

He gathered some of her hair in his fingers. Thick, silky strands the color of onyx. And her skin was silky, lovely, brown. Nothing at all like Fen's pale skin and red hair. He was sad that, at a time like this, he was still thinking of Fen.

"All right then. Why me?" he managed to ask.

She was so beautiful it hurt to look at her. "Why not you?"

"You know I'm fucked up." He made a fist with the hand that wasn't still holding his phone, trapping her hair in his fingers, and she had to take a step toward him. Her hands ended up on his chest, and she didn't try to free her hair, either. "Why me when you're all fucked up over Kynan? And he's fucked up over you."

She slid a hand under his shirt. He got an unintentional shot of her thoughts. He didn't mean it, but he was not in a safe place, and she wasn't blocking him and there he was in her head. Only maybe that little slip wasn't his fault because she smiled when it happened. "Kynan and I... We're very bad for each other, that's all."

"He's an idiot, Maddy."

"Thank you for saying so."

"He is." He let go of her hair and touched his thumb just beneath her lower lip. Maddy, beautiful Maddy the witch, turned her head to the side and caught the pad of his thumb between her teeth. She nipped him. Not enough to hurt. "Maybe," he said, "we can talk about Kynan afterward."

"Exactly what I was thinking." With one hand, she

took his phone, closed it, and slid it back into his front pocket.

And then, she reached to the top of his head and put the tips of her first two fingers on the first two of the stripes that went the length of his body and she ran her fingers downward. She took her time doing it, too.

And swear to Jesus sitting on a hill, for a moment he thought he was with Fen again, and his heart gave a lurch that was part joy and part fear and he thought for a minute that he was going to split in two all over again.

But she wasn't Fen.

Somewhere in the loss of separation between them he knew she wasn't Fen and that Maddy hadn't been the one to betray and destroy him.

But it was a close thing.

CHAPTER 28

Baker and Broadway, San Francisco

From the look on Durian's face when he put away his phone, Gray could tell he wasn't happy. She sat up on the futon and crossed her arms around her bent knees. She wasn't naked, but then again, she didn't exactly have on a lot of clothes. Before the phone rang, it had been her intention to get Durian into a similar state. "Was that Nikodemus?"

"No." He drew in a long, slow breath. He wore gray tonight. Dark gray trousers, charcoal shirt, a dark gray coat, and he looked too gorgeous for words. "We need to talk."

"Okay."

He scrubbed a hand through his hair and let out an exasperated sigh. "Somewhere other than here. With you looking like that."

"Wherever you want."

"Downstairs, then."

She dressed in jeans, a T-shirt and a sweater because this was San Francisco, after all, and they went downstairs. The living room was still being renovated and since the owner of the house was expected back from Mexico soon, there were kin she didn't know working at the repairs. A pile of broken furniture made a heap in the middle of the room. The windows had already been replaced. What was left of the doors still hung from shattered frames.

They bypassed the living room for the kitchen. He got two bottles of water from the fridge then quickly made and stacked four peanut butter and jelly sandwiches on a plate with two apples. Between the two of them, they carried the food outside to the terrace. One flip of a switch and floodlights came on that illuminated pink stonework and an infinity pool that overlooked the bay.

Gray sat on a padded wrought iron chair facing the pool. Durian was the kind of man who looked like he lived someplace like this house. If he were human, he'd be from old money. A fifth-generation lawyer or maybe someone who simply managed the family fortune. He sat across from her at a glass table with a huge fabric umbrella over it. He was limiting his connection with her and that meant he had something big on his mind. It made her nervous.

"Eat." He took one of the waters and one of the sandwiches and pushed the rest to her. She was hungry, actually. While she ate, he leaned over and rested his forearms on his thighs. His hair wasn't as long as Iskander's, say, or even Kynan's; it barely touched his shoulders because not so long ago Álvaro Magellan had shaved his head. "I have a proposition to make you."

She swallowed her bite of sandwich. "Let's hear it."

He shook his head. The light had to hit his hair just

right for her to tell it was brown instead of black. She polished off the first sandwich, then drew her eyebrows together. The breeze felt good. Wouldn't it be bliss to lie out here by the pool someday and just let the sun soak into her skin? Gray went for another PBJ.

While she ate, Durian remained leaning over, now with only one forearm on his thigh. He stroked the midline of his chest with his other hand, then pressed his fingertips to his sternum. He frowned. His thoughts came back from whatever unpleasantness they'd been to visit. When he looked at her, his irises were violet and she still didn't feel even the slightest hint of his magic.

He grabbed one of the waters and opened it. Just the sound of the cap twisting off made her thirsty. He handed her the bottle. Water condensed around her fingers. She tipped back her head and drank.

"First, there is the matter of your father."

Her heart set off banging against her chest. "This is going to be bad news, isn't it?" She squeezed her water bottle. But no, he didn't look like he was going to tell her that her fears for her father's safety had come true. "Is he all right?"

"Well enough. Considering." He told her about the reasons for his second visit to Piedmont, his encounter with her father, how he'd known about Christophe and Emily and how Christophe was now threatening him.

She could tell from his curt recitation that he hadn't liked her father. He was a mage, she thought; it stood to reason Durian wouldn't like him. But this seemed like something more to her. She thought about that and with a chill realized that Durian must believe her father had lied to him. "Sounds like Christophe," Gray said.

"Very much so."

She pushed away her empty plate and picked up one of the apples while she stared out at the pool and imagined how cool the water would feel on her skin. What the hell had her father done? "What do you need from me?"

"Your soul?"

She took a bite of the apple. "Besides that."

Durian stood and took a step toward the impossibly blue pool. He faced her. "That was Iskander on the phone earlier."

Distant sounds of traffic floated on the air. From where she sat she could see lights reflecting off the dark, dark waters of San Francisco Bay. Her chest tightened, and she had to concentrate on her breathing. "About?"

"The witch, Maddy, has learned that Christophe has plans to take a young boy. A child."

"A mage?"

"Uncertain. His mother is a witch. His father, however, is kin. It's possible he has both talents." His forehead creased. "That would be rare, indeed, but not unheard of."

"Shit."

"This is perhaps another reason he married your sister." Durian's expression hardened. "If the boy is a mage, Christophe will probably poison him so he can use the boy's magic. I expect he intends for your sister to raise him until he is of no more use to Christophe. If he manifests as kin, I expect him to take the boy mageheld as soon as practical. He won't be a boy, of course. We do not manifest until our twenties. In human years."

"It just gets better and better, doesn't it?"

"According to Maddy's information, he intends to take the boy sometime in the next few hours." He paused.

"Álvaro Magellan had Carson's family killed when he took her for the same purpose. Christophe will, I am afraid, kill this boy's parents."

"In other words, if we're going to do something, we need to do something soon."

"Yes." Durian licked his lower lip, and she followed the movement of his tongue. "If we are to prevent this, I need something of you, Gray."

"What?" She shivered even though she wasn't cold. He was more grave than she'd ever seen from him before.

"Do you know what a blood twin is?"

"No."

"Two of the kin who share a bond at such a basic level that, magically speaking, they are one and the same entity. Their twinned magic makes them that much more powerful. What one can do, so can the other. They share their magic and their lives completely and for that reason they tend to be solitary. With that bond in place, they don't have the same need for contact with other kin."

"What do you mean share everything? Toothbrushes? Bathroom towels?"

"I gain access to your abilities." He took a deep breath and let it out. "And you gain access to mine. Permanently. There would be few kin who could match us. Nikodemus could. Kynan. Possibly Iskander."

"Why would you want to do that?"

"Nikodemus bonded with Carson, a witch. She has the ability to sever mageheld and Nikodemus, since then, has become even more powerful. Carson, too. Alexandrine, a witch, is bonded to Xia, who was once a mageheld and is now free and sworn to Nikodemus. Now, like Carson, Xia can sever a mageheld. He and Alexandrine have also gained new abilities since they formed their bond." He gazed at her steadily. "You, Gray, are also magekind now."

"These others, they're blood twins, too?"

"Not blood twins. Though perhaps they have become something close to that. Carson was cut off from the magic she was born with, but Nikodemus is able to access it. Likewise, through a different set of circumstances, Xia controls Alexandrine's magic. Carson would have died had Nikodemus not acted. Alexandrine and Xia found themselves faced with a similar predicament, so I am given to understand. In neither case was the result entirely equitable. What I propose is that we attempt to combine our magic. We relinquish nothing of what we are and yet, if it works, you will share what I am as I share in what you are."

"So, theoretically speaking, you'd be able to sense magehelds, too."

"Quite possibly more."

"Jesus." Her body flashed hot. He was talking about something that would bind them far more intimately than her fealty to him. She leaned back, heart beating hard. "Is it dangerous?"

"Every ritual has the potential of going wrong."

"Sure. But I'm getting the feeling there's more to it."

"Blood twins share their lives." He hesitated, and she was pretty sure he flushed. There wasn't much that unsettled him.

"Spill, Durian."

He nodded. "Iskander was once a blood twin."

She frowned. "Was once. But not now."

"No."

"I thought you said it was permanent."

"His circumstance was extraordinary. His twin became

entangled with Rasmus Kessler. She was mageheld while Iskander was not. It is remarkable, actually, that he was able to maintain his independence from her." He stared at the pool for a while. "Ultimately, Carson Phillips severed him to preserve what remained of his sanity. But as I've said, his was an exceptional case." His attention shifted back to her. "What his situation tells us, however, is that when we have dealt with our situation, Carson or Xia can sever the bond."

"Not without risk, I assume."

"No, of course not." He gazed at her. "I understand your desire to rescue your sister, and I assure you we will do whatever is required for her safety and well-being. But, Gray, understand this. The kin do not leave our children behind. There are no tests to pass. They are not abandoned to the streets. If it happens they do not know what they are when they manifest, we do what is necessary for their survival. This boy is kin, and we watch over our own."

She pushed herself out of her chair. "Let's do it."

Durian stood up, too. She didn't think she was wrong that he looked relieved. "Not here."

CHAPTER 29

In less than four minutes Gray had her things packed in the battered leather satchel Durian gave her. Used to be she had to decide what to pack for a trip. Now, she could dump all her clothes in one carry-on-sized bag and it wasn't even full when she was done. A quick check of the bathroom confirmed she hadn't overlooked anything. She glanced in the mirror and ran a hand through her hair. Her dark roots were showing even more.

"All right, then," she said to the woman in the mirror, impressed with how calm she looked when she was shaking inside. She was intimately aware that Durian was putting himself on the line for her and it made her heart feel too big for her chest. He could have proposed that she allow him to take control of her magic as Nikodemus and Xia had done for the witches they were bonded with. But he hadn't because he knew she had not been given any choice with Tigran. He did not share himself easily, but he was offering her an access to him that she knew he'd never allow anyone else.

Even without her oath of fealty, she'd follow him to hell and back if he needed that from her.

She picked up her borrowed satchel and joined Durian. He was waiting in the doorway of the bedroom, leaning against the jamb, arms crossed over his chest. Her heart lurched. She smiled but it felt fake. "Let's go."

Very casually he took her hand, and Jesus, it made her want to cry, that he'd hold her hand like that. Her heart misgave her and she looked up, blinking to clear her vision. "Is this going to get you in trouble with Nikodemus?"

"Doubtful. If anything, the result will be of benefit to him."

"We don't have to do this," she said. "We can try this another way." Oh, damn. Those were tears burning in her eyes. "It's just I want my sister back safe and sound. I want Christophe to never harm anyone else, and I hate that I'm using you to get what I want."

His eyebrows lifted. He drew her closer and with his free hand ran his fingers through her hair. "More than I am using you, Gray?" His hand ended up touching the side of her face. "I asked for your fealty. And I proposed this to you, if you'll recall. If anyone should feel used, it's you."

"I'm glad you found me instead of someone else when I went after Christophe." She put her arms around his neck and held on tight, burying her face in his chest. Through his shirt, she kissed his scar. "I'm glad it's you."

He was still holding her hand, but his other one snaked around her waist and pulled her tight against him. "For the record, you may use me whenever you like."

Gray looked at him. He wasn't holding back the psychic connection anymore, and that meant he was an insistent presence in her head. "I'm going to do that. Just you wait."

When they walked out, he sent a current of magic into the repaired medallions over the left corner of the door. A *no strangers allowed here* command that spread from that one to the others. He did the same at the hallway door, and they walked out.

In the garage, he threw his bag and hers into the backseat of his car and they were off to, well, she had no idea. They didn't talk during the drive. She didn't even ask where they were going or when they would get there. They headed west, across the city. He jacked an iPod into the car stereo and put on some kind of edgy Latin guitar.

She waved a hand at the iPod. "Am I going to end up liking this?"

Without any change in expression he said, "You will acquire my superior taste, of course."

"How do you know you won't end up slumming with me?"

"Impossible."

"You may end up wearing jeans when this is over."

"You may find you like impractical shoes."

She laughed, and it felt good to be able to laugh. "Not hardly."

They ended up in the St. Francis Wood section of the city. Very expensive homes here. Eventually, he made a turn into the driveway of a house with a lawn that was larger than two normal houses. The house itself wasn't that large, but it was impressive, in a Georgian revival kind of way. He hit a button on a gadget clipped to the visor. They drove inside the garage and parked next to a shiny dark blue Tesla roadster. After a brief tussle over what could be wrong with her carrying her own bag, ten minutes later they were inside a house so clean she wondered if anyone lived here.

Durian threw his keys onto a table and they stood for several seconds, looking at each other. She gripped the strap of her bag and thought about why she was a fool to feel all the air rush out of her body just from eye contact. He was meltingly good-looking. She felt like a high school girl with a crush on the wrong boy. Except she'd had a taste. She'd seen him naked. She'd caressed him, gone down on him, and kissed him in places that got her hot just thinking about it. He hung his jacket in a closet near the door and walked into the main room with her following.

There was furniture here, a relief after that stark entryway. Beautiful antiques, too. Which was no surprise. He had a taste for old and elegant. They ended up in a kitchen where he got them both a glass of ice water.

"Perhaps you'd like time to think about your decision."

She shook her head. The ice cubes in her cup were tiny little squares. "Just think," she said. "Next time we do this, we'll be fighting over who gets which ice cube." She stuck her finger in her cup and jabbed at one. "Dibs."

"Enjoy it," he said without cracking a smile. "That is the last ice cube you will ever call your own."

She couldn't help laughing. With that they were five minutes after the storm instead of in the middle of it. This was the right thing to do. For both of them.

"This way."

They ended up upstairs. Partway down the hall, he took two quick steps ahead of her to open a door.

She walked in. A spray of coppery-red stars arched over the midnight blue wall directly opposite the door. In the light, they seemed to glitter. To the left was an impressive bed; a four poster complete with silk hangings that matched the walls. A gilt-framed still life of lemons in a brass bowl hung on another wall next to a Georgian-era highboy with what looked like the original finish. Her mother collected, so she had years of exposure to very old furniture.

"Nice."

"Thank you."

He walked to a curio cabinet and started taking things out of it.

Gray looked around. There wasn't much furniture, but she was used to less where he was concerned. What he had looked like it belonged in a museum. She knew a Queen Anne chair when she saw one. Like the three around the table there.

He walked out of the room with his arms full of items she couldn't identify. When he didn't come back right away she went after him through a small anteroom with nothing in it but tatami mats on the floor. She ended up in a room that was almost devoid of furniture. The walls were the same midnight blue here. His shoes and socks sat beside the doorway so she did the polite thing and removed hers, too.

This next room wasn't large, maybe ten by ten total. There were no windows. No more doors but the one behind her, and that one wasn't even a normal door. It stretched floor to ceiling, for one thing. There was no trim and no hardware. Just a quarter-sized medallion in about the same place you'd put a doorknob. Midnight blue on one side, coppery red on the other. She stepped through.

In there the walls were the color of an almost-new penny. The ceiling was brilliant white, the floor tiles a polished black stone that was cool and slick under her feet. Durian stood on the far side of the room, setting up a brazier on a recessed platform built into the wall. There wasn't much furniture here, either. Just a small couch pushed up against one of the walls and a cherry table with an empty copper vase on it.

"What are you doing?"

"Preparing." At the moment, the only light in the room came from the open door.

She looked around for a light switch and didn't see one.

"Please close the door then press the medallion there."

"Sure." She reached behind her and pulled the door closed. It clicked shut with the force of its own weight. She pressed the medallion and an electric zing shot up her arm. With no discernable seam, it looked like they were in a room with no way in and no way out.

Durian did something, she felt the magic, and all along the floor the walls shone with just enough light for her to see.

Her belly tightened. She had no reservations about what they were planning to do. None at all. She walked close enough to get a better look at the items he'd taken from the curio cabinet: a brazier, a fat-bellied stoppered jar about two inches high—alabaster, it looked like. There was also a box about the size of his fist that looked like it might be carved from lapis lazuli and various items required to heat the contents of the brazier. While she watched, he got the brazier going. He opened the jar and poured some of the contents into the bowl atop the brazier. The scented viscous material shone with rainbows of oil.

The smell was musty but not unpleasant.

They stood side by side, her shoulder touching his upper arm.

The blue box, it turned out, had no hinges, just an edged lid that snugly fit the bottom. The inside was blue, too, and it contained a golden-yellow substance. He took a pinch of the stuff and scattered it across the oil. Tiny gold sparks appeared on the surface of the liquid in the brazier. Durian bent over and breathed in.

When he straightened his irises were coppery red. Flecks of gold dotted his sclera. He must be holding more magic than she thought for his eyes to have gone straight to copper.

"You'll forgive me, Gray," he murmured. In one smooth motion he stripped off his shirt. He continued to strip down. "The ritual is a stressful one. If it happens that I change forms, it's best if I'm not clothed."

Her stomach clenched. "What about me?"

Durian folded his clothes and laid them neatly on the floor by what she could only call an altar. She did her best not to stare, but honestly, would she ever be tired of looking at his human form? "Since you cannot change forms, you may remain dressed."

He reached into the blue box and withdrew a sizeable pinch of the contents. He placed that on his palm, then did so twice more. He made a tight fist and held it for the count of five.

"What is that?"

"This," he said, unfurling his fingers, "is unrefined copa." He held his hand at his eye level. The substance had clumped together and was a smaller mass now than it had been. Gold flecks flashed in his eyes. "It's difficult to preserve in this state, but the experience is deeper. Richer."

"Isn't copa dangerous?"

"Not for the kin." He lowered his hand. "For the mage-kind, yes; it is eventually quite dangerous." He put the bolus in his mouth, made a face, then stayed motionless for some moments before he swallowed. His eyes, when they opened again, were even more vividly copper and gold. "Have you taken copa before?"

She shook her head. "At least not that I know of."

"Good." He took more copa from the box, less than before, did the same sort of compression with his closed fist and then handed over the portion.

She gave his hand a doubtful look.

"You have so little magic, Gray, that I think we are safe in believing there is no risk in your taking this. In the event, it's nowhere near the amount you'd need to cause ill effects. Leave it on your tongue until it almost completely dissolves."

She took the copa and set it on her tongue. The substance was so bitter her breath caught, but she let it dissolve. Before it was gone, the markings on her arm and temple flared hot.

Durian took her face between his hands. His fingers pressed tight to her temples, two of his fingers in contact with the tattoo on her right temple. Their connection came on with a saturated depth that took her breath. Her gaze met his and locked. "Are you ready?"

CHAPTER 30

Durian watched as the copa darkened her eyes from pale blue to turquoise. The tracery underneath her skin seethed in tight coils that whipped out and curled back. His fingertips sizzled from the contact but he didn't let go. He didn't want to. She'd become far more accepting of the kind of physical and mental touch that was so much a part of what the kin were.

She worked her mouth. "This is terrible."

"Yes." He was thinking about sex. And not vanilla kind. The kin's instincts for procreation were always aroused around human women, and that meant not keeping his human form. He had eons of experience in self-control. He told himself he wouldn't. That he didn't dare take that risk. For either of them. Her willingness to go there with him didn't make it safe or right.

She nodded.

"Very well." Durian lowered his mouth to her throat, pushing her head back enough for him to find the spot he wanted. He breathed in and smelled his shampoo in her hair, the light scent of her body only slightly masked by the scent of his soap. His stomach spiraled into white-hot lust.

There were words to say and to transform with magic so that they resonated with power. Reaching for her magic was easy. He knew her better than he'd known anyone in his long years of living. She was an extraordinary woman. Strong. Mentally tough. Determined. And, hell, when she touched him, he went up in flames.

He worked the magic he pulled up, shaped it, gave it the purpose he needed for the ritual and pushed it through to her. She gasped as the magic came through to her, darker, he knew, than anything he'd let her feel from him.

The pulse of blood through his veins slowed. His kind had been born to this magic. It was his nature to think of inhabiting her body, and having done so once, the lure of doing so again would be all the stronger.

Gray understood what was needed, because she did the same, sending her magic into him. As before, the effect was disorienting. Between those born kin, the magic was expected, the psychic connection practically mundane. With Gray, he was above all else aware of her as human. Other. Female. Beloved.

He breathed in, clearing his head of everything but the ritual he needed to complete. He began a silent chant, a recitation of words that had survived thousands of years and the centuries of depredations by the magekind. So much knowledge had been lost or locked away in mage-held fiends.

Her eyelashes fluttered, the edges of her mouth tight-ening. Durian stroked her shoulders and focused on maintaining their wide-open connection instead of letting go and simply taking over. He moved a step closer to her. Beneath his fingers her skin was fever-hot. She was reacting to the copa.

Now came the part that most worried him. He needed to adapt the ritual exchange to compensate for the fact that she was human.

"Gray." He drew a finger along her temple, and the sizzle of her magic took him right to the edge of the cliff. He stood there, poised to fall and praying to gods that no longer existed that he wouldn't. "I need your consent. For indwell."

She nodded, but her shoulders went tense and her now-turquoise eyes were wide and unfocused. His body tensed with anticipation. This was dangerous, wanting her so much. He'd regressed to a time when there were no rules about consent yet stood here in the future, expected to deny what he was.

"You have mine." He told her so there would be no question that he agreed to her indwell of him—if it could be accomplished.

His heart tripped because he didn't know for sure if he could open himself to her the way he needed to. His tension, the strength he needed to fight his instincts, were a barrier to what needed to happen. Leaving his other hand on her, he reached for the copa and shaped two more boluses. The difference between demonbound and twinned was vast and separated primarily by intent. The copa would, or ought to, relax him, and put him closer to his magic. He took the larger one and gave her the other.

Their minds were so entwined at this point that when she let the copa dissolve, the sharpness spread over his tongue, too. Different for humans than for the kin. Copa didn't taste as bitter for him as for her. She blinked once. A second time. By the third, the color of her eyes had deepened. His own resistence thinned.

"I can't see," she said.

"At all?"

"Not normally."

"Then it's now." His pulse thudded in his ears. "It's time." When she nodded, he slid into her mind. The world dropped away for him. This was like sex, the deliberate holding back in order to reach a higher peak. He wanted the shiver of power that came with an indwell. The fever excitement of a mind and body in his control. So much. Too much.

He wanted her with an ache. All of her. Bound to him. For the first time since he could remember, he let the copa take him over. He allowed himself to fall under.

When he opened his eyes, he saw the monochromatic glow of his own magic at the same time that he saw her. This *would* work. This had to work, because the alternative was Leonidas.

And you. He gave the thoughts to her without speaking. *Now.*

He held still, resisting his habit of closing off. She came into his mind. Not softly but with determination because that was Gray. Nothing timid. She touched boldly, accepting what she found. She became a part of his darkness. Just as he was now part of her magic.

Twinned.

He pushed aside her shirt collar and exposed the tender spot that was not quite the back of her neck and yet not the side either. He breathed in. So human. So frail and locked into a single physical manifestation. With the edge of a talon—the most he dared change—he scored her skin until blood ran, thick, red, hot with her life. She trusted him to see this through. Durian was determined not to fail her or himself. This was the only way he could bring out enough magic to complete the bond.

He bent at the same time he pulled her up and hard against him, exquisitely aware that he was male and bigger and stronger than she was. He licked away the trail of crimson from the cut he'd made. The taste of her blood hit his tongue with an explosion of heat and power.

She drew a breath that brought her torso in closer contact with his. He was desperate to have her naked against him. Desperate. How could he not be when he already knew how ferociously she made love? When he knew her private thoughts about him?

Durian reached between them to open her shirt because he needed contact with her as if she were fully kin. He pushed downward with the slice of a taloned finger and separated the buttons from her shirt. He did the same to her bra. He covered her breast with a hand, and his body shivered from the inside out from the first touch. Warm, human skin. Soft female curves. Her nipple grew taut underneath his palm.

Yes.

Was that her desire or his?

Skin to skin. Touching. Tasting. He fit his mouth over the cut and a low growl rose up from his chest. She held onto him, arching toward him. Their bodies touched. He wanted her to be as naked as he was. On her back, her body accepting his. As he was right now. And then more.

He separated from her, but the whole time, his free hand moved over her torso, down to the charm in her navel, the dip at the base of her spine. She let out a breath, soft and low. She accepted the forming bond, let it happen. The desire in the sound rocked him.

He opened a similar cut on his throat. Gray stretched to reach him and he held her, both hands around her waist, bringing her up to him. His head spun when she latched onto him and her magic swept through him like a wave. Her tongue touched the cut he'd made along his neck. Her teeth nipped at him, and—God yes. With the sensation of a lock sliding into position, the blood-bond between them settled into place.

When she released him, he bared his teeth, beyond himself with desire and the sense that he belonged to her. He flashed onto his memory of the day he first saw her. A defiant human woman on the verge of losing control of the magic he thought she'd stolen, and, incredible as it seemed, determined to kill Christophe dit Menart. He could have killed her for her attack on the mage, but he hadn't.

His instincts, it seemed, were not so untrustworthy as he thought.

He had not, as he had feared, lost sense of himself as an individual. Their psychic and physical boundaries remained. He was able to separate himself from her and yet he remained aware of her with a vividness that defied his ability to describe. At the same time, the distinction between her magic and his blurred. Gray was more alive in his head than anyone ever had been. More, even, than Nikodemus.

Gray slipped an arm around his shoulder. "No," she said in his ear. "You aren't alone, Durian." Her lips brushed his earlobe and then nipped. "Not even when you're sure you are."

She drew back. A drop of crimson glistened on her lip. He licked it away, and she pressed forward, and her skin was warm against his and her lust for him so inviting. She'd never been very shy about that, had she? Not even when she knew exactly what he was; a killer. And what he had been; enslaved.

He held out a hand, and she put her fingers on his palm. Without the need for words they used the silence to assess the change. The separation between them consistently blurred, though it was quite possible to keep the boundaries clear. *This* was him, and *that* was her. He suspected learning to do that would take some practice.

She ran a finger along the already healing cut on her throat, and he felt an echo of that touch. Her eyes closed halfway. Her physical sensations continued to mirror in him, and that was indeed something they must learn to deal with. He felt the icy pinch of the cut he'd made in her skin, caught the memory of her physical reaction to the taking of blood. She was not, he discovered, entirely at ease with the process.

She looked up with a steady gaze. "I don't regret anything."

He needed a moment to work out which one of them had spoken. A different problem arose when he managed to properly assign the various boundaries between them; the psychic, the magical, and the physical. Once he had placed himself in his body, and in turn, her in hers, his awareness of their differences intensified. Differences of origin, of bodies, of mind, and of gender.

He touched her, stroking her soft skin and feeling the pull of his kind for hers. When he had sex, he was always the one in control. Always. He never desired his partner more than she desired him. He never wanted more. He'd never given more, either. Now, all that changed.

He wanted Gray beyond anything in his experience. He leaned in and kissed her.

For about ten seconds, they were fine. Then he was in her head, or maybe she was in his, and all he wanted was her. He undid the knot that held together her shirt and, God, yes. She groaned when his hands found her breasts. Her head fell back, exposing her throat to him again, and he bit her. Not hard, but enough. She gripped his wrists, pulling him toward her, and his desire bubbled up and intermingled with hers, or maybe it was just the opposite.

In the next moment, she was on her back and he'd pulled himself over her and he was taking more blood. One of his hands slid down her belly to work at her pants while his entire body rippled with incipient change. That was him crooning to her, bringing her into his desire. Desperate that she could feel the way he did.

He pulled back and her ice-blue eyes fluttered open and then focused on him, laser sharp. He said, "I have a perfectly acceptable bed."

"So you do. Let's go."

He led the way to the bedroom. Once there, he pushed the door closed and pulled her into his arms so fast he had to lean against the door to keep his balance. They kissed for a ridiculously long time, and he kept his hands busy moving over her, underneath the back of her ruined shirt, back to her navel, over her breasts, down to the charm dangling from her navel.

It was all he could do to maintain his human form. He pushed off her shirt and bra then dropped to his knees, drawing his palms down her body, along her belly until he came to the waist of her jeans. The metal of the button was cold to his touch. He got her fly open, and he pressed his mouth to her navel and tongued the silver skull. She was soft and warm and he was unbearably aroused. He was cracking open, giving himself over to his impulses.

He circled his fingers around her right elbow and moved his fingers down her arm, touching, brushing, sliding along the markings that formed and reformed beneath her skin. His head filled with images of him sliding into her body when he wasn't human.

"Durian," she said, and his name was a plea that sent his lust into a tighter spiral. Through the magic that swirled just beneath her skin, he heard the thump of her heart hard against her ribs, her breath quickening, her anticipation. Her need.

He tugged her jeans down, and she helped him get them off, and then he leaned in and nipped her belly with teeth that were perhaps sharper than they ought to be. So close. He was so close to changing, and it was getting hard for him to remember why he shouldn't change. He picked her up and carried her to the bed.

This was going to happen between them. She understood what that meant for them both. He had her consent, and he was more than willing to accept the consequences. There wasn't any going back. She was his. Gray stretched on the mattress, arms above her head, toes pointed. Even when she was done stretching, he stayed distracted, arrested by all the curves of her body and what he wanted to do to them and with them.

Durian pulled himself over her and kissed his way down her belly. "If I bought you something for that thing in your navel, would you accept it from me? As a gift?"

She reached down and flipped the skull charm, but looked at him from under her half-closed eyes as she did.

"Could we talk about my tastes first?" She smiled at him. "Nothing gaudy."

"I have a number of loose stones." He slipped a hand along the inside of her thigh and followed that with kisses, paying a great deal of attention to her reaction so he could savor that and push it higher. "Sapphires. Spinel. A few emeralds. Some fine yellow diamonds. Among others. You choose. I know a jeweler who will make whatever you describe to him."

She brought up one knee and crossed her arms behind her head. She knew his secrets. He had nothing left to hide from her. He was a killer, and she knew that. He had been mageheld, nearly killed in a ritual murder and she knew that too, and did not blame him as he had blamed himself for so long.

"You're serious, aren't you?" she said.

He studied her without bothering to look at her face. Her knee shifted just enough and he set his fingers on her mons. He could lose his mind with her and it wouldn't matter. "Very."

The skin down his spine rippled and incipient pain quivered along his shoulder blades. She knew what that meant. Her tension flowed into him. He pushed back while he was kneeling between her legs. They were so closely linked right now that he was getting images from her. Of her and Tigran. Of him the day Nikodemus had bound her over. From the acuity of his vision, he knew he was closer to changing than was safe for her. Or him.

"Gray." He realized then that she wasn't afraid or panicked or repulsed. And that there was nothing she needed to be protected from. She knew the risks. Better than any human woman, she knew the risks.

She held his gaze, then slowly lowered her eyes to his torso, his belly. His penis. She didn't just let him know what she was thinking. She actively imagined what she wanted him to do to her, and how the hell was he supposed to suppress his reaction to those pictures of her accepting him into her body? She slid a bare foot along the outside of his thigh and smiled a lazy, lush smile while she thought about what she wanted to do to him. He looked at her, so beautifully naked, all the muscles of her body and the passion and desire coming back to him along their link.

"I can change back just before," he said.

"You could." Gray held his gaze. "Or we could take our chances."

He wanted to.

"After everything Tigran did to me, what if I can't even have a baby?" She put an arm around him and brought him close. "Don't go acting like this was never a possibility. It was from the start, and you know it. From the minute I sat on that couch and said I'd swear fealty to you, this was a possibility between us."

"There's a difference—"

She pushed him back to stare into his face. "I'll tell you the difference. The difference is this time I get a choice. And I choose you. I choose us. If you don't want this, then okay. But if you do, I've already made my choice."

He threw back his head until he was looking at the canopy, allowing his feelings to flow through him to her and back, and while he was doing that, she sat up and her hands skated over him. Touching him with the silk of human skin. He stretched his hands upward as he straightened and flickered into her head. He stayed in his body, though he saw with her eyes. One of her hands slid down his belly to his cock.

When her hand gripped him with exactly the right pressure, he let out a sound that was part growl, part groan.

The connection between them went hot with desire.

The traceries along her arm and temple glowed an unearthly green. "Do you want children some day?"

"I've never thought of it. Not in years."

"It's all right if you don't."

He touched her cheek and she turned her head and nipped his finger. "I don't want to hurt you. Or remind you of Tigran. Or bring back memories that are unpleasant for you."

"Do you ever learn? If you do any of that, I'll tell you."

He leaned in and bit her, and, yes, his teeth were sharper now, but he was in control of himself, and he kept tasting her while with his other hand he reached down and pushed her back until her body, pale against the dark coverings, lay beside him.

"Jesus, Durian."

He laughed to himself. To his long-dead god.

"Your choice now," she whispered. "Just make love to me."

He moved over her, his hips adjusting, her legs opening for him. Without preamble, he pushed inside her slick, hot body. He was still human. Barely. The pressure of her around him took his thoughts away from much besides this.

Better than before, and all the before with her had been very good. He got a hold of one of her hips and with his other hand gripped her head, and he was inside her body with her back pressed into the mattress, her arms holding him, and him so close. So close.

CHAPTER 31

Gray drew a breath as the weight of him on her increased, the texture of his skin changed. The heat of him sizzled where their bodies touched. Their psychic link went white hot and for a moment her vision cut out. She blinked and her sight was back because she was using Durian to see.

Colors were more saturated than she was used to. Gold underlay his copper-red eyes and bled into the whites of his eyes; she'd seen his eyes do that before, but never at such close range. Never while he was holding her. His breath came harsher now, and for a moment, she couldn't think. Maybe she didn't want to think.

His body was dark, dark, copper and, as with his eyes, flashes of gold gleamed as if there were shifting pools beneath the upper layers of his hide. He was just as beautiful as she remembered.

She bit her lower lip, but she didn't hold back her reaction, and that brought a growl rolling up from his chest. The scar down his chest remained and she trailed a finger along the twisting line. "I'm screwed up. I guess you know that."

"You are exactly as I prefer." Durian pressed his palm to her cheek.

She turned her head and kissed his wrist.

He circled her right wrist with a hand and she saw a flash of black teeth and tongue when he brought her arm to his mouth and traced one of the twisting whorls on the inside of her forearm. The effect was electric. He seemed to have known it would be, too. She couldn't suppress a gasp. He turned his head until he caught her eye. "Do you like that?"

She nodded.

"Mm." He went back to using his tongue to trace the whorls. Her own markings were moving now, the way the gold did underneath his skin, which was a fascinating similarity. He nicked her arm near the crook of her elbow. The touch of his tongue on her skin, the psychic echo as he tasted her blood, sent a shiver through her. He made a low sound in the back of his throat, and pressed her onto the bed, though he kept his mouth on her arm. He bit her again. The sharp pain didn't hurt the way it seemed it should, and then he braceleted both her wrists and pulled himself over her. Heat from his skin soaked into her palm, into her pelvis where his lower body pressed against hers.

His face and body were unhuman in a way that took her breath. You might turn the pages of some medieval manuscript and find creatures that looked like him; fanciful images—so humans supposed these days—drawn by some human scribe who had rendered his vision in disturbing and sensuous detail.

She was even more aroused than when he'd been

human, but then she'd known that would happen. Not repulsed. Not horrified. Nor afraid. Aroused. She wanted him this way. She wanted the danger and the beauty and lethal power of him. Her choice.

Durian lowered his head to her, nuzzling her belly and then sliding his mouth—such an unexpected sensation— up to her breast. She bowed off the bed at the pleasure of his mouth there, tonguing her nipple.

Gray pushed at his chest, and he let her push him away. She sat up, and he did the same, sitting on his haunches while she touched him. His skin was thicker, a smooth copper hide that was soft beneath her fingers. Muscle and sinew stood out in corded relief. There was no mistaking his strength. He had no hair anywhere, the tips of his ears lay flat to his head and when he opened his mouth his jet black teeth were sharp. His tongue flicked out to touch the side of his mouth.

He was different. His body was bigger, rougher, not quite as gentle, and she loved that about him. She spread her palm flat to his torso, just below the end point of his scar, then slid her fingers up until she touched his nipple. His eyes flashed bright copper and when she leaned in and licked him there, his hand came up to close over the back of her head. Talons pressed into her scalp. His other hand cupped her bottom.

He wasn't Tigran. He wasn't forcing anything. There was no compulsion but what came from her own desire.

His talons skipped along the side of her spine while she moved to his other nipple, licking, tasting and breathing in the heat of him. She slipped a hand between them and when her fingers circled his balls he spread his thighs enough to give her better access. She worked to keep her magic at a minimum because she knew what he wanted right now, when he was in this form, was the human part of her.

"Have I ever told you," she said, rearing back just enough, "how much I love the male anatomy?"

"No." His voice was deeper, rougher, and when he spoke she saw the sharp tips of his canines and incisors.

"Maybe I should show you." She curled her fingers around his cock.

"At your peril," he said. He reached out and hooked a tip of a talon through the ring that connected her skull pendant to the steel bar just above her navel.

The tug on her belly sent a zing of arousal to all the right places. She stretched her hands over her head and watched Durian's eyes fix on her breasts. "I've been told I give good head."

He cocked his head to one side and spread his hands wide. Gold shifted underneath his hide and wherever it did, the color highlighted the scaled markings on him.

His cock was different in texture and she savored the heat and salt, the flex of him in her mouth, the way his body stiffened, how his hands pressed the sides of her head and let her know when he wanted more force from her, more tongue. She reached with one hand and used her thumb to press against his anus. Her heart thudded in her chest when he let out a low, feral growl. His hips pumped forward and she took him deeper into her mouth.

She licked her way up his belly and chest, back to his nipples, his throat. He stretched his arms over his head and grabbed the top of the bedstead. The muscles of his upper body contracted with the tension of his grip. She straddled him and he bowed toward her when she lifted herself and brought his cock into her. She knew he wanted something else. Something more between them. His nature needed an edge between them but he was holding back.

This was nothing like what had happened to her with Tigran. There wasn't anything in her head that whispered softly of the horror of her life. Nothing in her fought the arousal she felt. No guilt. No hatred. She did not hate herself for this. He sat up, keeping a hand against her spine and himself inside her and kissed away her tears, a soft touch of his tongue to her skin.

Their eyes locked when he leaned back.

She could choose this. She did choose.

She put her hands behind her head and arched her torso toward him. After a slight pause, he did what she wanted, which was to kiss her breast, bringing her peaked nipple into the heat of his mouth with a pressure that set her on the edge. The pressure of his mouth increased; he held her tighter, pushed harder into her body, and she went right along.

"More," she said. "Durian. More."

He turned her over. The ferocity of his desire was in her, too, along with the knowledge that he was aroused by the gleam of her pale human skin. She saw what he did. Felt it. When he entered her from behind, he growled, a long low sound that sent a quiver of arousal up her spine. One hand spread over her back while the other held her hip, keeping her steady as he thrust into her. She pushed back to meet him. Harder and faster and she felt his body change again.

The weight of him was different. Denser. She started to come, so close. She was seconds from orgasm when he withdrew.

Then she was flat on her back and he pushed inside her, his big body straining to get deep inside, and she did come, in one long rolling wave of pleasure that he rode with her, drawing out the peak until she thought she'd never survive. When she could breathe again, she met his gaze. His eyes burned like fire and she grabbed his head and bit the side of his neck where he'd opened up a cut earlier. His blood tasted richer to her. She lifted her hips to his and let go. This time it was real. She wanted Durian. He wanted her. Her. Her. Her.

When he came, she held him close and refused to think about anything but right now and what she had chosen to do.

CHAPTER 32

St. Francis Wood, San Francisco

Less than an hour after Maddy called with the boy's location, Durian and Gray were on their way to an address on Clement Street, a commercial building with apartments upstairs. Though early enough to be dark, it wasn't early enough that there weren't worrisome numbers of humans on the streets. The joggers were first, along with those heading home after a night on the swing shift. And, for many of the humans who were out of their beds, their morning commutes were just getting started.

He let Gray deal with the locks on the barred door that led to the upstairs apartments. As expected, she opened them with no difficulty and left no sign of the building's security having been breached. Inside, they both stopped as the wrongness hit them. The air here was thick with magic that made their skin crawl. The hair across the back of his neck prickled. Beside him, Gray sucked in a breath.

It wasn't just the presence of the mage that brought them up short, but the magic that wafted down the stairwell. There were magekind here. More than one.

Gray glanced at him. "How many mages do you figure are here? Ten? More?"

He gave a tight shake of his head. "None of any strength. It isn't unusual for a human to register as a mage or witch yet have little, if any, usable magic. Nor to find that they end up living near each other, without any of them being aware of their latent talents."

From where they stood downstairs, locating the trail they'd followed here wasn't hard. There was an elevator, but getting on anything that might be interfered with mechanically wasn't the wisest course. Whatever mage was here, Durian didn't intend to telegraph their presence. He and Gray dampened their magic, and it was far easier than he expected. They hardly had to think about it.

They took the stairs. The higher they got, the stronger the stench of perverted magic. He and Gray shared senses and observations with almost no difficulty. They'd adapted to the duality to the point where he didn't need to flick into her head. He knew. He felt the way her other magic reacted to the presence of magekind.

Their destination was a sixth floor apartment. The scent of blood came raw and overpowering before they reached the final stairs. The apartment door was ajar. He examined the space around them for any traps and found none from either kin or magekind. Gray gave the door a gentle push.

The doorway opened onto a cluttered main room that at first glance appeared empty. They both knew that couldn't be. The air seethed with magic that set his skin to crawling.

Inside, someone softly sobbed, a heartrending sound.

"Christophe is here," Gray said.

"Yes."

Gray's other magic rippled through him, a foreign sensation but he recognized it for what it was. There were magehelds in here. They entered, with her beside him. To their right was an open kitchen; to the upper left a wall with two doors, one shut tight, the other ajar. He pulled as much magic as he could, to the point where his body felt light, and still there was more he could have called on. They could not yet see the crying woman, but she was here, off to the left, though not behind one of the two doors they could see.

Magehelds, when they attacked—and Durian did not doubt they would attack—would almost certainly come from behind one of those two doors. He wasn't sure how far their ability to sense magehelds extended, though he was confident he had a fix on the ones inside. They were a presence in his head. He could have pointed to them even if he were blind.

They moved farther in. The wrongness he and Gray had sensed downstairs intensified. Once they were past the front door, the rest of the apartment came into view. They were close enough now to identify the woman as a witch. One of the magehelds, a man with a newly and unevenly shaven head crouched next to the woman. A glow of magic surrounded them. The sobs weren't from her. They were coming from him.

Gray moved past Durian toward what was obviously a newly taken mageheld and the victim of his first command from the mage who now controlled him. He did not doubt that once the mageheld was done destroying the witch's mind, he'd kill her. Gray's expression was severe, a match for her psychic state. She was, rightly, appalled by what had been done here. The mageheld, it was heart-breakingly clear to Durian, was the witch's former lover and the father of the boy Christophe was after.

Durian stayed where he was. Gray had more than enough magic to do what was needed and she was fast enough to get her touch before the mageheld could hope to guess someone was close. They were going to have to drop the dampening of their magic in order to deal with the mageheld, but that had been an inevitability anyway. Once that was done, the mage would know they were here.

They didn't undampen until she got within range to touch the mageheld. She wasn't sanctioned for a kill, so all she could do was incapacitate him. Which she did. She caught the now lax body and lowered it silently to the floor.

She'd just turned to the witch when the open interior door swung wide and Christophe dit Menart emerged from the other room. His clothes were more soccer hooligan than elegant. Straight-legged jeans, pointy-tipped shoes, an AJ Auxerre jersey. Three of his mageheld bodyguards followed. Christophe held a dark-haired child in the crook of one arm, but he was also wiping his damp hands on a white towel. A slash of crimson stained the bottom of the towel. One of the magehelds carried a bright blue bag with a smiling train on the side.

The mage's grin faded when he saw the mageheld on the floor. "Ici!"

His remaining four bodyguards appeared from the other room, moving with alert eyes to spread out around dit Menart. He lifted the hand holding the towel. His magehelds stood still.

Durian crossed the room to Gray. He wasn't good at guessing the ages of human children, but he knew this one was quite young. Barely past the age when the magekind tested their offspring for ability. The boy's unnatural quiet was surely due to something Christophe had done to ensure he kept quiet. His gaze swept over Durian to settle on Gray.

"Nikodemus will not be pleased to learn you've taken a mageheld, Christophe," Durian said.

"In defense of my life, fiend. He attacked me." He waved his free hand. "I was well within my rights to act as I did."

"Put the boy down, Christophe," Gray said.

Christophe stroked the toddler's head. "Anna. How unexpected to meet you again." His smile broadened. "As to the boy, this is none of your affair. He is talented. Magekind. I've just confirmed that."

She lunged.

Durian tightened his grip on her wrist and yanked her back with enough force that he was afraid he'd hurt her. He pulled her close and spoke in a voice pitched to her ear. "Use your head. He hopes to provoke you." He squeezed her wrist. "We do not have his sanction."

"Not yet."

"You, Anna," the mage said. "You are . . . not quite what you were the last time we saw each other."

"Give him to me, Christophe."

"Give him to you." His smile got even bigger as he darted a glance at Durian. "Give him to you or what?" The mage laughed and ran his fingers through the boy's black hair. "He'll fit right in with my growing family. My wife is looking forward to taking in this poor orphaned boy."

Durian felt Gray go cold inside.

"I propose a trade," Christophe said. "I'll leave the boy here in return for her."

"No." Durian took a step forward. He and Gray needed to sell this moment. If Christophe didn't buy their reluctance to accept any deal, their chances of saving the boy and getting to Emily were going to be astronomically faint.

"Pity." Christophe resettled the boy in his arms. "I could be persuaded to accept you in lieu of her. In service to me as my mageheld, naturally."

"I serve Nikodemus, mage."

Light refracted off the faceted rubies that lined Christophe's ear. He waved a hand. The words tattooed on his hands flashed in and out of focus. "That would be immaterial if you were my mageheld." He waited. "A simple trade. The boy for one of you."

"Nikodemus won't like that much," Gray said. "No one's threatening your life right now."

"My dear Anna, my agreement with the warlord is that I won't *take* a mageheld while I am in his territory. Not without provocation." He made another dismissive gesture. "If one of you offers to submit to me and I accept, that's hardly what Nikodemus intended. And in any case not what I agreed to." The mage looked at him. "Well, fiend?"

"Very well. Give her the boy, and I agree you can try to take me."

"Durian," Gray said in a sharp voice. She was a far

better actor than he was. He believed she didn't want this to happen when, in fact, this was precisely what they'd hoped would happen.

"If you fail," Durian went on, "you leave him with us."

"Ridiculous." Christophe's magehelds took offensive positions near him. Durian held his ground. If the magehelds attacked, he was justified in defending himself and Gray. He would do so with lethal force if necessary. "I can hardly leave a young boy in the company of monsters." The mage narrowed his eyes. "You agree to become my mageheld?"

"I agree I won't resist you when you try." He would have killed Christophe where he stood if Durian didn't know that when his bond to Nikodemus broke as a result, Gray would suffer, too.

Christophe smiled.

He and Gray had planned for this. She withdrew from their connection so that anything Christophe did wouldn't blowback through her. He felt Christophe's touch, lightly at first, then like the slice of a knife. He centered himself against the instinct to fight. His chest burned along his scar, pulsing fire with each beat of his heart. His breath caught, but the nightmare that had once been his life failed to take hold. Dit Menart tried again and then once more. Each time the taking failed.

"Can this be?" Christophe flushed and made a sharp gesture that cut the air with the side of his hand. "You are not a free fiend?" His focus lasered in on Gray. "Surely, she's not the one who took you? She isn't capable. She doesn't have enough power for that."

Gray held out her arms and even though Durian knew

what she was going to say before the words came, still, his heart nearly stopped. This was a dangerous game they played.

"Leave the boy here, and I'll go with you."

Durian was afraid to look at Gray for fear he'd give something away. The mage had to believe. Had to. If this didn't work, if Gray were harmed in any way, Christophe would die. He would personally see to it. Xia could sever the blood bond and free him to kill the mage regardless of the consequences to him.

The muscles around Christophe's mouth and eyes tightened and an eager light came into his eyes. "A noble sacrifice, Anna."

Already her fealty to him was attenuating. "Don't do this."

She stared at the mage. "Put down the boy, and I won't fight you."

The air around them pulsed as the mage pulled again. He handed the boy off to one of his bodyguards. "When she's mine," he told the mageheld, "release the boy." He spread his hands wide. "There. Is that sufficient?"

Christophe signaled to one of his magehelds. The one with the boy took a step back.

"Gray." Durian met her gaze straight on this time because his feelings right now were exactly what Christophe would expect. Had events fallen out differently, he would have left her oath in place, but that option was now far too dangerous. As they had agreed, Gray was going to allow Christophe to take her mageheld. He pulled his magic, and it roared through him. "I release you from your oath of fealty."

They both felt her fealty to him vanish. The blood

bond, however, remained. He knew what would happen next. Dreaded it even knowing that this was the most likely outcome. Iskander had protected himself from a magheld blood twin. Durian intended to do the same. His world depended on it.

Another of the magehelds twisted her arms behind her and shoved her forward until she stood arm's length from Christophe. She glared at the mage with all the ferocity he'd come to love in her. Both he and Gray had accepted the risks of what they were doing, but he vowed to himself that if anything happened to her while Christophe had her, he would visit a thousand times worse on the mage. And then Durian would kill him.

Another of the magehelds got behind Durian and kicked the back of his knee so that he dropped to the ground. Dit Menart put a finger to his chin. "Her I can take." He tipped his head. "But you. You are somehow proof against me. This," he said, "I do not understand." He smiled. "Nor can it be allowed to exist. A fiend who cannot be controlled must be killed." He gestured behind him, and four of his magehelds stepped forward.

Gray looked at Durian, worried yet resolute, and he returned her gaze. He mouthed the words *I love you.*

The side of Christophe's mouth twitched—almost but not quite a smile. He was pleased with himself. Dit Menart's magic flared up and somewhere in the heat that blinded Durian in its intensity, Gray screamed. Her very soul convulsed with a pain Durian recognized all too well.

He felt the moment she was bound to the mage. The loss nearly crushed him. When he looked up he had to shove his emotions away. Gray's breath came in shallow pants. Her eyes were wide and staring. The traceries at her temple slowed and then stopped. Even as he reeled from change in the equilibrium of their twinned state, his relief that this had worked as they hoped swept through him. He continued to feel her magic through their blood bond, both the now stunted and deformed magic of his own kind and the foreign magic that had come from Christophe.

Christophe pointed to the mageheld who held the boy, then to two others. "You two with me. You—" He meant the other four. "—kill this one when we are gone."

"Leave the boy, Christophe." Gray faced the mage. "You promised."

Christophe backhanded her. "You will not defy me. Ever again."

Durian watch her leave the apartment with Christophe dit Menart. All he had to do now was survive whatever Christophe's magehelds had planned for him and then he was going after Gray.

CHAPTER 33

The moment the apartment door closed, Durian moved. A lunge and spin. Two down and out of commission. He ducked the only one to react before it was too late, then whirled, came in close and touched the last two. They, too, fell hard. His bond to Nikodemus prevented him from killing them outright, but even if he had been sanctioned, he wouldn't have because then Christophe would know he'd lost them while there was time for him to return and take matters into his own hands. The thought of the mage sending Gray against him froze his blood.

He and Gray had known something like this could happen, but he wasn't prepared for the despair howling through him, the paralyzing devastation of losing her or the fear that something would go wrong and he would lose her forever. One of the magehelds stirred, and Durian immobilized all four of them so that even as they returned to consciousness, they would not be able to move.

He pushed away as much emotion as he could. The magic required to maintain all four of the magehelds in this state was not trivial, but he hunkered down and assessed his status and reserves. His blood bond with Gray had survived whatever Christophe had done to her, and that was at once a comfort and a source of terror because of the horrible nullity where her magic had once been for him.

He took out his cell. There were ten missed calls from Nikodemus, eight voice mails and fifty-seven text messages. Nikodemus could wait. He'd go after Gray alone if he had to, but he didn't think he would. His first call was to Alexandrine. She picked up on the second ring.

"Hey, Big Dog." She didn't sound pleased to be hearing from him, but then no one ever did, did they? He didn't let it bother him. She'd answered. Xia probably wouldn't have.

He took a breath. In the back of his head, he felt the first stirrings of the effort of keeping Christophe's magehelds immobile and unable to touch their magic.

"Durian? Everything okay?"

He gripped his phone and almost blurted out, *I need your help,* but that would have been counterproductive. "I require assistance," he said. He was supposed to be rendering favors to Alexandrine, not the other way around. She was, as far as he knew, unaware that he considered himself as indebted to her as he was to Carson. "Your assistance," he said to clarify what he meant. He had to speak carefully. Too carefully. All four of the magehelds were awakening. Soon, he'd need all his concentration just to keep them restrained against the command Christophe had given them. "And Xia's."

"Whoa," Alexandrine said. "What's the matter?"

He hadn't been aware that the strain had shown quite that much in his voice, but it must have. Gray was so far away. Too far from him. "Please," he said.

"Xia's right here. Hold on a sec." The call went silent, and he considered disconnecting. They'd refuse to help. His pride would never survive the indignity. He could do this on his own. Without help. But Alexandrine came back on. "I've conferenced you in with Xia, okay? What's up?"

He related what had happened as clinically as he could. What he needed from them. His heart thumped in his chest the entire time he was speaking. And afterward, too. He couldn't stop thinking of how much more difficult things would be if Xia just told him to fuck off. The words had been said to him before.

"Where are you?" Xia said.

He told them that, too.

"Babe—" Durian knew Xia meant that for Alexandrine. "Get the others, would you? I'll be right down." Xia lapsed silent, but it didn't last long. "We're on our way. Thirty minutes, all right? Sooner if possible."

"I'm holding four of Christophe's magehelds," he said. He glanced at them. Three were already suffering under the strain of not yet having done as commanded; their mouths gaping open. The fourth looked calm enough. Under the circumstances. One touch from him and they would die. "If I am able to keep them alive, they may be of use once they're severed."

"Gotcha." Xia and Alexandrine disconnected the call.

The next call was to Maddy because she needed to deal with what was left of the witch. He left a message when she didn't pick up. He looked at the woman the mageheld had assaulted. Her eyes were open and tracking him. He stood with his phone in his hand. He didn't know whether she was capable of understanding much of anything right now, but he met that traumatized gaze and said, "I will get your boy back."

Then he called Leonidas.

His legs were shaky, but he went into the bedroom to get a blanket to cover the witch. He was afraid to move her. Maddy would have to take care of assessing what could be done for her. If anything. God help her if the mageheld had permanently damaged her mind.

In the silence he could hear the traffic that with every second was taking Gray farther away from him. The scar down his chest pulsed as if it were alive and made the darkness in him seem deeper than ever.

Restraining four magehelds under a compulsion to kill him wasn't the sort of magic he was used to carrying off, and he was feeling the strain. What he wanted to do was go after Christophe now. He wanted the mage dead. He wanted Gray back and safe and the boy returned to his mother or some other family member, if any could be located. Through the blood bond, he kept his link with Gray open. Whatever the cost, because she was drawing on his strength, and he would do nothing to deny her that.

She remained part of him, but Christophe's hold on her magic was taking a toll on his strength. The cost for her was, of course, exponentially worse. He knew what it was to be mageheld; the utter hopelessness, the knowledge that your life no longer belonged to you. If he relaxed his vigilance for even a moment, Christophe might discover his link with Gray and use it to get to him. Or to punish her.

Durian sat in the apartment with the stink of magic and the persistent sobs of the witch, holding on as best he could and not at all sure if his best would be enough. The constant pulse of Gray's loss ate at him, strung him high and tight. No wonder Iskander had cut himself off from his blood twin even if it came at the cost of his sanity.

He buried his emotions when he felt Xia and Alexandrine enter the building, staying as he was, kneeling and waiting. Holding on. Maddy was out there, too, but she didn't come in with the others.

Durian got to his feet when the apartment door opened. Xia must have ridden his Harley here because he was wearing his leathers. Alexandrine, too, had on a heavy coat. The two were serious but calm as they surveyed the four magehelds. What he recalled of the process of severing was not comforting.

"Hey," she said. She gave him a quick grin. "We met up with Maddy outside. She'll wait until it's safe."

Durian nodded. Wise, since a newly severed fiend might not understand or care that Maddy wasn't a danger to him.

"Can you let them go one at a time?" Xia shoved a pair of gloves in his coat pocket.

Durian nodded.

Xia stepped up to the four magehelds. "You ready, baby?"

"Yup," Alexandrine said.

Xia pointed. "This one first." Durian released the mageheld with the full expectation that the fiend, close to breaking from the delay in carrying out Christophe's order to kill him, would immediately strike. Xia and Alexandrine had refined their technique since the night Alexandrine had faced Kessler in his own home and had saved Durian in the process. The mageheld was severed before anyone drew breath. He went reeling back.

Xia pointed again. "Next."

They repeated the process until all four were severed. Alexandrine took care of making sure each one got Nikodemus' phone number and that they understood they were free to go or to swear fealty to the warlord if they were so moved. Durian said nothing as the first three were severed. They reacted badly to the process. The shock of freedom left them in a state of tenuous mental stability. The fourth, however, was clear-headed enough to keep his balance and say, "There is a witch nearby."

They all looked at the still sobbing woman.

"No," the fiend said.

"The witch you're feeling is with us," Alexandrine said. "Now, listen up. You need to understand what I'm going to tell you."

Durian interrupted her spiel on Nikodemus and the taking of binding oaths. He looked the fiend in the eye and said, "Will you swear fealty to me, fiend?"

"Whoa," Alexandrine said under her breath. Xia gave a low whistle. He ignored them both.

He ignored them. "You can wait for Nikodemus," he said. "But do you wish to stay unaffiliated long enough to get to him?" He met the kin's eyes. "Wouldn't you rather come with us to kill Christophe dit Menart?"

The fiend smiled. "Killing that mage? Yes."

Xia gave Durian a look, but didn't say anything. No objections. No smart ass remark.

The oath was finished with efficiency. By the end, Kynan and Iskander had arrived, too. They came upstairs with Maddy Winters. The witch shrugged when Durian gave them a questioning look. "Maddy thought we might need their help."

"Thank you," Durian said.

Then they got down to the business of finding out what Durian's newly sworn fiend knew about Christophe and his home.

CHAPTER 34

Gray didn't move when Christophe walked into her old room. There'd been some sort of crisis shortly after they arrived, the result of which had been Christophe shoving the boy into her arms and confining her here with a single uttered command. Just like the old days. She was sick to her stomach and more than a little disoriented. Hatred burned hot in her, beyond anything she'd felt in her life.

At the moment the boy—his name, she'd managed to discover, was Ian—was sitting on the floor. He had a pen and some old paper she'd found shoved in her old desk drawer. He was drawing pictures of monsters. He went still at Christophe's entrance. One of Christophe's magehelds came in with him and dropped the bag of Ian's things to the floor.

Christophe leaned his shoulders against the wall, bare arms crossed over his chest. She stayed on her old bed, sitting with her legs crossed. Nothing much had changed here. Same bed. Same dresser. Same battered chair. Her clothes were still in her doorless closet.

Habit could be a terrible thing. In this environment, she was in the habit of being afraid. Her fear permeated the room, and she hated that Christophe probably knew exactly how afraid she was. Hell, she half expected Tigran to walk in any moment, just like in the old days. Seeing the mageheld gave her a hell of a jolt because for a moment there she really had thought he was Tigran. He just dropped the bag and left. Thank God. *Thank God.* He wasn't Tigran's replacement. She worked to keep the fear from completely enveloping her.

She could, she discovered, draw strength from her blood tie with Durian, and with Christophe here, she borrowed what she dared. Not much, though, because number one, she didn't want Christophe to figure out what she was doing and number two, whenever she reached for her magic, her tie to Christophe choked her like a blight on her soul.

"Anna."

She didn't reply. What did he expect her to say to him? She'd spent too long wishing for his death, and she hated him too intensely. To be sitting here, in thrall to him made her sick. She wondered if Christophe intended to shave her head the way he did with his other magehelds. She stared out the window of her room, watching his reflection in the glass in between the bars that covered the windows.

Christophe, still leaning against the wall, rubbed his chin. "A dilemma."

She put her hands on her crossed knees and watched Ian. Her heart hurt for the boy. Christophe needed to die for this. He really did.

"You are not a true fiend, yet, I presume, since I have taken you mageheld, that you have their abilities." He frowned. "Physically you are human. I must doubt that you would survive if I treated you as any other mageheld. Look at me."

She did because she had to. Her bound magic compelled her. She hoped her hatred showed in her eyes.

"How is he doing?" He nodded in Ian's direction as he moved into the room to sit on the edge of her bed. "Well?"

She didn't answer. Her skin crawled at the thought of having Christophe so near her.

"Don't be difficult. It's unbecoming of you." He turned sideways so that he was looking at her but still had a view of Ian. "We've a great deal to discuss."

Her fingers tightened on her knees. Solidarity among magehelds, she thought. Any way she could resist him, she would.

"You will tell me what I wish to know."

Gray resented the hell out of the compulsion. Fine. He wanted her to talk, she had no choice but to talk. But, she was finding out, there was leeway in his compulsion of her. She already knew from her experience with Tigran that there was a gap between the literal words of command and the intent that drove a mage to issue the order. Christophe had just given her firsthand experience of the imperfection of compulsion. Like any mageheld, Gray intended to turn that gap into the Grand Canyon, if she could.

Christophe began. "All four of the magehelds I left behind are ... gone. Would you happen to know anything about that?"

She held his gaze. "I wasn't there when it happened."

"Four magehelds. Gone. This cannot be." He locked his hands in front of him, a lock of his dark hair falling over his forehead. "They had a simple task to carry out. Kill one fiend. They failed. Four of them."

She smiled grimly. "If you wanted Durian dead, you should have done it yourself."

"Explain." It was easy to forget how deadly Christophe was when he dressed like a soccer hooligan. Right now, though, she was well aware.

"He's not easy to kill."

He considered his next question. "What's wrong with his magic?"

"Nothing."

"He is a free fiend, yet I could not take him as mine. Why?"

"Rasmus Kessler beat you to it?" She tensed when his eyes narrowed. His hand lifted, but he glanced at the boy and didn't strike her. Duly noted. He probably wasn't going to hurt her in front of Ian.

"The only magehelds Kessler has left he got from me."

This was information to be tucked away; proof that Christophe was helping Kessler. They already knew Kessler was attacking in Nikodemus's territory and now she knew they could tie Christophe to Kessler's actions. "All I know is something happened when he was Kessler's mageheld, and he ended up like that. I don't understand it, either. I wasn't there." She couldn't help it. She grinned at him. "Too bad, huh?"

"Have you learned nothing from your experiences?" He shook his head. He moved closer to her, and there wasn't anywhere she could go to get far enough away from Christophe. "The demonkind, Anna, are not human. They are predators. Humans are their prey. You understand, don't you, that what Tigran did with you would have been a thousand times worse had he not been under my control?" He ran a hand through his hair. "They deceive by their very nature. They appear human, yet are not. As you know too well, they kill and rape. They destroy lives."

She glanced at Ian. He was so quiet. Too quiet. His life wasn't ever going to be the same. "Lately they've had a lot of help from you."

Christophe pried her right hand off her knee, turning her palm up to examine the markings underneath her skin. "These are new. Since your...transformation."

Heart in her mouth, she cut off her link with Durian. Jesus, it about killed her to lose that connection to him. The traceries weren't moving. If you didn't look close, you'd think they were tattoos.

"I often wondered why Tigran chose you. Did he ever tell you?"

"No." She hadn't even known the mageheld had been given a choice.

"It was necessary that he choose between you and your sister so that he would select the woman most likely to survive contact with him. Others did not, you understand."

Gray's stomach churned.

"You know how his kind feel about witches. I fully expected him to choose your sister. Much more powerful. A much greater allure, I would have thought. I was puzzled when he did not. Your sister should have been irresistible to him."

"Sounds like you had it carefully planned."

"Tigran knew what he was doing, I grant him that. Everything turned out for the best."

"I know Emily's alive."

His expression clouded. "I am aware of your encounter with her. That was ill-advised. She does not remember you." He shook his head. "She never will." He put a hand on her chin and turned her head from side to side, studying her. He paid extra attention to the mark at her temple. When he touched it, his magic sizzled through her, searing and white hot. She couldn't suppress a shudder. He went still. "I can make you want me," he said at last.

"We both know that would be a lie."

"Regardless of the genesis, the feelings would be real. You know that better than anyone, I think." Christophe ran the back of a knuckle over her cheek. "You are no longer completely human, Anna. If you were, you would not now belong to me."

"Fuck you, Christophe." Her stomach curled up and for a moment she remembered Tigran with heartbreaking clarity. The way he touched her, held her. Talked to her. He had died and given her what she needed to survive. She looked away, sickened by the thought that Christophe intended for that nightmare to begin again.

"There are not as many demonkind as there used to be." He gestured and she caught a flash of the words inked into his skin. "That is the goal of the magekind, to wipe out demonkind and so rid the world of a scourge."

"If you didn't need them around for ritual."

He nodded solemnly. "Every year, fewer and fewer mages of true ability are born. Did you know," he said in a low, harsh voice, "that this child is the first I've come across in the last three years, in Europe or America, who might legitimately be called gifted?"

"No," she said, because she was required to answer his question.

"He's nothing but a mongrel. The good Lord knows what effect his father's blood will have on him." Christophe didn't say anything for quite a while. "It is a pity about Tigran, but I wonder." He touched her arm. "What might we produce? The two of us."

That made her look at him. She wasn't prepared for the magic he sent into her, and the next thing she knew, she couldn't see. Her desire to kill him welled up so hot and fresh she could barely breathe. There was nowhere for the impulse to go. She could not act. No matter how much she wanted to kill Christophe, she couldn't. She was forbidden to harm any mage without Christophe's express order.

"Women have always been the future. I saw that years ago." The words inked on his forearm glowed as he waved a hand. "I sit here and see you, a woman who can bear my get. And I am curious, Anna, to know the result of that pairing. You are unique so far in how you were transformed, I feel quite certain of that. Later, of course, I'll use one of my magehelds with you. For now, I am curious to know if you and I would produce demon or mage."

"That's sick." More than anything she wanted to plunge a knife into his black, shriveled heart. She wanted to kill him with her bare hands. As long as she was mageheld, she couldn't.

"I've a few things to take care of, but we'll begin, you and I, later tonight." He stroked her cheek again and she leaned away from the contact. "You'll do what I tell you,

Anna. Oh. There is also the matter of the magic you stole from me. That, my dearest, will be returned."

She managed a nod, and didn't even care if she was anywhere close to looking at Christophe. The mage was right about Ian being a mage, she realized. Even blind, which she was right now, she could *see* him. His magical affect was different from one of the kin, but there wasn't any doubt what he was.

"Christophe?" The woman's call came from farther away in the house, but Gray recognized the voice. Her heart fell. "They said you were here. Where are you?"

Christophe went dead still. They listened to Emily walk down the hall, heading for them. His hand shot out and grabbed her chin in a painful grip. "You will do nothing to contradict anything I say to her. You will not tell her anything of what's happened to you in the past or today. Not how you were taken, where you have been or how you came to be here."

The door knob turned. "Christophe? Are you in there?"

He shot off the bed and walked to the door. "Erin. My darling. Whatever are you doing here?"

With Christophe blocking the door, Gray couldn't see her. Her voice was so achingly familiar that tears burned her eyes. "I locked myself out of the condo, and I can't get past your wardings, you know that. Can I get your keys? Please?" There was a silence. "Oh, Christophe," Emily said in a low, tender voice. "You should have called me."

Her sister walked inside, her attention focused on Ian. Gray didn't know what to do so she stayed where she was. "Hello," she said to Ian. Then she came in far enough to see the bed and Gray sitting on it. The color drained from her face. Christophe was at her side immediately, support-ing her.

"I know this is a shock, my love, but—"

"You. Anna, isn't that right?" She glanced at Chris-tophe. "What is she doing here? Has she come to bother you with her delusions that I'm her sister?"

"I've told her she's mistaken. Naturally. I fear she's been persistent."

"Call the police, Christophe." She ran a hand along Christophe's shoulder. "Get a restraining order."

"I might at that."

Emily frowned. A flicker of something passed over her face and vanished. Her eyebrows lifted, and she addressed Christophe. "The boy? Who is he? Did she bring him here?"

"No, darling. No. This is sheer coincidence. His father... Well. As you know. The worst has happened to him."

Emily seemed to know what that meant because she lifted a hand to stop Christophe from saying anything further. She faced the mage and said softly. "You let this woman near him? Christophe, what on earth were you thinking? She's mentally unstable."

"My love."

Emily crouched down as best she could in her condi-tion and addressed Ian. "Hello there, sweetie. I'm Erin. I am so very happy you've come to live with us."

The boy's hand around the pen turned white. He looked at Christophe with wide, frightened eyes and then he said, "He's here."

"Who's here?" Emily asked him in a soft voice. "Who are you talking about?"

Gray saw the moment her sister felt the free kin. Her

eyes flickered, and she straightened as quickly as she could. Then Gray felt it, too. Her other magic prickled through her.

Christophe whirled to the door. His body glowed with the magic he was pulling. After a moment, he grabbed Gray by the arms hard enough to pull her off her feet. His fingers dug into her upper arms. "If you are responsible for this intrusion, demon bitch, I will kill you, that is my promise."

"Christophe," Emily said. Ian looked between the three of them, eyes far too serious for a child his age. "Stop it. You're scaring the boy."

Gray stared into Christophe's face. "I don't know what you're talking about."

"Liar."

She laughed at him. True enough, she didn't know who, specifically, was responsible. Durian was unlikely to have come here by himself, and in any event, she didn't have enough of that kind of magic to distinguish numbers or individuals. "You know I can't lie to you anymore."

Emily frowned again, but she focused on her husband.

The mage pushed Gray hard enough that she stumbled against the bed. She had to slap a hand to the wall to keep her balance. He strode to the door. He glanced down the hallway then turned back to her. His magic burned hot.

"What's going on?" Emily asked. Her voice trembled. "Christophe?"

"You will not leave this room, Anna Grayson Spencer. Erin, stay here until I have this under control. Please, my love. I could not bear it if anything happened to you." He pressed a quick kiss to her forehead. Then he pointed at Gray. "You. Protect her and the boy with your life."

The tracings under her skin moved sluggishly as Christophe's compulsion took hold. She wanted to kill him. More than anything in the world, she wished she could follow him out of this room and plunge a knife into his heart.

"Christophe?"

"Later, Erin. My love. There is no time. We are under attack."

Emily paled. "Who?"

Christophe gave Gray a final command. "If any fiend not mine comes in this room, kill it. Understood? If you have to die yourself, kill it."

She nodded. Fighting the compulsion did no good, though she tried. The order settled into her very bones. She knew if Durian stepped foot in this room, she'd have to kill him. Or die trying.

As soon as Christophe was gone, Emily scooped Ian into her arms. The boy was sobbing, and she held him close, doing her best to soothe him. Her arms shook, though. "Maybe you should sit down, Emmy."

Her sister nodded and sank onto the edge of the bed. "You called me Emmy again."

"Sorry. I meant Erin."

"No you didn't."

She shrugged. "You'll always be Emmy to me. Even if you never remember who you are." Her mouth trembled and she had to work to get herself under control. "I'm so sorry this happened to you. I can tell you love him. Christophe."

"Yes. I suppose I do."

Gray stood there, watching her sister while she tried to sense something, anything about what was going on.

All she heard was Christophe barking orders from somewhere in the house. She felt the other magehelds, her sister's magic, Christophe's and faintly, magic she knew belonged to free kin. Durian had come for her.

"Your husband said his name was Aguirre. But Christophe called you Anna Grayson Spencer."

"That's my name."

Emily frowned until she winced as if her head hurt. "My maiden name is Spencer."

"Coincidence, I guess."

"Is it?" Emily stroked Ian's hair. "I know what my husband is, Anna."

"And you know what I am."

"You weren't mageheld before."

"No."

"When did that happen?"

Gray shook her head. "I can't tell you."

"Who's attacking us? And why?"

"He's an assassin, and he's going to take me home with him and return Ian to his parents, if they're still alive. If we can, we'll take you with us. If you want to come."

"You mean the man who was with you before, right? Andres Aguirre?" Gray nodded. "Ah," Emily said. Her mouth thinned. "And he's ordered you to kill the man you love?"

Her heart was in her mouth but somehow, she managed to croak out, "Yes."

Downstairs, something screamed. Heart pounding in her chest, Gray mastered her fear. "You need to take cover, Emily. This could get ugly fast."

"I'm sorry." She shook her head tightly. "My name isn't Emily."

"Sorry. But that's who you used to be." Every window in the house rattled. With a ping, the barred window in the room cracked from top corner to bottom.

Durian had come after her.

And she was going to have to kill him.

CHAPTER 35

He wanted maximum effect when they went after Gray. Though it would be preferable to kill Christophe, he was sanguine about his chances since he'd have to first get through the mage's defenses and bodyguards. While he did that, he wanted Christophe's magehelds busy fighting. Gray, when he got to her, needed to be off balance. According to Xia, an instant was all he needed. What he wanted was a personal campaign of shock and awe. So far so good.

Surreal as it was, Leonidas was at Durian's side, accompanying him to rescue one of the kin. The mage had made some kind of deal with Nikodemus that had resulted, unless he was mistaken, in the mage having sworn fealty to the warlord. Xia and Alexandrine were right behind them, taking the stairs two at a time. Severing Gray was Durian's primary goal. The longer she was Christophe's mageheld, the greater the risk.

He could hear Iskander continuing the disruption they needed to engage Christophe and distract him from his newest mageheld. Even with Iskander being a take-no-prisoners sort, Durian knew the other fiend would try not to kill the magehelds. Not when their freedom was so near at hand.

Kynan and Maddy were here, too. The warlord's job was to make sure Maddy was free to disable as many of Christophe's wards and protections as possible. Durian wasn't certain of the wisdom of that pairing, but so far they were doing exactly what was needed. He didn't have time to worry about anything else. Maddy and Kynan would have to cope on their own.

Durian had no trouble finding the room where Gray was being held. His bond with her led him unerringly to her. She wasn't alone, though, and that was a complication. The boy was there, too. And a witch. He stopped in front of the door to the room where she was being held. "Leonidas?"

The mage stepped forward, his eyes narrowed in concentration. He put a palm to the door and all the kin there, himself, Xia and, to some extent, Alexandrine flinched when he drew on his magic. Leonidas stood back. "No traps."

"Gray," he called. "Get away from the door."

He looked around him. "Ready?"

"Go." Xia's eyes were neon blue.

Durian kicked open the door. Anything to keep Gray on the edge until he had everything in place for the others. It felt good to destroy anything related to the mage. The general noise from downstairs, a great deal of shouting and screaming, covered the sound of the door shattering around the knob.

"I think you killed it," Xia said.

Gray was on the other side, crouched in the middle of the room. She was pale and shaking. Every instinct he possessed urged him to go to Gray, to find a way to take away the strain so evident in her eyes. But he couldn't. Not yet. Even if it killed him not to. There was no telling what Christophe might have done to her, or how, or what orders she may have been given, though he could guess.

If Christophe were here, he'd break his goddamned neck for this and damn the consequences, too. "Are you all right?" he asked.

She wasn't alone. Gray's sister, Emily, stood at the back of the room, holding a young boy and watching the door with suspicious, frightened eyes. She wasn't attacking, and that was a good thing. Neither could she be trusted.

"No." Her voice sounded strained. Knowing her, she had enough magic on hand to kill him. She knew him better than anyone. She knew his weaknesses and she would know, must know, that he would not willingly kill her. The markings on her arm and temple glowed. He didn't doubt that if he got close enough, she would try to kill him. No wonder she was shaking. She was doing everything possible to keep from attacking.

"Only a little longer," he said.

"Durian." Gray held up a hand. She looked like she'd been crying or maybe trying hard not to cry. "Don't come in here."

"I won't." He stayed on the other side of the threshold but made sure he stood sideways. He gestured to Leonidas who came to the door but judiciously stopped at the threshold.

"What were Christophe's orders to you?" the mage asked Gray.

"Don't leave the room." She scrubbed her hand through

her hair and left it sticking up in six different directions. The dark roots were more prominent than ever. "Kill any fiend who comes in who isn't his mageheld. Protect Emily and Ian with my life."

"You are still restricted from killing the magekind?"

She nodded. "As long as you don't harm them."

"Excellent."

"What's going on here?" Emily asked. She kept her arms tight around the boy.

"They're here to help us," Gray said. "I know Leonidas." She pointed. "Who are they?"

"Xia. And Alexandrine. I told you about them. They'll sever you when it's safe."

Gray nodded. "What's Leonidas doing here?"

"Whatever I can to help."

Durian thought it wise not to mention that the mage had sworn fealty to Nikodemus. Leonidas himself seemed to think so since he didn't mention it either. The mage walked into the room and there was a moment in which they all held their breath. She slowly straightened from her fighting stance. Leonidas bowed toward Gray's sister. "Mrs. dit Menart, I presume?"

Emily nodded. "What's going on? Mr. Aguirre?"

Durian nodded. "I'm here for Gray."

"I am Leonidas." The mage took a step closer. "Are you aware, Mrs. dit Menart, that the boy you hold has been stolen from his parents?"

"No," she whispered. She shook her head even as she cradled the back of Ian's head with one hand. "That can't be true. Christophe wouldn't do that."

Leonidas lifted a hand and made a graceful gesture in front of his chest. Durian couldn't see his face, but Gray and Emily's attention was riveted on him. "You have been tampered with."

Gray said, "Can you help my sister remember?"

"If it's possible, I will. But first, you." The mage put his hands on Gray's upper chest. The air grew slowly colder until there was a fine mist hovering over them. Gray started shaking.

Durian cursed, vilely. He didn't dare go in yet. "Xia? Can he sever her?"

Xia looked at him. "I don't know. I thought you knew."

"What are you doing to her?" Durian said, his voice rising to a roar.

The mist overhead thickened, and with a low cry of triumph, Leonidas threw his hands in the air. Gray took a step back, her hands on her chest where Leonidas had been touching her. Durian felt her magic burst into life, not as kin but as magekind. She swallowed hard. Her eyes were jittering and there were beads of sweat above her lip and along her temples. "Jesus. What the hell did you do?"

"Congratulations," Leonidas said. "You're now a full fledged witch." He turned to the doorway and met Durian's furious gaze. "It's only fair, Assassin. Now, I suggest you get her severed from Christophe before it's too late."

From downstairs, Kynan shouted, "Time to get it rolling, Big Dog!"

Durian crooked his fingers at Gray. "Come."

Gray shook her head and glanced back to where her sister and the boy were pressed against the wall. Her mouth was tense and the muscles of her upper body moved too stiffly. "I can't."

"Just to the doorway. No farther. We aren't leaving

here without Ian and your sister—" He darted a glance at Emily. "If she wants to come. I promise you that."

Gray approached the door up to the point where Christophe's compulsion to remain in the room got its hook deep into her. Leonidas backed up. Gray started quivering and had to take a step back until the reaction faded. "I can't come any closer."

"What's happening?" Emily asked.

"That's close enough," Xia told her. "Just stay where you are."

"They will sever her from Christophe. So that she is no longer his mageheld."

Durian locked eyes with Gray, and she said, "I hate this, Durian."

He looked over his shoulder at the other two. "Xia?"

Alexandrine touched Xia's shoulder and for an instant Durian was sure he saw her eyes flash the same neon blue as Xia's. Considering his size, Xia moved fast. He slid up to the doorway and Durian didn't even feel the magic. He saw and felt the results, though. From personal experience, he had a good idea of what Gray was feeling and that it wasn't pleasant. She gasped and staggered back a step, catching herself with a hand to the broken edge of the door.

At the same time, he felt their magic twin again, full on. He felt her other magic, too, as strong as any mage he'd encountered. Durian strode into the room and crouched beside her.

"Shit," Gray said. She bent over, sucking in air. She reached out with one hand and grabbed his wrist, holding on tight.

"Thank you, Xia," he said.

"No problem, Assassin," Xia said.

"Now!" Alexandrine shouted from the hallway. "We need to get out now."

Gray stood up. Still holding Durian's wrist, she addressed her sister, "The boy needs to go back to his family. Will you come with us?" Her voice got thick. "Please, Emmy?"

"He's my husband."

"He's a liar who took away what you are."

Durian took out the photo he'd taken from the Piedmont apartment, doing his best to straighten out the creases. The photo was of Gray in a white tutu and pointe shoes, full stage makeup outlining her eyes, her dark hair slicked back into a bun. Her arm was around Emily's shoulder. Both women were grinning like crazy. He handed over the photo. "She's telling you the truth."

The woman took the photo from him and brushed her fingers over the faces. "My God," she whispered. "That's me." She shook her head. Her face was ashen, and her mouth trembled. "It's me, and I don't remember this."

"Emmy?"

"There's no more time." Durian held out his arms. Taking Emily by force wasn't going to work. If nothing else, the doubts had been planted. "If you come with us, Gray and I will protect you." He sent their twinned magic into the words. The promise had power now, and Emily would have felt that. "Otherwise, I must ask that you return the boy to us. His father is one of ours. The boy belongs with us."

Cradling Ian in one arm, Emily stretched out her arm and placed her hand in his. Durian pulled her to her feet. She was awkward because of her pregnancy. He looked over at Xia, who was standing in the doorway with one eye on the hall. "You and Alexandrine sever as many magehelds as you can."

"Damn straight." Alexandrine poked her head around the doorway. "Everybody okay?" She caught sight of Emily and whistled. "Boy howdy."

Xia clapped Alexandrine on the shoulder. "See you back at the house then."

Durian watched the two with the sense that his old life had just been ripped away. "Do nothing to put yourselves in danger, Xia."

The big fiend paused outside the door long enough to grin at him. "You do the same, Big Dog."

"Move it," Durian said.

Emily stared at the photo again and then at Gray. "How could I not remember something like this?"

"Choose." Durian didn't have time to smooth away the gruffness. "Come with us and I will keep you safe. Leonidas will do what he can to restore your memories. Otherwise, don't leave this room until you no longer hear the fighting."

He didn't wait. She would come with them or not. In the hallway outside, they met Iskander jogging toward them. He pulled up and, grinning, put a bloody hand on the wall. His eyes, glowing blue, sidled to Emily. "You should be gone already."

Durian knew from the sudden awareness of new kin that Xia and Alexandrine had found wherever it was Christophe confined his magehelds. They worked damned fast, those two. "On our way."

Iskander straightened. His hand left a red print on the wall. "The mage let loose a shitload of magehelds with a kill order." He looked behind him. The noise level was higher even without Iskander adding to whatever was going on down there. "Kynan is insane." He looked back as he shook blood off his other hand. "He's an animal. Hey, Gray, good to have you back." His eyes went big when he got a dose of her combined magic. "Whoa. This is … unexpected."

Durian shoved Ian into Iskander's arms and gave Emily a push in the back. "Get them out of here and back to Harsh's house."

"The witch, too?"

He growled. "Do it."

"Whatever you say, Big Dog." Iskander pointed down the hall with a bloody hand. "That way."

Durian took Gray by her upper arms, intending to do what he could to prop her up, but she was unsteady and disoriented from being severed. "Go with Iskander." He gave a glance at Emily. "Someone has to make sure your sister and Ian make it out."

Gray looked at him, pale as death and shivering uncontrollably. "Don't let Christophe get away with this."

"I won't."

Iskander grinned down at the boy. Ian nodded and reached a hand to one of the blue stripes down his face. Iskander stilled, and the smile on his face vanished. "A mage?"

"A matter to be dealt with later," Durian said.

Iskander put a bloody hand on Emily's shoulder and looked at Durian with a definite smirk. "Come on, witch. Let's get a move on. Gray, I hear you might know a back way out."

She nodded. She wasn't drawing from his magic anymore because she knew he needed every bit of magic he had in order to deal with Christophe. "Leonidas." She gestured. "Go with my sister. Please? They need your help. You know that."

Leonidas nodded.

But they were too late. Christophe came running up the stairs, his bodyguards behind him. Leonidas lifted a hand and Christophe slid to a stop as if he'd slammed into something hard. He shouted. "Stop them!"

"Iskander," Durian said. He pulled his magic, feeling Gray's there too. Both kinds. "Take the boy and get out of here."

He obeyed instantly, turning on his heel and heading for the back way out of the house.

Christophe's tattooed arms came down, and he ripped through whatever Leonidas had done that had stopped him. He pointed at Gray. "Kill them. The assassin, the woman."

Gray stepped in front of her sister. "Emily, run!"

"Christophe dit Menart," Leonidas said. "Stop this. Before it is too late to save you."

"Do it now." Christophe motioned to his bodyguards. "You. All of you. Kill them all but Erin."

Emily walked toward Christophe. The hallway wasn't wide enough for his magehelds to carry out their orders without risking harm to her, and Christophe knew it because he raised a hand to stop them. His bodyguards halted.

"Who am I?" Emily said.

"My wife." Christophe held out his hands.

"And before that?" She held up the photo of her and Gray, her hand trembling. "Who was I before that?"

"A trick. That is a trick."

The air around the witch shimmered. "You're lying

to me, Christophe." She touched the side of her head. "You've lied to me all along, haven't you?"

"Emily," Gray whispered. "No."

"I love you." Christophe said. She walked up to him and put her hand on her husband's face. "I love you," he said. He didn't move. He could have saved himself. "Until my last breath, I love you."

"I loved you, too." And then she released her magic.

The fighting still going on downstairs cut off. Kynan cried out once. Just once, and then the house was silent as the grave.

Emily walked away from her husband's body. "Get me out of here."

CHAPTER 36

*A few hours later. Broadway near
Baker Street, San Francisco*

Gray sat up when she heard Durian come in the bedroom. Most of the drive from Christophe's house to here was lost in a blur of the aftereffects of being severed. More symptoms kicked in after the adrenaline rush of the events at Christophe's house wore off. Then she'd just about collapsed.

She didn't remember Durian bringing her here, though she knew he must have. Her brain felt mushy and her entire upper body hurt whenever she inhaled. The hallway door closed after him. She listened to the sound of him setting his keys on the desk in the anteroom. The silence closed in on her until she wasn't sure what to think or say or do. Durian walked into the bedroom.

She stayed where she was. He was blocking himself and that made her heart fall.

"Durian."

He faced her, expression unreadable. She felt cold to the bone. "How are you feeling?"

"You should know that," she said in a soft voice. If she sounded accusing, well, she was justified. The only reaction she got was a downward flicker of his eyelids. Jesus, her heart was going to crumble to ash. "But since you ask, I feel like crap."

He gave a slight nod. "Nikodemus is here."

"And?"

"We had a great deal to discuss."

"Like what?"

"We spent an inordinate amount of time going over the events of the last several hours. What happened exactly when and in what order." A wisp of frustration leaked from him. "In infinite detail."

"If I were him," Gray said, "I'd want to know where I stand with you."

He stilled, then walked closer to the futon. She stayed sitting. He stayed standing. "We discussed your sister."

"Is she all right? Where is she? What happens to her now?"

"Nothing. Nikodemus has no obligation to keep the magekind safe from their own."

"Thank God." Her sister was going to be staying here for the time being. Both Maddy and Leonidas had agreed that given Emily's pregnancy no one should push her to remember anything by means magical or otherwise. She'd remembered a few things. Nothing major, but the hope was that as the hold Christophe's magic had over her dissipated over time, she might recall more on her own. Gray's throat dammed up. When she could talk again, she said, "It's stupid for you to be standing up." She stretched out a hand and patted the bottom of the futon. "Sit."

After a moment's consideration, he did, facing her in a cross-legged position. She drew up her knees and folded her arms around her shins. He was relaxing, she thought, and not holding on so tightly to his blocks. Durian actually smiled, and he was just so beautiful she thought she might cry. He gave a small nod and then silence fell between them once again. He started to speak, stopped, then started again. If she didn't know better, she'd think Durian was having difficulty mastering his emotions. "Carson is here."

She didn't say anything right away. "Is she?"

"She has agreed to sever us. She's waiting downstairs."

"You're trying to be all noble and shit, aren't you?"

"I have very little experience with a situation like ours."

"Well, maybe you should cut it out and just go with it. Have you thought about that?" She got off the bed and walked to the stone table to stare at the photograph of the poppy. "I get that you're trying to offer me freedom from any bonds to the kin but the one to Nikodemus. That one has to stay in place."

His eyebrows quirked. "Yes, as to both."

"Maybe I should be all noble, too. Is that what you want? For me to be footloose and fancy free?"

Durian unfurled himself from the bed. He walked toward her. Gray held up a hand, but he kept coming. He didn't stop until he was inches from her. His hands moved around to her back, the fingers of one hand sliding under her shirt to touch her bare skin. Then he moved away, dropping his hands from her.

"We can do that. Both be all noble."

"Gray. This is not a decision to be made in passion."

"Why the hell not?" She put her hands on her hips. "Seems to me that passion is exactly what's called for right now. So, answer me. Total truth, Durian. Do you want Carson to sever us?"

He gave her the stare of doom.

She rolled her eyes. "Because it isn't what I want. I wouldn't have let you try to knock me up if I thought for a minute I wanted that." She crossed to him, grabbed his head and tangled her fingers in his hair. "You listen to me, I'm going to say this once and that's it. Think about what *you* want. Be selfish as hell. If you want us to be severed, we'll go down there right now and get it done. Otherwise, I'm not interested in what Carson has to offer."

"No," he said. "I don't want that."

"Good." She twined her arms around his shoulders but he didn't smile or look like they'd solved their issue at all. "Now what? Seriously, you are amazingly high maintenance."

"You have a great deal of magic. Of both kinds. You needn't live as I do. If you don't want to. It's enough for Nikodemus that your killing magic is bound over to him. You could choose to work with Maddy or Leonidas. If you so desire."

"Yeah, I guess I could." She stroked the side of his face. "But the way I see it, that's something we can do together. The way it is right now, it's our magic, right?"

"Yes." He stepped closer to her. "I will allow that you are right about that."

"I'm right about a lot of things." She exhaled slowly. "Let me be clear, Durian. I love you. Magic doesn't change that."

"You should be aware that as we are now, without your oath of fealty to me, you are sworn to Nikodemus through me."

"I'm okay with that." She pulled his head down until she could feel his breath across her face.

"Excellent."

The first touch of his lips on hers sent her mind spinning. She opened her mouth under his and kissed him back. His body was warm against hers, his mouth hot. She put her arms around his neck and brought them closer, sliding her tongue into his mouth to be met. God, yes. He kissed her tenderly, then not so tenderly, and his hands were on her ass, along her sides, over her breasts, then sliding over her nipples and he damn near drove her insane just touching her and kissing her.

One of his hands headed for the fly of her jeans, but she stopped him. "Isn't there something you need to do first, Assassin?"

He pulled away and looked directly into her eyes. "I love you, Gray. More than life."

She laughed. "I love you, too, but that isn't what I meant."

"What did you mean?"

"You need to call Carson and politely send her on her way. Tell her we decided thanks but no thanks."

"Ah."

She threaded her fingers through his hair and sucked in a sharp breath when he opened himself to her. The trickle of magic between them turned into a river.

"You are correct." He pulled out his phone and touched the screen. "I was distracted. It won't happen again."

His call to Carson was very polite. And mercifully short. Probably because while he was delivering his news to Nikodemus's witch, Gray was arranging herself on the futon, waiting for her immortal assassin to join her.

Dear Reader,

Iskander is finally getting his life back after his bond to his blood-twin was severed in order to save what was left of his sanity.

Most of the time he's completely normal. He works very hard at it. He has his own place and he can even spend time alone there without losing his mind. The woman who rents the apartment over his garage is completely normal. Just your average, everyday woman. But smoking hot, not that he would notice that. (Right.) She's also too nice for her own good. It's a testament to how far Iskander's come that he's always able to pass for human when she's around. Mostly.

Be sure to check out Iskander's story. It's called *My Dangerous Pleasure*, and it's available in January 2011. And for more information about Durian, Iskander, Kynan, and the others, check out my website at www.carolynjewel.com. You'll find character backgrounds, scenes that didn't make it into the final version and other cool stuff I happen to think of or that people suggest. (Hint! Hint!) If you have questions or comments, e-mail me (please!) at carolyn@carolynjewel.com. And thanks.

carolyn jewel

THE DISH

Where authors give you the inside scoop!

From the desk of Vicky Dreiling

Dear Reader,

The idea for HOW TO MARRY A DUKE came about purely by chance. One fateful evening while surfing 800+ channels on TV, I happened upon a reality show featuring a hunky bachelor and twenty-five beauties competing for his heart. As I watched the antics, a story idea popped into my head: the bachelor in Regency England (minus the hot tub and camera crew). The call to this writing adventure proved too irresistible to ignore.

During the planning stages of the book, I encountered numerous obstacles. Even the language presented challenges that meant creating substitutes such as *bridal candidates* for *bachelorettes*. Obviously, I needed to concoct alternatives to steamy smooching in the hot tub and overnight dates. But regardless of the century, some things never change. I figured catfights were fair game.

Before I could plunge into the writing, I had to figure out who the hero and heroine were. I picked up my imaginary remote control and surfed until I found Miss Tessa Mansfield, a wealthy, independent young woman with a penchant for matchmaking. In the short preview, she revealed that she only made love matches for all the ignored wallflowers. She, however, had no intention of ever marrying. By now I was on the edge of my seat. "Why?" I asked.

The preview ended, leaving me desperate to find out more. So I changed the metaphorical channel and nearly swooned at my first glimpse of Tristan Gatewick, the Duke of Shelbourne. England's Most Eligible Bachelor turned out to be the yummiest man I'd ever beheld. Evidently I wasn't alone in my ardent appreciation. Every eligible belle in the Beau Monde was vying to win his heart.

To my utter astonishment, Tristan slapped a newspaper on his desk and addressed me. "Madam, I am not amused with your ridiculous plot. Duty is the only reason I seek a wife, but you have made me the subject du jour in the scandal sheets. How the devil can I find a sensible bride when every witless female in Britain is chasing me?"

I smiled at him. "Actually, I know someone who can help you."

He scoffed.

I thought better of telling him he was about to meet his match.

Cheers!

Vicky Dreiling

www.vickydreiling.net

♥ ♥ ♥ ♥ ♥ ♥ ♥ ♥ ♥ ♥ ♥ ♥ ♥ ♥ ♥

From the desk of Carolyn Jewel

Dear Reader,

Revenge, as they say, is a dish best served cold. If you wait a bit before getting your payback, if you're calm and rational, you'll be in a better position to enjoy that sweet revenge. The downside, of course, is what can happen to you while you spend all this time plotting and planning. Some emotions shouldn't be left to fester in your soul.

Gray Spencer is a woman looking to serve up revenge while the embers are still glowing. She has reason. She does. Her normal, everyday life got derailed by a mage— a human who can do magic. Christophe dit Menart is a powerful mage with a few hundred years of living on her. Because of him, her life has been destroyed. Not just *her* life, but also the lives of her sister and parents.

After she gets her freedom at a terrible cost, the only thing Gray wants is Christophe dit Menart dead for what he did—before he does the same horrific thing to someone else that he did to her.

I know what you're thinking and you're right. A normal, nonmagical human like Gray can't hope to go up against someone like Christophe. But Gray's not normal—not anymore. She escaped because a demon gave his life for her and in the process transferred his magic to her. If she had any idea how to use that magic, she might have a chance against Christophe. Maybe.

The demon warlord Nikodemus has negotiated a

shaky peace agreement between the magekind and the demonkind. (Did I mention them? They are fiends, a kind of demon. And they don't take kindly to the mages who kill them in order to extend their miserable magic-using human lives by stealing a demon's life force.) Because of the peace, demons in Nikodemus's territory have agreed not to harm the magekind. In return, the magekind aren't supposed to kill any more demons.

Basically the problem is this: Gray intends to kill Christophe, and the demon warlord's most feared assassin has to make sure that doesn't happen.

Uh-oh.

After all that, I have what may seem like a strange confession to make about my assassin hero who is, after all, a wee bit scary at times. He's been alive for a long, long time, and for much of that time, women lived very restricted lives. Sometimes he is completely flummoxed by these modern women. It was a lot of fun writing a hero like that, and I hope you enjoy reading about how Christophe learns to deal with Gray as much as I enjoyed writing about it.

Yours Sincerely,

carolyn jewel

http://www.carolynjewel.com

♥ ♥ ♥ ♥ ♥ ♥ ♥ ♥ ♥ ♥ ♥ ♥ ♥ ♥ ♥ ♥

From the desk of Sophie Gunn

Dear Reader,

After years living in upstate New York, my husband got a new job and we moved back to my small hometown outside of Philadelphia. I was thrilled to be near my parents, brothers, aunts, uncles, and cousins. (Hi, Aunt Lillian!) But I didn't anticipate how close I would be to quite a few of my former high school classmates. Didn't anyone ever leave this town? My life had turned into a nonstop high school reunion.

And I was definitely still wearing the wrong dress.

One by one, I encountered my former "enemies" from high school. They were at the gym, the grocery store, and the elementary school bake sale. It didn't take long to realize two things. First, we had a blast rehashing the past. What had really happened at that eleventh-grade dance? What had become of Joey, the handsome captain of the football team? (Surprise, there he is now. Yes, he's the one walking that tiny toy poodle on a pink, blinged-up leash!) Second, we were still terrifically different people, *and it didn't matter*. We were grown-ups, and what someone wore or whom they dated didn't feel so crucial anymore.

Cups of coffee led to glasses of wine, which led to true friendship. But friendship that was different from any I'd ever known, because while we shared a past, our presents were still radically different. My husband started to jokingly call us the Enemy Club, and it stuck.

That was what we writers call an *aha moment*.

The Enemy Club would make a great book. Actually, a great series . . .

The rest, as they say, is history. Each book of the Enemy Club series is set in small-town Galton, New York. Four friends who had been the worst of enemies are now the best of friends, struggling to help one another juggle jobs, kids, love, heartbreak, and triumph as seen from their very (very!) different points of view.

HOW SWEET IT IS is the first book in the series. It focuses on Lizzie, the good girl gone bad. She made one mistake senior year of high school that changed her life forever. Now she and her teenage daughter get by just fine, thank you very much, with a little help from the Enemy Club. But then Lizzie's first love, the father who abandoned her daughter fourteen years before, decides to come back to town on Christmas Day. Lizzie imagines her life as seen through his eyes—and she doesn't like what she sees. She has the same job, same house, same everything as when he left fourteen years earlier. She vows to make a change. But how much is she willing to risk? And does the mysterious stranger, who shows up in town promising to grant her every wish, have the answers? Or is he just another of life's sweet, sweet mistakes?

I'm really excited about these books, because they're so close to my heart. Come visit me at www.sophiegunn.com to read an excerpt of HOW SWEET IT IS, to find out more about the Enemy Club, to see pictures of my cats, and to keep in touch. I'd love to hear from you!

Yours,

Sophie Gunn

♥ ♥ ♥ ♥ ♥ ♥ ♥ ♥ ♥ ♥ ♥ ♥ ♥ ♥ ♥ ♥

From the desk of Sue-Ellen Welfonder

Dear Reader,

Wild, heather-clad hills, empty glens, and the skirl of pipes stir the hearts of many. Female hearts beat fast at the flash of plaid. Yet I've seen grown men shed tears at the beauty of a Highland sunset. So many people love Scotland, and those of us who do know that our passion is a double-edged sword. We live with a constant ache to be there. It's a soul-deep yearning known as "the pull."

In SINS OF A HIGHLAND DEVIL, the first book in my new Highland Warriors trilogy, I wanted to explore the fierce attachment Highlanders feel for their home glen. Love that burns so hotly, they'll even lay down their lives to hold on to the hills so dear to them.

James Cameron and Catriona MacDonald, hero and heroine of SINS OF A HIGHLAND DEVIL, are bitter foes. Divided by centuries of clan feuds, strife, and rivalries, they share a fiery passion for the glen they each claim as their own. When a king's writ threatens banishment, long-held boundaries blur and forbidden desires are unleashed. James and Catriona soon discover there is much pleasure to be found in each other's embrace. But the price of their yearning must be paid in blood, and the battle facing them could shatter their world.

Fortunately, true love can prove a more powerful weapon than any warrior's sword.

There are a lot of swords in this story. And the fight

scenes are fierce. But passions flare when blood is spilled as James and Catriona showed me each day during the writing of their tale.

It was an exhilarating journey.

Catriona is a strong heroine who will brave any danger to protect her home and to win the heart of the man she never believed could be hers. James is a hardened warrior and proud clan leader, and he faces his greatest challenge when his beloved glen is threatened.

Because SINS OF A HIGHLAND DEVIL is a romance, James and Catriona are triumphant. Their ending is a happy one. Numberless Highlanders after them weren't as blessed. Later centuries saw the Clearances, while famine and other hardships did the rest. Clans were scattered, banished from their glens and hills as they were forced to sail to distant shores. Their hearts were irrevocably broken. But they kept their deep love of the land, their proud Celtic roots remaining true no matter where they settled.

Their forever yearning for home still beats in the heart of everyone with even a drop of Scottish blood. It's the reason we feel "the pull."

I hope you'll enjoy reading how James's and Catriona's passion for their glen rewards them with a love more wondrous than their wildest dreams.

With all good wishes,

Sue-Ellen Welfonder

www.welfonder.com